Ace Books by Dianne Sylvan

QUEEN OF SHADOWS
SHADOWFLAME
SHADOW'S FALL

SHADOW'S FALL

DIANNE SYLVAN

ACE BOOKS, NEW YORK

THE BERKLEY PUBLISHING GROUP
Published by the Penguin Group
Penguin Group (USA) Inc.
375 Hudson Street, New York, New York 10014, USA

Penguin Group (Canada), 90 Eglinton Avenue East, Suite 700, Toronto, Ontario M4P 2Y3, Canada
(a division of Pearson Penguin Canada Inc.) • Penguin Books Ltd., 80 Strand, London WC2R 0RL,
England • Penguin Group Ireland, 25 St. Stephen's Green, Dublin 2, Ireland (a division of Penguin
Books Ltd.) • Penguin Group (Australia), 250 Camberwell Road, Camberwell, Victoria 3124, Australia
(a division of Pearson Australia Group Pty. Ltd.) • Penguin Books India Pvt. Ltd., 11 Community
Centre, Panchsheel Park, New Delhi—110 017, India • Penguin Group (NZ), 67 Apollo Drive,
Rosedale, Auckland 0632, New Zealand (a division of Pearson New Zealand Ltd.) • Penguin Books
(South Africa) (Pty.) Ltd., 24 Sturdee Avenue, Rosebank, Johannesburg 2196, South Africa

Penguin Books Ltd., Registered Offices: 80 Strand, London WC2R 0RL, England

This is a work of fiction. Names, characters, places, and incidents either are the product of the author's
imagination or are used fictitiously, and any resemblance to actual persons, living or dead, business
establishments, events, or locales is entirely coincidental. The publisher does not have any control over
and does not assume any responsibility for author or third-party websites or their content.

SHADOW'S FALL

An Ace Book / published by arrangement with the author

PUBLISHING HISTORY
Ace mass-market edition / April 2012

ISBN: 978-1-937007-38-6

ACE
Ace Books are published by The Berkley Publishing Group,
a division of Penguin Group (USA) Inc.,
375 Hudson Street, New York, New York 10014.
ACE and the "A" design are trademarks of Penguin Group (USA) Inc.

PRINTED IN THE UNITED STATES OF AMERICA

10 9 8 7 6 5 4 3 2 1

ALWAYS LEARNING   PEARSON

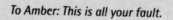

To Amber: This is all your fault.

PART ONE

Phoenix in Flight

One

"You are sure that this Prime is the one we have been searching for?"

From where she knelt below the dais, Lydia looked up at the woman sitting before her, into the cool pale eyes that held over a thousand years' worth of memory. "Yes."

"We have been here before, child, and you failed us . . . twice."

"I know, Mother. I have paid the penance you set out for me."

"You understand the consequences should you fail again. We are out of time, Lydia. If he isn't the one, if anything goes wrong, there won't be another chance. Everything we have worked for has led us to this."

"I understand. I give you my word as I have given you my blood—we won't fail."

The old one lowered her eyes, her hand moving unconsciously to touch the amulet at her throat; the same fire that had forged it had forged the Signets themselves, but hers was one of a kind, passed down through generations to a chosen successor, not by chance. She had led the Order for as long as Lydia could remember . . . and that was a long time. Once, she had intended to step down, leaving her power and her position to someone she had nurtured and loved as her own, only to be denied, betrayed. No one in the Order ever spoke of it, but Lydia knew the whole story, just as she knew the fate that awaited them all if she didn't complete her mission.

Did it seem, just for a moment, that the old one's eyes were bright with tears? Or was it a trick of the light? "I had hoped it would not come to this," she said, almost to herself. She seemed, too, almost transparent, as if her existence in the world were the last dried-out leaf clinging to a bare branch. "As I saw one piece of the puzzle after another falling into place, I prayed that I was wrong . . . yet here we are."

When she leveled her gaze back upon Lydia, however, it had hardened. "Go, then," she said. "Make sure he understands his role in all of this. Everything must come to pass exactly as it has been written—only then can we know for certain that our people will survive the coming fire."

Lydia rose slowly. "I am as always in your service, Mother."

With a sigh that sounded almost hollow, the old one held out her hands, and Lydia stepped forward to take the carved wooden box offered to her. One of the Priestess's hands lifted to touch Lydia's head in benediction, and Lydia closed her eyes.

"May the Dark Mother guide you, for you carry the future of the Shadow World."

Lydia smiled a little. "I will be home soon."

Their eyes met once more, and yes, this time Lydia was sure she saw tears. "Good-bye."

Night in California

Early summer breezes lifted the hem of the curtains and exposed, gently but immodestly, the bare sills of the open windows beneath. The waning night was cool and quiet, the faintest distant scent of the ocean discernible on the wind; the call of an owl was the only sound from outside and the rhythmic tapping of keys the only sound inside until a voice asked, "Coming to bed?"

Prime Deven O'Donnell looked up from the screen of his laptop. "Soon."

Jonathan leaned against the door frame, arms crossed. "What are you doing?"

"Ordering someone's death."

"I had to ask, didn't I?"

Deven smiled. "I told you years ago that you wouldn't want to know."

Jonathan shrugged. "I wanted to know everything about you. Back then I thought such a thing might be possible."

The Prime glanced down at the monitor, then back up to his Consort, who was disheveled and sleepy and absolutely the most gorgeous thing Deven could imagine in that moment. The only thing that would have made Jonathan look more enticing would be if he were holding a bottle of Scotch. "You know me better than anyone on this earth, my love . . . well enough to know that I'll always have my secrets."

Now Jonathan smiled. "And well enough that you should know you don't have as many secrets as you think."

They held each other's eyes. "Touché," Deven replied, extending his hand.

Jonathan walked over and took it, drawing the Prime up out of his chair and into the Consort's arms. Deven burrowed his face into Jonathan's shirt, inhaling the long-familiar scent of immortality, cologne, and Cuban cigars. That smell had always had the power to lift some of the weight from the Prime's shoulders, to let him feel at rest in a way he never had before Jonathan had come into his life.

"So who was it this time?" Jonathan asked, his voice rumbling against Deven's ear. "Dictator, business competitor, candlestick maker?"

"You don't want to know," he repeated, tipping his head back to meet Jonathan's eyes. "But it's worth four million dollars."

Jonathan's eyebrows quirked, and he whistled, impressed. "You're right. I don't want to know."

"Come on," Deven said. "Bed."

"It's only four thirty."

Deven gave him a dubious look. "Didn't you just say you were going?"

He grinned impishly. "Only if you were."

"Ah, I see." Deven laced his fingers through Jonathan's. "Lead on, then."

Jonathan looked surprised but, as usual, didn't object.

Deven couldn't say whether it was a genuine desire for more of his Consort's company, guilt over what had happened in Austin, or perhaps a bit of both, but he had made a concerted effort to let Jonathan know how wonderful he was in as many ways as possible in the three years since then. He hated the thought that Jonathan had lived with the foreknowledge of what would happen between Deven and David for months, uncomplaining, unwilling to upset the balance of future events. The precognitive "gift" was burden enough already; Deven wasn't going to add to his sorrows by acting like a spoiled brat—if he could help it, anyway.

There had come a point, the first year, that Jonathan had sat him down and said, "Don't get me wrong, darling, I love that you're jumping me all over the house, but if you're only doing it because you feel bad about shagging your boy, well, I'd just as soon you stopped."

Deven could defeat twelve vampires at once in hand-to-hand combat, but he knew quite well he was a disaster at relationships. He had ample evidence scattered throughout the centuries and over the face of the globe. And even though being Signet-bound guaranteed they would always love each other, that didn't mean things weren't downright horrid from time to time, usually because of his egregious misbehavior. They were still two people, after all, and while their souls might be a unit, their personalities definitely weren't.

About the only thing he could come up with to offer Jonathan was to have someone assassinated. Jonathan had passed.

Since then things had settled down. Deven still had to work at being openly affectionate, and they still fought bitterly on occasion, but overall their relationship had gotten much stronger, and Deven wondered from time to time if that wasn't part of why Jonathan hadn't spoken up about Austin before it happened.

It was hard to say; people with precog tended to have a strange outlook on fate. Every Consort Deven had ever met had struggled with it, and the wisest, like Jonathan, had learned to keep their mouths shut and let things unfold as they were meant to, because to disturb the order of things often brought far more dire consequences.

Of course, try explaining that to Miranda, for example, who was determined to forge her own destiny no matter what. It would take her a few decades to realize that seeing the future and having power over it were two entirely different things . . . assuming, of course, she didn't get herself killed first.

"What's wrong?" Jonathan asked as they entered the bedroom. "All of a sudden you're a hundred miles away."

Deven let the Consort lead him to bed and begin relieving him of his pesky attire, including the three concealed knives he wore, which by now Jonathan was well versed in ferreting out. "The Council meeting," he admitted reluctantly. He might as well be honest; Jonathan might not know everything there was to know about his mate, but he did know Deven's moods and expressions far better than Deven would have liked. "I have a bad feeling about it."

Jonathan smiled, gently shoving him onto the bed. "That's usually my line, darling. What exactly are you dreading about it?"

"Aside from everything?"

"I know you're not looking forward to being in the same room with Hart."

"He's planning something, Jonathan. He's been up there festering for three years. 8.3 Claret is in deep cover, and it's hard to maintain contact at this level; as far as I know, we have a handle on things, but Hart's unstable and could change his plans at any time. I can't predict his actions, and it vexes me. I'm vexed."

Jonathan settled beside him, propped up on one elbow. "And?"

Sighing, Deven added, "And I'm concerned about Miranda. That whole thing with the bloggers last year could have gone so much worse. People have tried to tell her she has to think ahead, but she's just not listening."

Jonathan nodded; he'd heard all of this before. "And?" he prompted.

They stared at each other for a moment before Deven said, "And I'm nervous about seeing him again."

The Consort leaned down and kissed Deven's throat just over the pulse. "Would you like me to see about getting you a chastity belt?"

Deven sighed yet again, but this time at the heady warmth of Jonathan's lips wandering over his skin. It grew increasingly difficult to concentrate on the conversation. "It's not that . . . you know that's not going to happen again . . . don't you?"

A chuckle. "I know you'd rather blow a rabid badger than deal with David right now, but you saw how well avoidance worked last time. I also know that circumstances would have to change radically for the two of you to go down that road again."

"So you don't have any predictions on that score? No visions of shag dancing in your head?"

"Just one," Jonathan said, one hand wrapping around the back of Deven's neck to pull their mouths together.

When Deven got a chance to come up for air, he panted, "Why, Mr. Burke, are you trying to distract me?"

"No," was the reply, somewhat muffled. "I'm trying to get laid. Now, if you wouldn't mind shutting up?"

Deven smiled up at him. "As you will it, my Lord."

* * *

From *Rolling Stone*:

Since Grammy-winning musician Miranda Grey's debut single "Bleed" devoured the charts, the singer has been subject to wild speculation about her closely guarded private life. Everything from her husband's career to the state of her health has been debated and dissected in the media, especially on celebrity gossip blogs like *Constellation*, which last year went public with a controversial interview with an unidentified former employee claiming that Grey is, in fact, a vampire.

For the most part Grey's PR team ignores the rumors, and when asked point-blank by a journalist if she's a vampire, Grey famously said, "Oh, absolutely!" with that wry smile she's become so known for.

Notorious for avoiding public appearances during the day—and avoiding interviews in general—Grey dodged the sci-fi theories about her mortality for nearly a year before *Constellation* uncovered another explanation entirely: Miranda Grey is ill.

The website reportedly paid handsomely for a set of test results and scans stolen from Grey's medical file revealing that her idiosyncratic behavior may not be caused by something out of legend, but something equally strange: Erythropoietic protoporphyria, an extremely rare condition caused by an enzyme deficiency, causes her skin to itch and blister on exposure to sunlight.

When *Rolling Stone* finally scored a one-on-one interview with the singer in a luxurious room at Austin's Driskill Hotel, it was first things first:

RS: So, let's get this out of the way.

MG: (laughing) Okay. Yeah, I'm totally a vampire. In fact in bed my husband and I call each other Louis and Lestat.

RS: Well, we're sitting here in this hotel room and I can see you in the mirror over there, so I guess that part of the legend is wrong.

MG: These days every aspect of people's lives is online, so I guess it was only a matter of time before my condition got out in the press.

RS: Why didn't you just come out with the truth in the beginning?

MG: It is kind of fun to go on the fan sites and see people arguing over whether I'm human, but I'd rather people think I was a vampire than some kind of invalid. I don't think of myself as a sick person, but people treat me differently when they find out. There was one guy, though, at a magazine I won't name, who tried to get me to prove I've got porphyria by sticking my arm out a window to see if it burned.

RS: What did you say to him?

MG: As I recall, I said, "Go fuck yourself." That was the end of that interview.

RS: Does your condition cause any other symptoms?

MG: It does. In fact, one of the documents that got circulated was a postsurgical report from when my spleen had to be removed. My red blood cells are defective, and processing them is hard on my organs.

RS: But going out in sunlight won't kill you?

MG: Technically, no. But it hurts like hell and makes my skin come off in sheets, so I'm basically nocturnal. It was never that much of a problem until the rumors started; how often do musicians do daytime concerts? But imagine going online and seeing ultrasound images of your insides on someone's blog—it was unsettling.

RS: Did you ever figure out who leaked the test results to *Constellation*?

MG: Yes. It was someone who worked for my personal physician, and that person has been dealt with.

RS: Speaking of which, you've worked with your medical team to establish a research foundation for porphyria—do you think you'll find a cure?

MG: Right now our focus is on learning more about the condition and helping people live with it. We've got a team working on a new form of sunscreen that's showing a lot of promise.

RS: Do you miss going out in the sunlight?

MG: You know, you would think so, but I really don't.

My life is very full and rewarding, and I love every minute of it. If I have to sacrifice having a tan for everything I've gotten to experience and achieve, well, redheads look better pale anyway.

RS: You didn't tour much in support of your first album. Was that a health-related decision as well?

MG: Yes. Travel isn't fun for me. I did a few dates in New York and L.A., but they were a nightmare.

RS: At the same time, though, you've found other ways to reach out to your fans.

MG: I love technology. Those same websites that were telling people I'm a vampire were vital in getting my name out there when I was new on the scene. That's the interesting thing about fame; the tide can turn for you or against you in an instant. One minute people are falling at your feet, the next minute they're driving a stake through your heart . . .

* * *

"My name is Miranda, and I am a vampire."

Two pairs of eyes, wide, were locked on her. She might have expected disbelief, but by now they knew better. They were experienced enough, and smart enough, to recognize the truth when they heard it.

The Queen of the Southern United States stood with her arms crossed at the front of the room, every inch of her from her black boots to her jewel-red hair laced with danger and power, an immortal menace arisen from the darkness to elicit fear in her prey.

At least, she hoped so.

"I'm here tonight because the two of you have been given a special assignment for the Austin Live Music Festival: namely, me. Your supervisor, Detective Maguire, has chosen you to act as liaisons between my security staff and the Austin Police Department. We felt it was important that you know what you're getting into in the unlikely event of an incident Saturday night."

She caught each of their gazes and held them until they looked away. She had found that humans had a hard time keeping eye contact with her; she wasn't sure what they saw, but she remembered a time when she couldn't meet people's eyes either, and she knew the power in that kind of contact.

Detective Maguire sat at the back of the room, keeping his distance from Faith, who was waiting for her cue. They could have sent another Elite to handle this meeting, but after what had happened to Detective Ojedo a few months ago, Miranda had wanted to make absolutely sure the two liaisons understood what they were dealing with.

"Do either of you know the circumstances of Detective Ojedo's death?" she asked. They all did, but she didn't wait for a reply. "He was investigating a drug ring that had hired several vampires as enforcers. He knew what they were, and he knew better than to pursue one alone, but he tried to play hero, and this"—Miranda opened her mouth and pressed her tongue against her canines—"is what happened."

One officer gasped; the other shrank back visibly.

When her teeth had slid back into her jaw and she knew she could speak without lisping, she went on. "In the event that you are faced with a vampire, either Saturday night at the festival or at any point in your careers, *do not engage.* You have each been given a code to send via text message, which will bring my people in ninety seconds or less, but under no circumstances—no matter who is in jeopardy—should you attempt to fight or shoot a vampire. You will piss us off and die."

She gestured to Faith.

The Second rose and walked down to the front of the conference room. The detectives hadn't known she was there until now, and it was clear they had guessed what Faith was.

"All right," Miranda said. "I want you to see why trying to fight one of us is suicide. We are stronger, faster, and much harder to kill than you are. Even in Kevlar with a nine-millimeter, you're basically just food to us. We will drain your blood until you shrivel, and we will walk away smiling."

Miranda nodded to Faith.

Faith shot her a grin, then took a swing at her.

The fight wasn't choreographed, but they had practiced slowing things down just a little so that the audience would still be able to track their movements instead of just registering a blur of activity. They also had to hold back enough not to damage the room; the training spaces at the Haven were much bigger, and they were used to fighting in alleys without ceilings or desks.

Miranda spun around and blocked Faith's kick, then backflipped in midair and landed about six feet away, dropping low so that Faith's boot whizzed past her head but didn't connect. They weren't using weapons, which put Faith at an advantage, but Faith had said she considered this part of Miranda's training, a chance for her to practice without a blade.

Not that the detectives knew that. To them, even the most amateur vampire warrior was Bruce Lee on an espresso-methamphetamine bender. By the time Faith and Miranda stopped their display, bowed to each other, and stepped back, one of the policemen was stark white, and the other one, a stoic Asian man who cleaned his glasses a lot, was gripping the sides of his desk with shaking knuckles.

"Thank you, Faith," Miranda told her Second. "I'll be out in thirty."

Faith nodded, bowed, and strode out the door, locking it again behind her.

Miranda turned back to the detectives. "Now then. I only have half an hour, so let's get down to it: Any questions?"

Two hands shot into the air.

David paused outside the conference room door, listening to the murmur of conversation inside. One woman, three men; three humans, one vampire . . . three detectives, one Queen.

He heard her say something, and the humans all laughed;

whatever they were talking about, their fear of her had been put aside in favor of the camaraderie of law enforcement officers who all had one goal: to protect Austin's citizens. Miranda had just expanded these detectives' definition of *citizen*, and now she was letting them see that not all vampires were evil or had death in mind for all humans; the Elite, and the Signets, existed to protect and serve just as the human police did, and the Signet of this territory wanted a good relationship with the authorities for everyone's sake.

Ojedo's death could easily have been avoided; in fact, David had seen the fight go down over the sensor network, and he'd sent a team, but because the officer hadn't sent out an alarm, by the time David realized something was wrong, it was too late. Ojedo had been dead on the ground when the patrol team arrived . . . but at least the vampire who had killed him had been apprehended and executed, and thanks to Ojedo's work the drug ring had been dismantled, arrested, and beheaded where appropriate.

It was important that they got along with law enforcement because these officers had a vital—if unwitting for the most part—part to play in keeping Miranda's supersecret identity super and secret. They had to be very, very careful whom they shared it with, and make very clear what their roles were; and in return for police cooperation in any sort of human security problems facing Miranda, the Signet stepped up Elite presence in violent areas of the city and helped the authorities deal with supernaturally related problems like the drug ring before more lives could be lost.

David didn't enter the room; they had seen enough for one night. He waited until the laughter and joking faded and he heard Miranda call an end to the session. When he heard the two detectives approaching, David moved back out of the way, holding himself perfectly still; they left the room and walked right past him.

"Coffee?" one of them said to the other.

"Christ, yes," was the reply. "As Irish as humanly possible."

David smiled. Once they were gone, he returned to the door and peeked in to see Miranda conversing amiably with Detective Maguire, an affable red-haired cop with a galaxy of freckles and a surprisingly good sense of humor for someone who worked in Homicide.

Maguire was chuckling as he took a piece of paper— one of the promotional posters for Miranda's performance this Saturday—from the Queen, who was capping a black marker. "Thank you, my Lady. She's been a fan of yours since the beginning."

Miranda smiled at him. "I hope it works, Detective. She's a lucky girl."

They shook hands; the detective was respectful but not afraid of her. It was a fine line they walked. The humans needed to fear vampires as a whole but also needed to know that some were fighting for them. They had to be willing to trust the Elite and the Signet but to be suspicious of any others.

It had already paid off handsomely for the Pair last year, when David had worked with APD to secure a floor at the Driskill for the *Rolling Stone* interview. That was, in fact, how they had met Detective Maguire, and so far David liked working with him more than anyone else he'd met on the force. Maguire had taken the existence of vampires remarkably in stride for a human, saying that he'd seen plenty of "weird crap" in his time.

There were a lot of irons in the fire that night, and any one part of the system failing would have destroyed the illusion that Miranda was human, but having APD on their side meant no interference from the hotel staff as David set up the cameras that projected Miranda's "reflection" onto the fake mirror, proving, as far as that proved, that she wasn't what she actually was.

Comparatively speaking, medical tests and surgical reports were much easier to fake. It was far easier to build celebrity gossip sites. Keeping Miranda's secret in the closet was mostly a matter of outguessing the rumor mill and making their speculations ridiculous by introducing an even more ridiculous "truth." Leaked reports, digital sleight of hand, and now Miranda was an inspiration to a generation of young people with illnesses, disabilities, and checkered pasts to overcome to reach their dreams.

It was only partly fiction. It had been Miranda's idea—in fact she had used her own money—to establish the foundation to research treatments for porphyria. She felt that having brought the illness into the spotlight, it was her duty to try to help those who really had it. Novotny had jumped at the opportunity, as most of the work he'd done for the Signet had been forensic rather than medical, and his first love was rare diseases.

Finally, Miranda finished her conversation with Maguire and approached the door; David took a step back, and as she walked out into the hallway, he was ready, holding Shadowflame out to her with both hands.

She smiled at him and took the sword. "My Lord Prime."

He bowed slightly. "My Lady. Shall we?"

She fell into step at his right hand, and they took the back hallway out of the precinct building, out to where Faith was waiting with Harlan at the car. As they hit the street, David noticed, with satisfaction, Miranda's bodyguards emerging from their positions around the building.

"I think it went well," Miranda said as Harlan shut the door and Faith slid into the front passenger seat. "They had good questions, mostly."

David smiled. "Who was the autograph for?"

She grinned back. "Maguire's daughter, Stella. They haven't been getting along lately, and he's hoping to bribe her to have lunch."

"I see."

Miranda sighed, leaning back in her seat, her fingers seeking to wind around his as the car pulled away from the curb. "I'm worried about them," she said. "I think I got the message across, but . . . we thought we did enough before, and Detective Ojedo paid the price."

"They won't all listen," David reminded her, squeezing her hand and then lifting it to kiss the palm. "We can't control that. We've given them knowledge that most Signets wouldn't bother with, and it's saved more than one officer's life. But some of them don't look before they leap with common criminals any more than they would with ours."

"Still . . . I can't help but feel responsible," she said. "If we'd taken down that drug ring the minute we realized they were hiring vampires . . ."

"We were working on it. Another two days and we'd have had them. Ojedo broke protocol. He knew there was a plan in place, but he charged in anyway. That wasn't our fault, Miranda. He made his choices."

She wasn't satisfied, but there was nothing he could say; she would have to work through it herself. She was disturbingly like him in that regard. People could talk until they were blue in the face, but once her mind was made up, it was made up, until she'd gone away and had time to mull things over. Stubborn, she was, to a fault; but once she realized she was wrong, she admitted to it readily and did her best to smooth over any hurt feelings . . . feelings being, of course, her specialty.

He hadn't expected that her clumsiness with this sort of thing would actually endear her to people, but it did; they saw that she sometimes struggled, that not every decision was easy and might not be right, but she genuinely cared, and she would happily take a bullet rather than have the consequences of her inexperience cause someone else harm.

"How are preparations going?" Miranda asked.

"Smoothly. The Haven is ready—they got the table set up in the Great Hall tonight, and the ballroom is prepared. I spoke with Esther and Matthew, and the staff is almost ready. The delivery from the blood bank is scheduled for Thursday evening, and the first arrivals will be late that night."

"How many confirmations?"

"Twenty-five," David said, smiling. "All but Demetriou and Dzhamgerchinov, and there's still a chance that Demetriou will change his mind . . . not that I particularly want him to."

Miranda took a deep breath. "I still can't believe we're letting Hart set foot in our Haven again."

"I know, beloved, but those are the rules. Everyone is invited to a full Council. I put in my bid to have this one in Austin ten years ago, and by the time things fell out with Hart it was too late to back out. But with the entire Council there he'll be on his best behavior. He won't risk losing support by making a dick of himself."

The Queen raised an eyebrow. "Or the Council meeting is the opportunity he's been waiting for to get revenge on us in some public way that forces us to react."

"I'm trying to be optimistic, here."

"What about Cora? How can we force her to sit in the same room with that bastard?"

He smiled. Miranda was very protective of Cora; indeed, the Queen of Eastern Europe seemed to bring that out in people. "No one is forcing Cora to do anything. Queens aren't required to attend the official sessions."

"I understand that, but I can't help but worry about her."

He leaned over and kissed her temple. "You can't fix everything."

"At least he's not bringing his . . . girls . . . this time."

"Not according to the Shadow operative in his Court, at least. For all that he's been nursing his grudge for three years, he's being very cautious not to tip his hand."

"Doesn't that concern you just a little?"

"A lot," he admitted. "I prefer Hart when he's being violent and out of control; it's easier to deal with than his fake charm."

"Sire," Faith spoke up from the front seat, "First-shift preliminary patrol reports are in. Everyone's reporting situation normal."

"Thank you." David took out his phone and did a quick systems check; situation normal there, too. With the exception of the Austin Live Music Festival and the Council meeting, the entire territory was almost eerily quiet this month.

He wanted to believe it was because of the territory-wide sensor network and new Elite protocols he'd put in place, but it felt far more like some sort of demented version of Christmas Eve, and he was waiting with growing dread to see what kind of havoc Hart would leave under the tree.

When he was finished, he looked over to see that Miranda had fallen asleep with her head leaning against the car window. He gingerly tilted her the other way so that she would be more comfortable on his shoulder, and with a sigh, she put an arm around him and settled in for the rest of the ride home.

Faith looked back over the seat and said quietly, "She must be exhausted. She had that appearance at the ALMF opening concert, then we had that disturbance over at the university campus—even though it turned out to be nothing—then our session with the APD."

David nodded. "She's been burning the candle at both ends lately . . . but try telling her to cut back and rest."

Faith made a noise of agreement. "Tell me about it."

"Sitting right here," Miranda muttered, eyes opening a slit.

David chuckled and kissed the top of her head. "Faith has a point, you know. You have been pushing yourself way too hard. You're immortal, remember? You have plenty of time to have grand adventures."

The Queen sighed, shook her head. "I'll take a break after the festival's over and all the Magnificent Bastards have gone home."

The Council would arrive starting Thursday night, and the opening meeting would be held Friday night, followed by a formal ball. The main meeting was Saturday night, and everyone would depart predawn Tuesday at the latest; Miranda was headlining on the festival's main stage Saturday night and would get home just before the Council got down to business, provided there weren't any delays.

As much of a clusterfuck as the timing was, it had been a calculated risk on his part; holding the Council during a festival meant that there would be thousands of additional humans in Austin, and therefore feeding all the Pairs, their servants, and their bodyguards would be much easier.

"I vote you take a vacation," Faith told them. "Make a state visit of it if you have to, but go somewhere for a few days and rest. New Orleans, maybe."

David felt Miranda perk up a little at the suggestion. "Could we?"

He frowned, reluctant at first to leave Austin so soon after the Council, but if they waited until midweek to be sure things were calm . . . "I don't see why not. I could meet with Laveau while I'm there and visit a few of our far-flung Court members."

"We can get a place in the Quarter," Miranda said, sounding more energetic than she had all night, "and I could stuff myself sick with beignets."

There was no way he could deny her anything that put such a spark in her eyes. "Sold," he said. "I'll call our travel agent and see what she can pull together."

"Thank you, baby," Miranda murmured, reaching up to nip his earlobe and then settling back down against his shoulder to return to her nap. "I'll make it worth your while."

Hours later and miles away, something jolted Deven out of sleep. His hand immediately snaked under the pillow for the knife he kept there, but otherwise he held himself completely still, senses on red alert.

Evaluation: They were alone in the room, and the disturbance had come from Jonathan. Deven relaxed his grip on the knife's hilt and turned toward his Consort, who had been curled up at his back.

Jonathan lay staring at the ceiling, eyes wide, forehead glistening with sweat. The energy around him was practically crackling.

Damn.

"Easy," Deven said softly, laying a hand against Jonathan's face to try to bring him back. "You're here in our Haven, in our room, with me, and you're safe."

For a long moment Jonathan was frozen, his vision fixed on something Deven was grateful he couldn't see, but as Deven continued to murmur to him, the sound of the Prime's voice reached him, and Jonathan slowly returned to his body, his paralysis turning into a nasty case of tremors as the fever that held him broke as suddenly as it had come and he went from blazing to freezing.

Deven acted on years of experience with this exact scenario. He pulled the blankets up around his Consort, pressing their bodies together and raising his own energy deliberately to transfer heat to Jonathan's skin.

"It isn't now," Deven told him. "Wherever you were, it isn't now. Now everything's all right."

There were few things that made Jonathan seem vulnerable, and this was the only one that Deven could do nothing about but offer comfort and safety. His healing power was useless here, and there was no enemy to impale or behead. All he could do was be there.

It took nearly twenty minutes for Jonathan to speak. This had been a bad one.

"I'm okay," he finally rasped.

"Like hell you are. Are you warm enough?"

A nod. "Coke, please."

Deven withdrew reluctantly—he hated to risk Jonathan getting a chill—but if he didn't get some caffeine quickly, he'd get a migraine that might last the whole next day. Deven fetched a soda from the fridge and brought it back to the bed, where to his relief Jonathan was sitting up and looking far more alert.

The Consort grunted his thanks and drank the entire can in one go.

"Aren't you going to smash it on your forehead?" Deven asked. That, at least, earned a weary grin.

They settled back down, this time with Jonathan's head on Deven's shoulder, and were silent for a while; sometimes Jonathan didn't want to talk about whatever he had seen, and sometimes he did, but if pressed, he would shut down and refuse to say anything. Deven waited, running his fingers absently through Jonathan's blond hair, soothing them both.

This time, however, was different. Though Jonathan remained silent for a long time, Deven could feel him struggling, could feel his fear. Whatever he had seen had been enough to terrify him . . . and that almost never happened.

Finally Deven couldn't stand it anymore. "What did you see?"

Jonathan shook his head and turned his face into Deven's neck. "I can't," he whispered. "I just . . . I can't, baby. I'm sorry."

"Am I going to die tomorrow or anything like that? Because if I am, I need to go cancel my massage."

Jonathan looked at him, his usually bright hazel eyes full of anguish. "Please . . . don't even joke about that."

Their eyes held. "All right," Deven said with a nod. "Do we need to call off our trip?"

"No. We have to go. It's not . . . it's nothing immediate, at least not for us. We're the least of our worries right now."

Deven sighed, lying back; now it was his turn to stare at the ceiling. "Let me guess."

"Pack extra eyeliner," Jonathan said. "We might be in Austin for a while."

Two

"Damn it, would you hold still?"

Faith managed—barely—not to roll her eyes at her boss. "Sorry, Sire."

The electrical hum in the room grew fractionally louder. It was starting to make Faith's ears ring. "Any closer?" she asked.

The Prime's eyes were on the bank of monitors in front of him, their light glaring off his glasses.

"You're staring again," he said mildly without looking up.

"Sorry." She held back her reaction, which was to flush at being caught, but there was no undertone to his words, just amusement. As far as he knew, she was staring at the glasses, and that was true . . . though not for the reasons he thought.

Vampire senses were designed for hunting in the dark, their pupils dilating to take in far more light than a human's could sense; that meant that bright lights hurt them, and they had found as technology continued to take over their lives that working in front of monitors for hours could cause a vampire as much eyestrain as a human. They recovered from it much more quickly, of course, and there was no long-term damage, but David had begun to have severe headaches after the network was extended throughout the

South, and he spent so much time calibrating it that Miranda had suggested, half jokingly, that he get glasses.

So he did. They weren't prescription, but antiglare, and had a magnifying strip along the bottom for when he was doing delicate work with his lasers and soldering irons. They looked like everyday human eyeglasses . . . and Faith had finally allowed herself to admit that they made him unspeakably attractive.

She took a long, slow breath. *Oh, for fuck's sake, Faith.*

"I know they look weird," David was saying, "but Novotny's lenses have really done wonders for me. I'm having him make pairs for the other network monitor Elite, too, so they don't lose productivity to migraines."

He looked up at her, and again she was struck by how the glasses completed his face, finally made him look like the genius he was. Put together with his seemingly endless collection of geeky T-shirts—tonight's bore an engineering schematic of the TARDIS from *Doctor Who*—it was a good thing he only wore them in his workroom. Faith wasn't the only person in the Haven who had noticed, and she was fully aware that Miranda had pinned him to the lab table more than once with a "Talk nerdy to me, baby."

There was a series of clicks, and David said, "I think that's got it. Now, on my mark, I want you to hold your arms out to your sides and turn very slowly in a counter-clockwise circle."

"What is this accomplishing, again?"

He sighed. He hated repeating himself. It amused her to make him do it. "I'm refining the camera technology that projected Miranda's image into that fake mirror for her *Rolling Stone* interview. I need to be able to use it for other applications."

"But we show up on camera—sort of," Faith pointed out.

David shook his head and clarified, "We show up in digital formats that don't use traditional mirrors. But the picture quality is almost always poor. People have recorded her on cell phone cameras at concerts, but if they try to blow the frame up larger or improve the resolution, it gets pixilated. The projector I used to fake out the *Rolling Stone* guy was . . . well, let's just say it's a good thing he didn't look at the mirror more than once or twice. If I can refine the signal a little further, we'll be able to show her on the big projection screens at larger concert venues, and I can help refine still-shot photography of vampires so she can do more photo shoots."

"Why?" Faith asked. "I mean, why don't we show up on film? Do we reflect funny?"

David smiled and gave her the rarest of answers, for him: "I honestly don't know."

"You don't?"

"No. Novotny and I have conducted all sorts of experiments, changing different variables, and we can't nail down exactly what it is that keeps us from reflecting in glass mirrors, water, or windows—but digital photography produces a slightly blurry image for most of us. I have no idea why. My concern right now is taking what we do know and making it work better."

"I heard it was because we don't have souls," she said softly, eyes still on the monitor where he worked.

A shrug. "Perhaps. I don't do mysticism."

Faith turned her head toward the screen where, presumably, her own image would show up eventually. "I haven't seen my own face in a century," Faith mused. "I barely remember what I look like, Sire."

He looked up at her. "Don't worry, Second, you're beautiful."

Now she *did* blush. Damn it.

"Have you seen yourself?" she asked, stumbling only a little over the words. "On camera, I mean?"

He gave her a rueful smile. "I can't," he said. "I've tried this thing on several people, and so far Miranda is the only one who's worked well. She's also the youngest. That's why I wanted to try you, to see if it's the age that matters; you fall right between the two of us."

"How odd."

"It has a sort of poetry to it," he replied, turning a knob

and entering a string of numbers. "The further we get from our humanity, the less of it you can see in images. Scientifically, however, I'm flummoxed. Now, hold still!"

Faith obeyed, closing her eyes for a moment and trying to be patient. She had a lot to do; the Haven was in chaos with the first Pairs arriving in a few hours, and though the Haven's staff and supplies were someone else's department, security was very much Faith's. She knew David was keeping himself occupied until the circus began so he wouldn't have time to fret, but that was the luxury of being in charge.

"Almost . . . got it . . . there!"

Faith's eyes flicked open, and she looked at the screen.

Her breath caught hard in her chest, and she covered her mouth with her hand for a few seconds while she took in what she was seeing.

She was staring at her own face.

It wasn't crystal clear, and the edges were definitely pixilated, but she recognized herself as the girl who had stumbled bleeding through the streets of Gion, so very long ago . . . but her face had changed. It was pale, yes, but also harder, colder. The wide innocence of her eyes was gone . . . her eyes were old.

"That's me," she said softly.

She heard David rise from his chair and come over to join her; a blur moved across the screen to her side, but it barely even registered as a visual anomaly. When he stood still beside her, however, he took on a more concrete shape, its edges a moonlit silver. He was, essentially, a living shadow.

"As I said," David told her with a smile. "Beautiful."

Faith stared at herself for a long time, trying to make sense of her face, and finally the picture began to lose its coherency. David turned the projector off to run analysis on the results. It was hard for Faith to look away from the screen even after the image was gone.

"We're in the early stages with all of this—up until the last couple of years I didn't have the technology to really study the phenomenon. Eventually I hope to be able to offer everyone living here a sort-of-mirror for their quarters," the Prime was saying. "Novotny's holographic projection system would offer a much clearer picture, if I can compensate for the age factor, but that will take more experiments and probably a . . ."

His voice turned into a murmur that meant she no longer had his attention and he had become absorbed in his work once more. She might as well talk to the empty screen.

"I'm heading out, then," Faith said. "Lots to do."

No reply.

Sighing, shaking her head, Faith left him to his toys.

After meeting with the shift team leaders briefly to go over the night's arrival schedule, Faith headed across the Haven to check in with Miranda, who had barely left the music room in the last week except when she had to go into the city. The Queen was scrambling to get ready for her big show on Saturday night; she and three other bands would take the main festival stage that evening, with her performance last since she was the biggest name.

The Austin Live Music Festival drew about fifteen thousand registered attendees every year, many of whom jockeyed for wristbands to the four-day event; there were close to a thousand performers on the schedule at outside stages, clubs and bars, and traditional music venues all over the city. The main stage would be surrounded by almost the entire congregation Saturday night. It was easily the biggest show she'd ever done; her album tour had focused on smaller, intimate venues and hadn't strayed far from the South.

Miranda was planning to get home from her show in time to attend the main Council meeting; while she wasn't required to attend, she was determined not to let it seem like she was unable to keep her two worlds balanced.

Faith shook her head. Modern women were able to vote, hold property, determine their own occupations, choose whom to marry, if anyone . . . but they were under a different tyranny now, the drive to prove to the world they weren't weak the way men had portrayed them for so long.

But that wasn't the whole story, Faith knew as well as Miranda did; Miranda's time as a performer was limited. She could perhaps eke out another decade before the questions became too hard to answer, and that was if nothing else went wrong. She would not age, she would not change at all, but the world would, and the world would notice. The mess with *Constellation* had rattled Miranda badly, even with David's quick solution. Miranda had the sense she was living on borrowed time . . . and she was right.

They hadn't really talked about it. For now there was a fragile détente between the two halves of the Queen's life, as if bringing up the impossibility of it all would send the entire house of cards crashing down.

Faith approached the music room with her ears perked; interrupting the Queen in the middle of a song tended to make her grouchy. There was, however, no noise coming through the door, and Faith knocked.

The door opened by itself a few inches. That was how the Pair indicated permission to enter rather than calling out.

Faith walked in to find the Queen standing on her hands.

Once in a while the thought crossed the Second's mind that she worked for some very strange people.

"My Lady."

Miranda opened her eyes and looked up at Faith. She was balanced perfectly on her hands, her hair spilling out all over the floor around her, and her bare feet were pointed toward the ceiling, her toenails boasting a cheerful coat of purple polish. Her Signet had fallen down to rest on her chin. "Hi, Faith. How are things?"

"Oh, the usual. Twenty-five Primes coming for a slumber party. What's new with you?"

Miranda grinned. "I'm balancing my chakras, obviously."

The new yoga teacher, Elite 83, was an extremely nicely

put-together vampire named Samir, and his classes were well attended by Elite and staff of both genders. Faith was looking forward to introducing him to the Queen of Eastern Europe, who, after her introduction to yoga while in the South, was a yogini adept in several schools. Miranda hadn't devoted herself completely to the practice, but she had learned enough to become even more gymnastic in her fighting style and, it would seem, to cope with the anxiety of the impending weekend. Faith had been pleased with the progress all the yoga students had made in their combat training and was in the process of starting similar programs in the other major Signet outposts in the territory.

Yet another thing the rest of the Council was chuckling about. Apparently the current view of the South was as some kind of free-love techno-ashram. Well, they were welcome to scoff all they liked; this weekend they'd see just how silly it was when the various guest Elite and the South's own took part in the fight tournament that coincided with each Council session. She would lay odds that by Monday other Seconds would be approaching her to discuss her training methods, just as several Primes had oh-so-casually inquired about the sensor network since it had gone live all over the South and crime had dropped to almost nothing.

Faith mused, "Do you remember that scene in *Return of the Jedi* where Yoda makes Luke Skywalker do Jedi yoga and float rocks with his brain?"

Miranda's grin turned mischievous, and Faith laughed as the pair of tattered Chucks on the floor nearby lifted off the ground. "That was *The Empire Strikes Back*, thank you very much," Miranda said brightly.

"Dear God, you two spend way too much time together."

The Queen dropped the shoes, then came gracefully out of the handstand. "Anything to report?"

"Nothing new or urgent. I was just checking in to see if you were ready for the festivities to begin. We're two hours out from Tanaka's arrival."

Miranda glanced up at the clock and sighed. "If by 'ready' you mean 'wishing to God it was over before it's even started,' then yes, I'm ready."

"We've done everything we can to make this go smoothly," Faith reassured her. "We've been preparing for this for over a year. Don't concentrate so much on what could go wrong."

"I have to," the Queen replied, returning to the Bösendorfer, which was no longer alone on its end of the room; Miranda had set up a bank of digital keyboards directly behind the piano bench. She flipped a few switches on the main board as she went on. "I don't get as freaked out if I plan for the worst-case scenario."

"What would you consider the worst-case scenario here?"

"Let's see . . . the last thing I came up with was Hart trying to kill me in the middle of the Council meeting."

"That's the worst thing you can think of? Honestly, my Lady, I'm disappointed." Faith crossed her arms. "If Hart did anything that stupid in full view of the Council, they'd cast him out then and there. And since when do you believe he could kill you even if he tried? You could take him in a fight. Let's not forget you threw him into a wall."

She smiled. "Yes, I did."

"My guess is that Hart wants to put on a show. He wants to come after you using the Council's power; otherwise, why wait this long? He won't try violence, not here and now."

"You're saying he's going to kill us with diplomacy."

"Politics has ended a lot of lives, my Lady. But honestly . . . you know what these meetings are really like? Tedious. They're a bunch of rich old men waving their dicks around. They get together every ten years to show off and bluster at each other, but in the end, nothing really happens. There's some redistricting and a few arguments, then everyone goes home and gossips for another decade."

"I keep forgetting you were in London ten years ago," Miranda said. "But you've never had to host one."

"The housekeeping staff has a much bigger headache in all this than we do."

"I have no doubt. I think the bonus pay will make up for it, though."

"I was thinking of buying a Ferrari with mine."

Miranda grinned at her and settled into a position that Faith had no doubt had benefited greatly from her yoga training: twisted slightly sideways so that she could reach the piano with one hand and the keyboard with the other and play both at once. She hadn't invented the move, but it allowed her to perform some of the more complex tracks from her album without needing a backup band.

The Queen had gone against the grain of popular music and opted for a stripped-down, emotionally raw style on stage instead of creating lavish theatrical productions like most solo female artists, and the gamble had paid off. There was now a generation of up-and-coming girls-with-pianos on the radio. The lack of pyrotechnics was practical as well—it enabled her to travel light, which meant she could come and go from performances without spending days on the road. Her touring retinue consisted of a single truck and a Signet jet, both with blacked-out windows.

Before she got into her work, however, Miranda looked up at Faith again and said, "I'd like it if you'd do me a favor this weekend."

Faith raised an eyebrow. "Name it, my Lady."

"I know we have extra surveillance on Hart's suite and the Elite are under orders to watch his every move, but . . . I'd like it if you would keep an eye on Queen Cora for me. Make sure she's never alone with Hart."

"You don't think she can handle herself?" Faith asked.

"It's not that . . . between Jacob and that giant dog of hers she's safe enough, but I'm more concerned about her emotional health. After everything Hart did to her, I don't want to put her in a position where he can hurt her in any way. It's one thing for them to make nice in front of the full Council, but I don't trust him not to at least lash out verbally."

There was protective steel in the Queen's eyes, and they had silvered at the edges as they always did when she mentioned Hart. Faith nodded. "Done."

"Good. Thank you. I don't know what to expect in all of this. I'll breathe easier knowing you're on watch."

"Of course, my Lady. Although . . . I doubt I'll be the only person with one eye on Cora."

Miranda cocked her head to one side. "You mean Deven."

For reasons known only to the Prime of the West himself, he had taken a special interest in Cora; Deven and Jonathan had been the second Pair to visit Prague, and Deven gave the Queen a rather impressive gift, a Nighthound named Vràna. Nighthounds, a breed of dog unknown outside the Shadow World, were traditional vampire companions, and giving one as a gift was a rare gesture for any Prime. It silently announced to the world that Cora was under Deven's protection.

Rumors about the two of them had flown for months; if Faith were more cynical, she might have attributed that to Deven's desire to downplay his tryst with David, which despite their best efforts had become a subject of Council gossip almost immediately. Anyone who knew Deven for more than ten minutes would find the idea of him courting Cora laughable, but still, it effectively shifted the spotlight.

"Why do you think he's so interested in her?" Faith asked, almost offhandedly.

Miranda shrugged. "Why does Deven do anything?" She struck a chord on the keyboard, frowned, and nudged a lever upward to adjust the sound. "Maybe he just likes her. Maybe he envies that she's held on to her faith despite everything that she's been through. Maybe she reminds him of his mother. Who knows?"

Faith nodded in agreement, then said, "Well, if there's nothing further, my Lady, I'll head back to my schedule and start escorting in the arrivals. I'll see you tomorrow night, then, before the ball?"

Another flicker of doubt passed over Miranda's face, and Faith raised an eyebrow, knowing exactly what the flicker was for. "You're sure the dress is right," Miranda said. "And you're sure you don't mind doing my face? We could have hired someone, but . . . I always love the way you do your makeup. You have such a good eye for color."

Faith smiled. "I told you, I'm happy to do it. I've already got a plan. You're going to break every heart in that Council tomorrow night. Just trust me."

She started to leave but paused as Miranda said, "I do trust you, Faith. In all things."

Their eyes met and held for a moment, and Faith got a terrible sinking feeling in her stomach, wondering if . . . but Miranda only smiled, and it was with the same warmth toward the Second as always.

"Thank you, my Lady," Faith said, then bowed and left Miranda to her rehearsal.

You are in love with my husband.

Miranda watched the Second's black-uniformed shape retreat down the hall beyond the music room door, and again came that treacherous thought, the one she couldn't deny—even given as hard as Faith was denying it.

Miranda had sensed it years ago, just after the Ovaska ordeal had ended, but for a long time she had tried to dismiss it, even though her gift had never been wrong. As the years had passed, it had become harder and harder to ignore . . . but Miranda tried. She didn't want to know this. She shouldn't know it.

Once, in another lifetime, the gift of empathy had driven Marilyn Grey mad and then a decade later destroyed the sanity of her daughter. Marilyn had taken her own life to stop the endless assault of voices and emotions that shoved their way into her, obliterating her own thoughts. Miranda had barely missed that fate, but by the end she *was* dead . . . and born again, a vampire.

The gift had always given her knowledge about people that she didn't want. It wasn't her right to know someone else's innermost fears and desires. She didn't want the power to take advantage of their insecurities . . . yet she could, and she did, first onstage, then as Queen.

She had long ago given up any pretense that her manipulation of her audiences was ethical, but she had felt better about it once she learned that the gift didn't work through recordings or over the radio. People had to be in her presence for her to read and shift their feelings, so she couldn't influence them to buy her albums except by making sure their concert experience was worth every penny of the ticket price.

It was assumed among the Signets that whatever gifts a Queen had, she would use to their utmost in service of her territory. Sometimes that meant deliberately invading people's privacy. Sometimes it meant keeping shields between herself and people she loved, for their own safety. Sometimes . . . sometimes things still slipped through.

Miranda's hands slid down from their position over the keyboard, then up to cover her face.

There were so many things she knew that she didn't need or want to know. There were so many things she knew that she couldn't tell anyone, not even David.

She lifted her eyes up to the smiling portrait of Queen Bess. "I miss Kat," she said softly to the painting. "Her daughter is two now, did you know? She's adorable."

No reply, of course, and for all that Miranda longed for someone to talk to, she was grateful that at least the paintings weren't talking back. She'd had enough of being crazy for one lifetime.

"Maybe I should tell Jonathan," Miranda went on. "He knows Faith . . . he could tell me I'm being ridiculous, or . . . not. But if he said I'm not, if someone else confirmed it and I knew it wasn't just me picking it up . . . I don't know what I'd do . . ."

The sad fact was that Faith would die before she'd admit the truth if Miranda were to confront her directly, and she knew—as did Faith—that David didn't have romantic feelings for the Second, so it wasn't as if they were destined for a repeat of the Deven incident. Faith's behavior was professional as always, and the only reason Miranda had to suspect anything was her gift, so really, there was nothing to be done about it but keep it to herself and hope nothing went wrong.

It wasn't herself or David that Miranda was worried about; it was Faith. Unrequited love was awful enough without the subject of that love being married in soul to someone else who was also your friend. Faith wasn't an emotional person, at least not where anyone could see. She and David were a lot alike in that regard, and Miranda had seen how hard it was for David to cope with powerful feelings for someone he didn't want to love.

Even now, and even with Miranda, David almost never brought up what had happened with Deven; he was still deeply ashamed of the loss of control that had nearly driven him and his Queen apart. They had talked about it but not because he wanted to; Miranda refused to let things fester as they had before. They had to be as honest with each other as possible—they had eternity to contend with, and that was a long damn time to harbor resentment.

For months, she had dealt with moments of rage toward her husband and the man that she knew he still loved . . . but in the end she had to make a choice, and living with that kind of anger was poisonous. She couldn't afford to lose her grip on her emotions, and David had realized that to be her Prime, he had to stay as strong as possible so she would always have an anchor.

She had to forgive, for her own sake, and they had to move on. David, she knew, was having a harder time with it than she was; even with all the lives he'd taken over the centuries, nothing had come closer to breaking him down with self-loathing than hurting her. He wanted to hate Deven, and couldn't; he wanted to change what had happened, and couldn't. Part of him wanted Miranda to hate him. Nothing Miranda could have done to punish him would ever be worse than what he did to himself.

If the departed Queen in the painting had an opinion on

the matter, she kept it to herself. It stood to reason she'd keep her own counsel; by all accounts Bess had been very wise.

Miranda stared at the portrait for another moment, wishing for any kind of reassurance before shaking her head and muttering to herself, "Your cheese done slid off your cracker, baby girl. Stop talking to dead people and get back to work."

She suspected Bess would agree.

She turned back to the piano and began running through one of her favorite covers, Concrete Blonde's "Bloodletting." She'd taken to playing it onstage after the vampire rumors started flying, at first just for the laugh; but after a few shows she had pared the song down to its bones and sang it in a half whisper with a soft accompaniment, and it took on a haunting sort of irony that she and the audience both appreciated for their own reasons.

As many times as she'd performed, she didn't really need practice, especially since she didn't have a band or backup singers to coordinate with as she had when recording the album, but she was working on a new song she wanted to debut at ALMF and it had consumed most of her rehearsal time this past week. She still wasn't happy with the last chorus. Songwriting had never been easy for her, and she'd done a number of collaborations to get around it, but the lyrics she wrote herself were always the biggest hits because they were the most personal. Crazy or not, human or not, people liked what they heard when it came from beneath her skin.

She finished the Concrete Blonde and transitioned seamlessly into the new song, tentatively titled "Landing."

> *The angel fell with tattered wings*
> *She flew too close to the sun again*
> *The sky is full of broken things*
> *Wishing for a softer place to land*
> *It's not the fall that kills you, darlin'*
> *It's not the fall that kills you . . .*

*   *   *

Custom dictated that there was no formal declaration of a Pair's arrival at Council until the ball; the Primes and Consorts would arrive at the Haven throughout Thursday night and early Friday morning before sunrise, then a few stragglers Friday evening before things got underway. At that point each Pair would be announced as they entered the ballroom, and from that moment the Council was considered officially convened.

Still, the Haven's staff made sure that each Pair was made to feel honored and welcome as they settled into their rooms, and David's closest allies would of course get there first and have a chance to meet privately. Other gatherings would doubtless occur among other Primes. Aside from the Magnificent Bastard parades, there were few chances for allies to meet face-to-face, so it was tradition to allow even one's enemies to get together . . . even if it meant they were conspiring against their host.

Whoever was hosting the Council was expected to remain as neutral as possible as far as etiquette went. It was considered a major coup to host, a vote of confidence in one's power rather like landing the Olympic Games. David had lobbied long and hard for this, and he was determined things would go as smoothly as possible. As old as he was, his tenure had not been long, and he was still looked at as an upstart newcomer in the Council. He was the first Prime to have won a Council convention with less than fifty years' rule under his belt. He knew that several of the Primes who had voted for him had done so more to see if he'd screw it up than because they liked him.

That was fine. He had built a career out of making other vampires eat crow. By Monday they would all have feathers in their teeth.

"Tanaka-san," David said, bowing. "Welcome. It's good to see you again."

The Prime of Japan returned the gesture and smiled. "Likewise, my old friend."

Tanaka was older than Deven, and given his age and status he could have easily been some sort of wise-old-Asian stereotype, but he coupled the bearing of an emperor with the wardrobe of a business executive. As parliamentary leader of the Council, he ran the meetings and had therefore given up his vote in most matters to maintain neutrality, but his influence among the Signets was formidable, and where his favor went, most of the Council tended to follow. He rarely spoke ill of—or heaped praise upon—anyone. His friendship, however, was coveted.

Each Signet territory's culture reflected its human culture, of course, and despite Japan's dense vampire population, it had been calm as long as Tanaka held it. Japan was known for its fierce warrior class and its elegant, highly ritualized Court. Tanaka dealt with his enemies quietly and swiftly, and though David knew there was gang activity there, no one would ever see it from outside. David had learned a lot observing Tanaka's leadership.

"I trust your accommodations are acceptable," David added.

Tanaka smiled. "Of course. I am honored that you remembered this was our favorite room. Not surprised, but honored."

"For you, anything." David turned to the woman who was directing the Japanese Elite on where to leave the Pair's luggage. "Is there anything you require, Lady Queen?" he asked.

Mameha didn't often speak English—in fact she rarely spoke at all—but it would be a mistake to dismiss her as servile or unintelligent, as some Primes tried to when they met her. She missed nothing, and David had heard that she carried several weapons concealed in her traditional kimono. David thought back to the last time the Pair had visited; Mameha was to date the only woman he'd ever seen visibly intimidate Miranda, and with good reason. It would never occur to anyone to treat Mameha with anything but utmost respect; her sheer presence demanded it.

She merely bowed, said that no, she required nothing, thank you, and went back to her business.

"I wanted to invite you to a private reception in my study," David said, returning his attention to Tanaka. "The West, the Plains, India, and Eastern Europe will be there."

"I shall be happy to attend," Tanaka replied. "I need to speak to Varati anyway to finalize a business transaction. And I am anxious to hear the latest news on your network progress—as are the others, I imagine. I know that as soon as you have the system ready for distribution, we will want to purchase a license."

"Absolutely. Of course I'd give it to you for free, but I'm sure we can strike a deal that will satisfy Council propriety."

"I look forward to it."

"Two A.M., then. I'll have Faith come to escort you to the study."

They bowed to each other again, and David left the suite with a nod to the Japanese Elite who stood guard.

Once in the hallway again, he paused.

The next suite to visit was California's.

David steeled himself. There was no reason to be nervous. They had talked frequently over the last three years, and as far as anyone was concerned, the whole horrible incident was behind them . . . but he knew, as did they all, that in reality it would never be done.

Just get it over with.

The door opened before he could even knock. "There you are," Jonathan said with a grin. "Come on in."

They shook hands, and the Consort ushered him into the room. He gave David a sidelong glance. "Relax," Jonathan said. "I'm here to chaperone."

Normally David would have been embarrassed to be so transparent, but really, it was something of a relief not to dance around the subject. He'd had no idea how this was going to go; phone calls were one thing, but face-to-face . . . but Jonathan's expression held only acceptance.

It had been three years since he'd seen Deven in person. Three years—and the last time they'd been in the same city, they'd surrendered to the demons that still bound them together. David wouldn't allow it to happen again . . . but he would never have believed it would happen in the first place. Nothing he had ever been sure of about himself held true anymore, and that was the most terrifying thing he'd ever had to face in his life.

The Prime stood at the window, watching the splendid view of the night; as David approached, he turned toward him, unsmiling.

They stared at each other.

"My Lord Prime," Deven finally said, bowing. "It's good to see you again."

David took a deep breath and held out his hand. "You, too. Welcome back."

Deven looked down at David's hand, then back up at his face; slowly, he offered his own, and they shook, neither one willing to draw any closer. David realized that Deven was as afraid of this as he was.

"Oh, for God's sake," Jonathan said. "You two are ridiculous. Just kiss already and let's move on."

"I don't think that's a good idea," Deven said quietly.

The Consort made an irritated noise. "If you start humping each other, I'll turn the hose on you. Cross my heart. Now stop acting like you can ignore all of this and it'll go away—we all know what happens when you do that."

David couldn't help but laugh a little. "All right, all right." Carefully, he moved closer and leaned down to bestow a kiss on Deven's forehead.

Dev raised an eyebrow. "Are you serious?" He put a hand around the back of David's neck and pulled David's lips to his.

The contact was electric . . . but David found it easy enough to keep the kiss brief and light, and when he drew back, they both breathed a little easier. He did, however, notice that Deven's ears were a little pink.

"There," Jonathan said. "See? We're all adults here. You were perfectly able to be friends before and nothing went wrong. You've got to trust yourselves."

Deven smiled. "All the same . . . thank you for putting us in a different room this time."

David gave him a slightly wicked grin. "Actually Hart's in that one. I thought that was appropriate."

"You are as delightfully evil as always," Deven replied. "Now, to the matter at hand."

David frowned. "What's the matter?"

Deven sat down. "A few days ago I lost contact with the operative I had in Hart's Elite."

David bit off a curse. "So we have to assume the worst—he knows you were spying on him."

"No, he knows the Red Shadow was spying on him. Even then, he'd have no idea why; the Shadow doesn't normally work for vampires, so he'd most likely believe a human hired us."

"Doesn't normally? Does that mean you've changed your policy?"

"Irrelevant, David. The point is that even though Hart has no reason to suspect my involvement, nor any way to know on whose behalf Claret was working, he knows someone was watching him . . . and more important, I no longer have eyes on Hart. Whatever his plan is, we're flying blind now."

David nodded slowly, straightening, determination stepping up to stomp out the stirrings of fear. "It doesn't matter," he said. "We proceed as planned. Whatever he's up to, we're ready for it. Let him try something. If he makes a move on us, he'll regret it."

Three

"There . . . all done."

Miranda took a deep breath. "How's it look?"

Faith raised an eyebrow. "As usual, I recommend you wear a bag over your head."

"Be serious, Faith! I can't see it!"

"I can help you with that."

Miranda looked up from the vanity—which wasn't much of one, considering it had no mirror—to see David in the bathroom doorway, mostly dressed, with his laptop and some sort of odd contraption that looked a lot like a video camera. "What's that?"

He gave her his "geek triumphant" smile and set the computer down on the counter, opened it, and plugged the camera into the USB port. "One moment, my Lady."

Miranda exchanged a look with Faith, who was both amused and bemused; Miranda remembered that Faith had been helping David with his new toys, and they'd had some promising results.

"Now, this won't be a perfect image, but . . ." David brought up a window and typed in a string of commands; another window popped up, this one a media player. At first it was nothing but shadows and fog, but David adjusted a dial on the camera and turned it toward Miranda. "Watch the screen."

As her eyes lit on the monitor, the foggy image in front of her flickered, and . . .

"Oh my God."

It had been a while since Miranda had seen her reflection—she'd seen the one in the mirror during the *Rolling Stone* interview for a few seconds—but she had found herself incredibly frustrated at having to get by without one; she had hair-and-makeup people for performances, but she never had any idea what they were sending her out looking like onstage. And for every night, she generally went without makeup at all and didn't try to do much with the unruly mass of her hair. She had yet to master Deven's ability to perfectly apply eyeliner by feel, and really, why bother when she was going to run and fight and sweat it all off?

The last time she'd seen herself, she'd been human . . . or a human on the verge of transition, with David's blood in her veins. She'd still been pasty and unhealthy looking, with dark circles under her eyes.

"I forgot about that scar," she said softly.

"I can cover it better if you want it to disappear," Faith said. "It's really faint."

"No," Miranda told her. "No . . . I want to see it. I earned it."

Faith had spent nearly two hours working on Miranda's face and hair for the ball and had wrought some sort of cosmetic miracle. The red tumble of curls had been secured atop her head, with a few tendrils artfully falling down into her face; the effect made her neck look longer, graceful, and even just in her bathrobe, she looked elegant and refined.

Miranda would never have left the house in half the color that Faith had applied to her face, but it was gorgeous. She'd used at least four shades of eye shadow, and Miranda's natural eye color was practically luminous against the palette. Faith had even fastened several tiny jewels, like Indian bindis, down Miranda's left temple. Her lips were a deep bloodred with a purple undertone.

Miranda felt her eyes start to burn. "I look like a Queen," she said.

David tipped her chin up with his hand so their eyes met. "You always do, beloved," he replied. "I just wanted you to see it."

"Don't cry!" Faith instructed. "I don't want to have to redo all of that."

Miranda stared into her own face for a long moment, swallowing hard. *This is who I am now . . . It's real.*

"Come on," Faith said. "Time to get you into your dress."

"I'll wait outside." David rose, leaving the camera where it was and giving his Queen a loving smile before he left them to their preparations.

"Did you feel like this when you saw yourself?" Miranda asked Faith, who was fetching the garment bag from where it hung on the back of the door.

"It was weird," Faith admitted. "It's been a lot longer for me."

Miranda sighed and stood up so that Faith could help her into the gown they'd spent four hours shopping for last week. Miranda had thought she should wear green, what with her hair and eyes, but Faith had quickly squashed that idea. Every redhead in the world wore green dresses, the Second told her. She had a better idea.

Still skeptical, Miranda stood still while Faith pulled and tucked and yanked various bits of the gown down over the insane bra situation that they'd bought. It was reasonably comfortable, though definitely not something she'd wear to fight or perform in. Still, she had refused to go anywhere totally unarmed, and Faith had chuckled and produced a small wooden knife that slid into a hidden sheath on Miranda's garter.

"Okay," Faith said. "Take a step back, and I'll move this thing so you can see the full effect." The Second took the computer and turned it sideways so that the image switched to vertical.

Miranda started laughing. "Jesus, Faith. Are you sure that's me?"

Faith grinned. "You plus some helpful girly scaffolding."

The gown was dark plum, almost black, and shimmered when it caught the light; it was fitted to the waist and then had a flowing skirt that was slit expertly to reveal glimpses of her calves as she walked. Her shoulders and arms were bare, and while she'd been afraid her skin would look pallid, it glowed; her Signet made the entire ensemble complete.

"All right, go blow your husband's mind while I finish getting ready," Faith told her.

Feeling faintly dazed, Miranda nodded and slipped on her shoes, then left the bathroom.

She heard a half-choking sound when she emerged, and had to hold back a giggle.

David was standing by the fireplace, staring at her with wide eyes over a glass of Scotch that he had apparently inhaled when he saw her.

Miranda smiled, put a hand on her hip, and said, "What do you think, my Lord?"

He set the glass down on the mantel and came up to her, still staring, and she half expected him to seize her arms and throw her down on the bed. His hunger for her was palpable, and his eyes were dilated and full of fire.

He looked as beautiful as she did—she'd never seen him in a tux before and hadn't thought it possible for him to look *more* sophisticated, but there it was. It was so attractive she wanted to rip it right off.

They stared at each other. "Faith will kill us both if you smudge my makeup," Miranda said, her voice husky with desire.

In response, David leaned into her, lips moving lightly along her neck while his hands encircled her waist and pulled her tightly to him. She sighed, eyes closed, and sucked in a breath at the sting of his teeth in her throat.

He took only a swallow, and by the time he lifted his mouth she knew the wound was gone. Carefully, so as not to smear her lipstick, she ran her tongue across his lips.

"I have something for you," David said, the words a whispered secret between them.

"I bet you do," she replied impishly.

Reluctantly, he turned away to retrieve a flat box from the dresser. He opened it and showed her its contents: a set of earrings and a ring, stones and setting a flawless match to her Signet.

"They're perfect," she said, letting him put the jewelry on her. He lifted her hands and kissed her fingers before slipping the ring on her middle finger next to her wedding band.

"Now you're ready," David told her with a smile.

A knock at the door, and the guard outside told them it was time to head for the ballroom.

"Faith," Miranda called.

"I'm right behind you," the Second returned. "Go on ahead."

Prime and Queen smiled at each other, and Miranda felt the first moment of genuine excitement she'd had in days. Whatever was going to happen, at least for a minute she'd get to dance with her husband like a Disney princess, something she would never have imagined possible for herself a few years ago. *This is who I am now.*

David bowed and offered his arm. She gave him an almost-graceful curtsy, laughed, and took it, and together they left the suite.

The first time she set foot in the Haven, she was a slave, wasting away from starvation and abuse. She was almost too weak to stand, and she lived in the quiet hell of eternal despair. She had no hope, no will to live, no will at all.

Then a woman had come into her life, and without saying a word, she changed everything. Her dark-honeyed voice, her proud shoulders, the purpose in her stride had awoken something . . . something fierce, something that would not go quietly into the darkness . . .

And the next time Cora set foot in the Haven, she, too, was a Queen.

"Are you sure . . . ?"

They stood near the end of the line of Pairs waiting to descend the grand staircase into the ballroom, she in floor-length velvet and he in his tuxedo. On the far side of the wide double doors she heard a booming voice announcing each Pair one by one. She recognized a few from their state visits three years ago; her Prime had many friends, and the array of names and territories had been dizzying.

Cora turned to Jacob. The syllables of her new home language—Czech—were still a little strange to her, but she tried to honor her Prime and her subjects by becoming as fluent as possible. "I am, my Lord."

He took her hand and kissed it, giving her that kind, nose-crinkling smile that warmed her to her toes. "I am proud of you," he said. "You are doing far better than I am with all of this."

She shrugged. Perhaps her stomach was quaking a little from nerves, perhaps not, but the truth was: "I have nothing to fear."

Jacob nodded. "That's right, my love. You are now the equal of anyone here. Not to mention you have your yeti to watch over you."

Cora held out her free hand, and in a few seconds a large, shaggy head bumped it. The servant standing nearby made a startled noise as Vràna the Nighthound, Cora's guardian, appeared from where she had been sitting in the corner and stepped up to her mistress's side.

Nighthounds had started out as Scottish deerhounds, but centuries of selective breeding had produced an uncannily intelligent creature the size of a pony that could run as fast as a vampire. They were imposing animals, to be sure, but usually quite docile unless called to defend their masters. Vràna rarely left the Queen's presence, though Cora knew better than to take the dog into the ballroom. Vràna would wait for her out here, quiet in her corner and completely unnoticed.

Cora scratched Vràna's head, then gestured for her to return to her post. The breeder Prime Deven had acquired her from had shown Cora a series of one-handed visual cues that Vràna had been taught to obey from puppyhood, though over time Queen and Hound had come to understand one another at an almost psychic level.

She wished she could take Vràna in with her. Hound on one side, Prime on the other, she felt safe . . . protected. She knew she wasn't weak, but she was not a fighter, and the thought of . . .

"He is in there," she said, almost too softly to be heard, staring at the doors. "In a few minutes I will . . . we will . . ."

Jacob touched her face. "We don't have to do this. As long as I come to the meeting tomorrow—"

"No," she said, perhaps too quickly. "I have to. This is my world now as much as his. I have a right to be here."

They held each other's eyes a long moment, and Jacob smiled again, shaking his head in wonder. "You surprise me every night," he said. "I would never have imagined your strength. I thank God every night when I wake beside you that we found each other."

She smiled back. "As do I . . . my love."

Now he was practically beaming; she was still hesitant to express affection and only very rarely solicited physical attention of any kind. They had made great progress together, but in many ways she was still trying to shed the restrictive skin of who she had once been, and he gave her all the space she needed, telling her just after they met, "We have years ahead to travel down those paths. There's no need to rush down them—think of all we might miss."

They moved forward until they had reached the doorway, and the uniformed guard acting as herald consulted his list and then verified their identities with Jacob.

"Here we go," the Prime said, taking her arm and leaning in to kiss her cheek.

Cora took a deep breath and closed her eyes in a second's prayer as she heard her name called. Her mind was racing, and all she could think to pray was, *God help me . . . God help me . . . amen.*

The ballroom opened out before her, a vision of formal dress and candlelight and music. The staircase ended at a red carpet that lined the room's center; on either side, watching each new couple enter the room, were the Pairs of the Council, applauding after names were announced. The orchestra was set up in the far corner, playing a regal but upbeat march. There was so much to take in, and Cora had never seen anything like it; she remembered all the fairy tales she'd heard as a child about princesses and masquerades, and indeed it all felt so unreal, as if she had stumbled into a fairy tale of her own.

Cora scanned the crowd as she and Jacob took the stairs, but she couldn't see Hart anywhere. One of the hundred terrors she had feared about this night was the thought of meeting Hart's eyes, tripping over her gown, and tumbling headlong down the staircase.   ·

Instead, she held her head up and smiled, nodding to the Queens she recognized and a few who were watching her curiously—sometimes logistics prevented a Pair from making a state visit, and there were some, like Japan and Australia, that had tendered regrets and sent gifts.

The variety of costume and facial features among the Council was astounding; while most had come in Western-style ball gowns and tuxedos, some were in traditional dress for their homelands, and the colors and luxury were enough to make her head spin. There were glowing stones everywhere; the Primes wore them in place of a bow tie. She had never seen such a diverse crowd before—every imaginable ethnicity was represented.

It seemed to take a year to reach the last step, but as soon as they did, the herald called out another Pair's names, and the room's attention shifted back to the top of the staircase. Cora let out the breath she'd been unconsciously holding. Jacob, smiling, squeezed her hand, and together they joined the throng of onlookers.

A moment later, the herald announced, "Prime Deven O'Donnell of the Western United States and his Consort, Jonathan Burke."

Cora found herself grinning in spite of her anxiety.

Both Deven and Jonathan looked absolutely splendid in their tuxes, though Deven as always cut an interesting figure with his facial piercings and spiky hair, which was, just now, shot through with violently red streaks. It was strange to Cora to see two men walking arm in arm the way all the other couples did, but it didn't bother her the way it seemed to bother a few of the others standing around her. She knew that Hart had considered Deven a deviant, but it surprised her anyone else would. Hart was a fool—surely they all knew that?

Still, there were a few uncomfortable expressions among the Pairs, and Cora frowned, feeling protective of the Pair. Deven had been a good friend to her, and she was quite fond of Jonathan, and if anyone had a problem with them, well, they were as wrongheaded as Hart.

Shortly thereafter, the herald made his last introduction: "The hosts of this decade's Council gathering: Prime David Solomon of the Southern United States and his Queen, Miranda."

Cora's smile returned.

This time the applause was practically deafening; the Council seemed determined to show appreciation, if not to win favor with the host Pair. Surely they were an impressive sight, elegant and regal, perfectly matched. Miranda's cascade of garnet curls was held up atop her head; she wore a shimmering gown that showed off every inch of her curvaceous figure. Prime David's blue eyes swept the entire room in a heartbeat, missing nothing, and the power radiating from the two of them was like a storm cloud of burnished silver.

When they reached the ground, the orchestra changed its tune, striking up a lively waltz; Pairs all around Cora joined in to dance.

Jacob leaned in and whispered, "Just this one, my darling, and we'll get you out of the center of attention."

Cora nodded her assent and put her hand on his shoulder. As they made their way around the room, she had to remind herself over and over to keep in step—it was hard not to get distracted with so much grandeur to stare at. She and Jacob had practiced dancing at home for weeks, and she had taken to it readily enough, though she vastly preferred her yoga; but waltzes had been the hardest to learn, and she had to count in her mind a few times to avoid stumbling.

At last the song was over, but the exhausting part of the evening had just begun; now it was time to make the rounds among Jacob's allies, meeting and greeting, and she kept a smile plastered to her face, though the whole time all she could do was cast anxious glances around for Hart.

Every Pair was different, though they all had the same air of royalty and immortal grace. She knew that the handful who were hostile toward the entire Signet system abstained from the Council meetings entirely, and because Signets were autonomous, no one could be forced to attend, but even among those who were here, she could feel the eyes on her with varying degrees of interest, lust, disdain, even vague hostility. Most of the men here were killers, with no regard for human life, and she could feel the menace from many of them—directed not toward her, but toward the entire world. She couldn't imagine giving her loyalty to them, but they all had followers, even fanatics. Again she sent up her gratitude to God for leading her to Jacob and not another.

"All right," Jacob finally said, leading her off to the side of the ballroom. "Why don't you rest here a moment out of the way and get your bearings? I'll get us something to drink."

She wanted to protest his leaving her alone, but on second thought she decided she didn't want to be that woman. She didn't want to be afraid or to demand that he stay by her side and protect her, as if she were some helpless child. She might not be a warrior, but as she had said, she belonged here as much as anyone else.

Cora moved as close to the wall as she could and tried to mimic Vràna's ability to become invisible. After a moment, she found herself watching the dancers and relaxing a little, admiring the way everyone moved together. Now, many were circulating and talking, while others danced, but some Pairs had swapped partners with their friends; she saw Prime David dancing with a gorgeous dark-skinned woman who Cora was pretty sure was the Queen of some other part of America, and Jonathan was with the Queen of South Africa.

The music was so beautiful, and the atmosphere so genial, that Cora found herself considering whether to ask Jacob to dance with her again, or perhaps even to approach Deven just to say hello—she couldn't stand here all night, after all, and there was no reason she couldn't talk to people as Miranda was doing, even without her Prime at her side.

Cora should have known something would go terribly wrong.

"Well, well . . . what have we here?"

Cora found that for all her brave words to Jacob, she couldn't move, couldn't react at all; time seemed to freeze the second Hart's hand closed around her arm, and she felt his hot breath at her ear.

"Aren't you a beautiful sight," he said to her softly, running his fingers down her shoulder. "I wouldn't have thought a sparrow dressed as a peacock would be so enticing." His grip on her arm tightened painfully as he added, "Of course, no matter how you paint it, it's still just a sparrow."

She wanted to scream, to strike him, to do anything, but she couldn't. She couldn't even breathe.

Suddenly Hart stiffened, and his hand pulled away as if it had touched something red-hot. Cora heard a woman's voice, low and deadly, speaking words she didn't understand; those words seemed to break the spell over Cora, who finally was able to wrench herself away from Hart and turn to face him.

To her amazement, Hart was pale. Beside him stood a woman resplendent in traditional Japanese dress . . . holding a wooden dagger to Hart's ribs. Her face was expressionless, but her eyes conveyed all the meaning required. They were full of cold fury.

"Is there a problem here?"

Cora felt the air rush back into her lungs as Queen Miranda and her Second, Faith, appeared on either side of Cora. Both were glaring at Hart with the same look as the Asian woman's.

"No, of course not," Hart said smoothly, recovering his aplomb as quickly as he always had after an outburst of violent rage. He cleared his throat and straightened his tie; as he drew back from Cora, the Asian woman removed her weapon from his side and it vanished.

"I was simply asking the young Queen here to dance," Hart went on.

Cora felt the first real stab of emotion since he had approached her: wrath. She held it in check, but straightened and said, her voice full of ice, "I'm afraid I must respectfully decline."

"Very well." Hart gave her an extremely shallow bow and a poisonous smile. "I'm certain we'll meet again soon."

The Asian woman, who Cora realized was wearing a Signet set with a milky green stone, gave Cora a silent nod, then turned and was gone, her footsteps as soundless as her imposing countenance.

Miranda sighed. "That bastard," she muttered. "Faith, what did Mameha say to him?"

Faith smiled a tad wickedly. "Basically, 'Lay a hand on her, and you draw back a bloody stump.'"

Cora's breath was coming in harsh gasps, though she tried to keep her calm; now that Hart was out of her sight, she felt her entire body weaken with relief and start to shake.

Miranda gave her a penetrating look, then touched her arm. "Come on," she said gently. "Let's get some air. "

Miranda led Cora around the perimeter of the ballroom, ignoring the couples that turned slowly on the dance floor to the orchestra's flowing music. There was a door half-hidden by a huge tropical potted tree, and she beckoned for Cora to follow her through it.

The hallway beyond was dark and quiet. She sat Cora down on an upholstered bench and let the Queen ground herself; Cora was no slouch at energy work, with her yoga experience, and before long she had slowed and deepened her breathing.

Not two minutes later Miranda heard something tapping along the floor and looked up to see Cora's gigantic dog trotting toward them. Miranda blinked in surprise; she had seen pictures of Nighthounds, but the real thing was even larger than she had expected. The dog's head came up to Miranda's shoulder.

Vràna gave Miranda a quick look of appraisal, deemed her harmless the way David's horses had once upon a time, and sat down at attention at Cora's feet.

Finally, Cora looked up at Miranda; she wasn't crying, but there was such sadness in her eyes. "I thought I could do it," she said.

Miranda nodded and sat down, crossing her arms and toying with her Signet. "Before I came here, back when I was human . . . I was attacked by some men in an alley. They did things that . . ."

She didn't look at Cora, but she could feel the Queen's eyes on her as she groped for the words and the will to continue. "When they were done, they intended to kill me . . . and for a minute, I wanted them to. I couldn't imagine living with that. All I could think was that at least it would be quiet . . . that I would be safe, and no one could ever hurt me again."

"But you escaped."

Miranda met her eyes again. "I killed them," she said. "All of them. There's this thing I can do . . . I didn't really understand it at the time, but I hit them with so much emotion, so much rage, that it snapped their lifelines. Their hearts just . . . stopped. In a way, mine did, too, and it took a long time for it to beat again."

Cora took a deep breath that was heavy with unshed tears. "You are saying, then, that you understand how I feel."

"What I went through was only one night, and your ordeal was years long. But I understand violation, fear, and anger."

The Queen tilted her head back to rest against the wall, regarding Miranda with something new in her face; after a moment she said, "If you were to face those men now, what would you say?"

Miranda smiled. "I would kill them all over again . . . but this time I would take a lot longer."

"I want Hart to die, Miranda. I do not like feeling this hatred . . . not even for such a monster. And I cannot kill him—even if I were able, I do not think I could. So I am doomed to face him every ten years . . . forever."

"Not forever."

"What do you mean?"

Miranda lowered her voice until it was barely a whisper. "All I'm saying is . . . if things continue as they are and Hart continues to bait us, his continued safety is in serious doubt."

Cora considered that, then asked gravely, "Could you kill him? Is it easy to take a life?"

Miranda started to say that she'd already killed quite a few people and yes, it was incredibly fucking easy, but something in Cora's tone made her pause. "I don't think about it much," she admitted. "I accepted that in this life there are things worth dying for and things worth killing for. I'm one of those things. My people are also. So are my friends and my Prime."

"I ask myself if I could kill Hart," Cora said. "If I were to stand over him with a stake, knowing the shot would be true, over in an instant, and the suffering of all his harem girls and servants and those killed by his legions would end . . . in that moment, could I do it? And, in doing it, what would that do to me? What would I become, then?"

Miranda found herself smiling softly at the irony of a vampire Queen who was, at this moment, hiding in a hallway outside a gala event, theorizing over the moral implications of killing a murdering rapist in a society of vampires. "I have to say, my Lady, you are the first person who has made me think about any of this since I became Queen."

Cora looked surprised. "I would think that such questions would be at the center of everything we do. If God has appointed us to this rule, we must be clear on where the lines are drawn."

"There," Miranda said with a smile. "There's the difference, Cora. You have faith in God, and that faith leads you to ask these questions about right and wrong. Most of us just bypass them and then deal with the consequences."

"So your way is . . . efficient."

"Yes. But it's not a moral high ground by any means. I . . . I admire you, Cora, more than you probably realize. I never had faith in God. I've only learned to have faith in my own strength. Where that comes from . . . I have no idea."

"But something saved you that night, when you lay upon the ground . . ." Cora's eyes grew cloudy, and Miranda knew she was Seeing something as her slender fingers rested lightly on Miranda's arm. "And when you were beneath the dark water, drowning . . . you found that God within you, that . . . Dark Warrior Queen, who came to you . . . a serpent."

Miranda stared. "How do you know about that?"

Cora let go of her arm with a sigh. "I touch people and I see things. Past, present, glimpses of the future. Lord Jonathan has visions. You feel emotions and know the hidden truth of the heart."

Miranda remembered how rattled Kat had been when Miranda read her; well, now she knew how that felt, and it *was* creepy. "So, I guess I had faith in something then. But right now, I'm doing the best I can without a higher power. So I envy you your surety."

Cora looked down the hallway at the ballroom door. "Do not envy me now, my Lady Queen."

Miranda stood up and took both of her hands. "Cora, look at me. The one thing you absolutely cannot do is let

Hart make you run and hide. You are no one's harem girl, no one's slave. So whatever you do, do it as Queen."

She pulled Cora up from the bench, still hand in hand. "Walk with me," Miranda said. "You and I will walk into that room together and let him see us both. He can hate us both until the sky falls, but he can't take away who we are."

Cora took a deep, slightly shaky breath and nodded. This time there were sparks returning to her eyes, and she squared off her shoulders and ran her hands down over her dress to smooth it out. "Yes," Cora said. "Let us walk, my Lady."

Miranda held open the door; the two Queens smiled at each other, and without hesitation, Cora walked back inside.

Faith alerted the guards to keep their eyes on Hart for the rest of the night; she had no intention of letting him out of her sight, but she couldn't be everywhere at once, as evidenced by the fact that somehow the bastard had cornered Cora before either Faith or Miranda could head him off. Thank goodness for Mameha and her dagger.

Aside from that incident, it seemed the evening was going smoothly. Faith took a moment to admire the splendor. So much power and influence in one room . . . and so many hidden agendas, fangs waiting to come out after a cordial smile and a few diplomatic platitudes. The ball was a chance for everyone to show off and make nice before the real power plays began.

Tomorrow night the gloves would come off.

A circulating waiter offered her champagne, and she took it without really intending to drink it; she was used to having a weapon at hand, and being here made her feel vulnerable and antsy. As beautiful as everyone was, she knew what really lay beneath, and in truth she would have vastly preferred to be in uniform along the walls with the other Elite.

At least she knew she could run and fight in her heels.

As she took a tiny sip of her champagne, something drew her gaze across the room, and she found herself meeting a pair of cool hazel eyes.

He obviously recognized her, and she was fairly sure she'd seen him before, too—the lack of a Signet around his neck suggested he was probably someone's Second, though with him being in a tux she couldn't tell whose. He, too, was drinking champagne and lifted his glass to her in silent salute, which she returned without smiling.

Something red caught Faith's eye, and she turned her head in time to see Miranda and David return to the dance floor, the Prime spinning his Queen out and then back into his arms, her dark gown twirling around her legs. Faith's heart caught at the sight of them together, and she lowered her eyes and took a long drink of her champagne before either could notice her staring . . . not that they would. They only had eyes for each other.

When Faith looked back over to where the man had been, he was gone.

"You must be Faith," someone said.

She turned toward the voice and saw that her hazel-eyed saluter was standing a few feet away. "I am."

Up close, he was really very handsome, with slightly feline features, white-blond hair, and a determined chin. He had the body of a seasoned warrior, flat-muscled but lithe, and seemed as ill-at-ease without a weapon as she was. He didn't look like he laughed very often; neither did Faith, come to think of it.

"Jeremy Hayes," he said, offering his free hand. He had an Australian accent that made him about ten times more attractive. Faith's pulse started up its own waltz. What *was* it about Australian men? "Second in Command of the Northeastern Elite."

Faith stared at him, heart sinking. "Oh."

His eyebrow quirked.

"You work for Hart," she said, not bothering to hide her distaste. As another waiter glided past, she reached out and swapped her empty champagne flute for a full one.

Hayes smiled. "And you hold that against me."

"Of course I do. Your Prime is a swine."

Hayes tilted his head to one side, considering her words, then nodded. "I suppose it would be impolitic to agree with you."

"Yet you're loyal enough to him to be his Second?"

A shrug. "It's a job."

She couldn't help but be shocked at his attitude. How could anyone advance all the way to Second without being fiercely devoted to his Prime? "It's not just a job," she replied coldly. "The rest of us understand that."

He didn't react to her tone. "I owe Hart a great debt," he said. "Those who owe him, he owns. One day I will have paid off that debt, and I'll be free of him."

"And how many innocent people will you have killed in the meantime?"

"Probably many. But the truth of the matter is, Hart gives his dirty work to specialists like the Inquisitor. I have one job: to lead the Elite. I'm a general, not a confidant."

She felt her own eyebrows shoot up. "He has his own *inquisitor*?"

He smiled. "Like you said . . . swine."

With a slow nod, Faith reached out and shook his hand. "It's . . . interesting to meet you, Second Hayes."

"Jeremy, please." He glanced over at the dance floor. "Shall we?"

"You want me to dance with you?"

Now he looked surprised. "That is generally what one does at a ball. I hate to think you put on that beautiful dress just to stand around and look wary."

She frowned at him. "I don't trust you."

"I'm not asking you to. I'm just asking you to dance."

After another pause, she nodded again and took his arm.

There was no nightmare quite like throwing a party.

David didn't especially like big social gatherings. He preferred to be able to see everyone in the room with him at once and know where the threats might be. A crowd of humans was one thing—they were hardly a danger—but even he had to admit that having the whole Council there, watching him, was unnerving.

Luckily he'd had years to prepare for this night. The staff had been drilled in their duties for months, and everything had been meticulously prepared, from the flower arrangements—selected to complement Miranda's gown—to the sequence of music, chosen by the Queen and the orchestra leader to create the rise and fall of the room's mood. At least they didn't have to feed everyone, just keep the alcohol flowing. Each Pair's suite had a fridge with a blood supply, but beyond that they had to hunt for themselves.

He watched Jonathan spin Miranda around the floor, the two Consorts laughing; David's heart beat wildly with love for his Queen, who was easily the most beautiful woman in the room tonight. He had nearly gone weak in the knees when he saw her in her gown earlier that evening. She was breathtaking. He couldn't take his eyes off her.

David became aware, distractedly, of Deven standing next to him, and rather expected Deven to ask him to dance, but the Prime was as fixated on their mates as David was.

They stood side by side for a long moment, neither speaking until Deven's gaze flicked to the left and he noted, "That's interesting."

David followed the tilt of Deven's head and made a noise of surprise. "Huh."

Most of the crowd was made up of Pairs, of course, but a great many had allowed their Seconds to join in the festivities, both as a perk of the job and as a way to show off the cream of the crop of their warriors. Mostly the Seconds hung around together—a lot of them knew each other and had friendly relationships or rivalries just like their employers—and were self-segregated to one side of the ballroom.

He saw Faith, and his first thought was that she looked

absolutely beautiful. His second thought was that she was dancing with Jeremy Hayes.

"That's Hart's Second," David said, brow furrowing. "What is she doing with him?"

Deven shot him a quizzical look. "Have you *seen* him? I'd be all over that, too, if I were Faith."

"But . . . it's Faith."

A quiet snort. "David, my darling, you can be as thick as a porn star sometimes. Faith is a flesh-and-blood woman, not a stone statue."

David continued to stare at the striking couple, conflicted. "But . . . Hart's Second? Surely she knows better than to trust him."

A shrug. "They're dancing. It's not a crime." He gave David a piercing look. "Don't you trust *her*?"

David felt himself flush sheepishly. "You're right. I'm overreacting." He turned to Deven and added, "But I think you might be underreacting. If your theory is correct, he's the one who exposed—"

Deven shot him a warning look. There were too many possible eavesdroppers here.

"—your friend," David concluded.

"Oh, don't worry," Deven said. "If I find out for sure it was him, I'll have his balls and then his head. But tonight, at least, I'm willing to let it go long enough for Faith to get that stick out of her ass for half an hour. Aren't you?"

David sighed. "Stop shaming me with your level head."

Deven grinned. "Jealous?"

"Of course not!"

The Prime of the West just gave him that look, the one that Southerners would refer to as a "bless your heart" expression, and returned to his crowd-watching.

Miranda emerged from the dance floor with Jonathan in tow and gave David a light kiss. "Ready for another round, baby?"

David smiled at her. "Are we talking about dancing?"

The Queen chuckled, then noticed Faith and said, "Would you look at that?"

Jonathan saw, too. "Wait, isn't that—"

"Yes," David said. He looked over at Miranda, expecting her to be concerned, but she actually looked relieved. He had no idea what to make of that.

"Come on," Miranda told the Prime, taking his hand. "Dance with me. I didn't put on this crazy-ass bra for nothing."

"I agree," Jonathan said. "Except for the bra part. Mine is perfectly comfortable."

Deven and David both snorted and happily acquiesced to their Consorts' desires.

I can't do this. I can't do this.

Oh, yes, I can.

She arched her back, letting his hand slide up to unfasten her dress and help her wriggle it off onto the floor.

Her nails raked long red lines up the length of his back, then curled up in the silvery strands of his hair and hauled his mouth to hers over and over again, her teeth sliding down to tear holes in his tongue and suck.

He shoved her back against the wall with a grunt. His shirt and jacket were somewhere near the door along with her shoes. They didn't bother removing any more than was necessary—she barely even got the black lace down past her waist before he had hoisted her up off the ground and pushed into her, hard.

And if she had been thinking about blue eyes instead of hazel . . . if she had imagined, just for a moment, that he was taller, that there was a black-line tattoo over his back . . . at that instant, she forgot.

She cried out, nearly wailing. They tore into each other, biting and clawing, bodies meeting with such force it was almost more pain than pleasure . . . almost. They slid down the wall together, and she pushed him down onto his back on the floor, twisting her hips in circles and spirals and eliciting a moan with each movement.

He tasted like whiskey and fire.
I can't do this.
Yes, I can.
I can.
I am.
Yes.

Four

Miranda's eyes were on the conference room screen, where a diagram that looked like a spiderweb spread out from a single name at the center: Marja Ovaska.

Lines connected the assassin with weapons dealers, martial arts trainers, spies, and alleged sorcerers of all stripes from all over the globe, but there was a noticeable gap. "So you still have nothing," Miranda said.

Deven shrugged and tapped the screen of his phone, causing the diagram in front of them to change. A new line connected Ovaska to something labeled *Morningstar*. There was no image attached.

"Morningstar," David mused. "That's the corporation you said was referenced in Ovaska's financial records?"

"Yes. No CEO is given, but there are at least three deposits from Morningstar into Ovaska's offshore account over the three-month span before she was killed. Each deposit was two hundred fifty thousand dollars. That's a standard payment for a Shadow contract . . . but not enough to kill a high-profile vampire."

"Oh?" Miranda asked. "What's the going rate on a Signet these days?"

Deven smiled. "I don't kill Signets. Too risky. The most we'd do would be to take out a high-profile Court member, and that would set you back at least two million. Even if she was driven mad by her need for vengeance, I can't picture Ovaska agreeing to kill a Signet for as little as three-quarters of a million."

"What if there was more money coming after the mission was complete?"

"Not how it works. I teach them from day one: payment in full up front. Ovaska was methodical and paranoid. I can't see her deviating from that."

"So what would that much money get her?" David asked. "Who would a Shadow operative kill for seven hundred fifty thousand dollars?"

"No one," Deven replied. "But we'd sure as hell kidnap someone."

Miranda nodded, looking back up at the screen. "Ovaska said she was supposed to deliver me alive—you were just collateral damage."

"Exactly. Now, I've had my people digging into this Morningstar thing, and that's where it gets interesting. Like I said, the Shadow doesn't work for vampires, so my assumption was that Ovaska's client was a human. But what would a human want with a live Signet? Kidnapping one of us would be ridiculously dangerous, especially for a mortal. I've been through the obvious answers: ransom, medical research, political leverage, but there's one thing I keep coming back to: magic."

David rolled his eyes. "Again?"

"Believe what you want to believe, darling, but the fact is, there are sorcerers out there. Whether their power is real or not doesn't matter in this case; what matters are the lengths they're willing to go to, to get that power. So I asked around, and apparently there's an entire subset of black magic that uses stolen life energy, usually in the form of blood sacrifice. In those sorts of circles, the belief is that the sacrifice of a human can open doors and summon demons—imagine what they could do with one of us."

"If that's true, why hasn't it ever happened before?" David wanted to know.

Now it was Deven's turn to look annoyed. "Don't you get it? It might *have* happened before. How would we know?

Signets die all the time. It's only in the last few decades we've been able to find out so much detail on how and why. For all we know there have been dozens of Signets killed for this kind of purpose—it's taken me three years to find out this much, so that tells you how far underground this is. I'm working my way through Morningstar, but there are so many shell corporations and false titles hiding whoever is behind it, it's like looking for a needle in a needle stack."

Miranda followed the web from Ovaska again with her eyes, then asked quietly, "What about Sophie? Was she involved?"

Deven's voice gentled. "No. She at least was easy to investigate. Ovaska's involvement with Morningstar didn't begin until after Sophie's death, and it has no connection to Sophie's history whatsoever. Sophie was just a woman in love, and aside from what she did for a living, there wasn't a sinister bone in her body."

Miranda and Deven's eyes met for a second, and Miranda nodded. "Okay. Well, as soon as you find out anything new . . ."

"You'll be the first to hear of it," the Prime told her.

Standing, Miranda reached over and squeezed David's shoulder. He caught her hand and kissed it. "I'm going to finish getting ready for tonight, then," she said. "Dev, tell Jonathan to meet me in the garage at seven."

David looked up at her. "Be careful," he said.

She grinned. "Aren't I always?"

He snorted. "Right."

"Have fun at the tournament, baby. I'll see you in a few hours." She kissed him on the top of his head, then looked over and gave Deven a nod of thanks, which he returned.

The Queen headed back to their suite to gather up her guitar and wriggle her way into the Lycra contraption and thigh-high boots she had laid out to wear to her big night.

Faith woke alone.

She sat up in bed, startled out of sleep by who-knew-what, and looked around, panting. The sheets were twisted all around her bare legs, and the comforter had gone missing; one pillow was still up by her head, but the other was on the floor.

"Hello?" she called hesitantly, but she knew even as she spoke that the room was empty. There were clothes tossed all over the place, but they were all hers.

Relieved, she flopped back onto the bed. Her muscles complained bitterly—her back, her thighs, even her neck were all sore, and she was starving.

Faith put her hand over her eyes to still the hangover she could feel building in her skull. She really should have stopped after her sixth . . . seventh . . . eighth? drink, but they just kept appearing every time her glass was empty. "God, what were you thinking?" she muttered. The sound shot pain through her head.

Her com chimed, and she groaned. "Star-three," she said. Her voice was a little hoarse—had she really done that much screaming? Good God.

"Um . . . Second Faith . . . are you all right?"

Faith frowned. "I'm fine. Why?"

"You were supposed to be here at the tournament twenty minutes ago. You're never late for anything, so—"

Faith cut Elite 20 off with a long, colorful series of curses and sprang out of bed. "Shit! Are we up yet?"

"No ma'am. Our first round is in thirty. You should make it in plenty of time."

"I'm on my way."

She stripped the sheets from her body and threw them on the floor, then bolted into the bathroom and into a freezing cold shower. The water hit her like bricks, shaking her the rest of the way awake, and she probably would have been humiliated if she'd had time to think about it. She washed the sweat and blood and man-smell off herself as fast as she could, not bothering with her hair—she was about to get it dirty anyway.

"Fuck, fuck, fuck," she said as she grabbed the clean uniform she'd laid out yesterday; she always had one ready to go in case of bloodstains or emergencies. She had it down to a science and was dressed in five minutes, though her clothes were sticking to her because she hadn't gotten completely dry.

Boots, weapons, phone. She grabbed her best sword from the cabinet that held her arsenal and strapped it to her hip as she hit the hallway at a trot.

She could hear the fighting even before she reached the Elite training building. Swords clashed amid the sounds of a crowd's murmur. Only about half the Primes and a handful of Queens would be watching the quarterfinals; the entire Council would attend the last round to see which Elite took home the trophy this decade. Most of the tournament took place while the Council was meeting.

It had started as a way for the Elite to pass the time while their employers were wrangling with politics. A few exhibition matches had evolved into an organized event; each participating territory sent eight of its warriors, hand-picked to represent their Elite. They competed in single and group combat and were judged by a panel of their peers—usually Japan, as Tanaka abstained from the tournament, which was a shame, since Faith had heard his Elite were a thing to behold.

For the past thirty years the trophy had been securely positioned in California, but Faith had spent most of her tenure as Second improving the training program in the South, and she was confident her team would at least make it to the finals this year. To be late for this . . . it was more than embarrassing, it was inexcusable.

She hoped against hope that the Prime wasn't there, but her heart sank as she slipped into the room and saw David standing at the edge of the audience, arms crossed.

Fuck, fuck, fuck.

Faith steeled herself and went to join her team.

"Cutting it a little close, aren't you?" David asked without looking at her as she passed him.

"I'm sorry, Sire. I was delayed."

The Prime raised an eyebrow. "You might want to brush your hair. It looks rather postcoital."

Faith flushed and yanked her hair back into a tight ponytail where it wouldn't matter if it was a little unruly.

She took her place in line with the other Southern Elite and tried to get a grip on herself. Aside from a few strange looks, it didn't seem like that many people had noticed she was late. Everyone's attention was on the first round of solo combat, between the Seconds of South Africa and China. A group competition was going on, on the other side of the broad room. She looked over at the grid where the upcoming matches were listed, and the brackets for the semifinals were still blank. Good; she hadn't missed . . .

"Son of a bitch," she said, startling Elite 20, who was standing next to her.

"Are you all right?" the Elite asked, concerned. "You look a bit flustered."

Faith tore her eyes from the bracket where her first opponent was written: *Jeremy Hayes, Northeast.* "I'm fine," she said curtly.

She looked around the perimeter of the room, where the upcoming teams were all waiting, each in a line with their leader on the right. Sure enough, there he was, standing at attention in full uniform, armed and ready to fight.

Faith felt a quiver in her stomach as flashes of the day before came back to her. Much of it was blurry with alcohol, but she knew one thing: If he was as good in the ring as he was in bed, she was in trouble.

Nonsense. She squared off her shoulders. No man was going to best her, not here. She'd made a mistake last night—fraternizing with Hart's Second wasn't against any particular rule, but it was inappropriate and ill-advised. But she didn't think he would mention it; they were both professionals. His boss probably wouldn't like it any more than hers would. There was no reason to let the whole thing rattle her. People met and slept together and parted company all the time at these things. There were even a few of her own Elite who had regular bed partners among other Elite that they met up with only every ten years. No need for drama.

He felt her staring and met her eyes.

Faith tried to look away but couldn't. In this light, his eyes were hazel, but in the dark of her room they had been smoky green, almost . . .

Almost too quickly to register, he winked at her, then returned his gaze to the ring where South Africa was trouncing China.

The match ended to applause, and Faith heard her name called. She cast a glance over to where David had been standing, but he was gone, either to sit among the other Primes or to deal with some other business. She rather hoped he wasn't watching, just in case.

With a nod to the judges, she stepped out into the ring; the audience cheered for her, and less so for her opponent, who joined her. Second bowed to Second and each drew a sword.

The bell rang.

Faith went into a ready stance, sword up, watching Jeremy with narrowed eyes, calculating his relative strength and agility from what she'd . . . observed. They both had an advantage there—they'd seen each other move, and he had no doubt sized up her physical abilities as she had his. She had cataloged everything, from the curve of his biceps to the pale scar across his stomach that looked like the remnants of some surgery—

The attack caught her off guard, and she bit back a curse and leapt backward as his sword slashed the air a scant half inch from her chest.

She countered, wrenching her attention back to where it belonged. This was no time to daydream! She could hardly represent her Signet mooning like a schoolgirl!

Circling slowly around her, Jeremy smiled. "Preoccupied?" he asked quietly with a knowing look. "You seemed a lot more focused yesterday afternoon."

"Fuck you," she hissed before she could stop herself.

"It's a date," he replied.

"Was all of that last night just to get under my skin?" she asked between swings of her blade, each of which he parried expertly.

"No," he said. "It was to get under your clothes. You're far too experienced to let one shag throw you off your game . . . aren't you?"

"Trust me," she snapped, "you're hardly worth losing concentration over."

He grinned. "Keep talking. I can go on all night."

"Since when?" Faith fought hard not to grin back, but something of a chuckle got past her guard; they spun around each other, steel striking steel, neither yielding the advantage. On the other side of the room she heard the crowd react to something in the group combat ring; those watching her and Jeremy were no doubt silent, waiting for one of them to screw up. Thankfully the noise level ensured none of the Primes could hear their conversation.

Faith threw herself into the fight, determined not to shame her Elite—even if she lost, they could still make the finals as long as the team didn't lose any other matches, but giving up a victory to Hart's team was unthinkable. She wouldn't do that to her team, or to David. It wasn't just her reputation on the table here.

She didn't have the psychic fighting skills that Deven and David had, but she hadn't gotten to Second on her good looks; there was a reason that the South was the envy of every Elite save, perhaps, the West's. She battled Jeremy back and forth through the ring, and though he was certainly strong and nearly as good as she was, she was better . . . and they both knew it.

Faith did one of her trademark backflips, earning a cheer from the crowd, and when she hit the ground, she whipped her blade in an arc that caught his and slammed it out of his hand. The blade clattered to the ground outside the ring, and she whirled around again, freezing with the point of her sword at his throat.

She heard the bell go off again and the audience—as

well as the other Elite—applauding loudly. The announcer called the round.

Jeremy didn't look terribly upset about losing to her. He was, in fact, smiling again as he bowed. "Good match," he said.

Faith nodded. "Good match."

As a show of sportsmanship, she retrieved his sword and handed it to him.

When they drew close enough to shake hands, he said, "Tonight, after the meeting's over . . . your place?"

She met his eyes. "Yes."

Then, taking a deep breath, she turned away from him and went to rejoin her team.

Isis, lithe and swift as a deer, leapt over the stream so smoothly that Cora barely felt the jolt of the Friesian's front hooves striking the earth on the far bank. Cora leaned into the horse's neck, her hands almost slack on the reins, letting Isis take the lead—the animal knew these trails backward and forward and, when allowed to run free, responded with a joy that Cora felt echoing in her own body.

Cora felt and heard the lighter impact of four paws alongside them; Vràna kept up easily, her tongue lolling out and her tail high.

The Queen knew she was going to be late for the party. She didn't especially care.

Jacob had taught her to ride almost the day they'd arrived in Prague. His love for his horses was infectious, and though the size of the beasts had intimidated her at first, she had quickly caught her mate's fever, and now she had her own Friesian, a gelding named Zimní—which meant "winter," though his full registered name was something like, "Damn, the Winters Here Are Hellish."

She had asked Jacob if he thought Prime David would mind her taking Isis out for a run; Jacob had told her she ought to ask him herself, probably to nudge her past her fear of the Southern Prime . . . of every Prime but Jacob and Deven, truth be told. She had screwed up her courage and approached David on his way to the Council meeting.

He had been thrilled to give her access to the stables; he still hadn't persuaded Miranda to learn to ride, and Isis was temperamental with most of the staff, so the mare got less exercise than David would have liked.

Cora was sure the horse remembered her. She had walked up to the stall and bowed, saying, "My Lady Isis, would you care for a run?"

Isis stepped delicately up to the gate, leaned over, and whuffled her hair; then she tossed her enormous head in an unmistakable nod.

An hour later, here they were, galloping around the perimeter of the Haven grounds, with Vràna keeping pace, all three of them practically whooping with happiness.

Cora would never have believed that one day she would love riding horses or doing yoga or running with her dog. The thought of enjoying anything had been ludicrous back when she lay beneath Hart. But thanks to the will of the Signets—which she was convinced was the will of God— she had stumbled headlong into a new, wonderful life, and whatever she had to do to keep it, she would.

Miranda was right. Her life was worth facing down Hart every ten years, assuming he lived for another decade. She knew war was coming . . . It might not be outright battle, as that was a rarity among Signets, but there were many, many ways to destroy someone, and she knew that Hart was a master at the slow torment of a lingering death.

As she, horse, and dog came around the last turn before the stables, she reluctantly pulled Isis back from her run and into a slower gait to cool her off; they'd take one last turn around the back loop before heading in to the pasture at a walk. Cora didn't want to go to the Queens' gathering; she didn't really want to have anything to do with the other Queens, who so far had mostly ignored her or looked down their noses at her. She had done nothing to deserve their ire, yet they apparently thought she was on a lower level of royalty than they were. She had promised Jacob she would try to make friends, mostly because he worried she was too withdrawn, but she was already anticipating an awkward, if not outright miserable, evening.

She saw in the distance that someone was standing at the pasture fence. Vràna identified the figure first and bounded over; it didn't take long for Cora to recognize him as well.

"My Lord Prime," she said, drawing Isis up by the fence. "Should you not be in the meeting hall already?"

"I was on my way," Deven said with a smile. He was standing up on the lowest rail of the fence, which enabled him to see over it. It was, she thought, absurdly cute, especially considering that he was probably armed to the teeth. "I saw you gallop by and thought I'd check in on you. We haven't had a chance to speak much this weekend."

Vràna stuck her head through the fence, and Deven bent to rub her ears. "You seem to be doing very well," he went on, looking up at Cora. "I must say you look magnificent on that monster's back."

Cora patted Isis on the neck. "Isis is no monster. She is a regal and proud lady."

Deven looked unconvinced, and Isis flicked her ear at him disdainfully, supremely uninterested in his opinion. Cora had to laugh at that.

"I wanted to ask you a favor," Deven said. "Feel free to say no for any reason."

Cora dismounted, facing the Prime through the fence. "Anything, my Lord."

"It's nothing dramatic. But tonight Jonathan is going into the city with Miranda for her concert, and that leaves me without ears in the Queens' gathering. I was hoping you might consent to carrying this." He drew something from his pocket: a tiny device about the size of a button. "I want to know what they're gossiping about. This will record conversations near you, and I can listen to them later."

Cora slid her hand through the fence and took the device. "Where do I put it?"

"There's a clip on it that will fit on the back of your Signet. Are you sure you don't mind?"

She turned over the device and her Signet, and sure enough, the clip was the perfect length to slide into the amber stone's setting. "I do not mind at all," she said, "as long as you do not wish for me to act on whatever I hear— I am neither a warrior nor an agent of yours."

His eyebrows shot up. "Now what makes you think I have agents, Cora?"

Cora gave him an amused look. "Why, nothing at all, my Lord."

Deven smiled at her slowly. "You are quite a woman, my Lady Queen. I look forward to a great many years as your ally."

"Perhaps you can offer a few pointers on how I might get the others to talk to me," she said. "Otherwise, I may not hear anything useful for you."

"Flatter them. Women love to be sincerely complimented, and it's a way to start a conversation: *I love your dress, that wart on your neck brings out your eyes*, whatever. If you don't like them, just pretend you don't speak whatever language they're using, and look preoccupied and mysterious."

"None of them seem to like me much," she noted, trying not to sound petulant. "I wish I knew why."

Deven snorted quietly. "By and large, Cora, Queens are shallow bitches who care about nothing but riches and power, just like their Primes. They look down on you because of where you came from, not because of who you are, which proves they're of no use to you. But they're not all bad. Aside from Jonathan and Miranda, I would advise you to at least stay on good terms with Mameha of Japan, Virginia Larimer of the Midwestern U.S. . . . Varati from India is a good friend of your Prime's, and his Queen is a brilliant woman. Most won't make the first move, though; that will be up to you, if you want your circle of allies to grow."

"I will try," she told him.

He reached through the fence and took her hand. "The most important thing is this: Even if they intimidate you, don't let them know they do. Walk in like you own the place. You've seen Miranda do it—and even the ones who hate her respect her enough to get out of her way. The Queens who would make good friends will be drawn to you, and you to them. Trust your instincts."

Cora squeezed his hand back and nodded. "I shall."

"Then you'll do fine, my Lady. Now, if you'll excuse me . . . I have to go pretend to find any of this interesting, and you should probably dehorse yourself if you want anyone to come near you."

He gave her a wink, released her hand, and was gone.

Cora sighed, her hand touching her Signet. She had no idea what he was hoping to learn through her tonight, but she would do her best to find it for him.

"Come, Isis," she told the horse, slipping a hand through her bridle. "Let us retire: you to your pasture and your mate, and I to my very first spy mission."

Once upon a time, in an era lost to the mists of history, the Signets had been something else: something real, something meaningful. There were no written records as far as anyone knew, but Deven knew that this pageant of peacocks going through the motions of civility wasn't why they were here.

Despite his age he was a relative newcomer to the Council, having been in power less than a hundred years, but even from the first meeting he had attended, he'd felt the lack of . . . *something*. Purpose, perhaps.

They had no real power over each other here; Primes could fight and kill each other from across the globe, but when a Prime wanted to hurt another, he did so secretly, using assassins and vampire hunters and by sending someone powerful to take down an enemy and perhaps take his Signet. Diplomacy as it was practiced by the Council changed little . . . but oh, how they loved their intrigues, their alliances.

Why did they bother with this charade?

None of the others knew anymore. More disturbingly,

no one seemed to care. They performed the ritual of assembling and arguing, then went home and ruled how they liked until the next time, and no one ever questioned *why*.

Deven watched the Primes assemble, some lingering in groups to chat, others already taking their seats along the great table. There were chairs for every territory, although a few Primes rarely, if ever, attended; Demetriou, Prime of the Black Sea territories, hadn't been brave enough to show this year, and to Deven's knowledge no one even knew what Dzhamgerchinov looked like . . . well, except Deven himself, who was probably the only Prime who had any sort of relationship with the oldest vampire in the Council.

The Prime of Russia terrified most of the others even though they'd never admit it. The vampires of his territory were nasty, brutish, and bloodthirsty; some of them barely looked humanoid. A combination of harsh environment and a Prime who had dispensed with the trappings of humanity centuries ago drew them to Dzhamgerchinov. The man himself was about as far from human as it was possible to get . . . but his friendship was useful.

Not even David knew that Russia and the Western United States had ties. Some things were best left undisclosed.

Human or monster, Deven would have preferred Russia's company to the oily presence of the Prime who came to stand next to him.

"Prime Deven," Hart said with that slight hint of disdain that was going to get him castrated one day.

"Hello, James," Deven replied mildly. "Had any consensual sex lately?"

"You know, you really ought to mind your manners," Hart replied, his tone calm, almost friendly.

Deven gave him a withering look. "Run along. The adults have business to attend to."

Hart's eyes narrowed. "Be careful . . . your boy over there is treading on thin ice, and you won't always be around to protect him or his shrew wife. Neither of you has as much influence as you think you do."

Deven actually laughed. "Oh, James. Your little grudge is so adorable." He turned his gaze fully on Hart, who had the good sense to look a little uneasy. "So the South gave Cora asylum, and Miranda threw you at a wall. So David's affection for humans threatens the status quo you've been exploiting to deal heroin and women all over the Northeast—yes, I'm well aware of how you make your money. So you think I'm a deviant: Get over it. You can't touch me, Hart . . . And if you try anything against the Southern Signet, you'll wish to God I had killed you here and now."

As he spoke, Deven's hand moved down to the hilt of his sword in silent reminder of all the heads Ghostlight had parted from traitorous shoulders. "Now go sit down like a good lad, drink your wine, and keep your fool mouth shut."

Hart glared at him for a moment before stalking off.

"That looked fun," David said, moving up beside Deven a few minutes later. "Everything all right?"

"He's feeling bold," Deven replied. "I don't like it."

"Neither do I."

They both watched as most of the Primes took their seats; Deven took the lead and started toward his own, David walking with him.

"Congratulations on making the finals," Deven noted. "We're going to beat you into next week, but still, you made a good showing."

David smiled. "Don't be too sure. Faith has been very driven this year—I think we have a good chance of winning."

"I hope not. I really don't want to pay India ten grand. He'd never let me live it down."

David checked his phone as they took their seats across from each other. When David was worried, a thin line appeared between his eyebrows; it was practically a canyon tonight. Deven knew why; across the city, Miranda was getting ready to perform in front of fifteen thousand people . . . onstage, vulnerable, and too far away to reach without a dangerous Mist.

Meanwhile, there was a gathering of Queens going on in another room of the Haven; most of them didn't deal in politics, so they had their own reception. Deven liked to imagine it involved doilies and drinking tea with extended pinky fingers, but Jonathan insisted he was wrong. Still, Jonathan had happily given up the doily party to accompany Miranda into the city, and Cora was Deven's informant tonight.

Jonathan never complained about being the only male Consort, but Deven was well aware how alienated he often felt from the others of his kind; no matter what, the Consort stuck out like a giraffe among zebras. He got along well with most of the Queens—his personality was the sort that made friends easily and made people feel comfortable despite their prejudices—but it was still a lonely place to stand. One thing Deven appreciated about Miranda was that she and Jonathan had been immediately taken with each other, and finally, finally Jonathan had a true friend among the Council.

David had felt better about Miranda going once Jonathan was with her. The Prime didn't doubt his Queen's strength or courage, but it took only one moment's lapsed attention, one shot, one unlucky night, to destroy everything.

One shot.

"Let us come to order, my Lords," Tanaka said from his position at the head of the table. "We will begin with the traditional roll call by territory. When I call the name of your region, please respond with your name . . ."

Fifteen thousand people, all under the same spell.

Jonathan had first seen Miranda play in her music room at the Haven. He had been floored by her voice, but of course she hadn't been working her empathy on him, so he knew the full extent of her abilities only via the sales figures for her first album. He had enjoyed watching her singles climb the charts and the CD go first gold, then platinum.

The Austin Live Music Festival main stage was outdoors in the middle of a public park, and the sheer size of the crowd should have generated an insane amount of noise, but just now they all seemed caught in silence, swaying silently back and forth while the muted strains of a piano melody floated out over them through a network of amps and speakers.

Miranda sang with her eyes closed and her hair down. Her fingers moved like a dreamer's over the keys, and her voice was almost a whisper, catching the lyrics of the song and spinning them into a spiderweb of wistful longing:

> *There's a crack in the mirror and a bloodstain on*
> *my bed*
> *Oh, you were a vampire and baby I'm the walking*
> *dead . . .*

The most amazing thing was that she held the entire audience rapt in the palm of her hand . . . and she wasn't using her empathy at all. It was her voice, her music, doing the weaving.

She transitioned from the cover song to an original piece seamlessly, without the pause to banter with the audience that most musicians would take. She tended to talk only when she switched from piano to guitar or while she was changing the settings on the digital keyboard behind her.

There was a hypnotic, drowning quality to her piano playing that was distinctly different from her guitar-based songs; the latter tended to be more fiery and sparked at the edges with emotional urgency. She seemed more at home behind the Bösendorfer than the Martin, but her skill was remarkable either way.

He was watching from the wings, not out in the audience where he'd be jostled and sweated upon by the teeming mass of humanity. There were Elite everywhere in addition to the Festival's considerable security staff. David had made sure to send as many warriors as he could spare, though that meant stretching them thin tonight as so many were required at the Haven. There was little chance of an incident requiring Elite intervention at the Council meeting, but while a handful were taking part in the tournament, the rest were on duty as a show of strength.

Miranda finished the song to deafening cheers. She rose from her piano bench and bowed, smiling broadly, face flushed with pleasure, hair soaked with sweat from the glaring stage lights.

A tech emerged from offstage and handed her her guitar. She stepped up to the microphone at center stage.

"Thank you," she said, quieting the applause. "I'd like to thank the Austin Live Music Festival for having me here tonight and all of you for your support . . . And speaking of support, as we mentioned on the website last week, we're now featuring a new T-shirt, designed by local artist Simone Veracruz, and one hundred percent of the proceeds will go directly to the Miranda Grey Porphyria Research Foundation."

Another wave of applause, along with a few shouts of "We love you, Miranda!"

"I have one more song for you tonight," Miranda went on, "but I'm going to need your help singing the chorus."

Her hand slid along the guitar's neck to find the opening chord, and she favored the audience with a mischievous smile.

Just as her pick hit the strings, Jonathan heard something strange: a faint pop and a whistle, then another.

The beginning of the final song screeched into discord as Miranda jerked backward. The microphone caught her gasp as she looked down.

Blood, berry-bright against her pale skin, blossomed from two round holes in her chest and in seconds had flooded down over her breasts and dripped onto the guitar's glossy wood.

For a few seconds, the entire crowd of fifteen thousand went deathly silent . . . but that silence turned to screams of horror as Miranda Grey crumpled and fell.

Five

Don't move. Don't move . . .

Pain engulfed her, but she fought to keep her mind moving: *Fall down. Don't move.*

The cacophony came to her distantly. Someone yelled to call 911; footsteps rushed all around her; thousands of people roared in fear and outrage.

Part of her was tempted to stay on her feet and reassure the humans. *It's just a flesh wound!* But she knew that if she were mortal, these wounds would probably kill her. She had to fall. She could only hope that her guitar wasn't damaged by the impact with the stage.

The fear around her was overwhelming. She bolstered her shields as best she could around the burning pain in her chest, giving her enough space in her mind to think semi-lucidly.

Bullets. Not wood. Can't heal them until they're out, can't dig them out with everyone watching. She could feel herself weakening from the blood loss, though it wouldn't kill her. The worst that would happen was she would lose consciousness while her body forced the bullets up to the surface and out of her body. She could feel them lodged in her muscles, each less than two inches from her heart.

Almost equally spaced. Perfectly placed shots. Not in the heart.

Sniper.

Faces moved in and out of her vision. The first she recognized was Jonathan's; he'd been close by so he'd reached her first. "Darts?" he asked.

She managed to shake her head. She was having trouble maintaining her shields; she had no energy left for conversation. "Bullets," she croaked.

Jonathan looked completely baffled. "Who the hell would shoot you with bullets?"

The Elite clustered around her, blocking the view from the stage as well as keeping the human security officers away. "We've got this," she heard one of the Elite bark at the police. "Paramedics are on the way."

"Miranda! What happened? Talk to me, beloved . . ."

David's voice from her com was a thousand miles away, but she heard Jonathan responding to it: "She's all right, David. Someone shot her. Stand by."

Something made the world go partly dark. Most of the stage lights had been doused. The sound of metal wheels on the backstage ramp was like nails on a chalkboard.

The Elite parted to let the stretcher through, and Miranda half screamed in pain as they hoisted her up onto it. "Get these fucking things out of me!"

To her surprise, the uniformed paramedic who peered down at her was a familiar, heavily bearded face with sympathetic brown eyes. "Let us get you into the ambulance first," Mo said. "Best not to have onlookers."

"What are you . . . doing . . . here?" she panted. There was so much noise . . . it was getting harder to concentrate . . . one of the EMTs fitted an oxygen mask over her face, and though it might have been for appearance's sake, she was grateful for the blast of air that shoved its way into her lungs.

"Our Lord Prime was concerned that something might happen tonight," the Elite medic replied, staying at her side as the "EMTs" rushed her off the stage and around to a waiting emergency vehicle. "He assigned me and several of the Hausmann staff to be nearby just in case."

There was another series of violent jolts as they loaded

her into the ambulance and slammed the doors. The rest of the staff peeled away, leaving only Mo and Jonathan with her.

Miranda had never been shot before. She had been staked more than once. Lead bullets weren't as painful or as deadly, but the wounds were still agonizing. Now that she was safe from prying eyes, she dredged up as much energy as she could and fed it into the wounds. Her muscles ejected the bullets much too slowly for her liking—she could feel them moving toward the surface, red-hot, until with one last push she forced them out. She screamed in pain and then heard the plink-plink of the slugs falling off to the side and onto the ambulance floor.

Mo had taken her arm and already had a needle in her vein; he hooked up a bag of blood and switched on the pump. "Five minutes and you'll be good as new," he assured her. "It's a nice fresh O neg."

He was, as always, very calm, even cheerful. From most people it would be aggravating in this situation, but from Mo it was incredibly comforting. Just as he had taken David's poisoning three years ago in stride, he didn't seem at all alarmed at the fact that someone had shot his Queen in full view of the entire Austin Live Music Festival.

"Someone shot me," Miranda said.

Mo lifted the oxygen mask. "Come again, my Lady?"

"Someone shot me!"

"The Elite are tearing through the place," Jonathan told her. He had one hand on her arm, squeezing almost too hard, but she was grateful for his presence. "They've already got a basic trajectory analysis based on how you recoiled when you were hit, so they know the shots came from somewhere up the hill and off to stage right. They're combing the grounds for shell casings."

"Someone in the audience?" she asked. The blood flowing into her arm was bathing the still-burning wounds in warmth, renewing the flesh and returning it to health. She tried to keep her breathing steady and let her vampire power and the blood do their work.

"Only if they somehow got past the police with a gun," Jonathan replied.

"This is Texas," Miranda reminded him. "It could have been anyone."

Mo was busy gathering up the slugs and slipping them into plastic bags. "We will know more once we have these analyzed," he said. "They appear to be from a handgun, not from a sniper rifle, but I admit my experience with human bullets was long ago and far away."

"Report!"

Both Miranda and Mo's coms blared out with David's voice this time, and she could hear the note of restrained terror in the words. She lifted her arm weakly and said into the com, "I'm okay, baby. I'm in the ambulance with Mo and Jonathan. The bullets are out and I'm healing."

"I've called an emergency recess. I'll be there in thirty minutes," he said.

"No—I'm fine, I promise. Stay there and do what you have to do. We've got Elite searching for the shooter and I'm out of danger. I'll be home soon." She dropped her arm with a grunt and shut her eyes for a moment.

"I'm headed to the server room," David said. *"I'll know in five minutes whether the shooter was a vampire."*

Someone knocked on the ambulance door, and Miranda nodded; Mo opened it, revealing a human in a suit with an APD shield hanging from his neck.

"Detective Maguire," Miranda said. "Nice to see you again. Did Stella like the autograph?"

"She's here tonight," Maguire replied. "I'd bring her to meet you, but I think now's probably a bad time. What can you tell me?"

"Got shot," Miranda told him. God, she was so tired. Such a large audience had taken more out of her than she thought; even before the shot, before their terror, they had been draining her. "It really hurt."

The detective actually smiled, though he was clearly focused on the matter at hand. "I've got uniforms all over the place and more on the way," he said. "The audience nearly rioted, but between APD and ALMF security we got things calmed down. There were at least a dozen people with cell phones recording the concert. We're rounding them up now to go over their footage—someone might have caught the shooter on camera."

Miranda's com went off, and David returned to the conversation. *"All right . . . I'm going back through the sensor data, and there were about thirty vampires in the audience, mostly in pairs and a few small groups. All of them arrived at least an hour ago, except . . . there's one signal that shows up midway through your set, working his or her way up toward stage right. The shot goes off, you fall . . ."*

"I'm okay," Miranda said again. "I really am."

David took a deep breath and went on, voice a little roughened with tension. *"Got him! Tracking northwest— he's in a cluster of humans who are walking toward the parking lot. He's blending in, not in a hurry. Detective, have uniforms in place for crowd control at the corner of Zilker Park Drive and the entrance to the botanical gardens. Try to clear the humans from the area. I'm sending all available Elite. Stand by."*

Maguire ducked out of the ambulance, and Miranda heard him yelling into his walkie-talkie.

Miranda found she was shaking—a delayed reaction, perhaps, but suddenly she was freezing and had the urge to curl up on herself and cry.

"Hey," Jonathan said gently, taking her hand. "You're all right. We'll catch the bastard and figure this out."

"My big night," Miranda said around the knot in her stomach. "Guess it's one they'll remember."

"Are you kidding?" He gave her a slightly uncertain grin. "You'll be a legend."

"If I live," Miranda said. "If I were human . . . wait . . ."

"What is it?"

No one in the Shadow World would shoot a Queen with bullets. They'd use a crossbow or stake launcher. And what human would want to kill her, assuming she was human? A deranged fan? The shots had been awfully well-placed . . .

but if a human was going to shoot her in the middle of a concert, why not aim directly for her heart or head? A vampire wouldn't bother, but a vampire would know that bullets wouldn't kill her . . . but it would *look* like she was mortally wounded.

"Whoever did this knew what I am," she said. "A human couldn't survive a shot like that."

Mo looked thoughtful. "If one had adequate and immediate medical attention, one could survive. These particular shots missed your organs entirely. It would be a grave wound regardless due to the blood loss."

Jonathan, with a stricken nod, said, "They wanted to end your career."

"Suspect apprehended," came a voice over the network. It was one of the Elite who had been assigned to the concert. *"There was a fight but no casualties."*

"Do you have an ID?" Miranda asked.

A pause, then: *"Partial, my Lady. The suspect is identified as Monroe . . . he's not talking."*

"He will," David replied shortly. *"Have him brought to Interrogation A. Did you recover the gun?"*

"Yes, Sire."

"Get it to APD—have them run prints and ballistics and check for registration. It's probably illegal, but we might catch a break."

"Shouldn't we send it to Novotny?" Miranda asked.

"Hunter Development doesn't have much on firearms," the Prime said. *"The human authorities will be able to get us faster information."*

"We've got quite a backlog in Ballistics," Maguire spoke up. "It could take days."

"Don't worry, Detective. I cheat."

Miranda sagged back on the stretcher, finally giving up on consciousness. "I want to go home," she sighed as exhaustion washed up over her and she closed her eyes. "Can we go home now?"

Mo's voice was kind. "Of course, my Lady. I will let the driver know we are ready—we are set to rendezvous in town so the press will not see you leave Austin in an ambulance and try to follow. A car is waiting for us there."

"Thank you, Mo."

The last thing she heard before she passed out was Jonathan speaking into his phone, the tone of his voice one Miranda had never heard before. "Deven . . . call me back. We need to talk. *Now.*"

As soon as Cora heard that something had happened to Miranda, she excused herself from the tediousness of the Queens' gathering and headed straight for the chamber where the Council had convened. They were in recess, the guard had said, and no one would notice if she was there.

Cora was both disappointed and relieved that she heard virtually nothing important during the party; she stuck to the outer edges of the group, making a little small talk here and there, but as she had predicted, few of the Queens were at all interested in her, and those who were didn't seem all that happy to be there either. Queen Larimer, in fact, excused herself after half an hour of obligatory circulating; she did give Cora a fairly warm smile as she left, which was encouraging. But Cora was far too frightened of Mameha to approach her, and India's Queen was surrounded by admirers—understandable, as she was stunningly beautiful and everyone seemed to want to know her.

Still, since she didn't know what Deven was looking for, Cora made her way around the room, sipping champagne and exchanging polite greetings, most of the time following the Prime's advice to pretend she didn't speak much English.

She was happy to leave . . . although she would have preferred a less dire reason.

Even though it was certain Hart would be in that room, she didn't care; she had to know what was going on, and that Miranda was all right. The rumor had spread among the Queens like wildfire even though none of them would admit who had first heard the news, and no one seemed to know anything concrete. Worse, they didn't seem all that interested in Miranda's fate except as a source of idle gossip.

Vràna at her side, Cora entered the Council chamber to a scene of quiet anxiety. A few Primes were seated at the giant table, but most were milling around talking among themselves. She did not see Prime David, but her senses zeroed in on Jacob immediately, and she was with him in seconds.

"She's all right," Jacob said without asking why she was there. "Someone shot her while she was performing. They caught him—it was a vampire."

"Shot her? With what?"

Jacob looked a bit bewildered. "With a gun. Regular old human-killing bullets."

"Why would anyone do such a thing?"

He took her hand and squeezed it. "I suspect they were trying to make it impossible for her to ever perform again . . . to kill her without killing her."

Cora felt anger stirring in her chest. "It must have been Hart, my Lord. No one else could hate her so much."

"We don't have any proof yet," Jacob reminded her. "David can't accuse him without some sort of evidence."

Even as Jacob spoke, however, Cora saw one of the doors into the room fly open, and David Solomon walked in, cold fury written in every line of his body. Without speaking or acknowledging anyone in the room, he strode up to where Prime Hart was standing with several other Signets . . . and punched Hart in the face.

A gasp went up. Cora felt her mouth drop open, and she looked over to see an expression of utter—and probably very rare—shock on Prime Deven's face.

Hart, knocked backward by the hit, was pulled upright by his associates, and for a wonder, he, too, looked astonished by David's actions. "What in hell has gotten into you, boy?" Hart demanded.

The Prime of the South was very calm, but rage hung from him like a cloak in a low wind; his eyes were pure silver, fixed on Hart with loathing. "You have committed an act of war against my Queen," he said, quietly, but absolutely heard by every ear. "Consider the gauntlet thrown."

"I don't know what you're talking about," Hart returned, his own ire rising. "I've done nothing to your woman."

"I know it was you," David hissed. "As soon as I've gone a few rounds with your trigger-happy minion, I'll prove it to the entire Council."

"You can't prove anything." Now a hint of a sneer had entered Hart's voice, and he made a point of regaining his calm. "I don't know why you have this paranoid delusion that I'm out to get you, David. What have I ever done to you?"

Cora was sure, for a moment, that David was going to kill Hart then and there. Hart either didn't notice or was deliberately ignoring it to make himself look like the saner party.

"Honestly, I don't know why you're surprised something like this happened," Hart went on. "Your Queen has been playing a dangerous game with the entire Shadow World. She's risked all our safety for her own selfish gain. Eventually something was going to go wrong—you should be glad it's over with and she can return to your side where she belongs instead of putting herself in jeopardy with these silly artistic notions of hers. She might have been killed for real."

David stared at him, then smiled slowly . . . but it was a venomous smile, one that Cora had to resist shrinking back from. "So this is your revenge for Cora," he said. "We took something from you, and you want to take something from Miranda. Well, James, you'll be happy to know, since you're so concerned for her welfare, that Miranda's wounds were not that grave, and she'll be able to return to the stage after her recovery."

"Ridiculous," Hart said. "Humans rarely recover from a shot to the head."

Something in David's demeanor changed completely; the anger seemed to drain out of him, and he looked over at Deven, who was watching the whole thing with obvious amusement. "Well, you know how it is, James," David said, smiling again. "Celebrities have better medical coverage than the average human."

With that, the Prime turned back to the assembly and said, "I apologize for my behavior, honored Primes. I would like to request, given the circumstances, that we adjourn for the night and resume our business tomorrow after sunset. We can all relax and watch the tournament finals."

The Asian Prime whom Cora recognized as Tanaka, the meeting leader, cleared his throat and approached the table, where he had left a wooden gavel at his seat. "Adjourned until sunset tomorrow," he said.

David shot another look at Hart and said, even more quietly this time, "This isn't over."

Hart smiled. "Of course it isn't."

Hart turned and walked out of the room, still smiling; as he passed where Cora and Jacob were standing, he looked at her, but she very deliberately avoided eye contact, squeezing Jacob's hand hard enough that she shook.

Jacob let out a breath he'd been holding and exchanged a glance with Cora, and together they went over to David. "I think you need a drink, old friend," Jacob said, putting a hand on David's shoulder. "It'll be an hour or so before Miranda's home and your Elite bring your suspect in; why don't we have a bit of a drink before we head down to the tournament?"

Deven echoed Jacob's motion on David's other shoulder. "Come on, darling," he said soothingly. "Let's get away from this nonsense for a moment before your head explodes."

Slowly—almost so slowly Cora was afraid he would bolt after Hart—David relaxed, looking from one Prime to the other before nodding silently and letting them lead him out of the Council chamber.

By the time the car pulled up to the Haven and Jonathan helped her out, Miranda was healed, but she was still so tired she could barely think.

"I think fifteen thousand might have been too many,"

she said wearily, leaning on the Consort as they took a side hall toward the Signet wing.

"You weren't using empathy on them, though, were you?"

"No . . . but I had to stay shielded through all of that, and it was a lot harder than I expected. Have you ever sung for an hour in front of that many people and then taken two bullets in the chest?"

"Can't say that I have."

He helped her into the room, out of her bloody clothes, and into the shower. "You look awful," Jonathan said. "You wash, I'll find you something to put on."

"I can take it from here," she began, but he shook his head, chin set stubbornly.

"I'll stay until David gets here. I'm sure he'll want to fuss over you himself. I just don't want to risk you passing out again and knocking your head on something. Broken necks are a bitch to heal."

She caught his arm as he started to leave the bathroom, gave him a tired smile, and said, "Thanks."

"I'd say 'anytime,' but this had better not happen again."

"I second that."

Jonathan was right—she was so worn out that she had to lean sideways on the shower wall several times as the steam and heat overwhelmed her. It felt like it took her forever to clean up and climb out into her bathrobe.

She was glad that David had taken his computer out of the bathroom; he was working on rigging a spare tablet to run the camera-mirror so she could use it when she wanted to. Right now she was sure she looked dreadful. For their kind, looking tired basically meant looking dead. The albino zombie raccoon look didn't really suit her.

When she returned to the bedroom, she saw that Jonathan was gone and David had arrived. The Prime was sitting on the couch before the fire, her guitar in his lap, carefully cleaning the blood off.

"You look really hot holding that," she said. "You should learn to play."

David looked up at her, and there were so many warring emotions in his eyes: relief, anger, love, fear.

"I'm going to kill him," he said.

She nodded. "I know." She made her way over to the bed and sat down, reaching for the yoga pants and tank that Jonathan had thoughtfully left for her there. "Shouldn't you be down at the tournament?"

"The final round doesn't start for another hour. I'm pretty sure it's going to be us versus California."

"Do you need me to be there? I want to watch it, but . . ."

"Don't worry, beloved. You've had a hell of a night already; no one will expect you to attend. Faith will certainly understand."

"Still . . ." She pulled the shirt over her head, noticing she was still stiff; the bullets had missed her organs but had gone deep into her pectoral muscles, and even after the wounds were gone, she could feel their ghosts remaining. Stakes did the same thing, she remembered; injuries that involved a penetrating object took longer to fully disappear and left more damage than, say, a cut from a blade. "That bastard is making me miss the sight of my Elite kicking Deven's Elite's ass. That alone is a capital offense." Miranda stretched her arms out, first above her head and then behind her back, trying to work out the kinks. "Do we have any evidence yet that Hart was behind it?"

"He must have been—"

"I agree with you . . . but we have to connect this Monroe with Hart, or it could just be some lone nut after me. God knows that's happened before, and a lot of people got hurt. A lot more will get hurt if we go after Hart without support. You're the one who told me that."

"Fuck the Council," David said. "I've had enough of their bullshit. What can they do? Gossip him to death?"

Miranda chuckled. "You sound like me, baby. I thought you were the diplomat here."

"I was until they hurt you."

She sighed. "I love you, too."

He set the guitar aside and came to her; she held up her

comb, and with a smile he took it and settled behind her on the bed to draw it gingerly through her wet hair.

"We can't throw our forces into a full-out war just because Hart had me shot," she said after a while. "I want him dead, too, but we have to be careful."

"I know." David leaned forward and breathed in the scent of her hair, arms moving around her. She relaxed in the embrace, feeling the sweet relief of contact soothe the frazzled edges of her nerves. "Let's see what I can get from our shooter, and then we'll consider the next step. For now . . . just rest, beloved. Rest and be safe."

She turned her face into his shoulder, and he held on to her and stretched out on the bed so they were curled up face-to-face. And finally, after everything that had happened that night and all the fear and pain and chaos, she let go enough to cry.

Six

An unexpected but massive early summer storm broke over the Haven just as the Elite tournament finals were getting underway. David was glad he'd had a triple backup system installed both for the servers and the electrical generators; the whole complex was on solar power, but he had other means in case of emergencies.

The roar of the rain made the crowd noise even harder to hear through inside the training room where the two combat circles were awaiting their last teams of contestants. It had come down to the South and the West, to no one's surprise, and first there would be the group competitions, then the Seconds themselves squaring off for the final fight of the night. Depending on how the teams scored, that last one-on-one might make the difference between the trophy going to Sacramento or, for the first time in a century, staying in Austin.

David took his seat on the top row of bleachers, where he had a perfect vantage point to keep an eye on the entire room. The two Elite teams were lined up along the far wall, waiting to be announced; the bleachers were full of Pairs and other Elite from the losing teams . . . including Hart's.

He could see the white-blond head of Jeremy Hayes on the front row, and he could see that Hayes was watching Faith.

Anger dug tiny claws into David's chest. Hayes must

have known that Hart was going to attack Miranda at the concert. A Second would always know the details of any complicated plan being conducted by his own Elite. Whatever sort of flirtation he and Faith had struck up would be done with now. Faith would see to that.

Or so he thought.

To his surprise, Faith felt Hayes's eyes on her, met them, then gave him a tentative nod. Hayes returned the nod as well as a partial smile.

The tiny claws of anger became talons, and David crossed his arms, wishing there were something handy he could break.

Across the room, one of the glass doors of the trophy case swung open suddenly, hit the back wall, and shattered.

David felt a pang of guilt as the servants scrambled to clean up the mess.

"That was careless."

He turned his head and frowned. "What are you doing up, beloved?"

Miranda settled onto the seat beside him, shrugging. She still looked so tired. He had hoped she would sleep the rest of the night and all the next day, until Sunday when the last Council affairs would be dealt with and hopefully Maguire would have come through with some evidence about the shooter and David would have had a chance to question Monroe himself, whatever that entailed. He didn't want her to worry about it; he'd get the evidence they needed to call Hart out, and she wouldn't have to deal with him.

"I couldn't sleep," she said. She'd dressed following what he'd put on before he left their suite earlier: black pants and a shirt, dressy but not formal. All in black, she was a creature of blood and darkness that, even with the tiredness in her eyes, looked ready to leap into combat . . . though she might prefer a nap.

He kissed her. "I love you," he said. "I'm glad you're here, even though you shouldn't be."

"I'm not going to let this stop me from doing my job. I'm here to support our Elite."

Miranda's eyes wandered throughout the room, and he sensed her doing a light sweep of her empathy, looking for anything they needed to know about; when she reached Faith, she hesitated, looking from Faith over to Hayes and back again.

"I bet she regrets going to bed with him now," David muttered.

Miranda gave him a sharp look. "Don't," she said. "Don't judge her like that. It's not as if you've never had an ill-advised affair. Besides, Jeremy himself hasn't done anything, either to me or to her. Would you really fault him for not revealing Hart's plan to the Second of his enemy?"

"Don't talk like Deven," David said. "It's really confusing."

"I'm just saying . . . Faith deserves our trust and our care. She's probably feeling pretty embarrassed right now, and we shouldn't make that worse for her. She stood by you when you—"

"I know," David said, nodding. "I know, beloved. You're right. She's never been anything but a true friend to me, and I'm acting as if she broke some rule—which she didn't. She just deserves better, even for a fling, than some thug of Hart's."

"That's for her to decide. And for us to stay the hell out of. As her boss, you have no right to pry into her private life, and as her friend, you should know better than to think she can't handle herself."

He smiled at her. "Again, you shame me with your level head. Aren't you supposed to be young and hot-tempered and charge into situations full steam?"

She smiled back. "I'm older than I look, beloved."

He watched her for a moment, weighing the truth of her words. She seemed to have aged far more than three years in these last three; physically she was the same, but emotionally, she had worn down a lot faster than he expected. He had seen it even as soon as Marja Ovaska's defeat. The aftermath of David's betrayal, and of losing so many friends, had taken their toll on the Queen.

She needed to rest, to rejuvenate; he remembered Faith's idea of a vacation, and it was sounding like a better and better idea all the time. If he could get her away from all of this even for a weekend, she might come back with renewed enthusiasm for their life; right now it felt to her like everything was aligning to destroy what she loved, and that she was going to have to choose between one life and another.

That might be true, but it didn't have to happen yet. There was still time for her to have what she wanted for a while longer.

He could make it happen, no matter what Hart's backstabbing or the media's hunger for fallen idols dragged them into. They hadn't even seen the beginning of his resources yet. For Miranda, he would throw all his knowledge, all his experience, into making sure she stayed "human" as long as she wanted to. The rest of the world could wait.

I will give you the world, my love . . . and no one will dare try to take it. No one.

"They're starting," Miranda pointed down at the floor. David took her hand, and she leaned into his shoulder, both watching the Japanese referees get everyone organized. "Do you think we'll win?"

David smiled. "Probably not, but if ever there was a time, now would be a good one."

It was a strange thing, seeing Deven's Elite go up against David's own—his Elite, trained mostly by Faith, who had been trained by Deven, as had David and Miranda themselves, Miranda indirectly. But David had seen Deven's style evolve over the years—it was an organic thing, adapting and changing as it needed to—so what he and Faith had learned at the Alpha's hand and what Deven's new Elite would do might be two very different things.

David had turned his training program over to Faith entirely, and she had revolutionized it; she had taken a mind-body approach, having all the Elite take yoga and meditation classes to teach them concentration methods, and everyone with even an iota of psychic power had been trained and shielded. Faith was determined to make the most of every individual Elite's abilities, rather than forcing them all to adhere to a single program as many other Signets did; in that way, the Southern Elite was made up of warriors, not soldiers, who were willing to follow orders because they were loyal to the Signet but could also make their own decisions. David had no use for mindless automatons, and Faith had made him proud.

There was more going on than simply knocking someone down; there was a complex points system at work, kept track of on the scoreboard on the far end of the room.

"This seat taken?"

David looked up to see Jonathan and Deven sliding into the bleachers, Jonathan next to Miranda. He kissed her cheek, and she grinned. On the far side of the Western Pair, Janousek and Cora had arrived as well, and Cora's dog settled with a grunt at her feet.

David had to smile to himself. There was something rather comforting about having allies around him like this, and he could tell Miranda felt the same way; she perked up a little as the match began, even whooping aloud when the announcer read off the names of their Elite.

The team competition looked, on the surface, like something of a melee, but both teams were actually highly coordinated, using attack patterns that the Seconds had mostly created. The two teams fought similarly: speed and agility, not hack-and-bash, and most of the team members were built like Faith and Deven, flat-muscled and slender like dancers. Indeed, the whole thing brought to mind a deadly sort of ballet.

One of the Western Elite spun and kicked his opponent so hard she flew backward and out of the ring; a whistle blew, and that warrior was done, leaving seven against six. Over at the South's bench, Faith clapped her Elite on the shoulder encouragingly; she'd fought well even if she'd been eliminated, and Faith didn't believe in the "drop and give me twenty, you maggot" method of leadership.

Deven's Second, Thomas, was watching with his arms

crossed, like a basketball coach. He frowned, and the crowd groaned, as one of the South sent one of his people rolling with a concussion and a broken leg; two of the Japanese refs came forward to help the Elite get over to the bench, and a servant brought him blood to help him heal faster.

"Is he okay?" Miranda asked.

"Just a femur," Deven replied, eyes on the match.

"Doesn't it take an insane amount of force to break a femur?"

He glanced at the Queen. "Your point being?"

The fight became more and more fierce the longer it lasted. Two more of the South went down, followed by another of the West: five against four, and the point tally was dead even.

David found he kept looking over at Hayes, who was watching Faith as much as he was watching the match; his expression was unreadable, but he certainly seemed taken with the Second, who was ignoring him. The more David thought about it, the more he wondered if hooking up with Faith had been part of the larger plan; was there something Hayes was supposed to get out of her? Information, perhaps?

A cheer jolted him out of his dark thoughts. In the blink of an eye the match was over: The Southern Elite had waited until there were only three of them left against three of the West, then, by some invisible signal, they switched their attack pattern and, each one moving so fast a human eye would barely have caught a blur of motion, spun outward, perfectly choreographed, and disarmed their opponents simultaneously. It was a simple, elegant move, and it left the South surrounding the West, swords held level at their throats.

The crowd was on its feet applauding. It was the first time in decades any team had beaten the West in group combat.

David looked over at Deven and gave him a smug smile. "What was that about kicking our asses?"

Deven, however, didn't look upset; he looked impressed. "That was fantastic," he said. "Well done."

"Faith deserves the credit," he replied, catching his Second's eye and giving her a nod of approval. She smiled slightly and bowed, but her attention was already focused elsewhere; she stepped into the empty circle across from Thomas, and the two saluted each other before the whistle blew.

It was a beautiful fight. The Seconds were the best of the best, and these two represented the finest warriors in the entire Shadow World. Within ten seconds it was clear why.

Sword met sword so rapidly that it sounded like Morse code. The entire crowd had hushed, absolutely rapt; enemy and ally, all of them were watching intently, territory disputes and ancient feuds forgotten for a few breathless minutes.

Miranda had her hand over her mouth, out of sheer nerves, and even Deven was glued to the action.

The fight was to disarm or disable; while the score was still in the South's favor, if Faith lost, the West would take the tournament. Neither combatant showed any signs of tiring, or of letting up on the other; they drove each other back and forth through the circle, neither missing a beat, but David knew eventually one of them would slow down just enough, lose a split-second's rhythm, and then—

Thomas kicked Faith hard in the shoulder, and she flipped backward, the audience on its feet when she landed scant inches from the boundary line; but she caught her balance just in time and threw herself forward, rolling and then coming up to her knees, her sword flashing—

Blood. Thomas made a choking sound as his midsection opened, the blade slicing neatly through his diaphragm. He went down on his back, and there was Faith, standing with her boot on his neck.

The applause was thunderous, deafening. David and Miranda both grinned at each other, then headed down to the floor.

The Southern Elite had gathered around Faith and were cheering, but she waved them off long enough to kneel next to Thomas and check his wounds; it was serious but not fatal by any stretch. The referees and the Western Elite were already moving, bringing towels to stanch the blood, and blood to heal the wound itself, though they had their work cut out for them; David saw the damage and gestured to Mo, who was on standby near the exit just in case.

Deven appeared at Thomas's side, and for a second David thought he might use his power on the fallen Second, but Deven wouldn't want anyone to know he had the ability unless absolutely necessary; he was speaking to Thomas, and the warrior nodded, grimacing against the pain. Deven patted him on the arm and moved back out of the way.

Faith, satisfied that Thomas would be all right, got back up again as well, and the rest of the team surrounded her. Miranda slid through the group and hugged the Second hard. Faith laughed.

The referees came back onto the floor, this time bearing the tournament trophy, which they handed to Deven.

The Prime of the West was smiling wryly as he presented the trophy to David, amid another round of applause.

"I think that's what they call 'passing the torch,'" David told his mentor, ex, and friend.

"Don't get cocky," Deven said with a laugh. "You'll pass it back next time."

"Whatever helps you sleep at night, my Lord," David replied, but he too was laughing, and for a precious few hours that night, nothing mattered but the heady validation of victory and the pride he felt; he had always believed they were the best, and now everyone knew it. It was more than just a trophy; it was validation, at long last, that after decades of decline under lesser Primes, the South had returned, with a vengeance.

In all probability, Second Hayes was expecting a different greeting than the one he got.

Faith opened her door at his knock. When she saw him, she grabbed him by the shoulders and slammed him into the wall.

"Congratulations on the tournament," Jeremy said breathlessly.

"You son of a bitch," she snarled. "I should kill you."

He shook his head, dazed. "For what?"

"You know perfectly well for what. You knew what Hart was planning—you had to. You had to know he was going to have my Queen shot last night."

"Oh, that."

She shoved him again, and this time he looked annoyed. "You have the nerve to show up here after—"

He kissed her.

Faith resisted, or almost did, but her blood was already hot from her victory, and from her anger at him for daring to even speak to her . . . she couldn't stop herself. She pushed him against the wall one more time, this time forcing her tongue into his mouth as she did so. Jeremy fought back, flipping her onto the floor, and they wrestled each other to the ground over and over, stripping off clothing, tearing at each other as if they were in the fighting ring again.

She pinned him on his back, her legs clamped on either side of him, her nails drawing blood from his shoulders as she rocked her hips forward and back. Neither of them had anything to say to the other, and words would only destroy everything. She didn't care. She didn't care who he was working for or what he had known; right now she only wanted one thing from him, and it had nothing to do with Signets or politics or loyalty. She wanted driving heat and sweat and screaming loud enough to peel the paint off the walls.

She wanted to forget.

It wasn't until she fell back on the rug, panting, her entire body pulsating with aftershocks, that reality tried to reassert itself.

For a while she pushed it away, reveling for a moment in the way their breath rose and fell in tandem, the waves of pleasure that were rocking them both.

Finally, she said, still out of breath, "Still . . . going . . . to kill you."

"Oh, shut up." He was actually smiling when he spoke, and it occurred to her he had a lovely smile—like hers, it was rare, and it had a pale shade of some kind of pain beneath it. "The world won't end because you took an hour for yourself, Faith."

"No life advice from you," she retorted, twisting onto her side to look at him. "You're the bad guy, remember?"

"Right." He sat up, groaning slightly, his hair falling haphazardly into his eyes. "It must be rather boring living in a black-and-white world."

She watched him silently for a moment as he groped for his pants and pulled them back on. "What does Hart have over you?" she asked. "Why are you doing this?"

"It doesn't matter." He looked around for his shirt, and wordlessly she handed it to him. "The path's already chosen, isn't it? You walk into a Haven, give yourself to a Signet, and your fate is sealed. Good Prime, evil Prime, in the end it's all the same."

She was still sitting on the floor as he stood up and finished dressing; there was something different in his movements, almost furtive, like he was fighting himself over something. She had her ideas as to what. "I could help you," she said.

Jeremy looked at her sharply. "No."

Faith frowned. "Do you want me to be your enemy?"

"Ideally, yes, for your own sake. You're loyal, Faith . . . too much so, perhaps. Being so devoted to someone is only going to cause you pain. But still . . . I envy you. You'll get to die believing in something. If I'm lucky at all, I'll get back what Hart took from me, and die knowing it's free."

"I have no intention of dying at all."

He smiled again, pausing on the last button of his shirt. "I'll hold you to that one day."

"Jeremy . . ."

But he was already leaving and stopped only long enough to look back over his shoulder and say, "Good-bye, Faith. It's been an honor."

Alone again, she sat back against the side of the bed,

grabbing one of the blankets down to pull over herself, suddenly cold. The storm outside continued unabated, and it had brought a chill to the Haven.

Sighing, Faith ran her hand through the tangle of her hair, contemplating a hot shower and an early bed; it was still an hour or so until dawn, and she was off duty, though she knew the rest of the Elite were still celebrating their victory with a lot of carousing out in the training buildings. Tomorrow night work would resume; she was to help the Prime interrogate the shooting suspect, and there was the last half of the Council meeting to contend with . . .

Bed it was, then.

She started to push herself up to her feet, but something caught her eye, and she reached over to pick up a tiny golden object: one of Jeremy's cuff links. The crest embossed on it was unfamiliar—it wasn't Hart's, and in fact she wasn't sure it was a Signet crest at all; his family, perhaps? Was that what Hart had taken from him?

She would probably never know. And she could find him and give the cuff link back, but what would they say to each other?

"Maybe in ten years," she said to herself, her voice sounding strange in the empty room, "if we haven't killed each other by then." She dropped the cuff link on her bedside table and went to take a shower.

Seven

"Well now," the Prime said to the man hanging by his wrists from the cinder-block wall. "What am I going to do with you?"

Monroe raised his head; he'd been beaten pretty severely and not fed, so his face was a mess of bruises and a few nasty lacerations. "I was thinking perhaps a bonus, my Lord."

A sigh. "You should be grateful I'm not abandoning you completely. Solomon is itching to feed you your own entrails, and it would be much easier for me to let him." He reached into his coat and pulled out a hospital bag of blood with a length of tubing still attached; he fed the end into Monroe's mouth and squeezed gently to start the flow. Monroe sucked as slowly as he could given how hungry he had to be, and neither spoke again until the bag was empty.

"You are a great many things, my Lord, but cruel isn't one of them," Monroe panted.

He laughed coldly. "You think you know me? Foolish boy. It wouldn't be a matter of cruelty, but one of efficiency, and you *know* I'm efficient."

The wreck of Monroe's face began to smooth out as the blood worked its way through his parched system. Soon he was more dirty than injured. Clearly the Elite had taken out their anger on him.

"How much truth am I to give Solomon?" Monroe asked.

"You remember what we discussed in the pre-mission briefing."

"Enough to indict on the shooting," the prisoner said with a nod. "What of my other mission?"

A smile. "What other mission?"

Monroe nodded again. "Understood."

A moment later the door to the interrogation room swung open, and David Solomon and his Second entered . . . then drew up short.

"What the hell are you doing here?" David asked, at the same time Faith said, "You've got to be kidding me."

Deven smiled. "Allow me to introduce 8.3 Claret," he said, gesturing at the chained vampire. "I would appreciate it if you didn't kill him."

David leaned tiredly against the edge of the table that held the implements he usually employed for interrogations, rubbing his forehead, exasperated. "Tell me again why I don't hate you?"

The Prime of the West considered the question as he helped his agent down from the wall, then said, "Because I'm really, really good in bed."

David rolled his eyes. "Just tell me that the shooting was Hart's idea, not yours, and I might not kill you this time."

"Of course it was Hart's idea, darling. I told you he's been up to something. You're lucky that I had Claret in his Elite already, or whomever Hart had pull the trigger *would* have shot Miranda in the head, and that would be the end of her career. This way she can 'recover' and stage a come-back, and you have a solid case against Hart."

"So your objective was to shoot her in the chest," David said to Monroe, who had straightened and was now standing at attention awaiting further orders, "and then to get caught so Hart's plot would be revealed."

Monroe—Claret—shot a glance at Deven, who nodded permission for him to speak. "Precisely, Sire," Monroe said.

"And everyone's just going to take the word of a turn-coat Elite over a Prime?" Faith wanted to know.

Now it was Deven's turn to roll his eyes. "Have you got ballistics back on the gun?"

"Still waiting," David said. "Maguire said he'd have something for me by the time the Council reconvened."

"Well, I believe you will find that the weapon in question was registered to a fellow by the name of Richter, who works as a courier for the import/export business we all know is a front for Hart's narcotics distribution ring. There's a clear and present paper trail between Richter and Hart."

"You're telling me Hart's enough of a moron to use a gun that could be traced back to him?"

"No. Hart's not a moron at all. He's a crazy bastard and a complete dickweasel, but not a moron. He simply expected his assassin to procure a human weapon. Given Monroe's record with his Elite, there was no reason to doubt he'd be able to pull off the job without getting caught. Sad, really." Deven looked at Monroe. "He's so going to fire you."

David glared at Deven. "One of these days your meddling is going to backfire on you."

"What exactly do you call Marja Ovaska? A resounding success?" Deven pointed out. "I had an operative in Hart's Elite. I saw an opportunity to thwart Hart's ambitions, and I took it. If I'd told you, you would have insisted I stop the shooting altogether, and you would be back to trading insults and punching him in the nose with no solid evidence that he's plotting against you."

David, losing some of his calm, said, "Do you have any idea what you put Miranda through? How hard it's going to be to manage the aftermath of all this?

He shrugged. "Miranda's not a child. Stop underestimating her—she can handle it."

"That. Is not. The point." David stepped forward so that his greater height towered over Deven—purely out of anger, not because he honestly believed the Prime would be cowed by him or anyone else. "You are not a god, Deven. You have no right to push us around your little chessboard."

They stared hard at each other. Finally, Deven said, a soft dare as well as an ultimatum in his voice, "Well then, my darling, stop acting like a pawn."

He vanished into thin air.

David heard Faith let out a breath. "Dramatic," she muttered. "As per usual." She waved a hand at Monroe, who was still standing silently. "What do we do with this?"

David forced himself to ground. "Leave him here for now. We'll act as if we questioned him—you are prepared to testify against Hart, aren't you, Claret?"

"Yes, Lord Prime."

"Good. Then I suppose I won't flay you. Faith, keep double guards on this door and another pair in the corridor—I don't want Hart getting any ideas about sending in another assassin to destroy the evidence. The Council is set to reconvene at midnight—Maguire has my private cell, but if he should contact the main lines, put him through to me immediately."

Faith bowed. "As you will it."

They left the interrogation room together, David securing the bolts behind them. "I'm going to go tell Miranda what the Littlest Magnificent Bastard has been up to this time."

Deven had been right, which made David even more irritated with him; Miranda took the news that her shooter had been acting under orders from the Alpha as if she'd been expecting to hear it all along.

She was in the middle of getting dressed for a night out on the town—she, Jonathan, and Cora were going into Austin and steering clear of the entire Council situation. They'd stick to the Shadow District where there were no humans to recognize her, since she was supposed to be in the hospital recovering from serious injuries.

She paused midway through lacing up her boot and sighed. "It figures."

"You aren't angry?"

Miranda laughed humorlessly. "This is the same person

who sent someone to teach me how to fight so I could take part in the battle that landed me the Signet . . . and who was spying on us through a yoga teacher, and who slept with my husband, and whose ex-agent killed half my friends . . . and who saved my life by giving me all his energy, and who saved Kat's life, and who saved my career last night. I'm sure it would pain Deven to know this, but he's pretty much lost the ability to surprise me at this point." She switched to her other boot and added, "In his own twisted way he's actually being kind of sweet."

David rapped his head lightly against the bedpost in frustration, earning a chuckle from his Queen, who patted the couch next to her. He joined her and kissed her temple. "He said I underestimate you," David said. "Do I?"

Miranda sat back thoughtfully. "Not really. You tend to overreact a little when it comes to me, but then, you've never once tried to stop me from doing something that was important to me—even when it might be better if you did."

He took her hands. "I want you to have everything you want in life," he said. "I'm willing to deal with whatever consequences arise."

She shut her eyes, and there was pain in her voice. "I don't want anyone else to get hurt because of me. Maybe I should just—"

"Don't even think it," David said quickly, changing his grip from her hands to her wrists. "At this point, you absolutely cannot quit."

"Why not?"

"Because you'd be letting Hart win. This is exactly what he wants: for you to doubt yourself and give up." David held her eyes. "I promise you, Miranda, if at any point it looks like you've gone too far and that the risk is too great, I'll say so. But I believe in you, and I'm not giving up, so neither should you."

She smiled, eyes bright. "Thank you."

He leaned forward and kissed her on the nose, then the lips. "Now, get out of here and go have fun. Try not to get into any more trouble."

"I thought you said have fun!" She stood up and fetched her coat and wallet. "I'd tell you to do the same, but . . ."

David rose with her and nodded. "If I have an ounce of fun tonight it will be because Hart is eaten by coyotes and shat out over a cliff."

She laughed and quoted one of his favorite phrases: "From your lips to God's ears."

Jonathan woke to an empty bed that evening, but that happened often enough; he rose and dressed for his evening out with the Queens, taking his time, trying to decide if he wanted to continue this half-assed silent treatment or act like an adult.

He hadn't managed to get his Prime alone since the shooting, and Deven had conveniently had his phone off during the Council meeting, ensuring that Jonathan's desire to speak to him about what he knew—he *knew*, even without precognition, because he knew his Prime—was going on would go unfulfilled until the next night. Jonathan had given up and gone to bed, and a few hours later when the sun had gone down and they would normally wake twined around each other like wild ivy, Deven had avoided him yet again.

Really, that was all the confirmation Jonathan needed, but he wasn't going to let this one go. As soon as he was finished dressing, he felt out along the Signet bond between them, and when he found his mate's presence, he had to smile: of course. Where else would he be?

There were underground tunnels connecting the Haven itself with the outbuildings, though for the most part the complex was purely nocturnal except for a handful of day guards. Deven had most likely taken them, but now it was safe to go outside; Jonathan followed the gentle pull of his mate's presence out one of the Haven's side doors and across the compound.

He found his Prime alone in one of the Elite training rooms running through a complex *kata* with his sword, Ghostlight.

The Consort paused in the doorway for a moment. He'd always loved watching Deven move; Dev was naturally graceful, but when fighting, he achieved a level of lyrical precision that was as deadly as it was beautiful.

Deven had studied for half a century in Japan and made his way around the East learning everything he could about martial arts before coming to America to fine-tune his skills with the warrior branch of the Order of Elysium. He had realized very early after becoming a vampire—and perhaps even before that—that he had two choices: Kill or be killed. By now, his style was purely his own, a unique blend of dozens of disciplines and moves that suited his size and speed.

This particular series of choreographed moves was one he had designed himself, and it was slower than the rest, more art than martial; Deven had created it as a form of meditation. It was a sequence he taught his agents to enable them to still their minds and cleanse themselves of distracting emotion.

Of course. Jonathan sighed to himself. Deven was feeling guilty, but no one would ever know, unless they recognized the *kata* for what it was: a confession.

Ghostlight flashed in the simulated glow of a false moon. The blade was, to date, Deven's favorite, and he was rarely without it. He swung it in a perfect arc as he turned, finishing the *kata* in the same position he started in, and Jonathan saw that his eyes were closed.

Deven stood still a moment before sheathing the sword and opening his eyes. He already knew Jonathan was there, of course, but he smiled when he saw his Consort.

Jonathan came into the room and kissed him lightly. "Are you all right?"

The Prime made an indefinite noise. "Fine. Are you? You had quite a night."

Jonathan crossed his arms and regarded him gravely. "You know, Dev . . . I love you. And I think we've come a long way since we first Paired . . . but you can't keep doing this to me."

Deven didn't bother feigning ignorance. "You weren't seriously surprised, were you?"

"I can't always tell you everything I see. And I don't ask to be told everything you're doing. But when my friends are in jeopardy, I want to know."

"You didn't see it coming? I thought you were the prescient one."

"Damn it, Dev, don't do that. Don't trivialize this. You could have stopped this whole thing, and Miranda wouldn't have been hurt at all. Do you realize what she went through last night? It was supposed to be one of the biggest nights of her career, and instead, fifteen thousand people saw her bleed all over her guitar."

"There are bigger concerns here than a couple of bullet wounds," Deven said sharply. "Do you want to coddle her or save her life?"

"How about if we let her fight her own battles?"

"She will. Do you think this is just about Hart getting back at Miranda? There's a whole world of awful coming toward this Haven, and it isn't just about Miranda or David . . . or even about Hart. It's about all of us. You know that."

Jonathan took a deep breath. He could argue with Deven until his voice gave out, but he knew better than to think he'd ever win.

"It's all changing," Jonathan said at length, looking away. "Everything we knew . . . ever since David took the South, something has been . . ."

"I know," Deven said, laying a hand on Jonathan's arm and running it up to his shoulder. "I can feel it, too, love, and I know we have to be ready for it. I tried to warn David. All I'm trying to do now is make sure that in the long run, we all survive. There might have to be collateral damage."

"We've known each other sixty years, and you still think I can't deal with whatever machinations you have going on in defense of our friends? Am I supposed to be like the other Queens and not dirty my hands in the unsavory dealings of the menfolk? Should I be at the doily party instead of at your side?"

"No."

"Then why can't you open up to me, Deven? Why does it always have to be you alone against the world? Why won't you let me help you while I can?"

Deven frowned. "What do you mean, while you can?"

"I mean . . . if this all comes to a head, we need to have plans in place for the worst-case scenario, and that means you let me in. Now. Do you not think I'm strong enough?"

"Of course I do," Deven said, looking surprised at the suggestion. "Jonathan, I trust you, and you have my full faith; I just . . ."

Jonathan waited but didn't back down, and finally Deven said, "You already have too many burdens, my love. Even in the name of those we care for, I can't stand to lay anything else on your shoulders. I see what you go through, just knowing what you know, and . . ." His wide eyes had darkened, a trait Jonathan had never seen in other vampires—all their eyes went silver when they were on the hunt, but Deven's actually became a noticeably darker purple when he was emotional . . . which was rare.

Whatever quirk of genetics had landed Deven healing power had also made him just a little . . . otherworldly, at times, like a strange wild thing wandered out of the mists of some ancient forgotten realm. With his being medieval Irish, Jonathan had joked once that Deven might be some kind of Faery changeling . . . and that was one of the few times Deven had ever gotten genuinely upset with him. Jonathan had never brought up the idea again.

Deven came closer to him, putting both hands on his chest, one over his heart. "I've already killed too much," Deven said softly. "I can't stand to hurt you, too."

Jonathan couldn't help it—it was so unusual to see that much emotion in the Prime, he had no choice but to respond, and kissed Deven hard on the mouth, taking his breath away. They melted into each other with a sigh. It was a beautiful thing, to be Paired, to feel that balance and solace just at a touch. Deven called it holy; Jonathan was inclined to agree.

"I have to go," Deven said after a few minutes, drawing back reluctantly. "David's going to present his evidence to the Council and move for a censure—and we know if they throw Hart out he won't go quietly."

"They can't excommunicate him from the Council, can they?"

"Technically no. A Prime is a Prime, no matter how fucked up. But they can have him suspended—or he gets tossed out this time, and next time his vote is null and void on every motion."

"That's barely a slap on the wrist for having a Queen shot."

"It's symbolic. It means no matter what he tries to get done next meeting, no one will side with him; he's essentially blackballed for as long as Tanaka judges he deserves it. And since all his friends are cowardly sheep, they'll leave him twisting in the wind if he wants to pull another stunt like last night's."

"Has anyone ever been thrown off for good?"

"Not for good, but for a good while. Why do you think Demetriou never shows? He got a fifty-year suspension for his involvement in Horak's death. He could have come back this decade, but his pride won't let him . . . and at heart he's too chickenshit to risk facing Janousek."

Jonathan had to laugh at that. "Demetriou's afraid of Jacob? Why on earth? He's like our own personal Jesus."

Deven grinned, but sobered quickly. "Jesus got angry, too, you know."

Suddenly, something very strange happened: It felt like the building shook, just for a second, and there was a muffled *boom*.

A heartbeat later, alarms began blaring all throughout the Elite training complex. Jonathan cast his senses around, heard footsteps rushing toward one end of the orderly rows of buildings, and he and Deven were out of the training room and headed down the hall with the guards seconds later.

Jonathan smelled the smoke before he saw it. They

came around a corner and ran into a huge crowd of Elite from several territories who had no doubt been holding grudge matches or showing off after the tournament; everyone was surrounding a hallway that led to a plain steel door, into a cinder-block outbuilding.

"Interrogation room A," Deven informed Jonathan, charging through the crowd to where Faith was holding everyone back from the scene. "What's going on?"

The Second looked utterly thunderstruck, but she was still issuing orders to get the area contained and cordoned off. "I don't know," she said.

"Was someone trying to blow the door and let the prisoner escape?" Jonathan asked.

"No," came David's voice, as he Misted right at Deven's elbow. "The smoke is coming from inside the room. Wait here."

Sword drawn, the Prime nodded to Faith, who already had her own weapon out; with everyone watching, the two slipped into the antechamber, where the interior door to the interrogation room was hanging partly off its hinges.

Jonathan tried to keep Deven from getting any closer, but it was as always a useless enterprise; Deven was in the doorway in a flash, and after a pause, Jonathan heard him curse loudly in Gaelic.

Faith was the first one out, and Jonathan saw immediately that her boots were covered in blood.

She looked up at him. She sounded like she was about to be sick. "Monroe."

"Where is he?"

Faith made a helpless gesture. "All over the place."

"What do you mean, it's *gone*?"

The line had appeared between David's eyebrows again, and his eyes were silver.

Deven sighed deeply and poured himself another bourbon.

Even before David hung up with Detective Maguire,

Deven knew what he was going to say; while he should have been annoyed at the complete and utter derailing of a very intricate and costly plan, the most he could drum up was resignation.

"The gun disappeared from Ballistics," David said, sinking into his chair. "The gun, the data, the report . . . it's all gone. There's no record of the gun ever being entered into the system, though several techs swear they had eyes and hands on it before it vanished. Maguire's having the entire department torn apart, but . . . it's gone."

"And 8.3 Claret was blown to vamp-jam all over the walls of the interrogation room," Deven added with a slow, amazed shake of his head. "You have no evidence whatsoever that Hart had Miranda shot, except my word that Monroe was working for me, and that would reveal my involvement with the Red Shadow."

"How in hell did Hart get anyone into that room to leave a bomb? And how did he get into APD's labs to steal the gun *and* hack their computer system?"

"I agree it makes no sense, David. Claret was undercover in Hart's Haven for years, and he never gave me any indication that Hart had this level of finesse. His businesses—the drugs, the human trafficking—he runs them like a street thug, with hired brute enforcers. The degree of organization this suggests is *not* like Hart."

"So either he's wised up a lot in three years and somehow kept it from Claret—which would mean he knew the Claret his people killed wasn't the real thing—"

"Or there's someone else involved in this," Deven concluded. "Someone Hart hired or who is on his side and working on his behalf."

"It has to be Hayes," David said. "He's the only player here we don't know enough about. Do you have a file on him?"

"Not much of one. He's been Hart's Second for eight years, originally from Australia . . . and in all that time he hasn't shown the kind of initiative an operation like this would take. He's loyal, as far as anyone knows, but there's nothing remarkable about him aside from brooding good looks."

"We need to know more. Can you do some digging?"

"Of course. I can access Claret's files; he kept them on a remote server. He would have had a way into Hart's personnel data, as well—I can give you that and you can do a bit of techno-sleuthing. All Claret ever told me was that no one had ever heard of Jeremy Hayes before he joined the Elite; but that's not so unusual. Vampire Elite are not exactly a sharing-and-caring breed."

"I've got Elite poring over every inch of that room for the explosives," David said, putting his head in his hands. "If we can find the blast seed, I can learn more about when and where the bomb was set. That won't link us to Hart, but it will tell us more about who we're dealing with here. It's possible that Hart brought Hayes on board to take his Elite in a new direction."

"A direction remarkably like yours," Deven noted. "Technology, intelligence operatives . . . the old bastard might finally be learning."

David ran his hands back through his hair and looked up at Deven. "I can't accuse him of anything at Council tonight. I have to let this go."

"Yes."

"How can I do that, Deven? How can I just let him walk out of here unscathed after what he did to Miranda? After I walked in and hit him like that, if I just let it go, I look like a fool."

"Why did you hit him, anyway?" Deven asked. "I don't think I've ever seen you just flat-out lose it like that in front of other people. That's not the cool-headed David Solomon I know."

"Apparently my cool head falls right the fuck off when someone hurts my Queen."

Deven smiled. "That's as it should be. I don't care how logical you are, darling, when it comes to your Queen, logic doesn't ever apply, no matter how much you want it to. She will always be the one thing that gets under your armor, the soft underbelly of your dragon's scales."

"So basically she's a handicap," David muttered. "That sounds like something you would say."

Deven leaned forward, locking eyes with David. "No, David. A Consort is a Prime's greatest strength. Our power is debilitating. Our responsibility is a long walk alone that ends in a violent death. Eternity—real eternity, not some romantic ideal—kills everything eventually."

"Is that why you and I . . ." David lowered his gaze, heart catching; neither of them had brought it up like this in a long time. "I still don't understand why it happened."

Deven knew what he meant. "A house remains haunted until the ghost inside it is exorcised."

"Then it's over with. You really believe that."

A smile, somewhere between sad and amused. "What you and I had was . . . is . . . love, I have no doubt. Even a heart as close to dust as mine is capable of loving more than one person. But we'll never be a Pair, for the simple reason that your Queen completes a part of you no one else can. Miranda is your human heart, still beating. Your soul, still alive. She is a miracle and a treasure, and in three years she's already made you twice the Prime you were—which is saying something, because you, my darling, are wonderful."

They held eyes for a while, and after a moment David reached over and took his hand, sighing. "Thank you."

Deven lifted his hand and kissed it, then let go. "Let's get to the meeting, then, and get this over with—then we can start our real work. This isn't over by a long shot; we're going to nail that bastard to the wall . . . but we'll start with Jeremy Hayes."

Eight

Musician Hospitalized
after Shooting

Austin, Texas (AP)—Grammy-winning artist Miranda Grey is in good condition at a private hospital after being shot twice in the chest Saturday night during her performance at the Austin Live Music Festival.

"Miss Grey is stable and will make a full recovery," Dr. Stephen Novotny stated at a press conference Sunday. "Both bullets were successfully removed. Because of Miss Grey's prior condition we are monitoring her recovery very carefully."

An investigation is underway into the identity of the shooter. A representative of the Austin Police Department said the focus of the investigation is on a series of letters the singer received from a possible stalker.

Local music producer and chairman of the Austin Live Music Association Grizzly Behr also attended the press conference and said, "The ALMA is cooperating fully with APD to find out how the shooter got past security. Attendees of future festivals can rest assured that it won't happen again. We're thankful that Miss Grey is going to be all right, and we're hoping she'll be back next year."

Grey's representative, Theresa Cuaron, urged fans to either donate blood to the Travis County Blood and Tissue

Center or make monetary donations to the Miranda Grey
Porphyria Research Foundation in lieu of sending flowers
or gifts.

*   *   *

No one knew what hospital Miranda Grey was supposed to
be in, and no one knew exactly where she lived. As invasive as the media were these days, somehow her manage-
ment was always a step ahead of reporters, paparazzi, and
other stalker types.

She absolutely had a right to a private life . . . but it did
leave her fans in a sort of limbo when it came to showing
their support.

Stella didn't tell anyone where she was going. Lark
would probably laugh at her, for one thing, but really, Stella
needed to do this by herself, and she wasn't sure anybody
else would understand. She took the evening off from the
store and hopped a bus down South First.

There was a steady stream of people in front of the Bat
Cave, the studio where Miranda had recorded her album.
An impromptu shrine had appeared at the base of the live
oak tree outside the studio, sheltered from the rain that had
passed through in the wee hours of the morning by the
tree's canopy and the lee of the building. In less than twenty-
four hours fans had left an enormous spread of candles,
teddy bears, handwritten signs with *Get Well Soon!* and *We
Love You!* in permanent marker, and other mementos.
Miranda's official fan club, whose members were known
facetiously online as "Bleeders," had been there, too; the
organizers had tacked a poster to the tree where visitors
could sign their names. Some of the offerings looked like
they'd been made by children, though most of Miranda's
fans were in their early twenties like Stella herself.

Sighing, Stella crouched by the shrine, looking over the
items people had left. She knew how dumb it had to seem
to outsiders, but really, this was less for Miranda herself
and more for the fans. Stella knew that she wasn't the only

person who had been wandering around lost until she found Miranda's music. The singer had touched a lot of lives . . . in ways she would never have guessed.

The grocery store bouquet of alstromeria was all Stella could afford, and it was dwarfed by the massive vase of roses at the center of the shrine, but it would have to do. She set it in among the others, then rose, pushing her bag back onto her shoulder and straightening her jacket.

"Thought I might find you here."

Stella sighed again. "Don't you dare make fun of me, Lark."

"I'm not, I swear. I just wanted to make sure you were okay."

Stella shrugged. "I'm fine."

Lark fell into step beside her, heading back toward South First. Stella kept her hands shoved in her jacket pockets, her left hand wrapped around her cell phone. It was a nice night for a walk; the storm had largely gone around the city, but there had been enough rain to keep things cool, a bit muddy but otherwise perfect for the festivalgoers that had clogged Austin for days. There were still a lot of events going on tonight, but Stella suspected anything at Zilker Park would be sparsely attended, assuming APD let anyone near the stage.

"Foxglove said you saw the whole thing," Lark said.

"My dad got me a festival wristband. I was in the fourth row. Of course I saw it."

"That sucks, babe."

"Understatement."

They were passing Slim Shaky's espresso bar, and Lark paused. "Want a coffee? I'll buy."

"Sure."

Once they were settled at a corner table, Stella with her soy mocha and Lark with her dark roast Columbian whatever, Stella said, "I know you think it's stupid. But when her CD came out I was in a really bad place. I'd just started practicing the Craft, my dad told me to go to hell, I had this . . . thing . . . and her music helped me make sense of it all. It was like she understood."

She braced herself for a sarcastic remark, but for a wonder, Lark was nodding. "I get it. When I was in high school, I was a total outcast—shocking, I know. I was the kid in black with the tarot cards reading philosophy in a town where the two big things were Jesus and football. If it hadn't been for the other Witches I met online I would have ended up in the nuthouse. Or worse."

Stella sighed, relieved. She hadn't realized until that moment how much she wanted Lark to understand where she was coming from.

Lark leaned on her hand while her other was busy pouring a rather disturbing amount of sugar into her coffee. Whatever kind of outcast Lark had been in her hometown, she and Stella both fit in perfectly here in Austin; she and Lark both had a semi-Goth, semi-geek thing going . . . but tattooed twenty-two-year-old weirdoes were the norm in this town. The rest of the state was scarily conservative, but Austin was a haven for freaks, geeks, progressives, gays, artists, vegetarians, musicians . . . anyone for whom the status was simply not quo.

She wondered if Miranda Grey had felt the same way when she moved here to go to college. She was from a small Texas town, too, and she had left her family and not looked back. There wasn't a whole lot known about her personal life except what was publicized on her website bio, but Stella liked to think Miranda had found a home here in Austin, too, a place to belong.

"I have to show you something," Stella said, pulling out her phone.

"New app?"

"No. Just watch." Stella muted the sound and hit play.

She didn't look, but she knew what Lark was seeing because she'd watched it at least ten times since last night: A wobbly, grainy video of the ALMF main stage, with Miranda talking to the crowd and then hitting the first chord of "Bored Now." Stella knew every note of every song on the album, and that moment was a surreal sort of Name That Tune . . . broken by a sound like a broomstick breaking. It was muffled by all the crowd noise, but it came from somewhere near where Stella was standing, up front but off to the right.

A split second after she heard the sound, she saw Miranda jerk backward just a little: once, two times. Miranda looked down, her face going white as she saw the blood just before the pain must have hit her. She looked so shocked . . . and the whole audience had felt the same way . . . then she fell.

Almost the second Miranda's body hit the stage, she was surrounded by people and the view was mostly blocked. The video went on for about thirty more seconds until the crowd had started to panic and it was too dangerous to stay there. Stella had wanted so badly to run to the stage, to try to . . . do something . . . but the police were already herding everyone away, pulling people aside for statements, and Stella found herself being grilled by her father, who was way more worried about her than he was about Miranda . . . but she didn't give him the video. She just couldn't.

"Jesus." Lark shook her head. "That's fucked up."

"Again . . . understatement."

"Weird—how come the picture's so bad? I thought your phone had way better resolution than that."

"*That's* what bothers you?"

"No, just . . ." Lark handed the phone back, looking sheepish. "I remember you saying she doesn't take a lot of pictures."

"She said in an interview once that she hates having her picture taken because when she was younger she had this bad reaction to one of her meds and it messed up her skin for a while, so she's felt self-conscious about it ever since."

"So she has magic antiphotography powers?" Lark asked dubiously. "I know you love this chick and all, but she seems like a grade-A weirdo to me."

Stella smiled. "I know. That's the point."

"Why didn't you give this to your dad? They might be able to analyze the angles or something *CSI* and figure out who did it."

"They've got videos of it—lots of people had their phones out that night. The police confiscated a bunch of them, but there are already some showing up online."

"Are you planning to keep that forever? Kind of morbid, Stell."

"No . . ." Stella stared down at the screen of her phone, considering, wondering . . . if there was anyone she could tell, it was Lark, but . . . it was crazy.

"What is it?" Lark wanted to know. "You're making that face."

"You're going to think I'm totally out of my mind."

Lark snorted. "Um, Stell? We're Witches, remember? I've seen you do stuff right out of second-season *Supernatural*. For people like us, 'out of my mind' is kind of implied."

Stella couldn't help but laugh at that. "True. But . . . some things *are* impossible, right? There are limits to what can really happen. Magic works according to natural laws, so most of the time it's not that obvious. The wind changes, the rain stops, the rope holds on long enough that the piano doesn't fall on your head. Stuff like that. But what if . . ."

"Spit it out, babe."

"Okay. You remember that thing last year with *Constellation*, where some jackoff said Miranda's a vampire, and then the stuff about her porphyria came out?"

"Yeah."

"I think there's more to it than that."

Lark apparently couldn't decide whether to laugh out loud. "What, like she's really a vampire?"

"Well . . . there's no such thing, right?"

She shrugged, fingering the pentagram necklace she wore—Stella had one just like it. "More things in heaven and earth, Horatio."

"I was watching the video, though, and there's this one place where . . . I thought I saw something. Right here . . ."

Stella fast-forwarded the video past the shooting, to where all the security and medics were swarming the stage. "See this guy?"

She pointed to the tall, burly blond who ran to Miranda's side and knelt next to her. He was in and out of the frame because other people kept getting in the way, but as tall as he was, she could pick him out.

"Cute," Lark said. "A little old for my taste, but still."

"Not the point. Notice the necklace he's wearing? The big emerald that looks like it's glowing? It looks almost exactly like the red one she wears. Why would they wear matching jewelry?"

"Okay, that's a little freaky, but not exactly newsworthy. Maybe that's her husband."

"It's not. He's supposed to have black hair. The thing is, if you're just watching like usual the guy's just talking to her, but if I watch it with my Sight . . . something happens."

"I didn't think the Sight worked on video."

"Foxglove always said it wouldn't, so I never tried it. But I always wondered if maybe digital photography was different. A lot of aboriginal-type cultures won't let themselves be photographed because they believe it steals your soul—there's lots of myths built up around the idea. And there's that legend that you can't photograph a vampire because cameras use mirrors. But that's all based on film photography, not digital. Anyway, I kept getting this weird feeling when I was watching this guy, and so I decided to give it a shot."

Now Lark looked interested; they'd both said at one time or another that Foxglove, who had taught the Wicca 101 class where they'd met and owned the occult bookstore where Stella now worked, was hopelessly old-fashioned and needed to get with the times. "What did you See?"

"You know how when I look at people with the Sight I can see how they're connected to other people—the threads of light? Well, this guy and Miranda are really, really connected. Almost like married people are, but not in a romantic way."

"So, like relatives or something?"

"More than that. It's kind of tenuous, like it's new. And what's even weirder . . . I've checked out her aura before onstage, and it always seemed pretty normal. But now I wonder if maybe that isn't just one hell of a shield. When she was lying there on the stage, for just a second, her aura went *black*."

"Black? I've heard of all sorts of colors, but . . . black?"

"Black and a sort of bluish silver, like mercury. And it was crazy powerful. Scary even. I've met a lot of Witches, and I've never seen one as powerful as she was—but then it's like she got her control back and she looked normal again."

"So you're saying she's a Witch."

"I don't know. She might not practice Witchcraft, but she's got a gift, and she's had training. She could just be a psychic, or she could be a Witch. But black isn't exactly the kind of aura you'd find on someone who worships a Goddess and practices healing arts, so I doubt she's a Wiccan like us. It felt . . . dark."

"Black magic is pretty dark, Stell."

"No, not black magic. Not evil. Just . . . darkness. I don't know how to explain it, but . . . when I looked at her, it was like . . . like looking at death." She met Lark's eyes, trying to impress on her how serious she was as she said, "I think . . . I think Miranda Grey *is* a vampire."

Anodyne fell silent.

The bartender smiled. "My Lady, it's good to see you again."

Miranda strode into the bar, her entire body burning with pleasure from the hunt, strength and purpose flowing through her veins again, smoothing away the weariness, letting her walk again as a Queen.

Signets made other vampires nervous. She walked in aware that every eye was on her—doubly aware, as she was doing it on purpose to distract the crowd from what came in after her.

Cora didn't respond well to large crowds, and Miranda was worried about being recognized, so they'd stuck to a smaller hunting ground for dinner—a park known mostly to joggers from the university who came out at night for a last run before hitting the midnight books. As part of the school, it was well lit and frequently patrolled, so there was little risk for the students . . . unless, of course, the city was full of vampires.

The youngest Queen was unused to hunting this way. She and Jacob depended heavily on bottled blood, especially during winter months when the weather made nighttime travel treacherous even in urban areas. Prague was hardly a backwater—Miranda had never seen a city as beautiful—but it was cold as hell for long parts of the year. Cora had never really learned the heady joy of drinking from a live human or the sweetness of having that deep itch soothed by their blood.

She took to it like a spider to a snared butterfly.

Miranda and Jonathan helped her draw one out, a petite brunette on her jogging round. "Just watch," Miranda told the Queen. "It's easy."

Miranda reached out to touch the girl's mind, and the jogger halted, blinking, confused. She looked warily at the three flashing-eyed strangers standing beneath a sweeping willow tree just off the path.

"Come here," Miranda said, barely whispering.

The girl obeyed. "Do I know you?" she asked.

She smelled like peppermint soap and sweat and . . . enchiladas, her most recent meal. Miranda took careful hold of her will and let it go slack in her grasp so that the girl's head tilted off to the side, exposing her throat.

Miranda remembered when David had done this with her, gesturing, showing her the places it was safe to bite. "Here," Miranda said, tapping the skin lightly. "Any lower and you don't risk hitting a major artery, but you also don't get much flow. This is best."

Cora nodded, leaning in, and Miranda placed her hands on the girl's back to support her. She gasped and pushed back, instinctively trying to escape; Miranda held her there, soothing her fears, letting her know she was okay, that no one wanted to hurt her, but that she was giving them something they needed, the only thing, everything.

"Good job," Miranda said to Cora as the jogger went on her way . . . walking this time and taking long swallows from her water bottle. Miranda had imprinted the usual instructions on her to go home, eat something protein- and iron-rich, and rest.

Cora's eyes were practically glowing with satisfaction. Heavy-lidded and half-open, they were the eyes of a predator sated.

One by one, all three Consorts went on the hunt. Jonathan always preferred young men—athletic, all-American cute, a far cry from the slender, dark creature waiting for him at home. Miranda, on the other hand, still had not regained her comfort with men, except her Prime, and so she, too, fed on women.

Afterward they all went for a different sort of drink.

The patrons of Anodyne had seen Signets before, but never three at once, plus dog. Miranda had had someone call ahead to make sure there were no objections to Vràna's attendance; the dog could have waited in the car, but she made Cora feel so much safer it would be a shame not to at least ask. There was no food served at Anodyne, and Miranda wasn't even sure that the health department came anywhere near the Shadow District, so no one was likely to make any noise over it.

They approached, two beautiful women and one handsome man, all dressed impeccably and carrying themselves like royalty, with an enormous shaggy Nighthound padding quietly alongside. No one would have had to ask who they were.

"I'll have a Black Mary," Miranda said. "O negative, if you have it."

The bartender checked the fridge. "My O neg is three days out, but I have a batch of AB pos just donated tonight."

She nodded, and he went about fixing her drink as well as pulling Jonathan's Shiner and Cora's glass of Merlot. Miranda was the only one having blood in her beverage, and though once the idea had grossed her out, she'd found after an experimental sip of David's one night that she liked them . . . a lot.

"Signet tab, my Lady?" the bartender asked.

"Yes, Miguel. Thank you."

They all retired to a corner booth where they could talk. "What do you think of Austin?" Miranda asked Cora.

The Queen smiled. "I think I have had a very interesting time here, and I am looking forward to returning to my home."

"So how are things with you and Jacob?" Jonathan asked, giving her mischievous eyebrows. "Any . . ."

Cora laughed. "We are . . . a work in progress, my Lord. But we care much for each other, and I think one day soon we will be truly married in deed as in word. He is a very gentle and patient man, and for that I am thankful." She sipped her wine and then asked, "How long was it for you, my Lady, before you were able to bear a man's touch?"

"Only a few months." Miranda let the coppery-acidic tang of her drink bite into her tongue for a second before swallowing it. "But it would have been never, except for David."

Jonathan looked thoughtful; when he saw they were watching him, he set down his glass and said, "I've never been abused, not in any form. But my Prime certainly has . . . and even though when we met he had a lover already, it still took him a while to feel safe with me. I like to think that between myself and David we brought him back from a private hell he might never have come out of."

Miranda smiled and held up her glass. "To good men," she said.

"To good men," the two Consorts affirmed, and they clinked glasses.

They were all laughing, enjoying the first slightly blurry effects of the alcohol, when Miranda's bladder complained loudly. She groaned. "Damn it, let me out, Jonathan."

"I swear, Miranda, you're the peeing-est vampire I've ever met." He scooted good-naturedly out of the booth, and she made a beeline for the ladies' room.

As she was washing her hands, she felt . . . just for a second, almost like . . . someone was watching her.

As Miranda extended her senses through the room she asked, "Who's there?"

No answer and no alarms from her psychic probing. Sometimes when she was out in public, she overreacted to things—often humans didn't have their auras under control and tended to project without meaning to, and some vampires were guilty of the same carelessness. She expected it from humans, since most had no idea they were even gifted, but for vampires it was careless because it could expose what they were or, at the very least, warn off potential prey.

She sniffed the air; nothing stood out among the competing smells of human bodies, urine, soap, tile cleanser, and wood polish.

She left the restroom just in time to see a dark coat exiting the back door of the bar.

Miranda knew she should have gone back to her table, but . . . something . . .

Curious, she peered out the door then stepped out into the crisp night. She knew there were Signet guards all around the building, and she was on high alert herself; she opened out her shields to let her senses sweep the entire area for other minds and found those of her guards, a few passing humans on the street . . . and one other.

"Who are you?" she asked, not raising her voice. "I know you're there."

She reached inside her coat and flipped the leather strap that kept Shadowflame safely in its sheath so she could draw the blade, but stood with her hand on its hilt, waiting.

It was a woman's voice that answered: low, ironic, with an edge of formality that immediately identified her as Not From Around Here. "So this is the Queen of whom the legends foretold, the Flame of the South, whose fate rules the fate of so many."

Miranda pushed back her coat so that her sword and her Signet were both visible; she'd learned that move from

Deven, as well as the studied indifference she injected into her voice. "And you are?"

"I come seeking your Prime."

"Well, he isn't here. You've got me. And five minutes before I get bored and my drink waters down."

The woman detached herself from the shadows and came forward; at first all Miranda could see was her coat. The woman reached up and pushed back her hood, revealing a shining cascade of blond hair around a fine-featured oval face. She had an almost Disney-princess kind of beauty, except for the darkness in her eyes . . . they were a clouded blue, with silver undertones, and an immortal depth behind their coolness.

The woman looked at the sword, then back up at Miranda's face. "I assure you, I am no threat to you."

"Now, if I believed everyone who said that, I wouldn't have a coat left without bloodstains."

She smiled. It wasn't a particularly pleasant expression, but it did contain some respect. "So young," she said. "I was young once . . . a thousand years ago and a thousand miles away."

Miranda held her ground, though she could sense the woman letting her own shields slip, letting a glimpse of her true power show through . . . and it was formidable. She could easily hold her own among the Signets who were, by now, gathered around the table in the Haven.

Miranda might have been frightened of her, but the fact remained: This was Miranda's territory. Here, she was Queen. Whatever this woman was, she might be a threat, and she was not to be underestimated . . . but neither was Miranda.

"I want your name," Miranda said. "And I want to know what business you have with the Prime."

"My business with the Prime?" The woman chuckled and stepped forward. "My business is that I have a gift for him . . . a gift that could guarantee victory over his enemies . . . as well as set him on the throne of the entire Council. My name . . ."

Just then the back door burst open, and Jonathan and Cora appeared, looking ready to fling themselves into whatever trouble Miranda had gotten herself into.

Instead, they stared at the woman, and Jonathan said, "I know you."

She met the Consort's eyes. "I should hope so. I should hope you've seen me in your visions for months now. Perhaps that means you even know who I am."

But Jonathan didn't have to say it. Miranda knew. The pieces came together, and the gnawing feeling of recognition in her gut—from her own scattered visions, months and months ago—suddenly fed her a name.

"Lydia," the Queen said. "You're Lydia . . . David's sire."

Nine

". . . all those in favor of Central Africa's redistricting plan, please raise your right hands."

David hadn't realized it was possible to be bored and angry at the same time. The last Council he'd attended—his first as a Prime—had been fascinating because it was all new to him.

In the back of his mind he made a note to propose that the next summit include something besides just sitting around a table; they could be having lucrative discussions on security tactics and learning more about each other's territories . . . hell, even a round of miniature golf would be better than listening to two Primes debate whether Chad should be considered North or Central Africa . . . again.

The evening was not going according to plan A.

Hart was gloating. David knew he was gloating, even though his facial expression was schooled to neutral. Every now and then David felt eyes on him and looked over to see Hart pointedly looking away with a slight smile.

It was the kind of smug little grin that David itched to beat right off his face.

Right now David should be presenting his case against Hart, waiting for them to judge whether having a Queen shot in public counted as a declaration of war or was simply worthy of censure. He'd figured that they would vote to suspend Hart for a decade or two; the Council rarely moved against one of its own without serious provocation. The punishment itself wasn't the point.

What David really wanted was to see Hart lose influence and lose face. The fact that Hart was unhinged enough to hatch a complicated plot just to get back at them for freeing Cora would make him seem like a petty amateur rather than the sophisticated noble he tried to present as. As Miranda had said, it wasn't worth losing more lives over . . . but it would be worth the look on Hart's face when he was scolded like an erring schoolboy in front of his peers.

Now that wasn't going to happen. Until he had information from the blast that had killed Monroe, David had no evidence linking Hart to the shooting. No gun, no testimony from Monroe, no case—just a paper trail for a weapon that no longer existed. Maguire was looking for the missing gun, but David knew better than to expect it to reappear; a gun was a tiny thing, easily disposed of in a town with a lake in the middle.

He felt his phone vibrate and surreptitiously reached down to check it, expecting a check-in from Miranda; but it was a text from Deven, who was seated right next to him.

Any minute now. Brace yourself.

David gave a slight nod.

"Motion carried," Tanaka was saying. "The last item on tonight's agenda is a late submission from the Northeastern United States. Prime Hart, you have the floor."

Hart rose. "Honored Chairman, my fellow Primes, I move that the Council bar Queen Miranda Solomon from performing in public."

Dead silence.

David's first impulse, of course, was to reach out with his mind, grab the nearest blunt object, and bash Hart's skull in; before he could even complete the thought, however, stabbing pain in his thigh brought him back to center, courtesy of Deven's fingernails.

"Gentlemen, I realize such an action would be unprecedented on the part of the Council," Hart went on, barely able to keep the self-satisfaction out of his voice, "but the

Queen has created a new threat to the Shadow World that we cannot allow to continue. Her very existence as a public figure risks exposure for all of us. As we saw last night, there are humans out there who are obsessed enough to act against her in full view of thousands of people—not to mention her near-exposure last year by the media."

Something occurred to David right then that he hadn't really considered before: Hart was behind the "leak" to *Constellation*. That had been his first attempt to get Miranda off the stage, and then his second, a far bolder move, had failed . . . leaving him with this as his new card to play.

The rest of the Council was staring at David, waiting for him to respond; the silence was more than a little uncomfortable. Tanaka had to go about business as usual: "A motion is on the floor; is it seconded?"

"Seconded," Australia chimed in. Not a surprise; Hart and McMannis were thick as thieves.

In Tanaka's entire tenure as chair of the Council, violence had never broken out, but it was clear he expected it to this time, or at least that he would have to break up a vicious verbal fight between David and Hart. He had a look of dignified resignation mixed with dread on his face as he said, "The motion is now open for discussion."

Janousek spoke first. "I'd like to go on record as saying I find it extremely distasteful of Prime Hart to raise this motion when Queen Miranda isn't here."

Deven made a noise of disgust. "I don't think the word is *distasteful* so much as *convenient*."

Hart shrugged. "She chose not to attend the meeting. This issue won't wait."

"Of course it will," Deven said. "You and your petty vendetta against the South is what won't wait. Are we really supposed to believe that your timing here is a coincidence?"

"Are you accusing me of something, Prime O'Donnell?" Hart demanded, outrage in his voice. "If so, I hope you or your pet there have sufficient evidence to back up such a serious claim."

"Do I really need to make an accusation?" Deven asked, still leaning back comfortably in his chair, unaffected by Hart's tone. He addressed the rest of the table. "Is there anyone here who honestly thinks it was a random human who organized last night's incident? Don't say anything . . . just sit there and look uncomfortable if you agree with me."

"If we might return to the point," Janousek said before Hart could respond, "I think that we should consider the larger issue here before we rush to legislate what Miranda can and cannot do with her life."

"What issue is that, Lord Prime?" McMannis asked.

"I believe it would be setting a dangerous precedent to approve such a motion. For centuries the Signets have enjoyed autonomy—our power over each other is, and should remain, limited. If we start saying a Queen can't be a musician, what's next? Rules about how the rest of us make our money? Restrictions on hunting? Who here wants to lose his freedom for the tenuous promise of security?"

There was a murmur of agreement among the Signets; Jacob had hit them where they lived. The Council was happy to get together and argue about boundary lines that meant nothing, but when it came to real change, especially real change that could affect them directly, they ran like rabbits.

"At the same time, however, we cannot ignore the possibility that Queen Miranda's actions may expose all of us," McMannis countered. "We are charged with maintaining the secrecy of the Shadow World and ensuring the safety of our kind—and some of us extend that to the humans who live in our territories as well, though that's an entirely separate debate."

"But what risk is there, really?" Deven wanted to know. "How has Miranda put us in jeopardy so far? A rumor started that was easily dismissed as fairy tale—without some kind of direct proof, the human world will never believe in us. We've come close to exposure before—we've seen what happens. Those who speak the truth are treated like lunatics. Without large-scale proof, our secrecy isn't in any real danger. And last night could easily be blamed on an obsessive fan; I'm sure Prime Solomon will be able to produce one. I see no reason to change our entire policy over something that is ultimately frivolous."

"Frivolous?" David asked. It was the first thing he'd said, and everyone hushed and focused on him.

"I'm sorry, David, but it's true. Miranda has every right to her ambitions, but in the long run, what difference does it make to any of us? The average popular musician has, what, a five-to-ten-year career? She's not exactly Bob Dylan. By the time this Council meets again I doubt anyone in the media will even remember her. She would have to retire by then anyway, before people noticed she doesn't age."

David glared at Deven, who remained unperturbed by the venom in his eyes and went on. "I'd like to propose an amendment to Prime Hart's motion—that Queen Miranda Solomon be barred from performing in public as of the next Council summit in ten years."

"The woman could ruin us all in ten years," Hart all but blurted, suddenly angry. "She's come damn close in three!"

"No, *you've* come close in three," David snapped. "Or at least you've tried. Every one of your childish schemes has failed you."

"You have no proof of that whatsoever, and if you—"

"There's something else to consider." Jacob came to the rescue of civility again. "If Miranda were to vanish from the public eye right now, there would be a lot of questions. The risk of exposure is greater in that case than if she were to go on about her career and then retire gracefully, or fade from sight, within the next decade. Right now the whole world is watching her."

"These incidents are only going to escalate," Hart said, looking directly at David. "It is in everyone's best interest, including the Queen's, to put a stop to her foolishness now before her need for attention gets her, or anyone else, killed."

David knew a threat when he heard one. So did the rest of the Council, for that matter, but he knew no one would call Hart on it.

He stood.

"Honored Council," he said, "I would like to make one thing perfectly clear."

Once again the silence was so complete it practically had a life of its own. David faced them all, catching each pair of eyes in turn to make absolutely sure he had their undivided attention.

"I have no intention of defying the Council's ruling on this matter," he said. "I understand that our collective security is in question, though I vehemently disagree with the idea that the Council should—or does—have any authority over its individual members. However: If anyone, at any time, makes a move against my Queen, whether human or vampire, Prime or otherwise . . . I will rip his spine out and hang him from it. If she is hurt again, there will be hell to pay."

He sat down.

After a moment of Primes staring at each other and trying not to stare at David, Tanaka cleared his throat. "All those in favor of adopting Prime Hart's motion as stated, please raise your right hands."

David counted five hands.

"All those in favor of adopting Prime Hart's motion with the amendment proposed by Prime O'Donnell, raise your right hands."

Everyone else's hand went up, except David's. He abstained. He could feel, even across the table, Hart's growing outrage.

"Amended motion carried," Tanaka said with obvious relief. "Now, let us move on to the closing procedures of our gathering . . ."

After what seemed like years, the Council was adjourned, and Primes began to get up from their chairs and slowly leave the room, disbanding for another ten years.

David got up from his chair and strode past the milling Signets toward the exit. As he passed the rest of the table, he glanced over to see Hart and paused.

The Prime was looking at him with such open contempt

that it was almost surprising; his handsome face was twisted, for just a moment, with rage, and it almost looked like he was about to spring up and come after David.

David flashed him a wicked smile. "Strike three," he said. "Now get the hell out."

Jacob and Deven were both waiting for David in his study, the Scotch already poured.

When he entered, Deven made a face and asked, "Rip his spine out and hang him with it? Really? Why not 'I'll tear your skin off and wear it as a diaper,' or 'I'll crack you open and feed your nuts to the squirrels'?"

"Shut up," David replied, flopping down into a chair and accepting Jacob's proffered glass. He drank it in two swallows and held it out for a refill. "What about that bullshit you were laying on out there? 'Not exactly Bob Dylan'? Were you trying to make me punch you?"

Jacob was shaking his head, but he was also smiling. "The two of you are a piece of work, you know that? Worse still, you've sucked me in."

David sighed. "I knew he'd try something. It was the most likely scenario. Tonight was his only chance to get the Council to act against Miranda, and he failed. God knows how much money he wasted bribing the others to vote his way . . . but he was forgetting one important thing. No Prime is ever going to give up a single iota of his own power, not even if the entire Shadow World is at stake. That autonomy everyone prizes so highly is as much a weakness as a strength."

"One wonders," Jacob mused, "what would happen if we were to work together for something for a change."

Deven snorted quietly. "The only way that would ever happen is if God himself came down and made it so."

Halfway through the bottle, the study door opened, and the three Consorts entered, all of them looking a little rattled.

"There you are, my love," Jacob said, rising to take Cora's hands. "Did you enjoy your evening out?"

She sat down beside him. "I think so."

David frowned and looked up at Miranda, who was hovering in the doorway uncertainly. "It's all right," he said. "Everything went as planned."

"That's not . . ." Miranda looked from Cora to Jonathan, then back to David. "Something else happened tonight."

"Good God, now what?" Deven asked. "How much more alcohol are we going to need?"

Jonathan, taking his own position next to his Prime, laughed a little. "That depends on whether David thinks it's good news or bad news," he said.

David reached out for Miranda, who slid her hands into his and sat down; he felt his entire body relax slightly at the contact, the way it did every time one of them came home to the other. "What is it, beloved?"

"You didn't have anything scheduled for Tuesday night, did you?" she asked.

He blinked. "Um . . . not that I know of. The last of the Pairs is leaving Tuesday—Jacob, I believe you're scheduled for a midnight flight?" At Jacob's nod, David asked hesitantly, "Why?"

"Well . . . you have a meeting that night. In town, at Anodyne."

Again, he blinked. "With whom?"

She met his eyes.

"Lydia."

"Lydia?"

Miranda nodded.

"As in . . ."

She nodded again. "As in, the vampire who made you. Lydia. She wants to see you. She showed up at the bar tonight out of nowhere and demanded to come to the Haven. I told her as politely as I could to kiss my ass, and that if she wanted to talk to you, she could take a number like everyone else. We settled on a public meeting, contingent on your agreement, of course."

David looked like he'd been smacked in the head, and it

wasn't entirely inaccurate to say that he had. "Good plan," he managed. "What in hell could she possibly want?"

"She said something about defeating your enemies," Miranda replied. "I have no idea what it meant. Do you know anything about her, Deven?"

Dev shrugged with one shoulder. "Nobody gives a damn about lineage except the underclass. The only thing that seems to matter when it comes to the Signets is that you were sired by a vampire of considerable strength; and at our level of power, whomever we sire has the potential to be equally strong. Unless it was a love thing, few people really make a point of keeping tabs on who brought them over."

"Do you know who your sire was?" Miranda asked.

Deven's eyes were as frosty as his voice as he said, "No."

It was a highly personal question, she realized, and not her business . . . and she should have known that Deven of all people wouldn't want to discuss the matter. Almost everything she knew about his past was painful; it stood to reason that however he'd become a vampire, it had been some kind of nightmare. "So it's not normal for this Lydia to come looking for David," she said, opting not to push.

"Maybe she wants to borrow money," Jonathan suggested with a grin. "You know how it is—get rich, become a Prime, and suddenly everyone's your long-lost sire."

"But why now?" David asked. "She's had years."

"She must want something." Deven looked thoughtful. "Perhaps she's in trouble of some kind—on the run or in debt or something else she thinks you owe her help with."

"*Owe* her?" Miranda said in disbelief. "She killed a bunch of humans and let David's wife get burned at the stake for it, and then she turned him and left him to roast without so much as a 'Hey, get some sunblock.' He doesn't owe her anything."

The Prime of the West shrugged again. "It could be argued that what he is now, he is because she made him. I'm not saying I agree, just that she might think so. We know nothing about this woman, her motivations, or her intentions. It's pointless to speculate."

Miranda heard Cora hold back a yawn, and smiled. "I think we could all use some sleep," she said. "It's been a rough few days for all of us."

The others agreed and went their separate ways. Miranda took David by the arm and all but dragged him to their suite, despite his protestations that there was still enough time before dawn to do a systems check and talk to Faith about the departure schedules.

"Bed," she insisted. "With me. Right this minute. That's an order, Prime."

He chuckled. "What a fool I'd be to deny the Queen her due."

She shut and locked the suite door behind them, then leaned back against it with a heavy sigh, taking a moment to luxuriate in the quiet warmth of the room. There had been so much noise, so much fear and unhappiness in the last few days . . . but it was over now. The Bastards were going home, and their life could return to normal.

Except that it couldn't, at least not yet . . . she couldn't go onstage again until enough time had passed that people would believe she'd healed from her gunshot wounds. In fact she was going to have to stay out of the city as much as she could, except the Shadow District itself, to make sure no one recognized her—and then there would be press conferences and interviews, more lies to tell . . .

And in ten years it would all be taken away from her anyway.

David had taken his jacket off and unbuttoned his shirt, and was watching her from near the bed. He knew, without asking, what was on her mind. "It will work out," he said. "Ten years is a lot of time for things to change. You would have had to retire not long after that anyway—you'll find other ways to keep your career going. We'll think of something."

"I know," she said. "And you were right; it gets the Council off our backs. It's just . . . the idea of all of those people sitting there debating on whether I should live my own life . . . It pisses me off, David. And so does the idea that they could have just up and decided to take away a part of me like it was nothing."

"Come here," he said gently, gesturing at the bed. She sighed once more and did, throwing herself down on her back, earning a quiet laugh as David sat down and set to unlacing her boots. "I wouldn't have allowed that. The whole thing was orchestrated to make Hart seem unreasonable compared to Jacob and Deven, and to remind them all that if they start doling out rules on Signets they might get one made against themselves one day."

"That doesn't make it okay."

"No," he agreed. "But it was the best we could do under the circumstances."

"Have you heard from Maguire or gotten a report on the explosion?"

"No. I didn't really expect to tonight—I'm going to examine the scene myself tomorrow. It's been cleaned, just to get all the . . . Monroe . . . off the walls, but there's still a lot I can learn from it. And the team got detailed images of everything first as well as samples sent on to Novotny."

He pulled off first her left boot, then her right, and she groaned with relief. Her socks went next, but then David paused.

"Don't," she said before he could speak. "Don't ask me anything about Lydia or bring up anything else about the goddamned Council . . . just lie down with me. The door's locked and the world can wait."

David smiled. He stretched out alongside her, burying his face in her hair, and sighed, arms wrapping around her.

Their eyes met. "Just kiss me," she whispered, "and we can pretend everything's all right."

He gazed down at her, still smiling softly. "It is all right," he said. "As long as you and I are together, nothing can break us."

"Baby . . . I've seen enough movies to know you shouldn't say something like that . . . as soon as you do, the whole world goes to hell."

"You're right," he murmured into her ear. "No more talking."

She curved her hand around the back of his neck and drew his mouth against hers. For some reason, though she hated Scotch, the taste of it on his lips was irresistible, warm and familiar like the feel of his body shifting over hers while his hands relieved her of her clothing.

The night after the ball they had come at each other like animals, but tonight was different. Neither wanted time to pass any faster than it had to, and they touched and kissed each other with a delicious slowness that could just as easily have driven her crazy with need . . . but right now she wanted the hour to be a hundred, the moment to be a lifetime.

He sighed contentedly against her neck and then lifted up her torso with one hand on her back to peel her shirt away, and she did the same to him, both of them so well acquainted with each other that they could undress each other in perfect concert. He knew exactly where the ties on her favorite shirts were, and she had unbuckled every one of his belts at least a dozen times—but it wasn't a tired dance they performed, not at all. She was sure that in a hundred years feeling his skin bare against hers would still be exhilarating, still as new as it had been the first time. They melted into each other, boundaries blurred, that connection that was still so strange to them both rising up and weaving itself around them as effortlessly as her hair spilled down over his shoulder.

Sometimes it felt like joining together physically was almost unnecessary—it wasn't as though they were ever apart, not really. But there was something so lovely about being in two bodies, bringing them together and apart, mingling skin and limbs and sweat; mystical unions were all well and good, but there was something to be said for the sticky parts.

They curled and twisted around each other in a double helix, rolling in slow motion from one end of the bed to the other. At last Miranda got her wish; time stopped in the darkened room, and there was no *him*, no *her*, not even an *us*, only *this* . . . and *this* was all that mattered, tonight.

After affectionate embraces with their hosts and a mostly chaste kiss or two, the Pair of the Western United States departed in their hired limo, supposedly headed for Austin-Bergstrom International like the rest of the Council.

"To the airport, Sire?" the driver asked.

"No. Take us to the Ambassador Hotel." Deven was watching the hill country roll by out the dark-tinted window, and Jonathan tried to relax despite the growing pool of molten dread in his stomach that had first started building when he realized who the blond woman in the alley was.

I was right. Oh, God, I was right. What do we do now?

Like Miranda, Jonathan had been unable to discern a motive in Lydia's sudden appearance. She could be a friend or an enemy or a little of both. She might not *do* anything herself—but her arrival would start the dominoes falling, for good or ill, and Jonathan refused flat-out to leave Austin until Lydia and David had met and she had declared her intentions. He knew just as strongly that he and Deven had a part to play in all of this, and if they weren't there . . . things would go badly.

He had expected at least a little resistance on Deven's part; it was difficult, and somewhat hazardous, for a Pair to leave its territory even for a weekend, and the longer the Haven stood without its leaders, the more likely it was that the vampires of California would get unruly . . . while the cat was away, the mice would eat everyone in sight. It had happened to at least one Prime during every Council meeting—usually not a disaster, but a pain in the ass to deal with once the Signet was home.

Deven, however, was different from his peers. People thought David's security measures were invasive because of the sensor network that tracked every vampire in the South, but in truth David had nothing on Deven's intelligence network. His Elite were ruthless, and there was no such thing as due process; the West, like the South, was a place where good vampires felt safe but bad ones felt hunted. Deven's Elite were practically invisible and left bodies and blood without so much as casting a shadow. They were everywhere and nowhere; everyone and no one. Whatever the other Primes might think of him, the average vampire on the street found Deven terrifying, all the more so because so few had ever actually seen him.

That meant that Dev and Jonathan could spare a couple of extra days without coming home to too much of a mess. They sent their Elite home ahead of them, and between their Second, Thomas, and the Haven's Steward, Deven wasn't worried. That was, after all, why his hiring standards were so ridiculously high.

When Jonathan said he wanted to stay at least until Wednesday, Deven had merely nodded and said they already had a room waiting in town at a Signet-affiliated hotel where they could keep an eye on things without intruding. The Ambassador catered mostly to wealthy humans, but it also had a special concierge just for Shadow World guests.

"You said we might be here a while," Deven said. "I booked the room before we left Sacramento. Besides . . ." His voice grew a bit impish. "When was the last time I had you all to myself?"

Jonathan gave him a smile, but it was a bit forced, and Deven's eyebrows quirked; he laid his hand on Jonathan's knee and said soothingly, "You don't know for sure something will go wrong."

Jonathan almost laughed. "Yes, I do."

"All right, you do, but you don't know what or how bad it will be or even when it will go down, just that Lydia showing up starts something. You could say the same for the Council meeting or just waking up in the evening. Everything begins something, and everything ends something. We can't be afraid of every possibility."

Jonathan met his eyes. "Have I ever been wrong?"

A sigh. "No. But your visions tend to be open to interpretation—remember how you were certain David was going to get Miranda killed?"

"He did."

"Yes, but she woke up and became Queen. I'm sure it was hell for her while it was happening, but wouldn't you agree it was a good thing, in the long run?"

"So you're saying I'm being silly."

"No. You said we need to be here, and I believe you. I'm just saying that a lot of things could happen, and they're not all disastrous."

"I should have told Miranda," Jonathan muttered, probably for the tenth time. "What if I could have stopped anything from happening?"

"Stop doing this to yourself," Deven said, cupping Jonathan's chin in one hand and holding his eyes. "You don't have power over the future . . . just a glimpse of it here and there, and then through eyes that can't know everything. You've never freaked out over your visions this much before."

Jonathan sighed. The car rolled to a stop, and a moment later the door opened; they disembarked in front of the imposing edifice of one of Austin's most exclusive hotels. "I've never had a friend like Miranda before," he said to Deven as hotel staff leapt to action to collect their luggage and take it inside. "I know it sounds stupid, but . . . this one time, I'd like to avert fate. I want her to be happy, Dev."

Deven's smile was a little indulgent and a lot affectionate. "I know. And we'll do everything we can. I promise."

They arrived at the check-in desk, where the concierge was already waiting for them. Deven flashed his Signet, and the human nodded and bowed.

"My Lord Prime," he said. "My name is Javier, and it will be my pleasure to attend to your every need during your stay here at the Ambassador. I've had the suite you requested prepared to all your specifications."

"Good," Deven said with a nod, beckoning Javier to walk with them to the elevator. "We have a dedicated system?"

"Yes, sir. The suite has its own private server, and you'll have all the bandwidth you can stand."

"And the fridge?"

"Stocked with a fresh supply of AB positive, as requested."

"Thank you."

The suite was as big as most apartments and had an entire room set aside for computer equipment. What appealed to Jonathan most was the enormous bed, calling out with the siren song of seven-hundred-thread-count sheets, but Deven made a beeline for the office while the bellhops brought in their things. Jonathan tipped them all heavily, then asked Javier, "Can I get a bottle of Woodford Reserve sent up?"

"Already done, my Lord," Javier replied, inclining his head toward the bar. "The Prime sent a list."

Jonathan raised his eyebrows, impressed. "Very good, then, thank you Javier." He handed the concierge a hundred-dollar bill; Javier smiled, bowed, and departed, reminding them they needed only dial 0 to reach him directly.

As soon as he'd helped himself to the whiskey, Jonathan joined Deven in the office, where the Prime already had his laptop plugged into a bank of monitors.

"What exactly are you doing?" he asked.

Deven smiled. "Linking up to the Red Shadow network—I'm checking to see which agents are between assignments so I can pull a few here. I've got one researching Jeremy Hayes, but I'd like another two or three in town and at least one finding out what the hell Lydia wants . . . 5.1 Carmine is in Dallas, that should work . . . her mission won't go critical for another week."

Jonathan scrutinized the interface on the main screen. "Where did you learn how to write computer programs?"

Deven snorted quietly. "Darling, I have neither the patience nor the desire to learn any such thing. I had our favorite fanged geek design it for me, which is why it looks familiar—it's based on the Haven system. From here I can keep an eye on every active agent, research past assignments, track the money, and recall anyone from the field."

"Handy boy, our David . . . but you know he probably left a door open in there somewhere so he can spy on your spying."

"Oh, I know he did. But he's assuming I use accurate information in the records; it's all encoded. Looking at this he'd think I have an agent in the Pentagon, for example, and another clerking for the CIA, but in actuality I have one in the White House and one in the FBI. I can't have him knowing everything I'm up to. There are a couple of agents who aren't in the network at all—special ops, you might say."

Jonathan shook his head. "It's refreshing to see two friends trust each other so completely."

"Trust is for the fucked-over, darling."

The Consort laughed. "You are something else, my love. You really are."

Deven tilted his head back for a kiss, and Jonathan obliged, then said, "I'm going to lie down for a while—I'm knackered."

"Go on," Deven replied, touching his face. "And don't worry . . . even if something horrible does happen, we'll be here for them. You can only see parts of what's to come—you don't ever see the ending."

"That's because nothing ever ends," Jonathan said tiredly.

"Precisely—and that's why there's always hope."

Jonathan, taken aback, said, "Did you just say something optimistic? *You?*"

Deven actually looked a tad sheepish. "Well . . . sixty years you've been at my side . . . I guess eventually you were bound to rub off on me. Miracle of miracles: Even I can change. A little."

Jonathan felt something in his chest unclench just a tiny bit. "Then perhaps there is hope . . . for all of us."

PART TWO

Ashes to Ashes

Ten

Telekinesis was not for wimps.

Learning to control the power she'd somehow gotten from David was every bit as grueling as her first lessons in shielding—which had been, once upon a time, conducted in this very room.

It was easy enough to throw things if she was angry and didn't care what happened to them; she did it from time to time when in pursuit of a lawbreaker in the city. That burst of emotion gave her energy but no finesse, and if she wanted to have any kind of control, she had to practice. Her ability had been tenuous when it first showed up, and it had taken her months to strengthen it. Even three years in she hadn't progressed as much as she'd have liked, but she had been a little busy with other things. She wanted to be able to do more than fling trash cans and asshole Primes.

She figured out pretty quickly that she had to change the way she shielded. Sophie had told her that different gifts required different kinds of protection, and though Miranda had gone along with it at the time, she hadn't really understood the difference until now. To use her empathy on an audience, she thinned the outermost layer of her shielding so that she could sense things outside herself, and it had to be able to go both ways; she had to draw in people's emotions and then reach out to affect them. To move things with her mind she didn't let anything in, just reached out.

It was a subtle difference, but trying to move something the way she worked an audience left her feeling wide open and vulnerable. Once she realized that she needed to change her approach, it was much less overwhelming.

David had taught her the fundamentals, but he wasn't an empath. When it came to the fine-tuning, she was on her own, using what he'd shown her and what she had learned from Sophie about using psychic gifts as a weapon.

Every night, if she could, she at least sat down and did a few exercises, working with her shielding, empathy, and telekinesis one by one. Most of the time she just did simple things wherever she happened to have settled for the evening, which usually meant the music room, but Monday night she wanted to do something a little more challenging to try to occupy herself.

Until the meeting with Lydia was over she was going to be a nervous wreck; something about it was giving her an uneasy feeling, and while she hadn't gotten very far in dealing with her half-woken precog ability, it was strong enough to drive her insane, and she knew the only thing she could do was distract herself.

If she was being honest, she would admit she had been trying to ignore the precog completely in the faint and childish hope it would just go away.

Miranda sighed, speaking to Shadowflame as she removed the sword and laid it on the floor in the training room. "So I'm a vampire, a musician, an empath; I sword-fight; I can move stuff with my mind and sometimes sort of halfway see the future. What's next? Hey, maybe I'm a fire-starter, too. That would be cool."

The unfortunate thing about swords was that they tended to be as good at conversation as paintings of dead people, as in, not at all.

She flopped down in the armchair a few feet away from where she'd placed the sword, her guitar, and her cell phone. She had the best luck starting with something small, then gradually moving to larger objects. So far she hadn't tried anything alive, at least not on purpose; throwing Hart had been simple brute force, and David had said living things were the hardest and that when he'd started, he had more or less sprained his brain doing too much too fast.

Miranda sat cross-legged in the chair and concentrated, first grounding, then lowering and raising her shields a couple of times just to stay limber. As always, the act brought a smile to her face. Four years ago this had been the hardest thing in the world to do, and now it took her five seconds tops to go through the entire routine.

In a hundred years, how easy would it be?

The thought that she might live a hundred years or two hundred or more still didn't really make sense to her. She knew she was immortal; she could feel it, feel the stillness in her body when she was walking down the street sur-rounded by humans, animals, and plants that were all aging. She was a constant. Unchanging. Sometimes she would stop where she was and watch them all going on about their lives—lives that would be measured out in decades, bodies that were already dying, each day moving immeasurably closer to the inevitable.

Most of the time she didn't think about it, but it was still strange to her and probably would be for a while, according to the others. But the thought of still being on the planet to see what happened to the world in a century—or, like Deven, most of a millennium—was still just a bit on the unbelievable side.

Okay, girl, not now. Get down to business. Miranda pushed the thoughts away and brought her attention back to the room, specifically to the cell phone.

Telekinesis wasn't just about pushing things over. That was certainly useful, but the juicy part came from learning to wrap her will around an object and, while holding on to it, shift it from one place to another. The kind of mental pull she exerted was similar to the one that moved her body from place to place while Misting, but Misting was more a matter of power than control, which was why Signets who weren't telekinetic could still do it. The hardest part of Misting was bringing her body back together when she arrived at her destination. Moving other things meant she had to both hold on to them and move them at the same time, which required two coordinated sets of mental "muscles."

It didn't take much effort to pick up the phone. She did that first, straight up into the air, then back down, then up again, then in a circle; up and down was easiest, but she was already used to tossing around things of its size. It was just a warm-up.

Now came the fun part. She tightened her focus to the phone's screen. If there had been actual buttons it would be child's play, but touch screens didn't respond to her mental "fingers." She was convinced that if she could figure out the right way to touch it, the right amount of pressure, she could dial it . . . but she had to be careful how much force she used, or she'd crack the screen. Again.

A couple of attempts and she already had a headache. She shouldn't be surprised—David wasn't terribly good with touch screens yet, and he'd been working on it as long as they had existed. She set the phone down with a sigh.

Next, the sword: She had to expand her energy-lasso out to either side, but the blade itself wasn't that heavy, so she could lift it, no sweat. The challenge came from drawing Shadowflame from its sheath . . . lowering the sheath back to the floor . . . holding the sword up . . . and spinning it in slow circles like the needle of a compass.

Miranda held on to it and counted, quietly aloud, to thirty before stopping the spin and putting the sword down. By then she was sweating just a bit. But she was pleased with herself. She'd kept it spinning five seconds longer than last time.

Last trick: the guitar.

It was big, yes, but still lightweight compared to, say, a chair. Once she had it hovering a few feet off the ground, she turned it to face away from her and closed her eyes.

She split her focus into three "hands": the bulk of her energy holding the instrument aloft, then a piece of it wrapping around the neck and another focusing on the strings as if she were standing behind the guitar holding it to her chest.

Miranda squeezed her mind around two of the strings and pressed them back against the fretboard. Then, she concentrated on her other "hand" and tried to strum.

"Shit!"

The guitar nearly hit the floor when it slipped out of her grasp, but she caught it and lifted it back up again.

"Sorry, baby," she told the instrument sheepishly. "I know you've been knocked around a lot lately."

Despite the pain between her eyes, she tried it again, and again, but each time she ended up losing hold of either the strings or the guitar itself. It was just too much for her to do at once. If she set it down, she could play a chord or two, but not while still keeping it afloat. Not yet.

She finally put the guitar down and sat back, her head throbbing. "Star-one," she said.

"Yes, beloved?"

"Are you busy?"

"I just finished meeting with the patrol leaders, and I'm about to go examine the interrogation room." She could hear him smiling. *"You're in the training room?"*

"Yeah."

A matter of seconds later the door beeped, and David poked his head in. "Clear?"

She nodded. "Thank you for coming. I think I overdid it a little."

He chuckled. "You? Never."

She stuck her tongue out at him, and he grinned and laid his hand on her forehead. She felt an inrushing of energy, and the headache vanished between one breath and the next.

David looked at the objects on the ground. "Did you try using your hands?"

Miranda glared at him.

"No, no—" He was laughing again. "I don't mean to pick them up, I mean, using gestures to help you focus, the way I do sometimes to lift heavier things."

"You want me to play air guitar?"

He sighed. "Like this."

He turned to the other armchair, which she'd pushed up against the wall, and held out his hand, then made an "up" sort of motion. The chair shuddered slightly, then rose a few inches off the floor.

"Oh, the Magneto thing! I had completely forgotten about that."

"Sometimes if you visualize your power as an extension of your arm, it can help. Or it does me—your mileage may vary."

"Well, I'll try it next time. I think I'm done for the night."

He leaned down, put one hand on each arm of the chair, and caught her mouth with his; she kissed him back enthusiastically, and they smiled at each other.

"What do you have next tonight?" he asked, offering a hand up from the chair, which she took.

Miranda fetched her guitar case, buckled Shadowflame back on, and put her phone in her pocket. "I have a video blog post to record . . . you know, from the hospital?"

"Ah. Well, if you need any help, just call."

She kissed his cheek. "My own personal tech support hotline. Emphasis on *hot*."

He groaned. "I want you to love me for my *mind*," he said, mock-offended.

"Oh, honey, I do." She slapped him on the butt. "Now let me watch you walk away slowly."

David rolled his eyes and took her arm, leading her out of the training room. They kissed one more time before parting, she to the music room to deposit her guitar, he to get bloody and gross with Faith.

Miranda met Mo on the other side of the Haven, in the Elite wing, where his clinic was; he rarely used the room that they were headed for, which was equipped with a hospital bed and the usual complement of medical machinery for life support, but it had saved more than one life since Miranda had been there, and it was much easier than having to go into Austin to the Hausmann.

"Here we are, my Lady," Mo said, flipping on the lights. "You can change behind that curtain if you like."

She took the hospital gown he held out to her. "Yay."

Once she had shucked her clothes and had the gown on, Mo set about wrapping bandages around her chest and arm. It occurred to her that she had known Mo for several years but knew next to nothing about him; almost every time they met it was in a dire emergency with no time to chat. "How long have you been a vampire, Mo?" she asked.

"Forty-seven years," he replied with a smile. "I came to America with my wife in the 1990s."

"Were you a doctor when you were human?"

"Oh, yes. Medicine has always been my calling. But Firuzeh and I both tired of identifying corpses blown to pieces. We wanted to spend our eternity someplace a little safer."

Miranda laughed. "So you came to work for a Signet?"

"It was harder to find a job than I hoped it would be. Vampires are even worse than humans with their prejudices sometimes, because we have them so much longer."

"Do people here at the Haven mistreat you? You'd say something, right?"

He shrugged. "I have been here long enough that it is not much of an issue."

"Does Firuzeh work here, too? I don't think I've met her."

"She lives here with me, but her work is in the city, at the university. She has a medical background, too, but now she teaches history. Night courses, of course. And she's writing a book." He patted her arm. "Now, lie back, and let us see how you look."

Miranda climbed into the bed stiffly and tried to find a comfortable position. "I'm glad I don't really have to deal with this. It's so awkward."

"If you did, you would have very good drugs," Mo replied, getting the camera and computer and setting them up on the bedside rolling table. David had modified a digital video camera to work with the program he'd created for reflections; a cell phone camera would have worked okay for a full-body distance shot, but she wanted a close-up, and for that she needed a clearer picture.

Mo moved around, switching on monitors and attaching various things to her while she used her free arm to get the camera turned on and did a test shot.

The little viewscreen on the camera showed up blurry, but David had said that would happen; the computer would translate the video through its various algorithms and produce a cleaned-up image it would record on the hard drive.

She'd done a few audio blogs for her website in the past, but up until now video had been problematic; there were cell phone videos of her all over the Internet, but they were shot at concerts from far enough away that for the most part the poor quality of the recordings had gone unremarked upon. Now that David had made headway into improving the picture, she figured it would work well enough. It needed to be believable, but no one would expect Academy Award–winning documentary footage from her hospital bed.

There were apparently fans staking out every hospital in Austin trying to figure out where she was being treated, and there was a lot of anxiety online and in the city over whether she was really all right; she wanted to get this out there before people started in with the conspiracy theories. Patrol units had sent in images of the shrine that had been erected at the Bat Cave, and looking at it left tears in Miranda's eyes.

She had to say something. The people who had supported her deserved to hear from her.

"All done," Mo said. "I shall wait out of the way until you need me to take everything off again."

"Thanks." She adjusted the angle of the camera in her hand, resting her arm against the bed rail, until she could at least see her whole head in the viewer. Under the lamp Mo had turned on she did, in fact, look half-dead; vampires were creatures that needed mood lighting. Fluorescent light didn't hurt them like the sun would, but the light was harsh enough to eyes used to darker rooms that she was likely to have another headache by the time she was done.

Miranda took a last second to work out in her head what she wanted to say, then hit record.

The cell where 8.3 Claret, otherwise known as Monroe, had been held—and had met his unfortunate and messy end—was built out of steel-reinforced cinder block and could stand up to quite a bit of punishment, but it wasn't designed so much for explosions. Something like, say, the bomb used by Marja Ovaska when she kidnapped Miranda and Deven would have blown the building to smithereens.

Whatever had been used to kill Monroe had been a relatively small charge, just enough to blast a body all over the walls but not enough to damage the structure. Even as hard to kill as vampires were, they were still flesh and blood— a lot of blood, from the look of it. Prime David had surmised that whatever the device was, it had been somehow placed on Monroe's body—or worse, inside—and then detonated.

Faith watched her commander in chief make his way slowly around the small room, examining the walls through a lens attached to some sort of scanning device. He was muttering to himself, which was a good sign; if he were completely stymied, he would be making an irritable growling noise every few minutes.

She was not pleased to be spending her evening in a tiny room that reeked of charred flesh and splattered gore even after the housekeeping staff had done a cursory cleaning in order to properly see to the remains. David had on gloves and a disposable lab coat that made him look like a mad surgeon to keep any remaining remains off his clothes, and Faith was keeping her distance, though one good thing about wearing a black uniform was that stains weren't much of an issue. She did, however, wish she had her coat; interrogation rooms were kept very cold, which was why David had been able to leave this for tonight.

The staff hadn't sanitized the place yet on David's orders, and the walls were blood-dyed as dark as the floor . . . but this time not from interrogation.

Plenty of people had died in this cell, but only two she could think of had done so against the Prime's orders. The first, the traitorous Elite who went by Helen, had self-terminated after her Blackthorn co-conspirator Samuel had slipped her a stake. David had made changes in Elite protocol to make sure that didn't happen again; now, only he and Faith had the code to enter the interrogation rooms, and they could transmit it remotely in an emergency, but otherwise nobody could get in or out of the cells . . . well, except for someone powerful enough to Mist.

Prime Deven, for example . . . and Prime Hart.

"Is Hart strong enough to Mist?" Faith asked.

David, startled out of his wall-scrutiny, turned to her. "More than likely. Most of us are. But those who aren't would never admit it."

"So he could have Misted in here and planted the bomb himself."

"Easily. That's the only theory I have at the moment as to how this happened—the lock was still engaged up until the door blew out. No one opened the door."

"But that doesn't prove it was Hart, just that it was a Signet bearer."

"Or one of a handful of non-Signet vampires powerful enough to Mist, yes."

"You mean, like your sire?"

He frowned. "Oh, hell. That hadn't even occurred to me. I honestly don't know if she's that strong—but it's possible."

David went back to his examination for a moment, then made a triumphant noise. "Aha. Tweezers, please, Faith."

She picked them up from the open zipper case of probes, lenses, and other . . . whatever the hell they were . . . and handed them to him. He crouched down and gingerly removed something that was embedded in the mortar between two blocks.

"Bag," he said.

Faith supplied a small plastic evidence bag that was already labeled with the date and location; the Prime had harvested several already that housed various bits of blown-up detritus that could be pieces of bomb or possibly pieces of Monroe, she couldn't tell which. A series of samples from the floor and walls had been sent for analysis yesterday to test for explosive residue and anything else Hunter Development could find. David's quest was to find evidence of the bomb itself.

He held up the bag and peered at the small fragment of metal he'd retrieved; it was a section of a disk about the size of a button, and she would have thought it *was* a button. David brought it over to the table, under the light, and, after switching one of the dials on his scanner, ran it over the button.

"Transmitter," he said. "In fact . . . I'll be damned . . . it's remarkably similar to the one that Hart brought to me last time he was here. Same technology, and I'll bet . . ."

Faith watched, wondering for the thousandth time— that week—about his sanity, as David leaned in close to the wall where he'd found the button and *sniffed* the bricks.

"Sire," she said, "you know how people think you're crazy?"

"Do they?" he asked absently.

"Well, I do, anyway."

David straightened and faced her. "Come smell this."

"Not a chance in hell, Sire."

He laughed. "All right, I'll spare you—it smells very faintly of acetone."

"Nail polish remover?"

"I don't think it's actually acetone. I do think it's a liquid explosive, something along the lines of nitroglycerin. Liquid nitroglycerin isn't as unstable as people think it is, but a good, sharp shock will still detonate it. Based on the spatter patterns . . ."

"I do love it when you talk spatter patterns."

". . . he was standing about right here and blew out in all

directions, which means either he was holding a bottle of the stuff, or . . ."

He trailed off.

"Or?" she prompted.

"Given that we haven't found any evidence of a container, I would have to assume it was taken internally. If this transmitter was the same as the last one, it had a tiny charge inside it, and if that went off anywhere on his body . . ." David made a *boom!* gesture.

"Wait . . . if he drank it, that means he killed himself."

"Unless he didn't know he was drinking it."

"But that kind of thing is highly toxic, Sire. He would have gotten sick."

David nodded, considering. "True. He probably would have vomited it up within minutes of ingestion . . . if he was conscious. If whoever Misted in here knocked him out first, then poured the explosive down his throat or even injected it with a hypodermic, then stuck the transmitter in his mouth, for example, and Misted out, then set off the charge, there would be no evidence left behind besides remnants of the transmitter itself."

"Why not just punch him in the stomach to blow it, then, and not leave any evidence? Or—here's a wild idea—stake him?"

"Stake him and you risk getting blood on yourself and being seen with stained clothes. This way he could set it off at a distance, and all that's left are a few fragments of metal and traces of chemical residue. Best of all, liquid explosives are easy to make from common ingredients. There's no way to trace them back to the bomber himself. And I didn't get a damn thing off the last transmitter even before it blew, so I doubt there'll be much on this one either."

"So we're nowhere, still," Faith said. "Fantastic."

"Not exactly nowhere."

"How so?"

David began gathering up the sample bags and his tools, and said, "I'm going to get a closer look at this fragment. If in fact it is the same design as the one from three years ago, we know the two were made by the same manufacturer. There aren't a whole lot of people who deal in this kind of tech. Chances are the same person who left behind the first one was responsible for this, too."

"But you said Hart didn't have anything to do with the first transmitter—that he found it by a dead Elite. Shadow intelligence was that whoever was killing Hart's people is still doing it, just only once in a while to spook him . . . Hart brought you the earpiece thinking you were behind it, right? Wouldn't that mean Hart *didn't* kill Monroe?"

"That's making the wild assumption that Hart was telling the truth about the earpiece in the first place," David reminded her. "At the time I believed him. He seemed sincerely disturbed by the loss of his Elite. But I admit I could have been duped. I'm going to have to revisit my notes from back then and compare them to whatever I can get off this. Finding its origins became less of a priority with everything else that was going on, but now that I have pieces of two of them, I might make more progress."

As they left the interrogation room and locked it behind them, David handed her the instrument case long enough to strip off the plastic coat and gloves and stuff them in the trash. Underneath it he had on jeans and a tourist-looking T-shirt advertising someplace called Jaynestown, Canton.

"If Hart didn't kill Monroe . . ." Faith began, not really sure where the sentence was going to go; she had no idea what the alternatives were.

"Then another Signet probably did," David finished for her.

"Sire . . ."

He stopped walking. "What's wrong?"

"We have to consider . . . it might have been Deven. He was alone with Monroe when we walked in on them. He gave him blood—what if the explosive was mixed in the bag?"

David lifted his eyes to the star-flecked sky, sighing wearily. "The thought had crossed my mind. I just don't see what advantage he'd gain by killing his own agent after going to all that trouble to get Monroe into Hart's Elite and having him botch the shooting, then get caught. It makes far more sense for Hart to have done it to destroy evidence connecting him to the crime. Plus, as you said, it would have been hard to get Monroe to drink the stuff—I've never tasted nitroglycerin, but I'm betting it comes through the taste of blood."

"Red Shadow operatives are more than willing to die on command, Sire."

"True. But again, why? Monroe was supposed to testify against Hart. Deven hates Hart as much as I do. And Deven, for all his faults, doesn't throw his agents' lives away without good reason. It would have taken Monroe decades to get to Claret level; that's a lot of time and training gone to waste."

"I don't know," Faith answered truthfully. "I'm just saying it could have been him. His agenda is about three miles past inscrutable."

"Acknowledged, Second. And as much as I don't want to believe that Deven would conspire against us, he was willing to let Miranda get shot, and although I think . . . or want to think . . . that his intentions are good, who knows? He operates from a rather skewed sense of morality. He's not above lying to me, that's for damn sure."

The Prime started toward the Haven again, and she fell into step beside him, frustrated. "I hate this," she said. "Is there anyone left who can be trusted?"

He offered her a smile. "Besides you? I doubt it."

She nearly tripped over a nonexistent pebble in her sudden discomfort. "I . . . I appreciate that, Sire."

David held open the side door for her. "At least I have something to work with. I only hope it's the only transmitter Hart—or whoever—left here."

Faith froze halfway over the threshold.

Expecting her to have entered already, David nearly blundered into her; he caught himself on the door frame and said, "What the hell?"

She stepped out of the way, brain spinning, and put her

head in her hands. "I'm so stupid," she said. "Stupid, stupid—"

"Faith, what are you talking about?"

Averting her eyes so she wouldn't have to see his face, Faith reached into her pocket and handed him Jeremy's cuff link.

Eleven

"Hi everyone . . . it's Miranda. As you can tell by my awesome fashion statement here, I'm out of commission for a while. I wanted to thank you all for your wonderful support. I heard today that the blood bank has had a record number of donors . . ."

Stella paused the video, biting her lip.

She'd always played it off as a trick of the light, or a reflection, but . . . the necklace *was* glowing. She could see it through Miranda's hospital gown, just barely, and there was no way *that* was a reflection. Especially now that Stella had seen that other guy's green one doing the same thing.

She grounded and centered herself, then lowered her shielding enough that she could See, and started the video again.

". . . going to be a while before I'm back onstage, but I'll be keeping you up to date here on the website. And since I can't really go anywhere, I've got plenty of time to work on songs for the new album . . . as soon as I can sit up and hold my guitar, anyway. But I did want to ask you guys for one thing: Please don't hang out at the hospitals. I don't want anybody to get in trouble over me. I'm at a private facility and not at one of the big Austin hospitals, so you're probably not going to find me anyway."

Miranda looked like crap. She was all bandaged up and hooked up to monitors . . . just like a normal human would be. And Stella couldn't See a damn thing, not even her regular aura; something about the video was weird. It might be the editing; Stella had tried Looking at some of the other footage she had downloaded of Miranda onstage at different times, but only a couple of them showed anything psychically, and they were all normal . . . sort of.

Stella had figured one thing out: Miranda was gifted. Watching her perform with her inner eyes open, Stella could See something when she played—it was subtle, and if she'd just Seen it once, she wouldn't have thought anything of it, but after poring over a dozen videos, she knew it wasn't a coincidence.

She just had no idea what it was.

Stella's gift was visual clairvoyance; she could See people's energy, and it told her a lot about them: whether they were lying, what kind of intentions they had, how strong they were. She could spot another Witch in a crowd of a hundred people, and often she could tell what kind of abilities they had, but whatever Miranda had . . . she'd never seen it before.

It was hard to detect and definitely rare . . . and Miranda was definitely aware she had it. The way it showed up, like soft tendrils reaching out to the audience, was too perfectly controlled, and the shielding around it was too organized to be purely instinctive. Miranda had been trained.

Stella's phone rang. She jumped, losing her hold on the Sight with a bitten-off curse. She looked at the phone and sighed: her dad.

She'd call him back later.

Maybe.

He was trying. She had to give him credit. She'd never expected him to be the one to reach out to her after months of hardly speaking, but he'd called her last week wanting to have lunch and even got her a signed poster and a wristband for the music festival as a tacit apology. They'd talked about the festival and the bands she was going to see; he'd asked about her job, carefully avoiding The Subject, and she'd asked him about work. He always had great stories—fewer now that he was a detective and wasn't busting naked crack addicts anymore, but still. It had felt good to talk to him again.

She wondered if he knew anything else about the shooting; there wasn't a whole lot he could tell her other than they had a guy in custody and had some letters he'd written Miranda, but he might be willing to offer up a little extra info if she agreed to go to lunch again.

"Nice, Stell," she muttered. "Way to use your dad."

She'd call him back. Later. She would.

She grounded again and went back to the video.

"*. . . just wanted you all to know I'm okay, and that I love you all. I'm going to sink into a nice Vicodin coma now, so . . . talk to you later.*"

Miranda smiled wearily at the camera. The video went dark. Stella hadn't Seen a thing . . . but Miranda being very obviously in a hospital bed like that went a long way toward proving she was human.

Unless it was staged.

Stella had absolutely no idea how to go about proving Miranda was a vampire. The only thing she'd been able to think of was watching the video footage for more psychic anomalies. She'd even done a web search for others who had similar theories, but the two she'd found were run by crazy people who had no evidence other than the *Constellation* article and its aftermath. One of them even thought there was some kind of conspiracy to hide the truth; he claimed that other websites trying to investigate Miranda Grey had been yanked off the Internet with no explanation.

Facts: Miranda never went out during the day. It wasn't just that she was a night owl; she had literally *never* been seen in the sunlight. She didn't travel—what was that thing about vampires crossing running water? She had some kind of scary dark energy underneath a flawless set of shields. No one had ever seen her eat, either. She was rarely photographed by the media; there were a lot of fan videos of her concerts, but she was almost never in magazines or on TV.

But the porphyria explained the daylight thing. And it would make traveling pretty awful. And she had a reflection—that much had been made clear in the *Rolling Stone* interview . . . assuming it wasn't staged, too.

It was absurd. There was no reason a normal person would think Stella was anything but nuts for thinking Miranda was anything besides a quirky celebrity and a great musician.

But that darkness . . .

Stella couldn't deny her own Sight. And she couldn't shake the conviction that came from somewhere deep in her heart that the woman in that hospital bed wasn't human. Maybe she wasn't a vampire, but . . . she was something.

Lark had been skeptical, but she also knew that Stella wasn't the type of person given to wild flights of fancy, so she must be on to something. She'd agreed to help if Stella could figure out which way to turn. So far, she had nothing.

She looked up at the clock. Shit—time to go to work.

Stella closed her laptop and straightened her socks. She gave herself a quick once-over in the mirror. Yep, still her. Still a bit of a chubby pixie, freckled and bespectacled, with a fire-engine-red bob with brown roots just starting to show. She had a black spiderweb tattoo on her right shoulder, with a cheerful cartoon spider hanging on a thread down near her elbow. She was wearing one of her favorite outfits: a ruffled pink skirt with a black skull-and-crossbones T-shirt, over-the-knee striped socks, and combat boots. Foxglove would roll her eyes, but Revelry didn't have a dress code, as long as her bits and boobs were covered.

She grabbed her bag and left the apartment, waving to the landlord, who was sitting out in front of the building with her ancient Pomeranian. There were only eight apartments on the property, which had been built about a century ago and was covered in ivy. The place was practically falling down, but it was crazily cheap for something in South Austin, and Stella had always loved it. It was also only a few blocks from the store.

Revelry, an occult book and supply store where most of
the Pagans in Austin came to shop at one time or another,
was in a small strip of funky businesses with an eco-
friendly paint store and a taqueria; it was adjacent to the
South Congress trendy shopping district but just removed
enough not to be mobbed by tourists on weekends. Revelry
hosted monthly Full Moon gatherings that helped introduce new people to the community, and it had a classroom
in the back where Foxglove held her Wicca 101, herbalism,
and astrology classes.

It was where Stella and Lark had met three years ago—
Lark seeking refuge at UT from small-town Texas, Stella
still living with her dad and attending community college
part-time—at one of Foxglove's Full Moons. Lark had
been a practicing Wiccan for a year by then, but Stella was
brand-new to both Witchcraft and the Wiccan religion . . .
all she knew was that she was different, and she had to
know more about her powers. Just as a spiritual path,
Wicca didn't require more than a year or so of classes, followed by a lifetime of personal exploration; but Witchcraft,
the art of spellwork, took years to master, as did learning
to fine-tune a psychic gift. It confused a lot of outsiders
that there was a difference between the practice of Witchcraft and the religion of Wicca, and that a person didn't
have to be Wiccan to be a Witch.

Normally Stella worked only during the daytime, but
on Monday nights Foxglove had started staying open till
midnight—that had been Stella's idea, and it had turned
out to be a great one. The other occult store in town closed
before sundown every day, which didn't make a lick of
sense; most magical activity tended to happen at night, and
that was when people would realize they were out of red
candles or copal resin.

Pagan basically described anyone who wasn't part of
one of the big monotheistic religions, and it was an umbrella
term; within the community there were Wiccans, non-
Wiccan Witches, Druids, Shamans, and a wide variety of
other traditions. Revelry sold books and supplies to every-

one and could special-order all sorts of rare ingredients for rituals and spells that were even hard to find on the Internet. Foxglove had widespread resources and was immensely popular, so the store managed to hang on even through depressing economical woes.

The bell jangled merrily over the door when Stella went in; she strode past the group of college-age girls who looked far too normal to shop there, and up to the counter, where Foxglove was waiting to leave.

"Hey, I'm here," Stella said unnecessarily. "You look nice."

The older Witch smiled, turning in a circle. "I have a date."

"Rock on," Stella told her. "Get some for me."

Foxglove gave her signature eye roll and departed. She reminded Stella a lot of her grandmother, who had died when Stella was nine: plump and maternal, with short curly gray hair and an abundance of silver jewelry. She was exactly the sort of nonthreatening person who made a great spokeswoman for the fringe religions of Austin, and she'd been on the news more than once to explain, for the thousandth time, that Halloween originated with a Celtic harvest festival called Samhain, and real Witches weren't evil or Satanists and didn't have baby-eating orgies. Stella had Foxglove's "Wicca, a nature-centered religion with over a hundred thousand practitioners, is the most popular neo-Pagan faith . . ." speech memorized by now.

Stella logged in to the computer, checked the till, and settled down on the stool to wait for the sorority girls to decide whether they were going to do a love spell on one of their boyfriends. She could tell they weren't actual Witches and were probably going to be really annoying, but it was better than the raving evangelists they got once or twice a week wanting to leave "Jesus Loves You So Don't Shop Here or Get an Abortion or Be Gay or Else He'll Love You Straight to Hell Forever" pamphlets.

Before long, the girls had giggled their way out of the store empty-handed; Stella did a quick check with her Sight to make sure they weren't shoplifting. Meanwhile a few other customers drifted in and out, and Stella's mind drifted, too, back through the video she'd watched and the mental grid of things she knew about Miranda Grey.

"Young Mistress Maguire," came a voice, and she looked up and grinned.

"Young Master Gandalf," she replied with a sweeping bow.

People called the elderly white-haired man Gandalf for fun, and occasionally he'd wear full wizard outfits to festivals and parties—complete with a certified replica of Gandalf the Grey's staff ordered from a catalog—but in reality, he was a serious scholar of occult history and was always asking Foxglove to order him strange volumes of ritual and lore. Sometimes they took weeks to find, and they cost a pretty penny, but Gandalf was one of their best customers.

"I expect you're looking for this," Stella said, bending down to pull a heavy book wrapped in black fabric from under the counter. "It came in yesterday."

His eyes sparkled with glee as he opened it, revealing a leather-bound book a good five inches thick whose title was written in gold ink in a language Stella couldn't hope to translate.

"Most excellent," he said, fishing out a credit card. "I wasn't sure Foxglove would be able to find this one, but she's a regular Sherlock Holmes."

As Stella ran his card, something occurred to her. "Hey, Gandalf . . . can I ask you a dumb question?"

"Let's find out!" he said gamely.

"Do you know anything about vampires? Like, real ones?"

He looked surprised. "What, aren't the movies enough for you, young lady?"

Stella rolled her eyes. "Real vampires, Gandalf."

Most people would have laughed at her—even here at Revelry, where everyone was a little weird to begin with— but Gandalf raised a feathery white eyebrow. "Why would you think there was such a thing?"

"I . . . I met someone, and she seemed . . . she had this aura."

Gandalf grew serious and shook his head. "That's not a road you need to go down."

She froze halfway through handing him the receipt to sign. "So they're real."

He took the strip of paper and the pen she offered and signed his name in a quick scrawl. "Listen, Young Miss Stella . . . there are some things you don't need to know. You go poking around under certain rocks, certain nasty things come out and bite you."

"I won't poke anything," she insisted. "I just want to know the truth—and how I can spot them. Isn't that a good thing? If they're around here, I'd like to be able to run like hell when I see one."

"Don't run from dark things, Stella. If you run, they chase after you." Gandalf took the book and slid it into his ratty old leather messenger bag.

She tried to ask again, but he waved her off, and before she could come up with a way to convince him, the phone rang, and by the time she'd told the voice on the line what Revelry's hours were, he was gone.

As soon as she was alone, she called Lark.

"Dude," Lark said, "I was just about to roll a joint—are you coming over?"

"No, I'm at the store. Look, I found something out. Gandalf came in and basically admitted there's really such a thing as vampires."

Lark whistled. "Well if anybody would know, he would."

"That's what I thought."

"So now what?"

"Well . . . I was thinking . . . maybe if I dug around at the vamp fetish clubs based here in Austin, I might find someone who knows the real thing."

"Oh, Jesus, Stella, you're not going to go to some place where people wear fake fangs and talk about the eternal torment of being sexy, are you?"

"Come on, Lark, they're harmless—they have to be or they get raided by the cops. Dad told me all the fetish clubs are really careful not to cause trouble or break any laws. And I'd stick to the public ones."

"But . . . leather corsets and people biting each other for fun?"

"Would you come with me?"

Lark didn't miss a beat. "Fuck yeah!"

"Why have you been carrying this?" David asked, not sure he wanted to know the answer but unable to help himself.

Faith looked absolutely beside herself with shame, standing in the corner of his workroom where they'd immediately headed as soon as she showed him the innocuous-looking gold piece. "I don't . . . I don't know."

"Do you have some sort of warm and fuzzy feelings for him, Faith?"

Her expression changed, and her voice hardened. "I don't think that should be at issue here, Sire."

"If your loyalty is in any way compromised—"

"It isn't," she interrupted. "I assure you. We met twice during the summit, and that was it. I found that on the floor after he left and stuck it in my coat pocket to return to him, but with all the drama I never got a chance."

They stared at each other. David knew she wasn't being entirely truthful. But Miranda had been absolutely right; it wasn't his business. Although . . . thinking about Faith going to bed with Hayes again made his blood boil. He didn't have any right to hold it against her, but he wanted to . . . and it bothered him.

David turned back to his worktable, where he'd put the cuff link in a blastproof scanner he'd built after Hart's earpiece had nearly taken his eye out. It was calibrated to tell him if there was any sort of charge or signal going to or from whatever he put inside it. Though it wasn't as precise as a handheld tool, it would at least tell him if the thing was dangerous.

He turned on the scanner beam and mentally reached into the case, lifting the cuff link up and passing it slowly through the green light, first one way, then another, then turning it in a circle to get the entire surface.

A moment later the computer beeped. He glanced over the scan results and let out his breath.

"What is it?" Faith asked. "A transmitter? A recorder?"

He very deliberately did not laugh. "It's a cuff link, Faith."

"What do you mean? It has to be some kind of techno-thing . . . right?"

The Prime gestured at the screen. "Look for yourself. It's solid gold. There's nothing inside it, no charge on it, no radiation coming from it. It's a cuff link."

"What if it has some kind of spell on it, like Ovaska's talismans?"

He had to grin at that one. "Whatever those things ran on, they still emitted an energy field that affected the surrounding environment. This scanner accounts for that. There's nothing here but metal."

She looked like she wanted the ground to swallow her. "It's just a cuff link. You're sure."

"Yes, Faith. Would you like it back?"

"No," she said quickly. "You should destroy it . . . just in case. I'd feel better."

"All right, I will." He returned his attention to the scanner to give her a moment to compose herself. He knew how much she hated looking foolish—as much as he did. "Regardless, Faith, I'm glad you gave it to me. It might well have been something dangerous. I hope if you find anything else like it, you'll bring it to my attention right away."

"I will, Sire." She sounded less flustered without him looking at her, so he stayed where he was, turning on the magnification to look at the cuff link again out of curiosity.

"Interesting," he said. "This symbol isn't Hart's."

"I noticed that. Is it a Signet seal at all?" she wanted to know.

"Not sure," he replied. "I'll run it through the database

to see if it matches either a Prime or any outside vampire organization. It might just be a designer's emblem, but it looks an awful lot like one of ours."

"You don't have them all memorized?"

David snorted. "I can name maybe half a dozen on sight. I've never really needed to know them all. Now that we don't write many letters, we don't use them nearly as often. A couple of Primes have them in their e-mail signatures, but for the most part they've fallen out of favor."

He pulled up the Signet database he'd been building for the past few years. It had all the information he could gather on the Signets, their territories, and their history; he was even keeping a timeline of Primes and Queens and their reigns. The Signet seals were already part of the database. He set up a quick search comparing the scan of the cuff link to the Seals.

A match.

"Australia," David said.

Faith laughed quietly. "Big surprise there."

"No, and yes. Why is he wearing the seal of Australia if he's working for the Northeastern United States?"

Now she frowned. "That is a good question. Maybe he used to work for Australia McMannis hasn't been in power that long; he might have been in the previous Prime's Elite."

David looked up Australia and paged back past the current Prime. "The last one was Bartlett . . . he and his Queen were killed eleven years ago, and the Signet was vacant for nearly three years before McMannis took over. I have Bartlett's Second listed as an Olivia Daniels, deceased. I don't have anything on the rest of his Elite, though. Maybe Deven will uncover something about Hayes that will link him to the Australian Signet."

"I don't think he's working for Hart because he wants to," Faith said hesitantly. "We didn't talk about it in any detail, but he doesn't like Hart. I think Hart has something over him, a debt or something he has to pay, but he wouldn't tell me what it was."

David was glad to hear that, though he didn't say so. If

Faith believed that Hayes was working for Hart against his will, it was probably true—and it meant that her judgment was better than he'd feared.

He could hear Miranda now: *David, baby, you're being a dick.*

Quite true.

He sighed inwardly. "Look," he said, deciding just to lay it out. "I have to tell you, Faith, I really, really didn't like you going to bed with Hayes. I know you're an adult and that you didn't do anything wrong, but I still didn't like it. And I know it's my problem, not yours—so I'm going to try not to keep being an ass about it. But you deserve honesty, and honestly, it pissed me off."

She blinked at him for a moment. "Um . . . thank you?"

"No, just . . . I apologize for how I've been acting. You've given me years of flawless service and loyalty, and I act like a jilted boyfriend over something that's not my business. And I'm sorry that we're investigating Hayes like this and that he has to be a suspect, but you know what's at stake here."

Faith had turned faintly pink, but she said, "I was never fooled into thinking he was a good guy, Sire. Whatever his reasons, I never trusted him."

David nodded. "If you think of anything else that might help us figure out who he is and where he's from, please let me know."

"I will, Sire. Now . . . if there's nothing further?"

"Nothing further, Second. You can go."

She ducked out of the room, looking acutely uncomfortable.

He turned back to the worktable, shaking his head; he'd have been uncomfortable, too, if his boss wanted to discuss his sex life.

Of course the last time he'd had a boss, that boss had *been* his sex life.

Suddenly, his com went off. *"This is Shadow District patrol leader Elite Twenty-four reporting an emergency code Alpha Seven."*

The door flew open, and Faith, who couldn't have gotten to the end of the hall before her own alarm erupted, came back in.

"Elite Twenty-four, I have the Prime with me," Faith said into her com. "Go ahead."

"We've discovered a dead human behind a club—he has obviously been fed on and drained. Male, African-American, driver's license lists him as Russell Barry, thirty-four years old."

"Has APD been alerted?" Faith asked.

"No, ma'am."

"All right, Elite Twenty-four, I'm on my way to the scene. Secure the area and have the team start gathering evidence. I want a full set of photos on the server in ten minutes, as well as a scan of the victim's license and anything else in his wallet."

"On it, Second. Elite Twenty-four out."

"Goddamn it," David muttered. "We do not need this right now. This had better be an isolated incident."

Faith already had her phone out to call their liaison at the police department. "Let's just hope it wasn't your sire," she said as she walked out of the room.

David put his head in his hands. "Let's hope not," he said, though he had a sinking feeling that was exactly who it was.

Twelve

Miles away, the mortal world was running at its usual frenetic daylight pace; thousands of people strode purposefully along the streets of downtown Austin while in offices and boardrooms all over the city contracts were signed, decisions made, hostile takeovers negotiated.

Negotiations between the Queen and sleep were rapidly breaking down.

Miranda lay staring at the ceiling, listening to the deceptive quiet in the suite. It was never entirely silent to her—if she concentrated, she could hear the slightest creak of the walls expanding and contracting with the weather, the distant sound of the day guards on their rounds, the wind outside, the birds; but closer to the bed, she could hear the whirring of David's computer and the faint buzz of the various technical gadgets on his desk. Even closer was the sound of the Prime's slow, even breathing at her side and of his heartbeat, the metronome by which she usually slept.

Normally he was the insomniac. The first year they'd been together she had gotten used to finding him awake during the day—too much on his mind, he said, though she couldn't imagine being able to outlast the ages-old pull of the sun. Their bodies were designed to rest when the sun was out. Most young vampires literally *couldn't* stay awake in the afternoon; they became narcoleptic and would drop off midconversation. She was strong enough to resist if she needed to, but once her nightmares had become less frequent, she'd been happy to tumble into oblivion as soon as the sun rose over the hills.

Then there were days like Tuesday, when sleep eluded her no matter how much she wanted it.

She could have gotten up and gone to the music room, but with David next to her, the weight of his arms around her so comforting, it was hard to justify leaving the bed. Plus, she hated to risk waking him. The last few days had drained them both.

It was so strange, and wonderful, to have the Haven to themselves again. The last of the Bastards was gone, and life could settle down.

If David ever even mentioned having the Council gather in Austin again, she was going to lock him up in a padded room.

The idea had been to impress the others and establish the South as a strong Signet . . . and she supposed they'd been successful. Not only had their Elite won the tournament, but Miranda was pretty sure that several Primes who had previously dismissed David as an upstart were more than a little wary of him now. Jonathan had told her, amusedly, that in the Council's entire history there was no record of one Prime punching another one in the face in full view of the entire assembly, and the level of drama surrounding Miranda's shooting and the explosion in interrogation room A had convinced quite a few Signets that the South was not to be toyed with.

Hart's machinations had accomplished one thing in their favor: By the twisted psychology of the Council, anyone who was hated enough to earn that kind of single-minded attention from another Prime must be a formidable enemy indeed. Miranda wasn't alone in thinking it was strange for Hart to focus so much energy on taking her down. Either he was obsessed with destroying her, or he had some other reason for his behavior.

Neither of those possibilities was helping her sleep . . .

and that was without factoring tonight's little meeting into the equation.

She sighed. The worst part? Now she had to pee.

Although she couldn't in all fairness blame that one on Hart.

Miranda rolled gingerly out of David's embrace, trying to move slowly enough that he wouldn't be jolted awake; he muttered something in what she thought might be Italian and turned onto his back, eyes still closed.

Once upon a time, she'd been the sort of person who banged her shins trying to get to the bathroom in the dark; now, the thought of turning on a light just to get there and back was just silly. Even with the metal shutters down over the windows, her eyes could pick out enough light to navigate the familiar terrain. The wood floor of the bedroom gave way to cool tile, and she yawned, wondering how weird life would be if being a vampire meant all her body functions shut down—the old walking-corpse variety of immortal as opposed to . . . whatever they really were.

David's theory was that they were mutants: still alive but with different hormone and enzyme concentrations and a variety of other changes triggered by the initial death of the human body. Death functioned as a reset button and rebooted the system, rewriting the programming as it went. Still, all his science had yet to explain *why* it happened the way it did, or how such a complicated form of asexual reproduction was possible.

Miranda liked to say it was magic just to irritate him.

When she returned to the bedroom, she sighed again. "What are you doing up?"

Without making a sound David had gotten out of bed and was now at his desk. "Just doing a—"

"Routine systems check," she finished with him, climbing back into the bed.

He smiled. "Am I that predictable?"

She straightened out the blankets. "You, my dear, are what is known as a chronic workaholic," she replied. "If you were human, you'd probably have a heart attack by age forty."

He made a face. "I've noticed you tend to lie awake more and more often the longer you're Queen. Shall I book us adjoining beds in the cardiac ward?"

Miranda stuck her tongue out at him. "Who would've thought that being responsible for the lives of hundreds of vampires and all the humans they feed on would be stressful?"

"I think there's a bottle of Xanax in the bathroom. Wash three of those down with a shot of Jack, and you'll sleep like a baby."

She snorted. "Right, until Deven finds out you still keep Jack in the house and bashes you over the head with the bottle."

He smiled, though his eyes were on the computer screen. She had to admit he made a pretty picture sitting there shirtless at the antique wooden desk, hair tousled from sleep. All he needed were those glasses . . .

David raised an eyebrow. "You're staring."

"I was considering whether to drag you back to bed and shag you stupid, or just drag you back to bed and make you sleep."

He shook his head. "Just a few more minutes. I got a final report from APD on the Alpha Seven from last night. They didn't find anything useful, no prints, no trace evidence . . ."

Miranda narrowed her eyes, concentrated, and shut the screen of his laptop firmly with her mind, barely missing his fingers.

"Miranda!" he said.

She sat up, hands on her hips. "Your wife just offered to shag you stupid. If you'd rather go over police reports, then you are already stupid."

"I said just a few more minutes."

Miranda rolled her eyes and got up, crossing the room to his desk to come up behind him; she knew very well that "a few minutes" would turn into first one hour, then two, and before he knew it, sunrise would come and he'd still be sitting there fretting and stewing. After the week they'd had, she wasn't going to let that happen.

She laid her hands on his shoulders and ran them down along his arms, tugging backward to pull the chair away from the computer, leaving enough room for her to slide her butt around onto the desk and effectively obscure his view of the laptop should he attempt to open it again.

Miranda made a show of removing her T-shirt and dropping it on the floor. "Do I have your attention, Lord Prime?" she asked.

His eyes wandered lazily from her belly to her face. "You win," he said. "You always win. But you don't play fair."

She gave him a mischievous grin. "That's why I always win."

He leaned forward and nuzzled her navel, then kissed a spiral up over her skin, hands traversing the landscape of her breasts. "I love how soft you are," he murmured. "Even with all this muscle, you're like . . . the Hill Country, all curves."

She laughed. "But with fewer rattlesnakes and scorpions."

David took hold of her hips and pulled her onto his lap, tangling his hands in her hair and kissing her deeply. She braced her knees on either side of him and lifted up to try to free herself of her panties, but after a minute of twisting and grunting, she lost her balance and fell out of the chair with a squeak of surprise.

Both of them were laughing as he caught her and, somehow managing to still look graceful, lowered them both to the floor.

"I'm just so damn sexy," she giggled. She laughed even harder when, in an effort to get her underwear off, he twisted his torso at just the right angle to smack his head into the side of the chair. The chair jerked and rolled a few feet from the impact, and David toppled over the rest of the way, his Signet swinging back to hit him in the nose.

All of that, and her panties still weren't off.

He gave up, shoulders shaking with laughter, and collapsed on the floor next to her, rubbing his head with his hand.

Their eyes met. Amid the laughter she could feel his love for her humming along the bond between them, and she returned it joyfully.

There was no need to say it, but she did anyway. "I love you."

He smiled. "I love you, too. You klutz."

She slapped him lightly on the back of the head. "Can we go back to bed now?"

"Yes, please."

He reached over and fetched her T-shirt, handing it to her as they both got to their feet and, arms tight around each other, curled up beneath the covers to settle into richly deserved sleep.

"The perimeter is secure, Sire. No sign of her yet."

"Acknowledged, Second."

The bartender looked a little nervous—he might be used to hosting the Signets, but having Anodyne locked down and surrounded by Elite wasn't something any entrepreneur in the Shadow District wanted to be known for. An appropriately sized stack of hundred-dollar bills calmed his fears, but he still wasn't happy with the situation.

Neither was the Prime. David joined Miranda in the corner booth and handed the Queen one of the two beers he'd brought back from his conversation with the bartender.

"I hope all this security doesn't scare her off," Miranda remarked. "Is it really a good idea to treat her like a suspect from the beginning? We don't have any reason to think she's our enemy at this point."

"A little healthy paranoia never hurt anyone," David said. "Besides, whatever her aim in coming here, she can't be fool enough to expect me to meet her without guards in place. Most Primes don't even leave the house alone, much less have a drink with a stranger of questionable intent."

"Sire, we have a female vampire approaching the building on foot. Should we detain her?"

"No, Faith . . . just let her through. I'll send up an alarm if we need help."

A moment later, David heard the door swing open and then close again. He took a deep breath and stood.

She looked exactly as he remembered her . . . though those memories were distant and worn around the edges, looking into her calm, beautiful face brought it back. He remembered her standing over him in the jail . . . remembered the look of appraisal she had given him, as if unconvinced he was worth her time . . . remembered her teeth as she smiled.

"My Lord Prime," she said, bowing.

"Lydia." Now it was his turn to size her up. She was powerful, true . . . very nearly Signet-caliber, though she was definitely not a warrior of any sort. And she was much older than he had originally thought. When she'd turned him, he had guessed she wasn't long out of her own humanity, but he could sense her age stretching back at least as far as Deven's . . . and further. "It's been quite a while."

She looked him up, then down, and nodded. "I see you have done well for yourself."

He didn't answer.

She went on. "Over the centuries I've followed your career, waiting for the day when you would find your way to the Signet."

Now he said, "I'm flattered that you've taken such an interest in me."

Lydia regarded him in silence for a moment. "Do you believe in fate, David?"

"No."

She smiled. "I knew you would say that."

"Why have you come, Lydia?"

Another pause, then: "May I sit?"

Wordlessly he held out his hand toward the booth. Lydia bowed again and took the side opposite Miranda. David, in turn, slid back in next to his Queen.

Lydia looked around the bar, eyes lighting on each of the Elite who were stationed around the room. "I am not your enemy," she said. "In fact, I have something for you that I believe you will find . . . intriguing."

She reached into her coat and produced a small, carved wooden box . . . very much like the box the Queen's Signet had once been kept in, which was still locked in the cabinet in their suite. She placed it on the table and pushed it toward him.

"Have you ever wondered where you came from?" Lydia asked.

He looked from the box to her face. "You turned me," he replied. "I was an average blacksmith in an average village until you had me arrested—and my wife executed—for the murders you committed."

She smiled slightly when he said *average*. "I was referring to where the Signets came from," she said. "Don't you question, sitting at the Council table, if there was ever a meaning behind the shadow-puppet theater it has become? If once . . . long ago, in a time lost to the mists of history, something . . . or someone . . . united you?"

She touched the lid of the box. "I represent a group of our kind who still remember, my Lord. And we want you to remember as well."

"Why?" Miranda asked, speaking up for the first time. "Why David? And why now?"

Lydia turned her gaze to the Queen. "Because it is time. Because things are now in motion that cannot be stopped, and because . . . the fate of all our kind is at stake."

Miranda looked dubious. "Seriously? You're giving us 'grand and glorious destiny' here? How about some real answers, Lydia? What exactly do you want?"

An edge of faint impatience entered Lydia's voice. "I am a servant of a greater power," she said. "Those whom I serve sent me to a backward village in England to find the one they had searched for throughout the centuries. Now, they have sent me to find him again—to give him this."

David considered the box, and the vampire, and said,

"Before I take anything from you, I want to know who you're working for."

"I believe the saying is, 'Don't look a gift horse in the mouth.'"

The Prime smiled. "I have a saying of my own. It goes like this:" Instantly, he had a knife in his hand, the blade held to her throat. "Tell me what the fuck is going on, or I cut your throat."

Lydia was neither surprised nor frightened; instead she looked almost bored. "Open the box."

David heard Miranda sigh, and the Queen flipped up the box's lid. "What is it?"

He lowered his eyes, then frowned. The velvet-lined box contained a flat silver oval carved with a ring of symbols. Around its edge were five prongs, like the setting on a pendant.

There was something familiar about the craftsmanship, but it was Miranda who figured it out: "It looks kind of like a Signet," she said. "Only without a stone or a chain."

Lydia nodded. "It was forged by the same hands that created the Signets themselves, thousands of years ago."

"And what hands were those?" David asked.

Lydia's answer was to open the box further and tap on the inside of the lid.

The wood had been carved with a symbol . . . something else he recognized.

Infinity and the moon.

This symbol was different from the insignia Deven had used, though; his bore only a single moon, a waning crescent; this one had the waxing, full, and waning moons, with the infinity symbol beneath it. The symbol was worked into a complicated design similar to a Signet seal.

"I've seen a version of this," David said. "I was under the impression it was connected to the Order of Eleusis."

"Elysium," Lydia corrected. "Named after the lands of the righteous dead, as ruled over by the Dark Goddess Persephone. The Order was founded by one of the original Signets . . . the Secondborn."

"If the original Signets were the Secondborn, then what's a Firstborn?" David asked.

"The sleeping darkness," Lydia replied. "They are said to slumber far beneath the earth. Even I know little else about them—they were gone long before I was made. But the Secondborn, the sons and daughters of Persephone . . . from them came all other vampires, and the Signets were given the power to rule over and guide them. But as the centuries passed, the old gods were forgotten, and eventually the Signets were sundered from one another, loving power more than they loved their Creatrix."

David snapped the lid of the box shut and put his head in his hands. "Religion? That's all? You expect me to believe any of this?"

"Believe what you will about the past, Lord Prime. What matters here is the future. Change is coming; that much your Queen could tell you. The Council has lost its way. A grave threat looms against all our kind . . . and when it comes, we will need more than a group of power-hungry egomaniacs to defeat it. We will need a Prime . . . a true Prime."

He looked at her, feeling a surge of strange sorrow. "That's why you sired me, then? To further some kind of ridiculous prophetic agenda on behalf of your cult?"

She smiled. "There is a little more to it than that."

"Such as? What is this thing supposed to be, anyway?"

"I am not sure. It can be activated only by the Signet chosen to wear it, so we have never been able to learn much; perhaps you will have better luck. The closest guess is that it functions as a power amplifier."

Miranda asked suddenly, "Why would someone use this symbol with just one moon on it as opposed to all three?"

Lydia said, "There are three branches of the Order, and each has its own version of the symbol. The Triple Moon is used by the priesthood itself."

"And the waning Moon alone?"

If Lydia thought it an odd question, she didn't comment.

"The warrior class," she replied. "The Swords of Elysium are known for their weaponcraft as well as their prowess in battle. Only those who have been initiated into the Order may use the symbol, and it carries a great deal of weight . . . in some circles." She was looking back at David as she said that. "You expect me to prove myself to you, to offer you some sort of empirical evidence to back up my beliefs and my words. I would expect nothing less . . . but alas, I cannot give you any proof."

"So you want me to take a strange object that may or may not have some kind of voodoo hex on it . . . on faith. You've come to the wrong Signet."

Miranda put her hand on his arm and said, "I'm afraid David isn't exactly the religious type, Lydia. And he has a hard time believing in magic."

Lydia looked the Queen in the eye. "And you?"

Miranda shrugged. "I believe the world is way bigger and weirder than I can possibly know. I don't know if I believe in any sort of gods, ancient or otherwise . . . but maybe I'm just not old enough to see my error."

Lydia's expression became speculative once again, and she reached over and pushed the box toward the Queen. "Then I give this to you," she said. "Do with it what you will . . . my task is done."

"What makes you think she'll take it either?" David asked, but Miranda had already done so, drawing the little box toward her. "Miranda—"

"Thank you, Lydia," Miranda said over his protest.

Lydia nodded; there was new respect, and appreciation, in her eyes. She stood smoothly. "You are welcome. I take my leave of you, then . . . and may the Dark Goddess bless and guide you both."

"Wait . . ." Miranda called after her. "This Goddess of yours . . . what does She look like?"

The blonde paused. "Everyone sees Her a little differently," she said. "Most often She is pictured as a warrior, with black hair and black eyes, accompanied by a hound at Her feet and a serpent coiled around Her shoulders."

David felt Miranda's energy change completely as Lydia spoke, from bemused to frightened; he turned to her, saw how pale she had become, and started to tell Lydia to wait right where she was—

But Lydia was already gone.

"Faith, track her," David said into his com.

"Sire . . . we don't have a signal. She's not showing up on the sensor network at all."

"Recalibrate based on Ovaska's amulets, then."

"Already done, Sire. Whatever she's got on her to block the signal, it's different from what Ovaska used. We could see her when she came in, but the minute she stepped outside . . . shit . . . Sire, I don't think she blocked the signal. I think she Misted."

"Well, then, search the area. I want her back here—she hasn't even begun to answer my questions."

"Yes, Sire. Right away."

David took Miranda's hands and peered into her face. "Beloved . . . what did she say? What's got you so spooked?"

Miranda was clutching the box to her chest with one forearm, as if to keep him from taking it away from her. "Nothing," she ventured, but the look of disbelief on his face made her half smile and amend her statement. "It's just . . . Cora said something to me the other night, and . . . it had to be a coincidence. I mean we're talking about mythology here. Vampire mythology. It's all just folklore, there's no truth in it . . . is there?"

"Well, you already know how I feel about it."

"But what if . . ."

"What if what? What if there really are old gods and sleeping Firstborn and the Signets were created by some moldy old deity?"

"David . . . you told me, years ago, that some power had created the Signets, and that meant some power could destroy them. What if that power is this Order of Elysium? What if they really are that old, and even if the myth is just a myth, aren't you dying to know what that thing really is?

How it was made? The David I know would be champing at the bit to get this box to the lab."

The urgency in her voice, the absolute need to make him understand, was as disquieting as anything else he'd heard that night. Miranda wasn't gullible, nor was she easily impressed; something in Lydia's words had struck her, had reached the precognitive part of the Queen that knew things it didn't want to know.

She was right . . . there was more to this than fairy tales.

"All right," he said. "We'll take it to the lab and check it out. But I'm not letting it into the Haven until we know it's not a bomb or a transmitter. We'll go by Hunter when we leave here and see what Novotny makes of it."

He started to take the box, but she flinched, her arm tightening around it. "No," she said plaintively. "Let me keep it . . . she gave it to me."

He stared at her for a while, then relented. "Okay, beloved . . . if it's that important to you, you can keep it on you . . . but you'll have to let it go for the lab to analyze it. Can you do that?"

She nodded. "I can."

He waited a moment for her to relax before asking, "Can you tell me why it feels so important to you?"

"I can't," she said in a half whisper. "I know it's irrational, and I know it's probably just a piece of random jewelry, but . . . the minute I touched it I was scared of what would happen if I let it go." She looked up at him. "Can Novotny analyze that? That could be part of the spell that's on it, to make me want to keep it."

Relieved that she was thinking at least a little logically, he nodded. "Come on, beloved . . . let's get to Hunter, then." He found he wanted to wrap his arms around his Queen to reassure her. The edge of panic he could feel from her worried him intensely, and he wanted only to make it better. If that meant keeping the damn box, so be it. The sooner they got it to Novotny—and away from the Queen—the better.

* * *

Deep in the night, Austin was quiet, for a city, its constant rattle and hum almost like the sound of the ocean.

Oh, how she missed the ocean . . . the peace and solitude of the Cloister, nestled in the coastal forests where once, the legend insisted, Elves had lived. And now a myth occupied the land once occupied by a myth, and who was to say what was real anymore? Lydia certainly didn't know.

She had been to Austin once, three years ago, to see for herself if the prophecy had proven true and the Prime she had sired was, indeed, the one they were waiting for. The minute she laid eyes on Miranda, and later David, she had known it was all true. She could feel it. And so she left Austin to set the next part of the plan in motion, to find someone who could do what must be done.

She walked the long road through Austin alone, her steps feeling hollow even on the concrete. How long had she been walking to this very destination, with single-minded focus on one goal: to deliver the Stone of Awakening to its chosen vessel and then . . . nothing? Her task fulfilled, her mission completed, she could now go home to the Cloister and find peace . . . but only if she stopped now, Misted away, and was not seen in Austin again.

"Did you do it?"

Lydia stopped walking and sighed without turning toward the voice. "I did, my Lord."

The man who came to face her was all too familiar, for he, too, had had a part to play in all of this. She had spent centuries carefully moving the pieces into place. The cause she worked for was not one the Signets shared, power-hungry as they were. The first she had found had agreed to help, only to be killed and replaced with one far less sympathetic to the Order. She had tried to win Hart to her side, thinking that his hatred of the South would make him want to help her, but he was smarter than she had realized. Just when she began to fear her plan would fall apart, she found someone who could do it.

That bastard Hart had nearly destroyed everything, but now, in Jeremy, there was hope.

Jeremy Hayes faced her with his arms crossed. "Good. Then I can do what I must, and all will not be lost."

"Let us hope not."

He had old, old eyes, aged by sorrow and agony. She knew the weight of what he had lost and the weight of what he was still forced to carry. "Did you bring it?" he asked.

Lydia nodded and held out what he wanted: a scroll, yellowed and crumbling from age, but still legible under the right light. "Here you will find everything you need, save a single item."

"Which is?"

Sorrow rose in her throat, threatening her voice. "A hammer," she replied. "You will need a hammer."

Jeremy looked at the scroll in his hand with something like fear. She would have feared it, too, if she were him; it was death, written out in ancient script, and his instinct would be to destroy it. It wasn't even a danger to her, and she wanted to stomp it into dust.

"Remember your promise," he said. "Once this is done—"

"I swear on my life I will fulfill my end of the bargain."

He nodded and melted back into the shadows.

A tear made its way from her eye as she continued her walk . . . a long walk, going nowhere. Her time was nearly come. She had played her part. She had pledged her life to the Goddess, and now the Goddess would collect; and though Lydia should have felt satisfied that things were at last falling into place, instead she simply felt weary, and sad.

The voice came just when she expected it to. "Miss Lydia?"

This time she stopped and turned toward the Elite who were standing there, waiting to escort her to her last meeting on this journey. "Yes."

"Come with us, please."

They surrounded her, and even had she not been willing,

it would have been easy for them to overpower her and drag her bodily into the huge, luxurious hotel across the street. She was strong, but they were many. They passed through the lobby unnoticed at this late hour; even the concierge kept his eyes on his ledgers as they walked by.

She was escorted into a beautiful, elegant suite of rooms, where her . . . host . . . was waiting, seated at the end of a table.

"Lydia," he said.

"Lord Prime."

He was such a young-looking vampire, born from the frail body of a boy who would in all likelihood have been murdered at the hands of the Inquisition if he hadn't vanished into the darkness of a Dublin night and emerged reborn . . . a healer turned into a killer. Did he feel the dissonance between one calling and the other?

He regarded her through those lavender-blue eyes— eyes whose rare color she knew the origins of, even if he didn't, and whose age betrayed the apparent youth of his body—as he toyed with a wooden throwing stake with an expertly crafted steel hilt. "I'm glad we found you before you had a chance to do what the Order called you here to do."

She chose her words carefully. "And what is it you think the Order called me to do, my Lord?"

"I don't know," he replied, just as carefully. "But I would advise you to tell me, Lydia, and persuade me not to do what *I've* been asked to do."

She sat down opposite him. "Someone has hired the Red Shadow to kill me?"

"I did receive an offer on your life." He turned the stake over and over in his hand. "But before I take it, I want to know why anyone would want you dead."

"I imagine there are a great many people who would like to kill me," she mused. "Anyone who wants to see the Order fail in our quest. Anyone who wants the current Signet system to remain unchallenged. That would include most of the Council."

"Tell me, Lydia . . . you are, essentially, the agent of the Order, yes? You do whatever dirty work is necessary to ensure that the future unfolds as they see fit?"

"It is not as *they* see fit," she insisted. "It has been foreordained that the Awakening will come and with it the war. I am burdened with the work of making sure that happens, by any means necessary. Certain events must take place. They cannot be stopped. Ask your Consort—ask him what happens when we try to circumvent fate. I am only an instrument of the Order, Lord Alpha. We have been trying to Awaken Her for centuries . . . and only now has there come a power that could do it."

"And in order to bring this about, you'll hurt or kill or destroy anyone you have to."

"You of all people must understand that."

The Alpha nodded, smiling a little. "You're right. I do."

There was something almost like sympathy in his face just then, if indeed he was capable of such a thing. They were kindred spirits in a way—each manipulating the entwined strands of probability to ensure an outcome . . . yet, though he would not admit it, his motivations were far kinder, born out of love. It was that love that would prove his undoing, ultimately. Unless, of course, he was the one who succeeded in saving them all.

He took a sip from the glass of blood on the table. "For most of my life I've wondered, do we truly have free will, or is it all an illusion? Having a Consort who sees snatches of the future complicates things even further. How much of what he sees is incontrovertible, and how much can be changed? I've done my best to make sure that God or no God, fate or no fate, those I care for will be taken care of and that anyone who tries to hurt them will pay a terrible price."

"I never wanted to hurt anyone," she insisted softly. "I'm trying to help all of us. If events do not unfold as they are meant to . . ."

"Lydia," he interrupted, just as softly, "There's something I think you've forgotten in all your grand plans and epic destiny-making . . . something you didn't see on the chessboard even as you lined your pawns up one by one."

She felt tears in her eyes again, and the quiet knowledge she had been waiting for. "And what is that?" she asked.

The Alpha held the stake flat on the palm of his hand. As she watched, it rose into the air and began to spin like the needle on a compass.

"You aren't the only player in this game," he said.

The stake whistled across the room, and Lydia gave a strangled cry of pain as it struck her in the chest.

Thirteen

Miranda stood with her arms crossed, watching the talisman rotate inside the imaging machine very similar to the one David had built at the Haven—but much, much larger and more powerful, capable of detecting submicroscopic traces of evidence. A matrix of lasers and other types of scanners passed back and forth over the talisman's surface, bringing screens and screens of data up on the monitor that were already being analyzed and logged by the database.

She was still holding the box the talisman had come in. Novotny planned to scan it, too, but could do only one thing at a time, so she had managed to keep her hands on it for a little while.

"Nice blanket, Linus." Faith came to stand next to her. "I hear you've lost your mind."

The Queen looked down at the box in her hands. "Honestly, Faith, I have no idea what came over either of us. The minute I saw this thing I couldn't take my eyes off of it. Weirder still, David didn't want to touch it. He didn't pick it up, didn't examine it, didn't express any sort of curiosity about it."

Faith looked surprised at that. "A possible relic from Signet history shows up, and he doesn't want anything to do with it?"

"My point exactly. You know how he is—he has to press every button and take things apart like a little kid.

Even now he's not acting interested. He's over there on the phone with APD about that dead guy. The only reason he even came here was to humor me."

"That is odd." Faith scrutinized the talisman inside the scanner. "What do you think it does?"

"I don't know. Lydia didn't seem to know either—she was just the messenger. But even if it's got some kind of curse on it, I think it's important to find out more. David was right not to want to bring it into the Haven, but I'm right, too. I know it."

"So you couldn't get anything off Lydia with your empathy? I thought there weren't a lot of people who could shield against it."

"There aren't . . . but if she is who she says she is, it makes sense she'd have more than the average training."

"Well, now, let's have a look," Dr. Novotny said, joining them in front of the machine. "It is a pretty little thing, isn't it? The carving's definitely a variant on ancient Greek—in fact it might even be an antecedent, given the shape of the vowels, as you can see."

Miranda smiled. "If you say so."

"Can you read it?" Faith asked.

"Hmm . . . apparently not. Lord Prime, would you mind having a look at this?"

David ended his call with a sigh and came over to where they were standing. "At what?"

"You read ancient Greek, correct? What do you make of this dialect?"

David frowned at the screen, eyes narrowing, and was silent for the better part of a minute. "That's . . ."

"All Greek to you?" Faith quipped, earning an eye roll from the Prime and a groan from the Queen.

David shook his head. "The interesting thing is that it's *not* all Greek. It's more like what would happen if you took ancient Greek, Latin, and at least one form of Gaelic and made evil mutant babies from them . . . but there's a fourth element to it, too, that I don't recognize at all."

"You can't read it?" Miranda was baffled. She'd seen

him effortlessly plow through handwritten Russian and Deven's half-drunk Irish.

"I can pick out a few phrases. Can I get a printout of the carvings?" he asked. "I might be able to translate it all, but I'll have better luck if I take it home and run it through a few searches to see if I can identify that fourth language."

Novotny nodded and hit a red button on the machine; across the room, a printer buzzed to life.

Finally, David was starting to get interested in the thing. "What else can you tell us?"

"From the initial readings, it's definitely silver and very old—in fact . . ." Novotny entered something on his tablet computer, bringing up a window full of numbers, and said, "Based on those scans you had me do of your Signets back when you first became Prime, I'd say the three are nearly identical in age."

"So you're saying Lydia was telling the truth," Miranda said, giving David a pointed look.

Novotny gave an indefinite shrug. "About the item's age, certainly. Its origins, however, will take a good deal more research to uncover. Just from the surface impressions the workmanship is also quite similar—but it could easily be a forgery from the same time period. We'll have to match the metals; I'll take a sample."

He touched the tablet's screen and something inside the imager whirred; Miranda saw a thin metal arm extend toward the talisman and scrape very lightly over its surface, then retract.

"Is it giving off any kind of energy?" David asked.

"Not so much as a quiver, Sire. It might as well be a paperweight."

"You're kidding," Miranda said. "There has to be something coming from it—some kind of magnetic field or something."

"I'm afraid not, my Lady. If you'll recall, the amulets used by Marja Ovaska to shield her movements from the network emitted a low-level electromagnetic field even once they had been used up. The only thing coming from this is the same kind and level of electricity you'd expect from a metal object, metal being a conductor and all. But unless there's some sort of energy we aren't equipped to scan for, there's nothing."

"Sometimes a cuff link is just a cuff link," Faith muttered.

But the Prime was staring at the printouts he'd fetched, looking unconvinced. "No . . . not this time. If I'm interpreting this the right way, the carvings are phrased in the imperative; it's a set of instructions."

"Like an incantation?" Miranda looked over his shoulder at the pages, but aside from being able to tell it was a diagram of the talisman, she couldn't make heads or tails of it.

"Maybe. Regardless, we need to keep that thing under lock and key until I decipher this." He looked at Miranda. "The box, too."

She started to protest, but rationality intruded just in time; they needed to analyze the box as much as the talisman. A lot more people had probably touched the box itself over the years; there could be all sorts of evidence in the crevices and grain of the wood. It would take several days to get a full battery of tests run, and it would certainly be safe here at Hunter Development.

She held the box out to David without looking at it. When he took it from her hands, she got a violent chill.

"Good Christ," David said, handing off the box to Novotny and putting his arms around Miranda. "Whatever that thing was doing to you . . . I'm glad to get rid of it. I don't like this at all."

Miranda buried her face in his shoulder for a moment, drawing on his strength and calm until she felt settled again and her insides stopped shaking. "Did you feel anything when you touched it?" she asked.

"No. Apparently it likes you better."

She looked over at the imager, at the seemingly innocuous piece of decorative jewelry that could be . . . anything. Was it her imagination, or did it feel like something inside it was . . . not sleeping, exactly, but . . . waiting for something?

"Can we leave now?" she asked quietly.

David squeezed her around the middle and let her go. "Yes. You go on down to the car; I want a word with the doctor, but the sooner you're out of here the better. Faith, accompany the Queen downstairs before you go back on patrol, please."

"As you will it, Sire."

It wasn't until she was safely in the car, a dozen stories away from the lab and the talisman, that Miranda felt she could breathe again.

Faith got in next to her for a moment. "Are you all right?"

"I don't know. Why is that thing affecting me and not David? And what exactly is it doing? What does it want?"

The Second scoffed, "Want? It's a hunk of metal, my Lady. It's not alive."

Miranda shook her head and tapped her Signet. "Neither is this, but it has a will. It knows who's meant to wear it. Ask any of us—they may not be alive, but they want things."

"And you think this thing wants you for something?"

"We need to find Lydia. She's the only one who can give us any answers. Divert as many units as you can to the search."

"Already done, my Lady. We've been combing the city since she disappeared outside Anodyne, but so far there's nothing." Faith checked her phone. "If there's nothing else, I need to get back on shift—the second I have any news, I'll let you know."

"Sure. Go on . . . I'm fine. Really."

Faith didn't look convinced, but she got out of the car, just as David arrived to get in. They had a brief conversation outside before David slid onto the seat beside Miranda.

He looked at her speculatively. "You know," he said, "I think before we go home there's somewhere we should stop."

"Oh? Where?"

He smiled and spoke to Harlan: "Take us to Amy's on Sixth, please."

Faith wasn't surprised to get the call; to be honest she would have been more surprised not to.

She stood in the elevator with her arms crossed, watching the floor numbers tick upward. A knot of guilt—small but still significant—had already formed in her stomach the second she left the Pair . . . but she wasn't really doing anything wrong. She was entitled to a hunting break every shift, which she rarely took. Everyone else took breaks, and who knew what they did on them?

Why was it that she spent so much time lately justifying her own behavior to herself?

The elevator dinged and the doors slid open, revealing a hallway with three sets of double doors; she didn't have to wonder which one she wanted, as it was the only one with two uniformed guards standing at attention outside.

She nodded to them, and they returned the gesture. They had been expecting her, but aside from that, she knew them both from the tournament. They were top-tier lieutenants who had both faced her team in the finals.

"Glad to see the femur's healed," Faith said to one of them, who spared her a smile before opening the doors for her.

Faith sighed resignedly and walked into the suite to face the two vampires waiting for her there.

"You summoned me, my Lords?" she asked.

Jonathan, who had a book open in his lap, smiled. "I'm sorry about the timing, Faith. I didn't think you'd be busy this time of night. Can I get you a drink?"

She shook her head. "I wasn't busy exactly, but I am on duty. It'd be best if I wasn't out of contact long."

Deven was sitting at the table changing out the wood shafts on several throwing stakes. "We'll keep this brief."

"What can I do for you?"

The Prime picked up one of the stakes and looked down its length, checking the angle. "You don't seem surprised that we're still here."

Faith smiled mirthlessly. "That's because I know you, Sire. And, if I may speak freely . . ."

"You may."

"The thought that you could stay out of all of this is, frankly, laughable. In fact, the only thing that would surprise me is if you didn't have something to do with Lydia being here in the first place."

He put the stake down and lifted his eyes to her. "As a matter of fact, I didn't. I was fairly sure she was working with Hart, but at the very least she attempted to collude with him."

"Wait—she was working with Hart? How? Why?"

The Pair exchanged a look, and Faith could tell there was a certain degree of tension, and disagreement, between them . . . not exactly a novel situation where they were concerned. "We're not sure," Jonathan said. "We found several notations in Monroe's files indicating Lydia met with Hart at least twice, but we don't know what for. I was of the opinion that we could learn a lot more from her, but someone apparently disagreed."

Faith didn't even try to hide her dismay. "You killed her?"

Deven shrugged. "She was a threat. She has resources, and if she was in collusion with Hart, she was a liability. And trust me, I've dealt with enough zealots to know she wasn't going to tell us anything useful. We're just lucky we found her before she completed her mission."

"I don't know about that," Faith said. "She gave Miranda some kind of metal talisman thing tonight before she disappeared."

"That much we knew already. I'm assuming David took the thing to one of his labs as soon as he could."

"Yes. Do you know what it is? Lydia said it was a power amplifier."

Another look passed between them before Deven said, "What you need to know, Faith, is that Lydia was a member of a powerful, and very old, vampire cult. They are true believers, and they believe a war is coming."

"A war between whom?"

"Good and evil, perhaps. Vampires and humans. Some vampires and other vampires. It doesn't really matter—the important thing is that they believe this war has to happen . . . and they are willing to *make* it happen."

Jonathan said, "Deven thinks Lydia wanted to win Hart to the Order's side, possibly with the goal of inciting war between Hart and David. I'm not so sure—at least, I don't think the entire Order is involved, just a fringe group that got tired of waiting for their apocalypse and decided to speed up the timeline. Up until Lydia arrived, we weren't aware they had any intention of acting; as far as we knew, the Order was not an immediate threat to anyone, just a bunch of monastics off chanting in the forest."

"What does that have to do with the talisman?"

Deven leaned back in his chair, crossing his arms. "Have you ever heard of the Goddess Persephone?"

Faith blinked. "Of course I have. It's Greek mythology. She was kidnapped by Hades and became Queen of the Underworld—most versions of the myth say against her will."

Deven nodded. "Well, according to the Order, not only was she willing, she sought Hades out. She was no sweet young princess, but a huntress, and a bloodthirsty one at that. She also had a twin sister, Theia, who was a sparkles-and-bunnies healer sort of Goddess, and the two were constantly at odds. So one day all the gods were hanging out at a bar or something, and they started discussing how those pesky humans were spreading like a virus and fucking up the planet. The two sisters decided to have a competition to see who could do something about it. Theia created a race of beings to help teach humans how to be nice to each other. Persephone created vampires to eat humans."

Faith frowned. She had absolutely no idea where this was going. "Okay."

"Well, time wore on, and humans forgot the old gods.

The Order believes that Persephone is asleep, basically, but they have a thousand-year-old prophecy that says she's going to wake up . . . or, rather, that they're going to wake her up."

"And this talisman has something to do with that?"

Deven nodded. "It's known as the Stone of Awakening—a misnomer, really, since it doesn't have a stone until it's connected to a Signet. My sources have discovered that the theory is it functions as a key. The priests of the Order have to channel enough power through it to break the lock and release their Goddess. They need a lot of power . . . Signet-level power."

"So what happens to whoever's wearing it?"

"They die," Deven said, leaning forward. "The Stone sucks all the power out of them—and, therefore, logic follows, whomever they happen to be bound to, say, a Queen. They've been waiting all these years for someone strong enough; their seers read the entrails or whatever it is they do and decided David was their chosen one. Lydia was sent to bring him across, setting the entire story in motion, and now that he has a Queen, they're ready to push over their first domino."

Faith shook her head slowly in disbelief. "The whole reason she made him a vampire was so she could have him killed."

"Yes."

"Do you believe in any of this?" she asked.

"That they can wake a Goddess from her cosmic nap? No. But whatever it really does, the Stone is definitely *not* an amplifier. It's dangerous, and whatever spell is really on it, they're going to activate it soon. Based on the intelligence we've gathered, my money's on the next new moon, which is this Sunday . . . and that is why we need you."

"To do what, exactly?"

The Prime fixed her with a hard stare. "I want you to steal it."

Faith couldn't stop herself; she snorted. "Are you serious?" She looked at Jonathan. "Is he serious?"

The Consort grinned tiredly. "I'm afraid he is."

"You want me to steal a Signet artifact from my own Prime."

"I want you to save his life," Deven said. "Miranda's, too."

"Why can't you just call him and tell him the thing is bad mojo? Why steal it at all?"

"Tell me, Faith . . . based on what you know about your Prime . . . if he knew what the Stone really was and what it does, do you think he would destroy it?"

"No. He'd keep it and study it, just like he's doing now. In fact he'd want to see what it does on the new moon."

"Exactly. We need to get that thing away from the Pair—if either of them are even in the same room with it when it goes off, it could kill them both. In fact, even the sources I have aren't sure what its range is or how it knows whom to drain; if it's anywhere near any Signet bearer, he or she is in jeopardy. That's why I'm not going to touch the damn thing, and neither are they."

Jonathan saw her expression and added quickly, "Faith, it doesn't have to disappear forever. Our information is sketchy, but one thing is clear: It can be activated only once. If it's not able to do its job, it becomes a chunk of useless metal. All we need you to do is get the thing and hide it for a few days, just to make sure David and Miranda are safe from it. It can be misplaced and then found again. But we need someone with security clearance to get into whatever lab it's being kept in, and you're the only one who has that. You can get in and out without anyone asking questions."

"No," Faith said.

They both looked at her.

"I'm not going to participate in one of your cloak-and-dagger intrigues," Faith told Deven. "I'm not one of your agents, and I don't work for you. If you want to get the Stone away from David, you call him and tell him the truth—keeping it from him is going to backfire, I promise you, and someone could get hurt. I won't be part of that."

Jonathan was holding back a smile. "See?" he told Deven, no little satisfaction in his voice.

Deven ignored his Consort and laced his fingers together, regarding Faith for a long moment without speaking.

Finally, he said quietly, "Faith . . . this is not a request. Either you'll help us avert this, or you'll sign the death warrant of the man you love. Not only that, but the entire balance of power in the South will fall, and thousands of people, human and otherwise, will die."

She felt ice in her veins at his words but stood firm. "If you want to keep them from getting hurt, you'll pick up the phone right now and tell David what you know. He's not a fool or a child—why do you keep treating him like one?"

"To be fair," Jonathan said wryly, "he treats everyone that way."

"And how dare you try to play on my emotions just to get your own way?" Faith went on. "This has got to stop, Deven. Either you trust your friends to make their own decisions, or you don't, which means you're no friend to any of us."

She knew it was dangerous to bait him; she had seen more powerful vampires than her fall to the ground bleeding for saying less. But her anger was too strong to stuff back down—that he would try that emotional blackmail bullshit on her and expect her to commit an act of treason just so he wouldn't have to be open with someone—the temerity of it was astounding. She had known him even longer than David had; she'd stood by and watched Deven manipulate everyone around him with a master's touch for years, even since before he was Prime . . . and even though she genuinely believed in his motivations, she knew that one day he would cross the line, do something that couldn't be forgiven, and where would that leave him? Where would that leave any of the people who had unwittingly danced to his tune?

Still, his face was expressionless as he said, "What if I said I would kill you if you don't do it?"

Now she rolled her eyes. She held out her arms to her sides. "Then do it," she said. "Go ahead. In fact, it would be the most logical thing for you to do, because as soon as I leave here, I'm going to tell my Pair everything you just told me, including the fact that you threatened their Second. And if you kill me, when David figures it out—and you know he will—he'll unleash hell on you like you've never seen . . . and Lydia will have her war. So what will it be, my Lord?"

Deven lifted one of the stakes, his eyes meandering from it to Faith and back, before he said, "Very well, Faith. You've made your allegiance quite clear."

"My allegiance is exactly where it should be. With my Prime and Queen. Whatever my emotional connection to him, whatever conflict I might feel . . . I am loyal to my friends. And that's more than you've ever been."

She bowed to him, then to Jonathan. "Now, if you'll excuse me, I have to get back to my shift. Unless you're going to kill me?"

Deven made a gesture of dismissal.

"Right. Good night, my Lords."

She stalked out of the suite to the elevator, hoping it would be waiting for her, but damn it, it was down several floors and she had to wait.

A moment later there were footsteps. She sighed. "I'm not going to—"

"Faith," Jonathan said softly, urgently, taking her arm. "Please listen."

He'd never been physically forward with her before; Jonathan tended to give women a wide berth and was very careful not to presume familiarity. But now he touched her, drew her to the side.

"Believe whatever you want about all of this," Jonathan said, "But please believe me when I say that Deven is right. I've seen . . . I know that the Stone is going to cause horrible suffering to whoever is wearing it when it activates. I don't know if any of the Order's doctrine is true, but I know someone is going to die. I don't know if it can be stopped, but if it can, this may be our only chance. Please, Faith . . . if you don't want to steal the Stone, just do the best you can to make sure David and Miranda aren't in the building with it on the new moon. That wouldn't be hard, and it wouldn't have to involve lying. Just . . . think about it, all right? This is me asking, not Deven making demands. Please . . . just think about it."

The elevator dinged, and he nudged her gently toward it, stepping back away from her. Faith got in reluctantly, her mind swimming with questions she knew he wouldn't answer . . . and when the doors slid shut, she felt unaccountably like she was standing inside a tomb.

They didn't speak for a while. Jonathan leaned back against the locked suite door, eyes closed, his stomach a bottomless pit of shame.

When he opened his eyes again, Deven had risen from the table and was coming over to him. The Prime laid his hands on Jonathan's shoulders, and their eyes met.

"She'll do it," Jonathan said softly. "I don't know what she'll tell them, but she'll do whatever she can to keep them away from the Stone."

"What did you say to her?"

"I told her the truth," Jonathan snapped. "I know that's a foreign concept to you. The choice is up to her—but I know which one she'll make. Does that make you happy? Everything's going your way again."

For a wonder, there was actual hurt in Deven's eyes. "That's all anyone thinks of me," he said. "Even my own Consort thinks I'm doing all this for selfish gain." He turned away, toward the window. "Is it so wrong to want to spare those I love certain pain? To have seen them suffer, over and over, and want to stop it from happening again?"

"Life is pain," Jonathan said. "At least, part of it is. By denying them the right to determine their own destinies, you deny them the right to truly live."

"Oh? That's a bit rich coming from someone who sees

the future and who wanted to stay here in the first place. If you saw someone about to step in front of a train, could you honestly say you wouldn't call out?"

"That's the thing, Deven. We don't *know*. We have the word of several spies within the Order who aren't high up enough on the food chain to know all the Mysteries. We have rumors and hearsay that's been tainted by thousands of years of history and hatred. We don't even know the whole creation myth, much less its fallout—and that's assuming it's more than just a bedtime story. If we told David about all of this, we could all work together to find the truth, but you have to keep going it alone, behind everyone's backs, the all-knowing, all-seeing Alpha. But you're not all-knowing."

Deven didn't face him, but Jonathan knew he was listening. Jonathan walked up behind him and put his arms around the Prime, tempering his harsh words with the gesture. He rested his chin on the top of Deven's head as he had a thousand times before.

"I love you," Jonathan said. "I know I must be a moron for it, and I probably qualify for sainthood, but . . . I do. And here I stand, watching you try so desperately to change things and keep people you love from getting hurt, but Deven . . . they'll get hurt anyway. You've succeeded at more plans and missions than I can imagine, but when it comes to all of us . . . your heart will never let you win."

Deven leaned back into Jonathan's shoulder, and when he spoke, it was barely above a whisper. "I'm so tired, Jonathan . . . sometimes I wish it could all just be over with. In a way I'm just like you . . . I wish to God I didn't know the things I know . . . and sometimes I regret even meeting David, let alone all that came after. It was so much easier when I didn't care about anyone."

"I don't think that would ever be possible for you," he replied. "Fight it all you want, but I know what you really are, my love . . . and it's not a monster."

"I had to kill Lydia," Deven said, though even his tone disagreed with the words. "If my theory that she was Hart's ally is true, we have to assume Hart still has people here in town waiting to tear into the Elite the minute that Stone awakens and the South is defenseless. She was going to help them somehow. We had to stop her. And even after that, her involvement with the Order means she wouldn't give up—she would throw in her lot with Hart again and again to get the war she wanted."

Jonathan nodded. "I agree with you as far as that goes. I know she was in town for more than just delivering the Stone. There was something else . . . something else she was supposed to give someone . . . but that's all I know. We didn't find anything on her body, and no indication of where she might have been staying, so whatever she was delivering must have been information."

"Well, she won't have a chance to deliver it now," Deven said with a sigh, turning his face into Jonathan's chest. "That much at least I did right."

Hot fudge, thick and dark as a dreamless sleep, dripped down from the spoon, onto a puddle of equally warm caramel sauce coating pecan halves, melting the vanilla ice cream underneath to an alchemical perfection that not even blood could outmatch.

Miranda let her eyes flutter closed and took another bite, allowing the flavors to mingle on her tongue with a moan of pleasure. "You really are a genius," she said to her husband around mouthfuls.

The Prime chuckled and lifted up his napkin to wipe a stray spot of caramel from Miranda's nose.

The ice cream shop was otherwise empty, but outside the streets bustled with the usual amount of human traffic for a warm night in early summer. Sixth Street was the heart of downtown Austin, and from where they were she could see the mammoth Whole Foods flagship store, the city's favorite independent bookstore, and a natural eco-friendly beauty products boutique. Here, in fact at this very table, she and David had had their first . . . well, "date" wasn't exactly the right word, but it was the closest thing she could come up with.

This time they leaned closer together, hands entwined, instead of trying to ignore the tension between them. This time there were Elite keeping the humans at a distance, as well as Miranda's empathy gently steering the mortals away from the store just until she and David were gone. It had been a risk coming here, but David was right; they needed to unplug for a minute. David had offered the employees each a substantial bribe to close the store for half an hour.

The last time she'd sat in this chair she'd been human.

Everything was so different now.

Well, not everything. David still got sprinkles on his sundae.

They smiled at each other. He kissed her nose. "Do you want a soda?" he asked. "I'm going to get one."

"Sure."

She watched him saunter up to the counter and speak to the . . . what was the word for an ice cream–scooper person, anyway? Coffee shops had baristas; bars had bartenders. Miranda absently reached into her shirt and fiddled with her Signet, letting her fingers trace over the stone, the metal. As David turned around, she dropped the Signet and returned to her ice cream.

David sat back down, two frosty cans and two plastic cups of ice—plus one straw—in his hands. She took the Coke he offered, knowing he preferred Dr Pepper, and took the straw. She loved how the bubbles in the soda perked up all over her tongue; had they felt like that when she was human? She couldn't remember.

She glanced over at the counter again, where one of the scoopers was wiping down the slab of stone where they pounded ingredients into the ice cream. He was mortal . . . she could practically see him aging, from where she sat. Was it ever going to feel normal, knowing she would never grow old? Somewhere in Dallas her father was recovering from a mild heart attack; the perfunctory e-mail from her sister, Marianne, had come about six months ago, and Miranda had sent perfunctory flowers. How long until he died . . . and then Marianne . . . and then her children . . . and their children . . . ?

She had to shake her head to clear away the thoughts; they never went anywhere, because she had nowhere to take them. Faith was right; she couldn't make sense of immortality yet. She had to take one day, one week, one year at a time, and deal with what was in front of her.

What was in front of her was even less comforting than eternity.

"I know a lot has happened in the last week," David said, "but honestly, we're in control of everything now. Please don't look so worried."

"Let's make a list," Miranda said, holding up her fingers. "One: We have a magic box and toy delivered by your sire whose origins and purpose are basically unknown. Two: Hart is conspiring against us, and we're having trouble figuring out who the hell his Second really is—it's like the guy's a ghost. Three: We had an Alpha Seven last night out of nowhere. Four: We don't know who killed Monroe. Five: I'm supposed to be laid up in bed for an undetermined amount of time, which means every time I want to come into town we have to do *this*." She gestured at the guards outside and the employees casting covert glances at their guests . . . who would wipe their memories clean before leaving.

David nodded. "All true. But the Alpha Seven was a random act, probably a vampire who came to town for the music festival to try to get away with killing. Big events like ALMF do three things: snarl traffic, help the economy, and bring out the crazies. Meanwhile, the lab will have full results on the talisman and box by tomorrow night at the latest. I'm running a search comparing the components in the liquid explosive used to kill Monroe so we can narrow down possible manufacturers—bomb makers tend to have signatures, and if I can link any of those ingredients with an R&D company working on transmitters like the two we've uncovered so far, we'll have a lead. If we're really lucky, the same people will be able to shed light on both Monroe's death and whoever's been killing Hart's Elite."

Miranda nodded. "What have we found out about Jeremy?"

"Not much. Deven's people are on that, and also on Lydia and the Order, but it'll take a couple of days to get anything back."

"I thought Deven was in the Order."

"He was a member of their warrior class, the Swords of Elysium—the group he worked with was secular and not directly involved with the priesthood that Lydia belongs to. He knows their basic philosophy and structure but never got any deeper in than it took to learn their fighting style and make connections with their weaponsmiths."

She stabbed at a pecan with her spoon. "I suppose it was asking too much for the Council to come and go without causing half our lives to unravel."

When she looked up, he was smiling at her, and his face held no worry, no stress, only love. She found herself blushing. "What?"

His smile broadened. "I was just thinking about the last time you and I sat here. You were lecturing me about not wanting to live in fear, and I was hoping to God I could get through the night without kissing you breathless."

She smiled back. "You didn't make it," she said, taking his hand. "Thank goodness."

"I wonder how much easier things would have been if I'd been able to admit from that first moment that I realized I loved you?"

"What moment was that?"

"I believe it was the first night I heard you playing your guitar in the Haven . . . sitting on your bed, in your pajamas, your hair falling all around you . . . I was, in that moment, undone."

Miranda held his fingers to her lips. "Do you remember what I was playing?"

" 'Rain,' " he replied, without having to think about it.

"Patty Griffin." He took a bite of his sundae with his free hand, then asked a bit mischievously, "When did you first realize you loved me?"

"I'm not sure," she said truthfully. "I was so messed up back then . . . I think on some level I knew almost from the moment we met, but I couldn't really acknowledge those feelings until much later, when I was ready to face them. I think . . . it didn't really come together, and I didn't really understand, until you were on my couch quoting Shakespeare at me."

He held her eyes. " *'Silence is the perfectest herald of joy . . .'* "

She smiled and finished the line. " *'I were but little happy, if I could say how much.'* "

David's smile faded a little. "Are you happy with me, beloved? If you had it to do again, would you, knowing what would happen?"

"Knowing my friends would die or leave . . . knowing you'd go to bed with your ex three months after marrying me . . . knowing I'd end up killing people . . . knowing I'd get shot . . . knowing I'd be at the center of events I don't even understand?"

He looked down at the table. "Knowing all of that."

She laughed and took both of his hands, catching his eyes with hers. "I would, absolutely, without a doubt, do it all again . . . because as hard as it's been, as much pain as I've been through and as much uncertainty as there is . . . I am happy. Don't ever doubt that, David. This life with all its weirdness and all its burdens is where I belong. I may have my doubts about my own strength sometimes, but I chose to be here . . . and I have yet to regret that choice."

"I hope you never do," he said softly.

"Let's go home," Miranda said. "I want this date to end the way our first one did."

He leaned forward and kissed her; they could each taste the other's ice cream. Miranda found herself cursing the number of miles between downtown Austin and the

Haven . . . but a little anticipation, she had learned, made the having that much sweeter.

"Let's take these to go," she said, pointing at her sundae. "I have plans for them later."

David's eyes lit up, and he all but flew to the counter to settle the bill.

Fourteen

Faith knew that Wednesday night would be the ideal time to steal the Stone, if she so chose; it was her night off, the lab would be finishing up the data, and it would be easy for the item itself to vanish in between Hunter Development and the Haven. A witless courier, an improperly filled out chain-of-custody form, and the Stone could slip between the cracks and be found a couple of weeks later, no harm, no foul.

If she so chose.

But Faith hadn't lived as long as she had by letting her emotions get the better of her. Even if what Deven and Jonathan said was true, even if the Stone would be deadly, David and Miranda had a right to know. What if they wanted to bring it into the Haven? Faith's information could save their lives and would do so without forcing her to betray their trust in her. No; she absolutely could not steal the Stone.

And so, as soon as the sun had set, she headed for the Signet suite, determination in her steps, spine straight. She would tell them that Deven and Jonathan were still in Austin, and that Deven was trying to play them all—again!— and that she had refused to take part. Then David and Miranda could decide for themselves what to do with the information. It was her job, as Second, to report this kind of thing.

That didn't mean she didn't have doubts. So rarely had Jonathan ever looked at her like that, and he'd never, ever pleaded with her, with so much seriousness in his eyes. Deven's threats, she could deal with, but Jonathan . . . he wasn't duplicitous. She wasn't sure he knew how to be.

It was a little early to be knocking on the door, but Faith didn't want to wait. They needed to send the Stone away, preferably out of Austin entirely, until they were sure these Elysium crazies couldn't open their magic voodoo lock and kill the Pair. Faith didn't believe in goddesses any more than she did in God-with-a-capital-G, but she did believe in magic, and she believed in precaution over all.

Faith nodded to the door guards and rapped lightly on the door; no answer. She was about to try again when she noticed the door was slightly ajar already. Good; she'd been admitted.

She poked her head into the room, about to speak . . .

. . . and froze.

The firelight flickered golden and warm, bathing the room in its glow, perfectly illuminating the bed, whose curtains were drawn back partway . . . enough to see through them, to the rumpled sheets and comforter within.

Faith watched, transfixed, unable to tear her eyes from the bare skin, marked with lines of black ink, almost translucent in the firelight . . . his long capable fingers tangled in strands of red, the curve of her belly and breasts rising and falling against the hard plane of his chest, her hands on his shoulders, back arching . . . the flash of his teeth in her neck, letting a few precious drops of blood trickle down over her skin, his tongue lapping them up with a soft growling noise.

Their eyes were closed, but they were both smiling, such peace between them, such perfect and fulfilled desire . . . the waves of pleasure they were giving off were hard to resist and hit Faith like bricks, first in her belly, then hard in her chest.

She stumbled backward out of the door, catching herself so she didn't slam it; she left it just as it was and, ignoring the inquisitive eyebrows of the guards, turned and walked away as fast as she could without running.

She reached the garage, where her car was waiting; she'd already intended to go into town for a drink later. There was no one else out, and she sagged back against the side of the car for a moment, shaking.

Fool, fool, stupid weak girl, get yourself together . . .

No one had ever touched her like that, with such complete devotion. She'd had plenty of lovers, but had she ever been *loved*—the way Miranda was loved? Did Miranda have any idea how lucky she was?

Damn it, Faith!

She couldn't go back in there right now, that was certain. Talking to them would have to wait . . . she was going to need some vodka before she could even think about looking either of them in the face.

That was all right. They could be at it half the night anyway, and a few hours weren't going to make that much difference. She'd go to one of the bars the off-duty Elite favored, relax a little, and when she got back she'd meet with them. Maybe she could even find some nice vampire lad to work out her frustrations on.

It had worked with Jeremy . . . for a little while.

She threw herself behind the wheel and backed out of the garage, eager to put as many miles between herself and the Haven as she could for a few hours.

"Oh my God, that was so fucking lame," Lark groaned. "Please don't ever make me do that again."

Stella grabbed Lark's arm and steered her away from the building. "Come on, let's just get out of here."

Lark, who was a little on the tipsy side—the side of tipsy that was more like wasted—loomed over Stella and said in her worst Dracula impression, "I am a creature of the niiiiiight, and I will make you my eternal briiiiiiide."

Stella couldn't help it—she shushed Lark and hauled her away from the bouncers, but she was already giggling.

For some reason she got a mental flash of what she would look like to her dad. She and Lark were both decked out in black leather—corsets, skirts, boots, with fishnet stockings and their faces painted perfectly Goth white-and-black with bloodred lips. Stella liked the look, actually; the corset pushed her boobs up front and center, and since they were the primary upside to being plus-sized, she liked occasionally taking the twins out for a ride, as Lark would put it. She'd gotten a lot of ogling in the club.

She didn't think Detective Maguire would be as keen on the costume.

"You look freaking hot," Lark remarked fuzzily as they staggered down the street. "You're rockin' those beasts tonight."

"Beasts or breasts?"

"Yeah, those. Let's try another one!"

Stella laughed. Thank God she'd stayed mostly sober; otherwise, they'd be totally lost. Neither of them had ever been to this part of town, which was mostly fetish clubs and smoky bars with black windows. The place they'd just been was full of exactly the kind of stereotypical fake-fang emo poets she'd hoped they could bypass to find something at least a little real.

"Okay," Stella said, pulling Lark off the sidewalk into an alley—still in the solid glow of a streetlight; she was no idiot—to check the hastily scribbled map she'd made based on the one useful conversation so far tonight. A skinny boy she was pretty sure was a heroin addict had given her the basic layout of the three or four blocks that made up the "Shadow District." She'd tried not to snort at the cheesy name.

"If we keep going down this street, we'll hit a big dance club called the Black Door," Stella said. "If we turn right, there's a bar called Anodyne, but it's really exclusive. Across the street is another one, Nepenthe, and it's supposed to be easier to get into. Just a bar, no dance floor. So do you feel like dancing or drinking or both?"

Lark checked her lipstick in her purse mirror. "Well, if

you want info, someplace quieter's probably better. I couldn't hear shit in that last place."

"True. Let's check out Nepenthe, then if it sucks, we can at least go dance at the Black Door—that dude Jonas said they have killer margaritas."

Lark gave a thumbs-up.

They headed east, down a street that was slightly darker and less populated than Third; it was a weeknight, but in the summer the clubs tended to be crowded all week, and several were having ladies' nights and other specials.

Nepenthe on first glance didn't look like the sort of place her dad would ever, ever let her go into, which meant it was the first sort of place she would have run to a few years ago. It looked safe enough, but kind of . . . deliberately seedy, made to cater to the crowd that wanted to be able to say they'd been to "that kind of place." Stella looked over at the front of Anodyne, which looked like a fairly upscale, typical bar, and sure enough, a couple came out dressed to the nines and the valet brought their Lexus around.

They probably couldn't afford to get into Anodyne anyway. Stella sighed.

The bouncer stopped them. "ID?"

They both held up their cards, and he scrutinized them, then the girls themselves. Stella wasn't sure what exactly he was looking for, but after a second he nodded and unclipped the velvet rope to let them in.

"No cover?" she asked.

"Not for you ladies," he said with a wink.

"Nice," Stella muttered. "Nice and skeevy."

A blast of air-conditioning hit them as they entered the bar, which was as dark and forbidding as the last place had been cheap and cheesy. The bar itself was sparsely populated, but there were booths lining the walls that seemed to have a lot going on in them.

Instantly, Stella's senses went into overdrive, and fear clenched her stomach in a tight fist. *Oh shit. Not safe. Not safe.*

"We need to go," she said softly to Lark . . . who was already headed toward the bar.

"Oh come on, Stellybean. One drink."

Stella looked around the room, feeling as if dozens of eyes were on her, but when she turned her gaze on the figures in the booths, no one was looking at them. There were bats fluttering madly around in her chest, but she couldn't put her finger on *why*; no one in particular was giving off a threatening vibe, and while it was dark, it wasn't any worse than any other bar she'd ever been in. There was just something . . .

. . . dark . . .

Oh Jesus.

Lark had ordered a gin and tonic and had gotten Stella a Diet Coke with rum, but Stella barely sipped at the drink as she looked around, eyes wide.

She could feel them . . . watching her . . . and they were hungry.

"Lark," Stella whispered. *"They're here."*

But when she looked over at her friend, Lark was gone.

Stella grabbed the bartender. "Did you see where my friend went?" she asked, trying not to sound as borderline hysterical as she felt. "She was just here!"

He shrugged. "Maybe to the bathroom? It's in the back."

Stella dug out her cell phone and called Lark's number, but it went straight to voice mail.

Okay, Stella. Take a deep breath. Check the bathroom.

She slid off her stool and walked toward the door the bartender had indicated . . . and as she walked, she could feel eyes on her again, gazes moving over her body, greedy, wanting, and not in that sleazy frat-boy way . . . This was primal, a need so deep it made her shake from her very bones.

More than anything in the world, she wanted to run, but she heard Gandalf's words in her head: *"Don't run from dark things, Stella. If you run, they chase after you."* What had she been thinking? God, what difference did it make what Miranda Grey was, if finding out meant Lark getting herself killed? Whatever was going on in this place it was bad, really bad, and they had to get out of here.

She started to open the door, only to have Lark blunder out into her with a drunken laugh.

"Shit!" Lark said. "Sorry, Stell. You know me—when I drink, I piss like a racehorse."

Stella's heart about burst with relief, and she threw her arms around her friend. "It's okay, let's just go," she said. "We need to go."

But the thought of walking back through the bar, past all those eyes . . .

"This way," Stella said, pulling Lark toward the side door marked *EXIT* with glowing red letters. "Let's get outside, and I'll call us a cab."

The night air wasn't as cold as inside the bar, but it was free air, and Stella gulped it in gratefully even with the smell of garbage from the nearby Dumpster.

"This might be the stupidest damn thing we've ever done," Stella said.

Lark snorted loudly. "Stupider than the time we got fucked up on absinthe and went Christmas caroling on Halloween?"

"Much stupider," Stella replied. "At least we got candy that time."

"Can I help you ladies?"

Stella yelped and spun toward the voice; she hadn't heard anyone come up behind them, but a young man was standing at the top of the concrete steps to the bar's back door, watching them with mixed amusement and curiosity. He was dressed all in black, big surprise, and had dark hair and pale skin . . . with no makeup, she realized.

"Um, no," Stella said. "We were just leaving. Thanks, though."

"Oh, come now," came another voice from the mouth of the alley. "It's so early."

Stella's heart was in her throat; there were two more people, one man and one woman, approaching them, and she saw it in their eyes as she had felt it in the bar: *hunger.*

The young man on the steps said to the others, "Remember the rules."

"Fuck the rules," the woman said. "And fuck your Signet for good measure. We'll do what we want here, and nobody's going to stop us."

The young man frowned. "We'll see about that."

He disappeared back into the bar. "Wait!" Stella said. "Wait, help—somebody help—"

"Shhhh," the other man said, drawing closer and closer. Stella backed up until she hit the wall of the bar. "There's no need to be scared, pretty girl. We're not going to hurt you."

Stella craned her neck sideways to see Lark in a similar position with the woman, who was smiling cruelly—and as Stella stared, the woman's teeth . . .

Stella had often wondered what she would do in a life-or-death situation; would she freeze or fight or what? She'd taken self-defense classes for women at her father's behest, but when it came down to that moment, what would she do?

Apparently she would freak the fuck out.

Stella screamed and tried to wrench away from the man, but he had her in his grasp; she struggled as hard as she could, and when she heard Lark cry out in pain, Stella's fear seemed to erupt from her body, and she flung herself forward at the man, clawing at his eyes the way she'd learned in class. The man jumped back to avoid her nails, and she bolted, blindly running toward the light at the end of the alley where surely someone, anyone, could help.

Rough hands seized her arms and dragged her backward. She screamed again and flailed, fighting, but the man was so much stronger than her, her efforts were more pathetic than anything else. He hauled her back into the alley and threw her hard against the wall.

"Please," she sobbed, "Please don't hurt me—please don't hurt my friend—"

A hand grabbed her chin and jerked it back. "You two bitches were asking for it, walking into this place. The only reason humans come here is they want to be food, little girl. Lucky you—you get your wish."

She tried to get out another scream, but it was too late; she felt a piercing, burning agony in her throat, and the pain was so intense she couldn't think, couldn't move, couldn't fight anymore.

I'm going to die. I'm going to die here like this— Will they call Dad to the scene? Will he identify my body? Oh please Goddess someone please help—

"Step away from the human!"

A snarl, and the mouth on her neck pulled away to let out a feline hiss. Distantly Stella heard his companion drop something heavy on the ground and take off running; she could also hear other feet pounding after her.

"Make me," the man said.

Stella's vision was blurred, her consciousness wavering, but she saw someone . . . no, two someones . . . three . . . standing in the streetlight, wearing some kind of uniforms . . . holding . . . swords? Were those *swords*? "You're surrounded," one of them said. "You are under arrest for public feeding with intent to kill—release the human and your punishment will be lighter."

"How 'bout I just break her little neck?" he asked.

"How about you piss yourself and die?" another voice, this one female, came from directly behind the man. Stella felt a hard impact in the man's body, and he screamed, the sound making thunder rip through Stella's head. The man fell away from her, tumbling to the ground, and she saw a cylinder of wood jutting out of his back.

Stella's knees gave out, and she started to fall, but the woman reached out and steadied her. Stella tried to focus on her; she was Asian, not in uniform like the others but no less imposing.

She held on to Stella with one hand and lifted her other arm to her mouth and said into her wristwatch, "Dispatch, I need an ambulance at these coordinates, transport to the Hausmann for two humans, emergency code Alpha Six, authorization Star-three."

"On its way, Star-three."

Stella fought to squeeze the woman's arm to get her attention, but she was too weak. "Please," she gasped. "Is my friend okay?"

The woman looked over. "She's breathing. One of my Elite is seeing to her until the medics arrive. Don't worry, Miss . . . you're going to be okay. Help is coming."

As the world began to go gray and sound became distant and watery, Stella murmured, "Miranda . . ." and fell forward onto her rescuer, who caught her with strong arms and eased her to the ground.

"What the hell is going on in my city?" David demanded, slamming the car door. "Three attacks in as many days, out in full view of the entire Shadow World?"

Faith walked beside the Prime up the steps to the Hausmann. "Sire, it actually gets worse."

He paused. "I hate it when you say that."

"One of the victims . . . it's Detective Maguire's daughter, Stella."

David let out the breath he'd been holding. "Christ. Has he been notified?"

"He's already here. The Hausmann contacts APD after every vampire-human incident just to keep open a line of communication, and they gave her ID—Maguire was here in ten minutes. He's, well, a little upset."

"Well, no shit, Second," David said.

The Prime steeled himself for what would no doubt be waiting for them inside the clinic. The receptionist bowed as he passed, headed right into the treatment area, where two of the beds were curtained off. At the foot of one, in a plastic chair, sat the detective, looking pale and anxious . . . and angry.

"What the hell is going on here, Solomon?" Maguire all but thundered, on his feet the second he saw David. "I thought your job in this city was to keep things like this from happening! I swear to God, if—"

"Sit. Down."

David fixed his eyes on the detective's and spoke very calmly; Maguire went white as a sheet and dropped back into the chair without another word.

"Now, tell me what happened," David instructed.

Maguire swallowed hard and coughed.

"Jackie," David said, catching the head nurse as she walked by, "would you have a coffee brought in for the detective?"

"Yes, Sire, right away," Jackie said with her infectious grin. "I just put on a fresh pot before we got the call."

He returned his gaze to Maguire. "Go on."

"I don't know exactly," the detective stammered. "I got a call on an Alpha Six outside Nepenthe. I don't know what the hell they were doing there. But the bar manager said there were two vamps outside threatening a couple of girls, acting like they didn't intend to obey the laws. He didn't like the look of them so he hit the emergency patrol call button in the bar."

"And the girls?"

"Both will be just fine," Jackie said as she returned, handing Maguire a cup. The detective's hands were shaking, but he drank it anyway, and it seemed the bitterness helped him focus on the nurse's words. "The taller girl, Renee Sutton, lost a good deal of blood, but we got to her just in time—she's having a transfusion right now. Stella fared better; I don't think her attacker had as much time with her. She's bruised and scratched, so I think she put up a hell of a fight."

Maguire's eyes were full of tears. "That's my girl," he said.

"And the assailants?"

Faith stepped up. "I killed the one who attacked Stella, and the patrol unit took out the other. They're finishing up at the scene now, but as far as we can tell, there's no connection between these and the Alpha Seven the other day; the only commonality is that both occurred in the District. We could easily be dealing with vampires who came to town for the music festival looking to free-feed, or Signet groupies here for the Council meeting."

David didn't say it, but he knew Faith was thinking the same thing he was: This was not random, not groupies. There was something in the air, an unease and electricity he remembered from when the Blackthorn had terrorized Austin.

He put his hand on the detective's shoulder. "She's going to be just fine," he said, echoing Jackie's words. "And we'll wipe her memory so she won't even have nightmares—it'll be like it never happened."

"No . . . you won't . . ." came a harsh whisper.

David pulled back the curtain from the bed to reveal a lovely red-haired girl of perhaps twenty-two, freckled like her father, her hazel eyes dull from painkillers but focused on him with almost alarming clarity.

He felt the power in her as soon as he laid eyes on her. *Oh, bloody hell.*

"Stella," Maguire said, pushing himself past David to grab his daughter's hand. "How are you feeling? Are you okay? They said you're going to be okay."

Stella nodded and gave him a wan smile. "I'm glad you're here," she whispered.

Maguire looked up at David plaintively. "You can make her forget, right?"

Again, Stella spoke. "No, Dad . . . they can't. Mind control stuff doesn't work on me . . . I'm psychic like they are. And I'm a Witch."

Maguire shut his eyes tight and turned his face away. "Stella, we'll talk about that later . . ."

"I'm afraid she's right," David said. "She's obviously shielded and trained to her gifts; not to mention she's very strong. We can deal with her friend's memories because she's unconscious and not nearly as powerful. There's no way a typical compulsion like ours could overcome Stella's barriers. Luckily . . . I know someone who's not typical."

"No!" Stella exclaimed, the effort clearly making her dizzy. "You can't do that to me. You can't screw with my mind like that—I want to remember. And I want to know . . . I want to know about Miranda."

David raised an eyebrow. "What about Miranda?"

"She's one of you. I know she is. I know she is . . ." Stella's strength was failing her; she had been through a lot and was drugged for both pain and anxiety. It was possible she would forget most of this on her own because of the trauma.

David started to say something, but before he could, a soft presence moved up beside him, and with a flash of red hair, Miranda was standing over the bed, peering down at the young human who had whispered her name.

Stella's eyes went huge, and her hands clenched the sheets. David knew she was seeing . . . and Seeing . . . more than just her musical idol, although that would have been enough excitement for anyone.

"You must be Stella," Miranda said gently. "I'm told you asked for me."

Stella burst into tears.

Miranda Grey was sitting by Stella's bed, holding her hand, as if it were the most natural thing in the world.

Miranda Grey, a vampire.

She'd cleared everyone else out of the room, and they all obeyed without question, even Stella's father, who reluctantly shuffled out to the waiting room for a moment.

Miranda's hand was warm against Stella's, not cold like a corpse's. Her eyes, the same gold-flecked green as in the few pictures Stella had seen, were kind, but there was something alien in them as well that Stella doubted any of her fans had ever been close enough to see.

She was every bit as beautiful in person, up close, both smaller in stature and more massive in energy than any normal woman would be. She listened as Stella told her how she had come to be at Nepenthe with full attention, concern and anger in her eyes when Stella got to the part where the other vampires attacked them.

"I'm sorry that happened," Miranda said. Her speaking

voice without a microphone was so soft, but Stella had a feeling it could be imperious and hard when it needed to be. "We work very hard to make sure people are safe here—this kind of thing is pretty rare."

"Are there . . . are there a lot of you?"

A smile. "More than you would expect. The South is heavily populated because of the weather . . . we like the heat."

"Because . . . you're dead."

"No, Stella. I'm alive. Just different. My kind live in a world that touches yours, but they aren't meant to intersect; we take what we need to survive and try not to destroy anything . . . or most of us do. I'm a little different in that I chose to have a presence in the Day World, even if I can never walk there."

"And this thing you have, this psychic gift? What is it? I've never Seen anything like it."

Miranda looked surprised. "You can see it?"

"It's my gift. Sight. I See things about people—that's how I Saw your aura change when you got shot." Stella took a breath; she was tired, but she couldn't stand the thought of missing a moment of this conversation. "I'm sorry you got shot, by the way . . . I bet it hurt. I hope they caught the guy."

"I've had worse," Miranda replied with a smile. "And yes, he's been . . . held accountable."

Stella might have done some dumb shit tonight, but she wasn't dumb enough to follow up on that sentence. "But I watched videos of you performing, and I could See you doing something, but I didn't know what."

A slow nod. "I'm an empath," Miranda said. "I have been since I was human. I can sense and manipulate emotion."

"Is that how you could get past my shields and wipe my memories?" Stella asked uncertainly.

"Yes. Empathy as strong as mine is difficult to protect against because it's so rare. I get in through a different door than the others."

"Please . . . don't do it. I don't want to forget this."

Miranda sighed. "It's for your own good, Stella. People can't know what I really am. A lot of lives depend on our secrecy."

"I promise I won't tell anyone! I swear."

There was sympathy, and affection, in the singer's eyes. "I believe you." She gently let go of Stella's hand and straightened out the sheets, then laid her palm on Stella's cheek. "Rest now, Stella . . . would you like me to sing to you?"

Stella's heart was about to burst again, but this time with the sudden upwelling of joy after what had to have been one of the worst nights of her life. "Yes . . . I'd love that. Thank you so much."

Miranda leaned down and kissed her forehead, then sat back down and said, "Close your eyes."

Stella obeyed, and as Miranda's voice wove its honeyed way through the clinic's cold air, it wrapped its shadowy tendrils around Stella's mind and coaxed her toward a darkness that was made up of sleep and healing, not fear, a place where she could wrap herself in the song and dream . . . and forget:

> *I have no fear of heights,*
> *No fear of the deep blue sea . . .*

Fifteen

Like most of its cousins, the Haven of Eastern Europe stood just at the edge of the city proper, where the comings and goings of its denizens would be less noticeable. They could in fact bypass Prague entirely to reach it from the airport, but Jacob had business in town, so as their driver guided the car along the streets, Cora watched Prague Castle glide by lit up like a cathedral in the night, and seeing it gave her a sense of homecoming she had never felt anywhere else.

She was coming to know the city little by little. She stayed home most of the time, as she was even more sensitive to the cold than most vampires, a consequence of years spent shivering in slow starvation. But as she gained in strength over the months, she grew braver, and as Jacob had pointed out, it was unlikely anyone would bother her with Vràna trotting alongside her.

"Feeling better, my love?" the Prime asked as the car pulled to a stop outside their broker's office.

Cora nodded. "I really hate flying."

He smiled and kissed her cheek. "Luckily it should be quite some time before we have to do it again. That's the nice thing about Europe—to get anywhere in David's territory he has to fly, but we can tour the entire East via train." He looked her over. "You still look a little green. We'll be home soon, and you can have a long rest in a warm bed. I won't be long."

Jacob straightened out the blanket she'd had wrapped around her, which had gotten a bit tangled as she dozed, then ducked out of the car quickly so as not to let out too much heat. It was cool at night here year-round; she didn't long for the hundred-plus-degree summers of Texas, but she had enjoyed the May nights. There had even been a late snowfall here yesterday.

Vràna grunted in her sleep and pawed at the air. "Chasing rabbits again?" Cora asked, scratching the Nighthound's head with a smile. It was quite remarkable that in spite of the dog's size she could fold herself into a very narrow space in the car, though she did tend to jam her bony knees into Jacob fairly often.

Cora leaned back and watched the night go by out the car window for a while, feeling herself relax; the last few days had been far too much excitement for her taste. She had to smile at herself. There had been a time she had worried that she wouldn't be warrior enough for her Signet, but it turned out a warrior was not what Jacob needed, and she was quite satisfied with the comparatively boring life she had. Perhaps Miranda was a more memorable Queen and had a more interesting life, but given the toll it seemed to take on everyone around her, fame and fortune weren't as blissful as people were led to believe.

"I do not know how she does it," Cora murmured, partly to the dog, partly to herself. "How any of them do. I rather like not having so many mortal enemies."

Oh, she was sure that if Hart had the opportunity, he would gleefully kill Cora, but at least for now she had escaped the madness of his true wrath. Across the ocean and living quietly behind stone walls, Cora wasn't much of a target.

What was it, she wondered, that had made Hart fixate on Miranda so strongly? Was her outspoken nature, and her Prime's attachment to mortals, really that much of a threat? Yes, things were changing in the Council, but surely Hart had nothing to fear from a few Primes following the South's example. It had to be something else, something personal. Cora was neither an empath nor a strategist, but she knew Hart's capricious temper. He held grudges—cherished them—but he didn't jeopardize his own power in their pursuit. He genuinely fancied himself a true nobleman above getting his hands dirty. His behavior in this whole matter was . . . far too coarse, too petty.

She was still brooding when Jacob returned. "Oh dear," he said. "You have that look."

Cora blinked. "Look, my Lord?"

"The sort of look Vràna gets when she's on the scent of a particularly fat and tasty rabbit . . . or perhaps the look of a Queen on the verge of knowing too much."

She chuckled. "Perish the thought."

He waited, and finally she said, "I was thinking about Hart, my Lord . . . his obsession with the Southern United States is unlike him."

Jacob looked surprised for a moment but nodded. "And you suspect there's a larger game afoot."

"I cannot imagine what it could be. What would he have to gain by destroying them? There is no territory to annex, no riches to steal. He is possessed of a foolish pride, true, but the risks he is taking are extreme."

"I agree," Jacob said, knocking for the driver to resume the trip home. "My experience with Hart in the political arena is that he'd rather work behind the scenes and make life miserable for them than try to go after Miranda's career publicly. The leak to the media last year—that's Hart. Having her shot was pushing it. Making a play in Council seemed like an impulsive last-ditch effort. David's not going to go to war over something like this, so Hart's going to have to let the matter drop . . . but like you, I keep thinking there's something else he's trying to accomplish, or that his actions were a smokescreen for something else."

Cora sighed. "Jonathan told me he thinks something is coming . . . that Miranda becoming Queen was like a stone falling into a still pond, and that things are going to change for all of us. I have a feeling he is right."

"Whatever it is, I'm sure we're safe for now," Jacob assured her, brushing hair from her eyes. "Things have been peaceful here for centuries."

"I just wish I knew . . ." Cora trailed off as Vràna's head jerked upward, the Hound's teeth suddenly bared with a low growl.

Jacob started visibly. "Good Lord, Vràna, you have more dreams than any two-legged person I've ever—what is it?"

Cora's stomach had lurched, and she felt cold all over, then hot, then cold again. Her heart clawed up into her throat. Something . . . something was not right . . .

"Jan, stop the car," Jacob said. "Cora—"

An image flashed in Cora's mind: a small metal disk, the smell of exhaust, a beep . . . fire . . .

"Out," she gasped. "Get out of the car!"

Without asking a single question, Jacob seized Cora's arm with one hand and Vràna's collar with the other.

Cora felt the world spinning out of her view, and before she could even take a breath to cry out, her face slammed into a snowbank.

The cold jolted her out of the reflexive nausea that accompanied a Mist; she'd done it only a few times and usually with far more preparation. Jacob had tandem-Misted with her before, but he'd never brought the dog along.

As she lifted her head, she heard a roar and felt the air vibrate with blistering heat. She was grabbed again, hauled sideways underneath her Prime, who held her down until the blast was over. Cora screamed into his shoulder, feeling something impact with his back. She heard Vràna barking in panic from near her head.

Moments later the shaking stopped, and the smell of burning flesh assaulted her nose. Cora whimpered, clinging to Jacob, terrified for a second that he was dead, but he made a pained noise and shifted off her, allowing a large furry shadow to insert itself between them and start licking Cora fiercely on the face.

"Enough, Vràna," she croaked. "I'm fine."

She could count on one hand the times in the last three years she had heard her Prime curse, and this was one of them.

Cora forced herself out of the fetal position and tried to understand what she was seeing, but her mind had frozen—until she saw the blood.

Nausea gripped her. She might have passed out, but Jacob's voice intruded: "Cora, I need your help."

Cora admonished herself sternly in a mental voice that she noticed sounded much like Miranda: *Get ahold of yourself, Queen.*

"Yes," she said. "Hold still."

There was a large piece of black metal sticking out of Jacob's back just out of his reach; it wasn't very deep in, and nowhere near his heart. Relieved, she gripped it with both hands and pulled.

"Mother of Christ." Jacob shook himself and asked, "Are you hurt? I didn't feel anything hit you."

"No," she said. "What . . . what did I see? Metal and fire? I do not—"

"A bomb," Jacob replied, pulling his phone out of his coat pocket.

Cora turned her head toward the source of the heat and stench, the still-smoldering hulk of their car. She could hear sirens in the distance as she stared at the scene, unbelieving. Jacob put his arm around her and pulled her close while he called the Haven, the police, and a variety of other people. She wasn't really listening.

Cora jumped a mile as her pocket began to vibrate; the last thing she'd been expecting was a phone call. Hands numb from shock and cold, she dug it out and answered it with chattering teeth while trying to focus enough to raise her body temperature from the inside.

"What the hell just happened?" came a familiar voice. *"Are you all right?"*

"I think someone just tried to kill us," she said. "Did you have a vision?"

Jonathan let out his breath audibly. *"Not exactly—I woke up from a dead sleep with my hand already on the phone to call you. What happened?"*

Jacob gestured to her, and Cora hit the button to switch the phone to speaker mode. "The car blew up," he said a bit tersely. "Are you sure you weren't aware of it in advance?"

"Good God, Jacob, if I'd seen something like that, I would have warned you," Jonathan replied. *"Deven and I both sat bolt upright at the same time—we felt something happening."*

"I don't suppose you felt who did it," Jacob said. He was, as usual, keeping his head, though Cora had the urge to dig a hole in the snow and hide, or possibly throw up.

"What can you tell us?" Another voice joined in: Deven.

Jacob eyed the scene. "It looks like it originated near the front seat," he said, frowning. "The back is still mostly intact. That's a bit odd."

"Why?" Cora asked.

Jacob got to his feet. "We were in the back. So is the gas tank. I'm going to have a closer look—the fire's mostly out, and the police will be here in a few minutes." Cora grabbed his arm to stop him, but he gave her a smile. "I'll be fine. I just want to see what I can before the authorities arrive and disturb the scene."

"I'm coming with you, then." She struggled up in the snow until he took her arm and helped her get her balance. Vràna kept close as they picked their way past bits of the car's chassis and motor-type things, the stinking remains of a tire . . . an arm.

"Jan," Cora said softly. "Poor Jan."

Jacob's phone rang shrilly. This time they both jumped. "Janousek. *Prosím*," he said, then smiled wryly. "Ah, David. Lovely to hear from you." He glanced over at Cora, who was still holding her phone up where the West could hear. "No, we're all right . . . a bomb, as far as I can tell.

We've got Elite en route as well as inspectors . . . yes, if you wish. Let me call you back."

The approaching fire trucks and police cars were drowning out conversation, so Cora said, "We have to go now, Jonathan—we will call you later with more information."

"As long as you're all right," the Consort said.

"We are. Don't worry."

"Right. Of course not. People try to blow up my friends every day." Jonathan sounded uncharacteristically morose as he hung up, and she felt a pang of worry for him as well.

Cora joined Jacob nearer the wreck, where he was staring into the driver's seat. She was reluctant to see what might remain of Jan—and despite the obviousness of the answer, she asked, "Is he dead?"

Jacob sighed. "Spectacularly. We'll have to notify his family." He was taking pictures with his phone. "For David," he said to her.

"Did he have a 'feeling' about the bomb, too?" she asked.

"He said Miranda woke up in a fit and demanded he call immediately."

Cora bit her lip and, suddenly aware of how tired she was, sank down on the low stone wall that ran alongside the road. "Jonathan said he and Deven both knew something was wrong at the same time."

Jacob joined her, taking her hand. "Four Signets having the same premonition . . . Is it strange that I find that more worrisome than the fact that we were just blown up?"

She met his eyes. "So do I."

Together, with Vràna standing guard, they waited in the frigid night for the cavalry to arrive.

Stella wished fervently that she had been born with healing talent instead of Sight.

Sunlight glared through the front windows of Revelry, revealing every speck of dust on the inventory and elevating her headache from vicious-and-pounding to purely murderous.

She leaned on her elbows on the counter and rubbed her temples. Of all the stupid times to have a day shift.

"Hey, do you have any more red pillar candles?"

Stella cracked one eye at the woman with orangey-red dyed hair and a saucer-sized pentagram necklace. "Do you see any on the shelf?"

The woman made a noise of irritation and turned away, muttering.

Stella heaved a sigh and reached down into the drawer under the counter, rummaging for the bottle of Advil she was pretty sure Foxglove had stashed there. She groped past an assortment of office supplies and what felt like a bundle of dried sage until her fingers closed around the bottle; meanwhile, her other hand grabbed her coffee cup.

"Aw, hell," she said, realizing the cup was empty, just as the bell jangled to announce another customer. The sound sent a snarl of pain through her head.

"Here."

A take-out coffee cup appeared on the counter, and Stella seized it with a groan and popped four pills with a swallow of the blessedly hot liquid. "Perfect timing."

Lark looked about how Stella felt. She, too, was clinging to a giant cup as if her life depended on it. "Figured you had a hangover as nasty as mine. How drunk *were* we?"

Stella stared at her friend, taking in the dark circles under her eyes and her marginally groomed appearance. "You don't remember anything?"

"I remember we went to that fetish club. Where did we go after that?"

Stella found herself staring at Lark's neck, where there was a faint gummy-looking residue. "Did you hurt yourself?"

Lark reached up and touched the spot. "I dunno. I found a Band-Aid there, but there's nothing under it but a bug bite. What do you remember?"

"About the same." Stella drank her coffee, looking out

over the store at the handful of customers, most of whom were regulars. "Look, Lark . . . I'm sorry I got us into all that crap. It was stupid."

"Wait . . . you mean you aren't going to keep looking? I thought you were dying to know . . . that thing you wanted to know."

Stella shook her head. "That was before you got hurt."

"I'm not hurt, Stell, I'm hung-the-fuck-over. That happens at least once a week. Come on, there's got to be more to this—don't you want to find out?"

"I'm done, Lark. This whole thing is just insane."

Lark stared at her. "You're serious."

"Yeah. I'm serious. I'm done."

The look on Lark's face said she clearly didn't believe Stella, but she said, "Well . . . okay, if that's what you want. But if you change your mind after your hangover goes away, I'm up for another try."

Stella managed a smile. "Thanks for sticking with me through this. You're a good friend."

"And you, sweetie, are a certifiable nutbar. But I love you anyway." Lark leaned over and bestowed a kiss on Stella's forehead. "I've got to split—I've got class. I'll call you later, okay? We can go for falafel."

"Sure, sounds good."

Despite Lark's condition, as she left Stella heard her singing softly:

> *I have no fear of heights,*
> *No fear of the deep blue sea . . .*

Stella didn't breathe freely again until Lark had gone. She needed time to think, without worrying what her best friend might hare off and do impulsively on her behalf. Stella glanced, for the tenth time that day, at the paper-wrapped volume sitting on the shelf below, and as luck would have it, when she looked back up, the bell was jangling again to announce the arrival of a certain wizard-looking fellow.

"Young Mistress Maguire," Gandalf said with a bow as he approached the counter. "I hear that you have another package for me—from Genoa, I believe."

Stella nodded and retrieved the book, setting it carefully on the counter between them but leaving her hands on it for a second.

Gandalf peered at her curiously. "Are you well, Miss Stella? You look rather, as my uncle Larry would have said, 'rode hard and hung up wet.'"

Stella grinned. "I'm hungover, Master Gandalf. Majorly. But I'll be okay. Actually . . . there's something I want to ask you."

He frowned. "You're not still poking about in places angels like you should know better than to tread, are you?"

She held his eyes for a minute, then wordlessly reached up to her shirt collar and pulled it aside, showing him the very, very faint pink marks on her neck. At the rate they were healing, they'd be gone by nightfall, but she knew he could see them, because his eyes widened and his face paled a shade.

"Gandalf," she said softly, "I need you to tell me what you know about the Signets."

Faith did not like the way her boss was looking at her.

In fact, if they hadn't been in an elevator with nowhere to run, she probably would have backed away slowly.

"Why didn't you tell me this last night?" he asked, with that calmness in his voice that she had learned, after years of serving him, placed her on dangerous ground.

"I was going to," she insisted. "I was. But the incident with Maguire's girl distracted me, and there were the bodies to deal with afterward, and then this evening we were waiting for news from Janousek—"

"You should have come to me the minute you left the hotel," David cut her off. "What if we had already gone to pick up the Stone from the lab and one of us put it on? You could have put us both in danger, Faith."

"Yes, Sire. I'm sorry."

He was glowering as the numbers on the display ticked upward, but just as it reached the floor where Hunter was headquartered, he said, "Forgiven, Second."

"What do we do now?"

"First, we get the results from Novotny's tests. Then we have him lock the damn thing up for at least a week, preferably with monitoring equipment so he can measure any effects the new moon has on it."

"And then?"

"Then I drop in on the Pair of the West," he said darkly. "I think we need to have a little chat."

She crossed her arms. "Deven thought you would want to study the Stone and that you'd want to see what it does firsthand."

"That's because Deven apparently thinks I'm an idiot," David snapped.

"Jonathan agreed with him about the Stone."

The look on the Prime's face changed slightly, from angry to thoughtful. "Did he?"

"Yes. He was definitely shaken up by it—he suggested that if I didn't want to steal it, I should at least try to distract you from it until after the new moon. He really seems to think something terrible will happen."

The doors slid open and they headed down the hall. "The important thing is that you told me."

Faith shook hear head, saying, "I can't believe they thought I would keep it from you."

David gave her a piercing look. "You're assuming that your telling us wasn't their intention all along."

"But why . . ."

"I don't know. But when was the last time Deven did anything without six ulterior motives? His own plans don't trust themselves. Why should we believe anything he says?"

"Because Jonathan wouldn't lie," Faith pointed out. "That's why Deven never tells him anything—so he won't have to choose between loyalty and honesty. Jonathan certainly wouldn't fake a precognitive insight."

David strode through the lab's main door. "I hope he wouldn't . . . but I'll find out for sure after we're done here."

Novotny was waiting for them. "Good evening, Sire, Faith. I received the photos you sent earlier—is everything all right in Prague?"

"Yes," David said. "The human authorities swept both Janousek's remaining cars for explosives but found none. Do you agree with my initial assessment of the situation?"

"Oh, definitely." Novotny led them through the lab to the area where evidence was kept locked in vaults in the wall; he kept speaking as he walked over to where he was storing the Stone and began entering the passcodes. "Given the blast pattern in the photos, I would conclude it was the driver himself, not the car, that was rigged to go off. If what the Queen said about her vision is accurate, I would say the same person who killed your shooter Monroe is behind the attempt on the Pair's life. I can't be a hundred percent sure until I get samples for toxicology analysis, of course, but I'd wager the driver was either carrying or had ingested a similar explosive."

"This is looking less and less like Hart," Faith said. "He's not Janousek's biggest fan, but making an outright assassination attempt is another story altogether. He wouldn't be that obvious—not so soon after the Council meeting."

"Agreed," the Prime said. "Which leads us squarely back to Lydia and her Order, assuming Jeremy Hayes hasn't gone rogue. Neither of those possibilities comforts me."

Faith started to tell the Prime what else she'd learned from Deven—that Lydia was dead—but Novotny spoke first.

"Well, if you find this Lydia, there are a lot of questions about her object that remain unanswered," Novotny said, pressing his palm to the scanner; it beeped and Faith heard the lock on the vault disengage. "Either she was greatly exaggerating its importance, or whatever mystical properties it has are completely dormant. As far as any of our tests can tell, it's just a piece of—"

He pulled the drawer open and lifted the lid . . . revealing an empty nest of foam.

"Where is it?" David asked.

Novotny had gone ashen white, and to Faith's bewilderment, he actually stammered his reply: "I . . . I have no idea."

Sixteen

Deven had always found David irresistible when angry. Often when they were together, Deven would piss him off just for the makeup sex.

He also knew how to push the Prime's buttons—he had installed quite a few of them himself—such as allowing David to rage at him without so much as batting an eye.

"Where is it?" David all but thundered, not bothering with greetings as he and Faith burst into the hotel suite where Deven was going over a transcript of the recording Cora had gotten him during the Queens' gathering, and Jonathan was again reading his battered autographed copy of *Les Misérables*.

Deven looked up from the monitor. "Where is what?"

"The Stone, Deven. Where is the Stone?"

Deven's eyebrow quirked. He looked at Faith. "Did you get it?"

Faith narrowed her eyes. "I told you I had no intention of stealing the Stone," she said. "And I didn't. It must have been you."

Jonathan's book slid off his lap toward the floor, and he caught it, saying, "Us? We don't have it. What's going on, David?"

"It has to be you," David growled. His irises were the leaden color of a sky before a blizzard. "It was in the lab last night, and tonight Novotny opened the vault to find it had vanished. We have security footage of one of the interns opening the vault and taking the Stone out—but the intern has conveniently lost any memory of doing so, and there's no footage of where he took it."

Deven closed his laptop and folded his hands on its lid. "If I had known it would be that easy to get my hands on, I would never have asked Faith to take care of it."

David's eyes burned into his. "You're telling me you didn't steal it."

"I did not." Deven leaned back in his chair, crossing one leg over the other. "But I think we owe a debt of gratitude to whoever did, given what the thing does."

"Which you had no intention of telling me," David said. "Because you think I'm incapable of making my own decisions."

"I understand that you're angry—"

"No, I don't believe you do. Or at least I don't believe you care."

Deven considered that. "No, I don't, really. I don't mind you being angry with me as long as you're safe from the Stone. Once the thing is useless again and I don't have to worry about you getting yourself killed, then I can worry about apologizing."

David bowed his head for a moment, then said quietly, "I don't think so . . . not this time."

"What do you mean?"

Their eyes met again. "Deven . . . you know how much I care for you. And I value your friendship both personally and politically. But I can't do this anymore. Either you and I are equals, or we aren't. I want a friend who is an equal. I don't want whatever this is you're trying to be."

"I am trying," Deven said just as quietly, "to save your lives."

"Then tell me why. And how. And everything you know." When Deven didn't answer, David nodded. "That's what I thought."

David straightened, looking from one vampire to the

other. "You told me I should stop acting like a pawn; well, you were right. I would like for the two of you to leave my territory as soon as possible . . . and not return."

Deven started to speak, but David went on: "I would like to continue to honor our alliance in Council, but I have to consider our personal relationship at an end. I won't have a friendship without trust."

Their eyes still held. "I understand," Deven said.

Slowly, David nodded. "Please be gone by the end of the week."

He turned and walked out of the suite, and Faith—looking utterly amazed by what she'd just witnessed—followed him, closing the door behind her.

Silence, for a moment, while the humming anger of David's presence faded from the room.

Then Jonathan said, "You have no intention of leaving, do you?"

Deven sighed. "We'll do as the Prime requested after the new moon has come and gone and we can be sure they're safe. After that, we go home, and give David another few years to fret and stew before he realizes he needs us."

Jonathan was looking at the door. "You know, love . . . I'm not really sure that's going to happen this time. He may have finally had enough of you."

"He may have for now. But not forever. I don't really understand this thing that binds us together that keeps bringing us into each other's orbit over and over . . . but I know it can be denied for only so long before it pulls us back together again. Friends, lovers, whatever—there's some part of each of us that can't let go. And however much he may wish he could hate me . . . in time, he'll see that I was right. That's the one real advantage of what we are, Jonathan . . . we have all the time there is, years upon years, decades crumbling into centuries . . . never ending . . ."

He trailed off, and it was a moment before he realized Jonathan was staring at him.

"You're getting lost again," Jonathan said gently.

"Oh . . . right." Deven rubbed his temples against the headache that had formed there. "Whatever. He'll get over it. But he'll still be alive—that's what matters. I can deal with him pissed off for a while as long as he and Miranda stay alive."

He heard Jonathan rise and cross the room to where Deven sat, felt him go to his knees in front of Deven's chair. "Look at me," Jonathan said.

Deven sighed and obeyed.

"I've heard that the oldest vampires don't end up being killed by outside forces," Jonathan said, brushing stray hair from Deven's eyes. "They kill themselves slowly . . . they lose their will to go on. Immortality consumes them, and they just sort of fade away."

"It happens," Deven replied. "That's why Primes have Consorts . . . to make eternity less of a burden."

"Then I'm not doing my job," Jonathan said with regret. "I want to help you. I want to be what you need. But you won't let me."

"Do you want to know the truth?"

"Please."

Deven laid his hands on Jonathan's head, twining his fingers through his Consort's blond hair. "A part of me was ready to die before I met David. I had been alive too long, seen too much. He woke me from a living death—and in doing so, made me ready to find you. And you do make me want to live, my love . . . but nothing can take away the past. You can give me new life every day, but you can't heal me. No one can."

There were tears in Jonathan's eyes. "I hate it when you talk like that," he said.

"And that's why I don't."

"That's what I get for falling for an older man," he muttered.

Deven leaned back again, still stroking Jonathan's hair, and said, "None of them understand . . . they can't see the enormity of time the way I can, the way it swallows all our striving . . . they want to live solely in the moment, not realizing that for our kind the moment never ends. Empires have come and gone, continents have been discovered and populated from shore to shore, men have walked on the moon, wars have consumed the planet . . . everything dies, but we remain. We are witnesses to the endless decay of the world. No matter how high we rise, eventually . . . ashes to ashes, we all fall down."

Miranda finished pulling her comb through the tangle of her damp curls, then plaited the whole mass into a messy braid to keep it out of her face.

She'd spent as much of the night as she could working out to try to alleviate some of the tension that seemed to have taken up permanent residency in her body, and once she was good and worn out, she took a steamy hot shower and scrubbed herself raw.

It didn't really help. Once she was done, she was again at loose ends, with too many hours left in the night and too little to do.

She had to be careful about leaving the Haven for a while yet, though she was making sure that the public knew her recovery from the shooting was proceeding beautifully with no complications. That afternoon, lying awake with David after she had woken practically screaming with fear for Jacob and Cora, they'd discussed her "recovery" and decided she should stay home for a full month, going into town no more than once a week to hunt fresh blood and stave off cabin fever. If she didn't feel satisfied with donated bag blood brought from town, they could figure out a way to bring in live humans a few nights a week. But she had to stay out of sight.

But if she was being honest with herself . . . that wasn't the real problem right now.

She was so restless she was practically throwing off sparks. She needed to either get drunk or go pound out her frustrations on the piano. At least the piano would offer an opportunity to work on the new album.

There was also . . .

Miranda sighed heavily and left the suite barefoot in her pajamas, all but running down the hall to the music room; she unlocked it with her com and slipped into its welcome silence, heart pounding as if she'd broken out of prison.

Instead of hitting the overhead lights, she walked around the room lighting the candle sconces—well, technically they weren't real candles, but they flickered and gave the same soft illumination as a real candle without risking an accident should she forget to put one out. She tended to fall asleep in here a lot, or to wander in and out in a daze after working deeply with her gift, so it was best if they avoided real fire in a room with so much valuable wood and paper.

She sank down at the Bösendorfer and laid her head on its lid for a while. Anxiety drained out of her, through the piano, and into the floor, where she imagined it being transformed into something useful; she had learned from David how to ground and center, but the piano offered her an even more solid ground to stand on, one she needed more and more often these days.

She looked up at Queen Bess. "Things are getting very weird around here," she said.

Again, as she often did in this room, she thought of Kat. The blonde would have known what to do; she always knew. She had the right words, the right ideas, the ability to look at a situation with equanimity and make decisions rationally. Miranda had always jumped into things, unthinking, and trusted—God? Herself? She had no idea anymore—that there would be water to meet her, not rocks, when she tumbled down.

"Wish you were here, Katmandoo," she whispered. "Maybe you could tell me what the hell I'm supposed to do."

Miranda sat up and lifted the piano lid, reaching inside its body to retrieve the small wooden box she had tucked inside.

She held the box in both hands, contemplating it, tracing the carvings with her fingertips. Why did she have it? Why had she taken it?

She didn't know.

No one questioned the Queen when she requested it from the lab. They simply jumped to her orders and brought it out to her. Miranda put the incident out of their minds afterward just in case any of them mentioned seeing the Queen. She had in fact been leaving the lab when the call came in about Stella; with all the commotion she had forgotten about it, until she felt the corner of the box jab her in the ribs under her coat on the way home. While David was in the shower, she slipped off to the music room and hid it, hoping to keep enough distance from the thing that she could think logically again.

It hadn't worked. The box and its contents were all she could think about. And right now David and Faith were on their way to retrieve it . . . David was going to be good and pissed off when he figured out what she'd done, but that hadn't stopped her. Novotny had found no trace of a spell drawing her to it, but *something* was. Something made her want it in her hands beyond all reason.

Something made her flip open the lid and take the talisman out.

"What are you, really?" she asked it, turning it over in her hands. It was heavier than it looked, just like the Signets, and warmed to her touch. She could feel the carvings, each line practically burning her fingers with some kind of energy that neither David nor science itself could detect. Why did it want her? And what for?

Lydia had known. Miranda was sure of it. There was more to this thing than "power amplifier," and Lydia knew it—but she had vanished. A sweep of the entire sensor network had turned up nothing; she might as well have dropped dead and taken all her secrets with her. But if Lydia knew, then someone else in her Order would, too, and all they had to do was find that someone. It couldn't be that hard.

She examined the prongs on the talisman, wondering

how it was supposed to work—she was pretty sure it attached to her Signet, but where? The front or the back? She held it in one hand and flipped her Signet over with the other, looking for any sort of . . . wait.

She'd never noticed before, but there were tiny indentations along the Signet's outside edge, lining up exactly with the talisman's prongs. She tried to remember if she'd ever seen anything similar on David's Signet, but truthfully she'd never looked that closely at the back of it. Basically it looked like it just clipped on.

With a soft snap, the talisman clicked into place perfectly, fitting flat against the Signet. From the front nobody would even be able to see it.

As Miranda stared at the talisman, she could feel the metal growing warmer and warmer, until it practically burned in her hand; then, to her astonishment, she could see the carvings . . . *glowing.*

"Oh shit," she muttered. "Way to go, Miranda . . . you found the motherfucking Ring of Sauron."

She pulled on the talisman to detach it . . . and couldn't.

"You've got to be kidding me—" Miranda slid her fingernail in between Signet and talisman, trying to pry them apart, but they wouldn't budge; she couldn't bend back the prongs either, even though she could have sworn the metal was soft enough to let her do that a minute ago.

She was still trying to get the thing off when the music room door beeped and David entered, clearly distressed.

"You're not going to believe what I have to tell you," he said, dropping into his usual chair. "I just threw Deven and Jonathan out of Austin . . . and I think we broke up."

She dropped her Signet back in place on her neck, eyebrows shooting up. "You did what?"

"They've been here this whole time."

Miranda rolled her eyes. "No kidding."

"They tried to persuade Faith to steal the talisman from the lab."

Her hand closed around her Signet. "Oh?"

"And now it's gone—someone did steal it, but not Faith,

and not Deven. The goddamn thing just up and vanished, and I have no idea what happened to it . . ."

"I . . ."

"But it's probably a good thing, since apparently it's going to kill whoever's wearing it."

She froze. "Um . . . say again?"

He stared at her for a moment before he spoke again. "Miranda . . . please tell me you didn't do what I think you did."

Biting her lip, she turned her Signet over.

"Your head's going to explode now, isn't it?" Miranda said.

David put his face in his hands. "Possibly."

"You want to know what possessed me."

"Yes, please."

"I don't know."

He gave her a measuring look and then nodded. "May I?"

She unclasped the chain of her Signet and tossed it to him. Both of her hands moved up to her neck . . . she felt wrong without it. She hadn't removed the Signet for any reason in three years . . . its weight and presence were a comfort, and without it she felt exposed, vulnerable, smaller.

She watched silently as David did as she had done, trying to remove the talisman from the Signet. "Wait here," he said. "I'm going to try something."

"Crowbar?" she asked.

"Laser," he replied.

She sat on her piano bench, feeling alternately scared and stupid, settling on a combination of both. Could the thing really kill her? It didn't make sense. And it didn't feel right; something about the thought sat wrong with her, and she wondered where David had gotten the intel. If it was from Deven, it might be suspect . . . but why would he lie about something potentially deadly? Did he want the talisman for himself?

Slightly sick to her stomach, she called Jonathan.

"Yes, we're still in Austin," he began, *"but—"*

"Can this thing really kill me?" she interrupted.

She could hear him doing a double take. *"What?"*

"This talisman. Was Deven telling the truth?"

He took a deep breath. *"God, Miranda, you didn't . . ."*

"Yes, I did."

"Why on Earth would you—?"

"Not the point," she snapped, anger getting the best of her. "How about a better question? How about you tell me why you didn't say anything about this before? Or why you told Faith to steal it but didn't bother warning us that it might *kill us*? Why don't you ask your Prime what kind of bullshit game he's playing that's worth my life?"

"Miranda, you weren't supposed to—"

"You know what? Forget it. Just . . . fuck you. Fuck you both."

She was crying as she threw the phone at the floor, where its screen cracked and several bits of plastic flew off toward the corners of the room.

Miranda curled up on herself and wept until she heard the door open again and, a moment later, felt David's arms around her.

"Easy, beloved," he murmured into her hair. "We'll figure this out."

She knew, without asking, that he hadn't been able to remove the talisman; she lifted up her hair so he could place the Signet back around her neck for the time being. Having it where it belonged was a relief, but it didn't soothe the mad terror and anger warring in her heart.

David said, "Assuming Deven was right, we have until Sunday to get the thing off—that's when it's supposed to activate. Tomorrow night we'll take it to Novotny and see what he can do. I'll call everyone I can think of who might know something. There's no reason to assume the worst, though; Lydia could have been telling the truth, and Deven's source could have been lying or mistaken. At this point we can't be sure."

Miranda sniffed, wiping her eyes impatiently, trying to pull herself together. "I don't suppose I could just not be wearing it that night."

"I doubt it. You're connected to the Signet as long as you're alive—I don't think taking it off changes that. But I'll drop the damn thing in the river before I'll let it harm you."

She nodded. "I know."

"Did it do anything when you attached it? Did you feel anything?"

"The carvings lit up, and it got really hot . . . then nothing. I can't feel anything now at all."

David kept his arm around her as he lifted the other to speak into his com: "Star-three."

"Star-three here, Sire."

"Report to the music room, Faith . . . *now.*"

Miranda pointed to the remains of her phone and said guiltily, "I broke another one."

David smiled. "Don't worry. Last time I wised up and ordered five more."

The Second arrived in less than five minutes, and when she saw the state Miranda was in, Faith's eyes widened. "Is everything all right?"

"Not exactly," David said, giving Faith a look that contained far more anger than she probably deserved. "We've found our thief."

Miranda showed her the talisman, and Faith went ghostly pale and sought sideways for a chair. "Oh my God."

"Very reassuring," Miranda said irritably. "Thanks."

"This is my fault," Faith answered softly. "If I had said something as soon as Deven told me . . . I should have come to you immediately, Sire, like you said . . . this is my fault."

The Prime shrugged. "Would you like me to fire you, or would you prefer we cut to the chase and behead you? We really don't have time for histrionics."

Faith's voice was disturbingly unsteady as she asked, "What should I do?"

David took out his phone and glanced at the time. "There's not much we can do tonight, but for now I want you to go back over everything Deven told you about the Stone."

"What Stone?" Miranda asked.

"That one," David told her. "It's known as the Stone of Awakening."

"But it doesn't have a stone."

"Don't ask me," he muttered. "Apparently I'm on a need-to-know basis with anything that might potentially destroy our lives. We need to widen our search for Lydia—"

"Lydia's dead," Faith said.

They both stared at her.

"Three guesses who killed her," the Second added.

David took a long, deep breath, and Miranda could feel him clamping down on a rather alarming wave of wrath that she sensed he would keep reined in until he could unleash it on a more deserving target than Faith. Heads were, quite literally, going to roll if he had his way . . . and David always got his way in the end.

"All right," he said very carefully. "Faith . . . start from the beginning."

"Sire—Sire, please wait a moment—"

The concierge was panting as he caught up with David and Faith, who had headed straight for the elevators.

David was in no mood. "What do you want?" He turned on the human, who blanched and stuttered for a moment before he could speak.

"I must inform you that Prime O'Donnell and Lord Burke are no longer with us," the man said. "They checked out before sunrise this morning. There are already new guests in their suite."

David managed not to snap the man's neck . . . barely . . . and the concierge darted away with a sketchy bow, putting the lobby and the front desk between himself and the Prime as quickly as he could.

David pulled up Deven's phone number and called it . . . no answer . . . and none on Jonathan's either.

Verging on desperation, he tried Deven's again . . . and this time, there was a reply.

"I'm sorry."

David didn't raise his voice, but he knew his rage was only marginally contained in his words. "Get your lying, manipulative ass back here and help us."

"You have to trust me, David. I had no idea she would take the Stone—but I'm going to fix this. Don't worry—I have a plan. Everything's going to be fine."

David felt a curious, detached sort of calm descend over himself; he had, it seemed, finally found his breaking point, and there was only one thing left to say. "Deven . . . go to hell."

Seventeen

There were vampire bars like Anodyne that catered to the wealthy, influential members of the Court; there were trashy places like Nepenthe; there were even two bars that catered primarily to off-duty Elite and other Haven employees. The most popular of these, Deep Six, was where Faith usually went for a postshift beer. Everyone knew her there—she even had her own spot at the bar like Norm on *Cheers*.

That wasn't where she went tonight. Tonight she wanted anonymity. She wanted to disappear.

Easier said than done in a city where the entire Shadow District knew who she was, but Faith had been to every vampire-owned establishment at least once on inspection rounds, so she was familiar with a couple of out-of-the-way dives where even a Haven vamp could fade into the background.

It helped that she was in civilian drag instead of her uniform. Her Elite fatigues were a huge part of the persona of Second in Command; in normal clothes she could feel her spine relax, her shoulders unclench . . . a little. She left her hair loose and wore long sleeves that covered her com. She could have been anyone.

She slumped on her bar stool and worked on her second beer, trying very hard not to think about work . . . but what else did she have to think about?

She was lucky she hadn't been fired. Any other employer, on finding out she had failed to deliver important information before it was too late, would have thrown her out on her ass. She was almost angry at David for not being angrier at her. Perhaps he knew that as angry as she was at herself, he didn't really need to be.

Then again the Prime tended not to waste emotion; he had changed a lot since meeting Miranda—some of the Elite were muttering that he had gotten soft, which Faith found rather laughable—but he was still way more centered than most people. He had decided, quite wisely, to focus on the problem at hand: finding out how to stop the Stone from killing Miranda and, by extension, him.

David had said he didn't blame Faith. But Faith knew that if they failed, it wouldn't matter; she would blame herself.

She would also blame Deven, of course.

"If we do die," David had said that evening, "I hereby order you, Second, to hunt down Deven and kill him just on principle."

"As you will it, Sire."

He'd been only partly joking. There was going to be hell to pay after the Stone was dealt with. Faith didn't envy Deven the consequences of his actions.

They had no idea what Deven was planning. He and Jonathan had both dropped so thoroughly off the grid, even their own Second claimed not to know where they were. Whether the Pair was trying to help or had set the whole thing up, there was no way to know. In fact the only person who didn't seem to think Deven had fucked them all over was Miranda.

It was a mystery of the Queen's personality that she held fast to her opinion of the Prime of the West no matter what kind of crap he pulled. Was it her empathic gift telling her the truth about him, or did she refuse to believe David would cheat on her with someone unworthy of his affections? Probably not the second, given that Miranda had been willing to forgive their trespasses when neither could forgive himself. Faith wouldn't have been so forgiving . . . but then, she wasn't a Queen, wasn't bound to David for eternity . . . at least, not the same way.

Faith rested her forehead in her palm. She wasn't drunk enough yet for these thoughts.

"What can I get you?" the bartender asked nearby.

"Bootlegger Brown Ale for me and another Guinness for the lady."

Faith automatically started to turn the offer down, but the words died on her lips as she recognized the voice . . . and the accent.

Her head snapped up in time to see Jeremy Hayes sit down on the stool beside hers.

She gaped at him. The bartender whisked her glass away and replaced it with a fresh one and gave Jeremy a bottle. Jeremy handed the bartender a folded bill, then turned to Faith, smiling slightly at the expression on her face.

"What's a nice girl like you doing in a place like this?" Jeremy asked, then frowned. "No, let me try again: Heaven must be missing an angel . . . wait, do angels travel armed? I don't remember my Bible very well."

She recovered enough to ask, "What the hell are you doing here?"

"Having a beer with a beautiful woman, last I checked."

"How long have you been back in town?"

Jeremy smiled again. "You're assuming I left."

"Have you left Hart's service or are you here on his behalf?"

He took a swallow of his beer and pondered the label for a moment. "It's funny: I find I quite like Texas beers, but I don't care much for Australian." He tilted the neck of his bottle toward her glass. "Always hated Guinness—it's like drinking moldy bread."

"What are you doing here?" This time she put a note of command in the words. He didn't seem to notice.

"There was a time when I favored more upscale, snooty bars than this . . . like your Anodyne, I believe. Nowadays . . . I'd much rather be around people who make an honest living. You might be surprised—most of Hart's Elite are a lot like yours. Not politically . . . they're all as pigheaded as he is up in the North . . . but when you get them out of uniform, they're just regular people who do a job, then want a beer."

Faith had no idea what game he was playing. If she went just by his tone and posture, he seemed tired, resigned. But he wasn't just here for a drink. She knew better.

"I'll ask you one more time, and then I'll get testy," she said.

"No need for either." He set the bottle down and faced her directly. "I shouldn't be here at all, but I felt that, given our recent history, I owed you at least this much."

"A beer?"

"A warning." He reached up and touched her neck, fingers light; she didn't let herself react. "And an apology. Whatever happens . . . I'm sorry to bring all of this to your door. I wish things could have been different."

Faith held his gaze. "What are you going to do, Jeremy?"

He sighed. "I never wanted to hurt anyone. For what it's worth . . . I would have liked to sit across the table from your Prime and call him an ally."

"Jeremy—"

"Leave town, Faith. If you value your life, leave Austin." Jeremy slid off the stool, smiling as he shook his head. "I know you won't, of course . . . but I had to at least try."

Again, their eyes met. "Loyalty," she said.

He nodded. "Unto death."

Then he vanished into thin air.

Faith stared at the place he'd been standing for a long minute before she pulled back her sleeve and said quietly into her com, "Star-one . . . Sire, we have a serious problem."

Before the Prime could even reply, alarms began to erupt from her phone and her com:

"This is Elite Twenty-six reporting an Alpha Seven near the intersection of . . ."

"Patrol Team Three is under fire! I repeat, we are under fire!"

". . . reported at Nepenthe. Team Eight and APD are en route . . ."

". . . requesting immediate backup! This is not a drill!"

". . . at least three dead humans, in full view of a crowd at the Riviera nightclub . . ."

Faith hit the ground running.

"Fan out!" David ordered. "Thirty-eight, Nineteen, Twelve—I want you blocking off the back exit and side windows. Anyone you catch fleeing the scene, you bring them to me. Forty-four, get those hostages secure and report back."

He barely paid attention to the affirmative responses on his com; he was otherwise occupied. The front of the building, which had not long ago been a Mexican restaurant, shuddered as the doors ripped off their hinges and crashed in opposite directions.

Three vampires emerged from the gaping hole, blades drawn, murder in their eyes. They didn't even blink when they realized whom they were fighting . . . but then, he didn't give them much time to blink.

David took the first one's head on one swing, the second's on the follow-through, then spun and rammed his sword through the third vampire's midsection, eliciting a scream of pain. The vampire went down, and David kicked him onto his back and stood on his neck.

"Who are you working for?" he demanded.

Gurgling, the vampire tried to push him off balance. David made an impatient noise, drew the wooden stake from his coat, and killed him.

He heard something whistling toward his left ear and snatched the crossbow bolt out of the air, snapping it in half with a growl. "Forty-four, the hostages?"

Elite 44 responded, *"Secured, Sire. All alive."*

"Good. Hold your position. Faith, where are you?"

"On my way, Sire. The fire at Nepenthe is under control— three casualties, one fatality, no mortals present."

There was another voice, this one male: *"This is Elite Seventy-two reporting an Alpha Six as well as an Alpha Seven at Corsican and Tenth. We've got two vampires cornered and are requesting backup."*

Faith said, *"Team Fourteen, reroute to Corsican and Tenth."*

"Acknowledged."

David retrieved his stake and sheathed it as he entered the building, where he met Elite 44 and the others he'd ordered to breach the place. "Report."

"Four assailants," Elite 44 told him. "We took them all out."

"Get the hostages to the Hausmann for assessment and then report to Faith."

"Yes, Sire!" they all said in unison, and dispersed.

David spared a moment to call Miranda. "How's the network holding up?" he asked.

Her voice was tight with tension. *"Fine. I'm watching the entire spectacle at a nice, safe, useless distance."*

"Good," he replied. "I don't want you anywhere near the city tonight. As many humans as we've had to rescue, you'd be recognized in a heartbeat. The Hausmann is already at capacity."

"I recalled every off-duty Elite in the city," Miranda said with a sigh. *"We've tripled patrol teams, and I have the entire District on lockdown. Every club and bar is closed and being searched, and every vampire is being questioned. Do we have any idea where all these bastards are coming from?"*

"All I know is they're in league with Hayes. No one seems to know his endgame—they were all hired in small groups over the past week to cause chaos, but they're not organized in any significant way. There are similar situations in a few other cities, though nothing like we have here. The idea seems to be to spread us thin and wear us out."

"Well, it's working," Miranda observed. *"We've lost two Elite and have four more injured. As good as we are, we're not equipped for this kind of mass insanity."*

"Don't worry, beloved. They have to stop at dawn, and

that gives us time to plan. Right now we're catching them as fast as they—"

"Sire, we've got another Alpha Six in progress about two blocks from your location. What are your orders?"

"Send me the coordinates, Faith," David answered. "Miranda, I've got to go."

"Be safe," she said. *"Please come home in one piece."*

David hung up in time for the location of the attack to come up on his phone and, without giving himself time to think about how exhausted he already was, Misted directly there.

As he emerged from the darkness, sword drawn and blood on his mind, he saw that the situation was already under control; a group of vampires clad in Elite uniforms had surrounded two others, who had been in the process of feeding out in the open on a pair of young women who looked like they were on their way home from clubbing.

The Prime paused. The Elite on the scene were all unfamiliar. In fact, they were wearing—

"My Lord Prime," one of the warriors said, bowing. "We have this one under control."

"Who the hell are you?" David asked.

"Elite Thirteen, Western United States," the warrior said. "At your service."

David frowned. "You're Deven's people."

"Yes, Sire. We were dispatched from San Diego at sunset by the Consort and ordered to place ourselves under your command."

David momentarily considered telling the Elite to shove off, but the truth was, they needed the help, and he knew firsthand just how accomplished the Western Elite was. "Very well." He quickly brought up the network on his phone and set up a temporary loop to Elite 13, which he patched in to Faith. "My Second will be with you in a moment. I don't suppose . . . your boss didn't let you know where he was, did he?"

"No, Sire. The West is currently in our Second's capable hands, and the situation is normal."

"Lucky Thomas," David said. "Thank you for coming."

Faith arrived a moment later. "You don't have any reservations about trusting them, given the current situation with Deven?" she asked.

"I'll worry about that after the city finishes imploding. Get them to work. I want a sit-rep in thirty minutes."

"As you will it, Sire."

Faith darted over to the guest Elite and began issuing orders while the team she'd brought saw to the humans who had been attacked as well as the corpses of their attackers.

Whatever Jeremy's intentions, he was getting a lot of his own kind killed. There had been two Elite lost, yes, but more sobering was the number of dead who were responsible for the violence—fifteen so far. They had about two hours before the sky lightened . . . how many more lives could be lost in two hours?

David's eyes narrowed. Now was not the time to care about the body count; now was the time to make it higher . . . and as soon as Austin was secured, he was going to find Jeremy Hayes and make him pay for each and every death he'd caused.

The Queen understood that the sensor network, which now covered the entire Southern territory, was a thing of breathless technological beauty. She had heard half the Primes at the Council gathering singing its praises and expressing their desire to have something like it for themselves—those same Primes who had found David's reliance on technology childish were now foaming at the mouth to buy copies of the software. David had no intention of selling it to them, of course; he was working on a second version with about half the features that he would license to other Signets, but the real network, the sprawling labyrinthine creation of David Solomon, PhD, existed in exactly one territory.

Miranda knew it was a stupendous achievement. She just had no idea how the hell it worked.

She sat in David's chair in the server room with two monitors up at the same time; one showed the city's sensor grid and all vampire activity therein, and the other basically showed the user manual . . . what there was of one. David had made copious notes during the network's creation, but all of the coding and a lot of the details were locked in his head along with all of the passwords to get into the actual programming code. From the manual she could figure out how most of what she was looking at was set up. He had taught her the basic functions and how to interpret the grid, but there was so much going on at once in the dozen or more interlocking programs that made up the whole system, it kept giving her alerts and alarms she had never seen before.

But if this was all she could do right now, by God, she was going to do it right. The Elite were depending on her to keep an eye on the city while they dealt with each individual threat. David couldn't monitor the network and fight at the same time, and it was clear from the start that they needed all swords on deck.

It was a frustrating role reversal for the Pair. For the past three years Miranda had been the one stalking the streets more often than not. She had earned her reputation quickly in Austin—first because she was so angry at her husband's infidelity that she didn't want to be around him, and then because he had devoted his entire attention to expanding the network throughout the South. He was so busy with his servers and gadgets that Miranda became the presence the Shadow District recognized as its Signet.

That had worked fine until now, when she was stuck at home feeling like a fifties housewife and he was off bringing order to the streets.

She knew that what she was doing was important. Someone had to run the servers in a situation like this, to watch for anomalies and help Faith dispatch the Elite teams to where they were needed. It could be done from the field if necessary, but with the Haven's servers behind her Miranda could work much faster and see a much larger area at a time. David and the Elite were limited to what they could do with phones and coms. Already tonight Miranda's keen eye had helped stop a murder before it could happen, based entirely on her gut feeling when she saw a particular group of vampires converging on an area that she knew was populated with families that time of night.

She wasn't helpless. She was doing her job.

But which job?

Miranda sat back a moment, eyes still glued to the array of colored dots representing her people and the enemy all over downtown Austin.

She should be there. She could fight, and the Shadow World knew she was fearless; she and David together were terrifying. They could clamp down on the whole city and have this mess dealt with by morning, no problem . . . but she couldn't risk being recognized by one of the humans they'd saved. Even after a memory wipe it was too risky.

For all their planning and contrivances, she had stumbled into exactly what she'd dreaded the most: Her two worlds were at odds, and no matter what she did, one of the two would suffer for it. She could go into the city and fight and possibly cause a media firestorm, even risking the exposure of the Shadow World; or she could sit here and protect her musical career while people died.

The worst part was that unless something miraculous happened, none of it was going to matter. The new moon was tomorrow night, and so far no one had been able to find a solution to the problem of the Stone of Awakening. It was still stuck firmly to Miranda's Signet, and as far as anyone knew, it was still going to kill her.

Janousek had an operative who, he said, had information that might help, but they wouldn't hear from him until this afternoon, which was evening in Europe. Laveau was questioning a small branch of the Order of Elysium that operated out of Baton Rouge, but so far, she'd found no evidence that anything out of the ordinary was going on. If the Order was planning to do the Awakening ritual, it was being kept hush-hush; the priest that Laveau had spoken to said that for something so important, only the highest echelons of the Order, the High Priestess and her Acolytes, would be allowed to know anything about it. If the Pairs wanted to learn the truth, they had to find the High Priestess, and the only person who might have known where she was, Lydia, was dead.

As the night waned, the city quieted somewhat. Come dawn the entire mess would be forced to a halt—the question was, would it begin again at sundown? They would have about twelve hours to figure out a more cohesive strategy than simply putting out fires.

To that end, Miranda had been taking advantage of what she'd gleaned from the user manual and was compiling readings on the attacks so far to see if they had originated at a common point. That point would most likely be Jeremy's headquarters. It was looking pretty random so far—as much as she hated to admit it, it might take another night like tonight to get enough data points.

"Star-two, this is Elite Forty in the underground garage, reporting that the Prime's vehicle has just pulled in."

Miranda sighed. "Thank you, Elite Forty."

She issued the command to reroute authorization to David's laptop and locked down the server room before taking the stairs up to the ground level. She was just in time; the Prime was making his way down the hall toward their suite, and she ran to him, catching him as he wobbled from sheer exhaustion.

"Jesus, baby . . ." Miranda put her arm around him and held him up the rest of the way to the suite. "Are you hurt? I didn't feel any serious injuries."

"I'm fine," he insisted. "Just wrung out. I had a few cuts but they're all healed. I'm just kind of disgusting—I called ahead to have Esther run a bath for both of us."

"Smart move," she replied. "No way you're standing on your feet much longer. Come on . . . let's get you cleaned up and you can rest."

He shook his head. "Can't. I need to review the data and go over reports from the team leaders, then coordinate with APD for tonight's response—"

"And you can do all of that after a bath and a nap," she said firmly. "We can't do a damn thing about this for a good twelve hours, and you have got to rest or you'll do something stupid and get us killed."

"Oh, you mean like stealing a talisman with a hex on it?" he muttered.

She punched him in the shoulder a little harder than she really intended to.

David grunted in pain. "It was a joke."

"A bad joke."

"I know, love. I'm sorry. Here, can you help me get my shirt off? My shoulder's gone all fucked."

"Here . . ." Miranda placed her hands on either side of his neck and closed her eyes, breathing out slowly, letting energy pass from her to him. The power shored up his waning strength and helped ease the various aches and pains he hadn't had the time or concentration to heal while out in the field. Still, she helped him undress slowly in deference to his weariness. She'd never seen him so worn out.

"It wasn't your fault," David was saying as she helped him into the steaming hot tub. "You didn't know what the talisman was supposed to do. For all we knew at the time, Lydia was telling the truth. She still might have been. She was part of the Order, after all—I'd believe her story before I'd believe Deven's."

"Yes, well, right now you'd believe the Easter Bunny before you'd believe Deven. We don't know where his intel came from either. But they can't both be right."

Miranda stripped off her own clothes and slid into the water beside him with a sigh. "God bless Esther," she murmured, groping sideways for the washcloth and body wash she knew was on the side of the tub. As she had done a number of times before, she lathered up the cloth and began scrubbing David's skin, revealing its pristine ivory beneath the dried smears of blood and grime. He was in better shape than he'd been in after that first battle at the Haven, but this time he was way more tired; the Elite had been all over the city all night long, and he had spent profligate amounts of his energy Misting from place to place to try to stop attackers from killing humans or other vampires.

"Jacob said to expect a call just before sunset," she told the Prime. "He sounded fairly optimistic."

"What else did he say?" David asked, eyes closed, body relaxing gradually under her care.

"He said they have a suspect in custody for the car bomb—one of the servants, a recent hire. They're pretty sure he was working for someone, but he won't talk, even under interrogation."

David snorted quietly. "Jacob is not an interrogator. They should send the bastard to me."

"Don't underestimate him," Miranda admonished gently, taking a moment to rub some of the tension out of his shoulders. "Jacob can be fierce when he needs to be."

"Well, there's not much need for it anyway," David said, his voice growing more and more drowsy the longer she worked on him, her hands moving in slow circles down his arms, then over his back, under the water. She leaned him back to wet his hair and set to massaging his scalp, and finally she caught a ghost of a contented smile on his face. "I think our mysterious bomber's been identified."

"Jeremy Hayes," Miranda agreed. "If Faith really saw him Mist, it explains a lot . . . except who the hell he is. For that we need more information . . . we need . . ."

"Don't say it," David said suddenly, eyes opening, gaze hard. "Even if we can find them, I'm not asking for their help. We'll figure this out on our own."

"I know," she replied soothingly, nudging him back into the water. "I know how you feel. I wasn't suggesting otherwise. We've got resources of our own, and we'll find out who Hayes really is . . . just rest for now, baby. Just rest for a little while, and then we'll go back to work."

He sighed and let her go back to her ministrations without further comment. Before long, he was sound asleep.

Miranda rested him back against the side of the tub while she bathed herself, watching her husband sleep, wondering in the back of her mind where the hell Deven and Jonathan had disappeared to right when they were truly needed . . . and hoping against hope that whatever they were doing, they weren't out there making things even worse.

The Cloister had stood for hundreds of years, hidden among the forests of northern California, surrounded by mist and the scent of the sea. Within its hallowed walls were kept the secrets of the Order of Elysium—their history, their laws. About two dozen vampires made up the priesthood of Persephone, and they were among the few immortals left on earth who kept Her religion safe from the vagaries of time.

The Order had traveled to these shores back in the days of the earliest human settlers, hoping to escape a period of vampire-hunting hysteria that swept through Europe in the Age of Inquisition. Since then it had mostly been left behind by the Shadow World, a relic of an age long forgotten, drifting through the years until their time would come again to step forward and lead their people back to their Goddess. They were patient. They watched the stars for omens, and they waited.

The High Priestess, Eladra, was more than a thousand years old. Her disciples, known as the Acolytes, had not left the confines of the Cloister for centuries. They, and only they, had access to the ancient rituals that had once defined vampire civilization—rituals that, it was said, had helped create the Signets themselves. Legend had it that the Acolytes were each as powerful as a Prime, if not more so.

But for all their power, they died like every other vampire.

Eladra sank to her knees at the foot of the altar, her hands at her chest, groping for the wooden shaft that jutted from her sternum. Her eyes were wide with agony, but there was no real surprise on her pale, lined face as she stared up at her killer. She knew the omens, she watched the stars, she knew that death was coming for her . . . and death stood over her, impassive, and watched her die.

The stone walls of the Cloister had kept out the world, but now instead of a shelter, they were a tomb. One by one the Acolytes fell that night—by the sword, by the stake, slaughtered one by one, until the entire priesthood of the Dark Mother lay dead, their blood running thick over the cold floor.

In the silence that followed, he knelt in front of the altar where the collected ritual texts of the Order were kept in an enormous leather-bound book. Each branch of the Order had a copy of the common liturgy and rites, but this one was the one that held the secrets of the Awakening; only the inner circle of the priesthood had been trusted with the future of their kind. There might be others with the texts, or the arcane ability, but as far as anyone in the Shadow World knew, only the Cloister had been prepared to perform the ritual at the appointed hour. They were the only chance vampirekind had to call their Goddess back.

As the pages went up in flames, beatifying the dead in a golden halo of firelight, Deven turned to the High Priestess's body. He stared at her for a long moment while the flames spread over the tapestries that hung behind the altar.

"Forgive me, Mother, for I have sinned," he said softly, then closed Eladra's vacant eyes in benediction.

Eighteen

When the Cloister caught fire, it could be seen for miles, even among the dense rain forests of the Northwest. The smell of burning wood—and burning bodies—would hang heavily in the air for days and nights. The humidity of the coastal forests and the stone walls of the Cloister itself kept the fire from spreading. The walls would still stand, but there would be nothing inside them but blackness.

Jonathan stood at the brow of the hill, watching it from far away, almost hypnotized by the beauty of the flames—pink and orange and almost white, such butterfly colors to signify the end of one of the few things about their world that was still beautiful. From this distance it looked small and insignificant . . . until it burned.

He waited a while longer, then gave up his vigil and went back into the cabin.

If anyplace counted as the flat-ass middle of nowhere, this was it, a private getaway owned by someone who owed the Signet a favor. No phones, no Internet, intermittent cell service. It had unreliable electricity and running water from a well for part of the year. But they had come prepared.

Jonathan set about building a fire; the first quiet drums of rain had already begun, and soon the little ramshackle room would be freezing. He banked the coals from earlier and fed them.

He cranked up the water in the ancient shower to let it

run until it grew as hot as it could get, then closed the room to hold in the steam. He fetched blood from a bag and warmed it in a plain glass tumbler, probably risking life and limb by using the tiny microwave. It was human blood, which had pleased them both; this far out in the middle of nowhere they'd been lucky not to have to make do with deer, but lumberjacks, it seemed, hurt themselves regularly, so the local clinic was well stocked.

Jonathan went about the duties of a typical housewife, preparing a comfortable home and meal for his bread-winner, who would come home exhausted and distant, and need his helpmate to whisk away dirty boots and bring him a glass of whiskey.

Jonathan tried not to think about it in those terms. He tried instead to focus on what Deven was going to need—and better yet, what shape he would be in when he got back from tonight's grisly errand.

David and Miranda might find fault . . . no, they almost certainly would. But this time the fault lay in both Prime and Consort's hands. Jonathan had agreed with the plan. It was ugly, but it was necessary. If the ritual to activate the Stone could be performed only once, on this new moon, then it had to be stopped. The only way to be sure of that was to make sure no one was alive to perform it and that the text was destroyed. Goddess, demon, whatever the rite tried to summon . . . her chance was long gone now.

Finally, finally, Jonathan heard the back door to the cabin swing open and shut, and he reached back with his senses to verify the energy signature of his Prime. He waited a moment to see if Deven spoke.

Nothing.

Jonathan heard him slowly removing his weapons and laying them out on the table where a length of cloth already waited to hold them while they were cleaned. Ghostlight, its blade wiped cursorily but still smeared with dark blood; four hilted stakes, each with wood shafts that would need replacement; two long knives, bloody; two wood-tipped throwing stars, bloody.

He didn't interrupt. This was a sacred ritual to Deven, one of the few he had left. Jonathan let him keep it in silence.

Ghostlight was cleaned first, sheathed, and placed on the mantel. The other knives got similar treatment, but the stars and stakes would have to be refitted with new wooden parts and sharpened, and they'd keep until later. Dev placed them all together in a locked box until he had a moment to care for them.

Jonathan followed him into the bathroom, where he began the next phase of purification: his clothes. Red Shadow standard black BDUs, soaked and stained with blood and grime, stripped off and dropped with far less ceremony than the weapons; they were essentially disposable. The only thing Deven kept were his boots, of course, wiped down carefully and lined up by the door near the rest of the weapons.

When he was undressed, Deven climbed into the shower, and still, neither of them spoke as he scrubbed and rinsed smear after smear of blood from his body, none of it his.

Jonathan picked up the discarded clothes and looked them over. No rips or slices. The Cloister had no armed guards. It depended on its remote location and secrecy for protection; it had apparently not occurred to the priesthood that any of the Order's members might want to hurt them. The blood was mostly splatter, except for what looked like a handprint around the left ankle . . . had someone in her death throes begged for mercy? Had Deven given it?

He probably had . . . but Deven's brand of mercy was to deal out a swift death, not a long life.

Jonathan had clean clothes waiting when Deven emerged from the steam a very different creature: softer, smaller somehow, his hair falling into his weary eyes, his thin body looking frail instead of graceful. Jonathan held out a huge towel to fold the Prime into and held on to him for a long moment, feeling the mix of emotions twisting around themselves in Deven's mind. Satisfaction, yes, and triumph, but also a deep sadness he was trying not to let surface.

"I'm fine," Deven said, almost sounding angry. "Stop looking at me like you think I'm going to keen like a widow. I've been an assassin for most of seven centuries—why should this be any different?"

Jonathan just looked at him for a moment before he said, "You just killed your sire, Deven."

"So?" Deven withdrew from Jonathan's embrace. "She wanted me to be her successor—it's really rather poetic when you think about it."

Another long look. Deven shook his head, losing patience, and turned to go to bed, where a special sort of nightmare would likely be waiting for him this time.

Deven paused at the bedroom door. "Call Miranda," he said softly. "Tell her not to worry anymore."

Jonathan nodded.

Miranda leaned the side of her head against the chimney and sang quietly into the darkness, punctuating each line of the song with a sip from her beer:

> *The stars at night are big and bright . . .*
> *Deep in the heart of Texas . . .*

Out there, in the glow of the city far below the stars, her husband and her friend were in mortal peril, again, trying to bring the city back under control. This was the third night of the insanity. Somehow Jeremy Hayes had brought in dozens, if not hundreds, of vampires he had hired to tear the city down, and ordered them all to strike, to cause utter chaos, to destroy the Pair's hold on their own territory using the bodies of innocents whenever possible.

Last night David had given up trying to coordinate from the Haven and moved an entire mobile command unit to the Hausmann, one of the few vampire-owned establishments that hadn't already been vandalized. From there he ran the sensor network and coordinated all the teams, including the visiting Elite from California and, in a surprise move, another cadre of loaner warriors, this one from Eastern Europe.

Jacob wanted answers about the explosion. David needed help getting things under control so he could give Jacob answers. It was logical, then, for Jacob to send as many Elite as he could spare, which amounted to only a dozen, but that was damn fine by David; the sooner they got this over with, the sooner they could turn their attention back to the explosion and what the hell was going on in the bigger picture.

Miranda knew that David had been reluctant to accept outside help, for fear of appearing weak, but the word had already gone out that the South was under a massive and coordinated attack, and rather than delighting the Council by falling into riot and looting, the South had circled its wagons and was eliminating the threats one by one with a ruthless efficiency that had, Miranda could tell, shocked the shit out of most of the other Primes. David enfolded the loaner Elite into his own troops seamlessly and already had half the city back in hand that second night. The uprisings in other cities had been far easier to put down, but it was still just a matter of time. Tonight, the new moon, there were only pockets of resistance left in Austin, and while David ran the network and dispatched teams to hot spots, the vampires of the Haven showed the world once again what they were made of.

Faith had thrown herself into the fray like a berserker; she was at the head of every major operation, kicking down doors and slicing off heads and hauling in witnesses without breaking a sweat.

Miranda was worried about her. There was something wild and almost desperate in her eyes these last few days— like she was looking for one fight too many. David was pretty clumsy with emotions, but Faith did her level best to make it seem like she didn't have any at all; Miranda, however, could feel Faith's all-business exterior cracking, and it was only a matter of time before she did something stupid. If they could just get the city calmed down again, Miranda would talk to her.

Then there was Miranda, poor left-behind Miranda, too chicken to fight in case someone might see her and figure out her super-secret alter ego.

She really did try not to be angry at or feel sorry for herself. There was more than just her career at stake, here—until they found a way to stop the Awakening ritual, she was vulnerable, and there was no telling what was going to happen to her when those Elysium crazies did their magic hoo-hah and tried to suck the life out of her.

But so far there was no deus ex machina ringing her up to deliver good news and tell her that the truth was the Stone was really just a very Goth paperweight or change purse or something. She didn't know what to expect or when to expect it . . . Would she just drop dead? Would it hurt? Would it really kill David, too? Or had there been some kind of mistake, and Lydia was right all along?

As the hours ticked by, her hope that Jacob—or even Deven—would call with a reprieve diminished, until it was just Miranda, sitting on a roof, singing to the sky.

Her phone rang.

Miranda listlessly dug around for it in her pocket. "Hello?"

"Don't hang up," came a British accent, almost unrecognizable in its gravity.

"Okay," she said. She no longer had any fight left in her. The enormity of her own failure in all of this, confronted with the insanity of the thought that she'd ever get to choose what life she wanted to lead, had drained all the fight from her body and voice. Maybe it would be better if . . .

"It's done, Miranda."

She frowned. "What's done?"

"The ritual . . . the Awakening. It won't happen. It can't happen. Ever. You're safe. I give you my word."

She stared out over the Haven grounds, uncomprehending. "Wh . . . what did you do?"

Jonathan sighed. "I did nothing, Miranda. Don't worry about the details this time . . . This time just let it go, all right? The ritual can't be performed."

"Why not?"

He paused, then said quietly, "There's no one left to perform it."

Miranda felt herself go cold. "He killed them . . . all of them . . . to save us."

"Down to the last Acolyte. Down to the servants. Twenty-eight total. He slew them all and then burned their bodies and their texts. The priesthood of Persephone is no more, Miranda. That thing around your neck is just metal and will be forever."

She clutched her beer bottle as if it were a life preserver. "Just like that . . . he just . . . killed them all . . ."

"Yes. Every last one, with his own blade. He couldn't trust an agent to do this."

"And . . . what will that do to him?"

"Why do you care?" Jonathan asked harshly. "He doesn't have feelings, right? It's all just a game to us both."

Miranda caught herself halfway through a sob, and Jonathan's voice immediately gentled. "I'm sorry, Miranda. I don't mean to be a bastard."

Miranda was crying, though why, she didn't know; it could be relief, but it didn't feel like relief. It felt almost like capitulation, like she had lost something precious, some chance she'd never get again.

"Thank you for letting me know," she half whispered. "We'll talk later once things settle down, okay?"

Now he sounded relieved. Deven getting David's forgiveness would take a while, but at least Jonathan still had a friend in Miranda. "Yes. Of course. I'll check in on you tomorrow night."

They hung up, and Miranda wiped at her eyes.

She looked down at her Signet, turning the amulet over and exposing the Stone. She was glad, of course, that she wasn't going to die, but . . .

What if they'd been wrong about what it did? What if . . . what if Lydia was the one who knew the truth, and now all those vampires were dead . . . What if Deven had destroyed the entire Order of Elysium and all the knowledge of Signet history they might have been able to share—

knowledge they still needed, even if this Awakening never took place—and it was all for nothing?

She took a deep breath. Right or wrong, it was done.

The ruby in her Signet shone gently in the darkness, its light comforting to her frazzled nerves. After a moment she took a deep breath and dialed David.

"Can't talk now, beloved—kicking ass," he said a bit breathlessly, and hung up before she could reply.

She had to smile. Such a strange life she'd stumbled into. She would never have thought she would consider her own life worth the lives of two dozen others . . . and she was hardly proving that worth right now, sitting here doing nothing. Far more than twenty-eight lives were at stake right now, and it was supposed to be her duty to protect them.

Her smile faded, and she tucked her phone back in her pocket and touched her Signet again. David and Faith were out there defending the city. She should be there, too.

And if someone recognized her, they'd deal with it somehow . . . She couldn't worry about that now, with so much at risk. If the entire Order of Elysium had died so she could remain Queen, and all her Elite and her Prime were risking life and limb to protect Austin's people, immortal and otherwise . . . what was she doing here?

Miranda stood up on the roof, heartbeat quickening with a sudden and overwhelming sense of purpose.

To hell with this. I have work to do.

She left the roof and ran down to their suite, took up Shadowflame, and headed for her car.

Some people found their way to Witchcraft because of spiritual longing. They weren't satisfied with mainstream religion and yearned for something different: something that honored the divine feminine, perhaps, or that didn't threaten to cast them into hell for falling in love with the wrong person. In Wicca and the other neo-Pagan faiths that practiced the Craft, they found something that had been missing from the church services of their youths.

Then there were Witches like Stella who went hunting for something a little different.

She had known she was strange from childhood, of course; people looked at her funny when she said certain things, and one of the questions she heard most often, usually in an accusatory tone, was, "How did you know that?" She tried to explain it for a while, but eventually she realized that what she was Seeing scared people and she had to cut it out if she wanted to have friends and not end up in the nuthouse.

Most kids with psychic gifts went one of two ways: They clamped down on their talents until those talents disappeared, or they went crazy. Stella knew that mental hospitals were full of people who had been medicated out of their gifts, who couldn't make sense of what they knew or told the wrong person and got sent away for it. She could only imagine the kind of hell that would be.

Stella was one of the quiet ones . . . but her gifts never went away. She never denied them. She just learned when to keep her mouth shut . . . until she got to college and learned there were people out there whose entire religion was built around the idea that the kind of thing she could do was perfectly normal. Not all Wiccans were outstandingly psychic. Lark, for example, could do magic but didn't have a strong individual gift like Stella's Sight. Those who weren't psychic learned to use whatever they had, and those who were found their way to teachers like Foxglove.

Well . . . most did. A few still went crazy. But at least in the Pagan community they had a fighting chance.

She remembered when she'd been a new little Witchlet and had been determined to share her discoveries with her father. She'd worn a giant pentagram and carried her books around proudly. It wasn't as though they'd been devoutly religious before that. The last time she could remember being in church was for her stepmother's funeral.

Still, tell an Irish Catholic guy his daughter's a Witch, and the result was pretty predictable.

Now they circled around each other on tiptoe, carefully avoiding The Subject. And in the handful of days since

Stella and Lark were attacked, her dad was even more careful with the eggshells he walked on. Apparently seeing her in a hospital bed had shaken him up enough that questions of Satan were no longer quite so pressing.

Stella sat at her altar, which was basically a wooden banana crate with a piece of discounted sari fabric draped over it, decked with her favorite religious knickknacks and, just now, a deck of tarot cards.

She stared at the resin statue of the Goddess in front of her; it depicted the two faces of the Goddess Persephone, one a maiden with a loving smile and the other a raven-haired queen holding a basket of pomegranates. Stella hadn't been sure when she bought the statue whether the nice half was Persephone's alter ego, Kore, as she was known before she was taken to Hades, or her little-known twin, Theia, whom Stella had only seen mentioned once or twice in really esoteric out-there literature and who, most archaeologists agreed, had never been widely worshipped.

It wasn't that Stella worshipped Persephone, exactly—she just liked the image, and it made her feel grounded and safe to meditate in front of Her. Stella wasn't really sure she believed in gods the way some other Pagans did; she believed in the idea of God but wasn't sold on the specifics. Luckily like most religions Wicca—in theory at least—didn't focus so much on everyone believing the same way as it did on everyone celebrating the same holidays.

Persephone, Queen of the Underworld . . . Stella bit her lip, her eyes shifting sideways to another image she had kept on her altar for years: the cover shot from Miranda Grey's CD. The image of the singer had been painted, not photographed.

Now she knew why.

She knew why she had been drawn to Miranda, why she'd felt like Miranda would understand what she was going through as someone who was different. Even before she was a vampire, Miranda had her gift, and it made her crazy—at least that was what Stella had gleaned from their all-too-brief conversation and her own intuition. Empathy, untrained, could drive someone to suicide really easily. Stella had never met anyone with it, but she'd heard stories.

She's a vampire. An honest-to-God, blood-drinking, daytime-sleeping, fanged vampire. What the hell has gone wrong with your life, Stella Maguire, that this is your reality now?

She still wasn't clear on exactly why Miranda showed up on cell phone cameras but didn't have a reflection, but from what Gandalf had told her, a lot of the old vampire lore either was misguided or simply didn't apply, and modern technology had changed a lot about how the immortals lived. For example, every vampire in Austin was being monitored by some sort of network to make sure they didn't hurt anyone, and that was how the good guys— Stella shook her head bemusedly at the term—knew she and Lark were in trouble.

In the picture Miranda wore that same ruby amulet, the Signet, her badge of office . . . but there was more to it than that, Stella knew. Gandalf didn't know much about the Signets specifically, but he knew the basic organization of the Shadow World and had reluctantly told Stella as much as he could, hoping, she figured, that it would scare her away.

She was pretty sure his idea had worked. The thought that there really were vampires out there—hundreds of them, eating people, right under everyone's noses—made her question every alley she'd ever walked past that gave her the creeps, every shady-looking person staring out at her from a doorway, every trick of the light that made her wonder if someone was there. What was stopping them from coming into everyone's houses and killing every human they wanted to? Why should they care about taking lives if they really were that strong and fast?

Miranda.

Stella remembered the look on Miranda's face as she heard about what had happened. There was a determination there, an authority; and she remembered Miranda's rarely-seen-in-public husband, David, having that same aura, the same quiet nobility. Somehow they had power over every vampire here and kept them from killing. Those glowing amulets made all the difference. The way Stella's dad had deferred to David, the way they'd spoken to each other . . . she had never seen her father cowed before, especially not by some guy in a trench coat looking like a cast extra from *The Matrix*. But Maguire had listened to the Prime and to the Queen . . . though he didn't seem so much afraid as respectful.

Dad knew. He knew all along.

She wanted to call him. She wanted so badly to call him and tell him straight out that Miranda's vamp-mojo hadn't worked and Stella remembered everything. A few details were hazy, but everything in the clinic was crystal clear. Everything about Miranda was etched in stone in her memory and would stay there the rest of her life. She wanted so badly to call her father out on it, to demand that he tell her everything. How long had he been working with them? Did they obey human laws at all, or was it just a courtesy that they spoke to APD?

At least now she knew why her dad had objected so strongly, at first, to her rabid Miranda Grey fan-girling. He'd known what Miranda really was. No doubt he'd wanted Stella to stay as far away as she could.

"Too late now, Dad," Stella whispered into the silent room, her breath causing the candle on the altar to flicker. She'd sat down to try and clear her head. That was what the cards were for. Normally she didn't need them, but as Foxglove had explained in her classes, tarot cards and runes and other oracles didn't make someone see the future; they acted like a contact lens for your third eye, helping you to See more clearly and, at the very least, listen to your own intuition. Sometimes when she was confused, she would get a sensible answer from the cards even though her conscious mind was riding the Tilt-a-Whirl.

"What do I do?" she asked, eyes on Persephone again. "Do I pretend it never happened and go on like normal? How can I do that? Do I tell Lark? Do I try to talk to Miranda, or would she just try to Etch-a-Sketch my mind again? Would they hurt me if they knew I know? Or will they hurt me anyway? What do I do? Please . . ."

She shuffled the tarot cards mindlessly for a moment, trying to stay calm, then laid out three in a row for a quickie reading. At least she could get a direction to steer her thoughts in.

The first card was the Tower.

Stella swallowed hard. The Tower spelled violent upheaval, disaster, a total reordering of reality. It usually was for the best, a needed change, but it came at great cost and often through suffering.

"Awesome." She sighed.

The next card: Death.

Most normal people always freaked out when they saw the Death card, but in truth, it didn't usually mean actual death so much as irreversible transformation. It had foretold a few literal deaths, she was sure, but that was rare. Still, with the Tower . . . someone had a shitty hell of a time coming, and soon. Stella hoped it wasn't her.

"Okay, who's it for?" she asked. "Can you tell me that?"

She turned over the last card:

The Queen of Swords.

As soon as she saw the image on the card, she threw herself backward, seized with fear, and with *knowledge*. In her deck, the Queen of Swords stared at the viewer standing sideways, her long katana-like sword at the ready, her flame-red hair caught in a wind that carried with it autumn leaves, spun from a tree and falling. All around her were the colors of flame, and beyond the fire . . . darkness.

Miranda.

She's in danger.

Stella felt herself rocking back and forth, trying to shake her way out of the knowledge, and as she did, the candle flared up so brightly it almost looked like the Queen of Swords herself had truly caught fire.

And from somewhere deep inside Stella's heart, some corner she had barely even known existed, the voice came: *Go to her, child. Go to her now. Go to her.*

Stella was on her feet before she could think, grabbing her backpack and a flashlight and her can of Mace, and pulling on her boots. "Where? Where do I go?"

She strained to hear an answer, but her vision felt dragged back to her altar, where it fixed on the image of the Tower.

The Tower was burning as it fell. The world was burning as it fell.

Stella snatched up her cell phone and ran for the door.

Nineteen

The Shadow District had never been so quiet.

Miranda steered her car through the streets of Austin past landmarks that were usually mobbed this time of night, even on a Sunday. There were no valets outside the Black Door, and no line of patrons waiting to enter. The windows of Anodyne were dark. There were people about— she saw a few humans passing through on their way to or from somewhere, no one lingering, probably remarking to each other that it was quiet . . . too quiet. Aside from that and a few Elite standing watch, the District was a graveyard.

She pulled into a space in front of the Hausmann. She sucked at parallel parking, but there were no other cars on the entire block, so she was unlikely to aggravate anyone.

As she got out, buckling Shadowflame to her belt and making sure the car was locked, an Elite approached her. "My Lady—we weren't expecting you in the city tonight."

Miranda looked around. Eerie. There might as well be tumbleweeds rolling down the street.

"What's the situation?" she asked.

"Things have been calm for the last half hour," the Elite replied. "The Prime just returned from putting down a nest of hoodlums who were trashing the Plague Rat."

Miranda snorted. "How could they tell it was trashed?"

When the warrior failed to reply, Miranda sighed and asked, "What about the Second?"

"She's still out on the streets—we got word of a potential human attack and she took her team to snuff it out before anyone could get hurt."

"Thank you," Miranda said, taking the steps to the clinic. The guards out front bowed and let her pass.

The cacophony shocked her. She wasn't expecting the clinic to be full, and the wall of noise and emotion that hit her nearly knocked her off her feet. She had to pause and bolster her shields, take a breath, and get her bearings.

Every curtained cubicle in the clinic's main area was occupied. Nurses in black scrubs moved gracefully from one to another, poetic in their efficiency, checking IVs and making notes on charts. They were all calm but tense. About half the patients were vampires and half were human, in a variety of conditions. One person looked like she was in a coma. Most were bloody. In one cubicle the figure on the stretcher had been covered head to toe in a sheet.

Miranda had no idea where to go; she was about to grab the nearest Elite and ask where David was, but one of the nurses in the bay to her left shouted, "I need a hand here!"

The Queen was closest. She darted into the cubicle. "Where?"

"Right here—keep pressure while I clamp this off—"

Miranda did as she was told, sticking her hand out to press down on the pad of gauze the nurse had indicated that seemed to be all that was holding a vampire's blood vessel closed. The Elite on the gurney had been stabbed in several places including the thigh, and Miranda thought it might be the femoral artery she was holding, but she really didn't know anatomy well enough to be sure. There was a veritable ocean of blood soaking the vampire's uniform and the sheet below him, and his eyes were glazed with agony.

The nurse was doing something with a pair of steel clamps that Miranda couldn't really see given how she had to hold her arms. They must have gotten the Elite stabilized enough in the field to transfer him here, though she couldn't imagine how.

"Harder," the nurse commanded. She still hadn't looked up from her patient. "Hold for another ten seconds . . . nine . . . eight . . ."

By the time she reached one, the bleeding had stopped. The vampire's healing ability had caught up with the wound thanks to two people holding the vessel shut. Miranda watched the artery close itself and let out her breath in relief.

"All right," the nurse said. "I'll stitch this up to help it heal faster, but I think you're out of the woods, Lieutenant. I'll get you something for the pain—" She looked over at Miranda. "Thanks for the . . . oh."

Miranda managed a faintly seasick smile. "You're welcome. Do you need anything else?"

"Um . . . I . . . no . . . I . . . no, my Lady. I can take it from here if you'd like to wash up."

Miranda looked down at herself. She was bloodstained from belly to knees, and her hands looked like she'd dipped them in paint. She took the towel the nurse offered to stop the dripping and moved back out of the way, heading for the restrooms.

There wasn't much she could do for her clothes, but she got her arms clean in the sink. Beyond the ladies' room door someone cried out in pain, and she heard monitors beeping shrilly. For some reason she thought of the video she and Mo had made for the blog, and her heart felt heavy. Had anyone who had watched the video ended up here at the Hausmann this week?

She forced herself to leave the restroom and turn to the offices in the clinic's rear. She could sense David nearby underneath all the other presences, a calm center in the storm orbited by the staff.

He had taken over the admin office. A huge monitor showed the entire sensor grid, and another had a readout of Elite designations and their statuses. The Prime himself was at the desk on the phone.

". . . under control," he was saying as she came in. "I assure you, Chief, your presence on the streets here would only put your men in danger. I would advise you to keep patrolling the outer perimeter of the District and keep anyone from entering."

He looked up at her approach, and his eyebrows shot up at the condition of her clothes—he would have known if she'd been injured, so the question in his eyes was *Whose blood is that?*

She tilted her head toward the clinic's main room, and he nodded.

"I understand, Chief. Yes, we're following several leads on the source of the problem . . . You'll be the first to know."

He hung up without any pleasantries and leaned back in the chair with a groan. "God, as if we needed any more trouble—APD wants to help." Then he sat forward, looking at her. "What are you doing here?"

"My job," she answered.

A frown. "Oh?"

She dropped into the chair facing the desk. "I got a call from Jonathan."

Again: "Oh?"

"It would seem that we have one less thing to worry about."

She told him about her conversation with the Consort, watching his face. His expression, to the average person, didn't appear to change, but she saw his eyes turn silver, then back to blue. He didn't say anything for a while, but after a minute he crossed his arms and sat back.

"I don't know how to feel," Miranda said. "On the one hand I'm glad we're not going to die, but . . . it just feels wrong."

"Twenty-eight dead should always feel wrong," David muttered. "Even if it's right."

"Was it right?"

"I don't know, beloved. But I do know one thing . . ."

"Deven doesn't go murdering innocents for no reason,"

she finished for him. "At least not that you know of. But can you be sure?"

"He has more regard for life than most people think. And even after everything the Church did to him, he still has a soft spot for clergy. The thought of him . . ." He shook his head. "I don't know what to think either."

She half smiled. "Most people apologize with a card or flowers."

"Signets say it with slaughter," David replied resignedly. "How hopelessly romantic."

Miranda watched the network monitor for a moment. "You know, it really reminds me of Pac-Man."

"Are you going to tell me why you came here?" he asked. "I suppose I can guess, knowing you as I do. You got tired of sitting on the sidelines."

"Exactly."

"And if someone recognizes you?"

"We'll deal with that when it happens," she told him. "If the worst thing that happens is that we have to spin a situation with the press, I'm willing to deal with that. There are a lot of lives in the balance here, not just mine."

He smiled. "All right, then. At the moment the situation is under control, but if we get another alert, you can handle it."

"Damn right I can. I've had enough of that bastard and his flunkies. We're in charge here."

Another smile. "True."

She raised an eyebrow and said, "I appreciate your not lecturing me about my duties and responsibilities as Queen."

He sat back, arms crossed. "You're a grown woman, Miranda, and only you can decide what to do with your power. There's no rule that a Queen has to fight—you're one of the few who do, if you'll recall. I was reluctant to have you out here, I admit. I worry about you being hurt, but in any sort of battle I'd be a fool not to want you at my side."

She grinned. "That's why I love you."

"I thought it was because of that thing I do with my tongue."

"You should get it pierced."

David shuddered. "Needles. Hell no. I'll leave the pin-cushion antics to . . ."

Their eyes met. "Forgive him," Miranda said. "You'll have to eventually."

"Not everyone is as forgiving as you are."

She shrugged. "You didn't leave me much choice."

He practically flinched at the words as if she'd slapped him, though there hadn't been any venom in the statement.

"I don't mean it like that," she said quickly. "I just mean that with this gift of mine, I have to learn to keep my own emotions stable, or it's that much easier to knock me off center with other people's. Especially yours since we're so tightly bound. And if that happens . . ." She shook her head, uneasy just thinking about it. "I can't lose myself like that again. I might not come back."

Now, he smiled again. "Have I told you today how proud I am of you?"

"You don't have to. I know you are. But it's nice to hear all the same."

There was a knock, and one of the nurses poked her head in. "Sire, we've dealt with all the wounded—we only lost one tonight. Two humans are being transferred to the hospital for observation, but the rest can go home as soon as the Elite are finished blurring out their memories."

"Thank you, Jackie. Send Mo in when he has a free moment, would you?"

"As you will it, Sire."

His com chimed. "Star-one," he said.

"Sire, Faith here. The situation on Eighth was a false alarm, but Elite Forty-seven just called for backup in the warehouse district—I'm headed there with my team now. Sounds like she's taking crossbow fire."

"Proceed with caution," David replied.

"As always, Sire."

Miranda snorted softly, and he looked at her. "What?" he asked.

"Caution, my ass."

David nodded. "I've noticed. She's still blaming herself for you wearing the Stone. Speaking of which, I should tell her it's dealt with so maybe she can loosen up a little."

"Yes. Don't wait. She needs to know."

"Star-three, come in please."

There was no reply. David frowned. "Star-three."

Nothing.

Miranda took out her phone and called Faith's; it went directly to voice mail.

"Can you pinpoint her on the monitor?" she asked.

David was already on it; he hit a few keys on his laptop, and one of the dots on the grid blinked, its designation appearing beside it: Star-three. Next he pinged the other Elite who were with her. Only one seemed to be responding.

"Elite Twenty, what's your status?" the Prime demanded.

The answer was so much garbled noise that Miranda couldn't understand a word of it. That was strange and disturbing; there were sophisticated audio filters on the com network to get rid of background noise and amplify the speaker's voice.

"Elite Twenty, please repeat."

Nothing again. Now David looked genuinely worried; he accessed Elite 20's transmission and played it back, running additional filters over it.

This time Miranda caught a few words: *". . . heavy fire . . . several wounded . . . requesting backup . . ."* The sentence ended in a thud, coupled with a noise that sounded like a cry of pain.

"Shit!" David spoke into his com again, this time on broadcast mode. "All available teams proceed immediately to 9798 Third Street East. We've lost communication with Second Faith and her team. Situation unknown."

"Team D-Nine on our way, Sire."

"Teams B-Six and South-Twenty-one on our way, Sire."

Miranda's heart was pounding. "We need to get out there," she said. "I have a—"

"—bad feeling about this," David concluded, standing and reaching for his sword. "Let's go."

*   *   *

As Faith threw herself sideways and rolled out of the way of a third crossbow bolt, it occurred to her that this was the part in the movie where she should be yelling "GET DOWN!"

Her Elite knew they should get down, however, and they did—as soon as the arrows began to rain down from the roof above, her team darted in all directions and ran for cover.

"Twenty, Sixty-six, I want you on the roof taking those bastards out!" she barked into her com. She saw two shadowy figures scrambling up the side of the building.

She stayed crouched behind the Dumpster but reached down to her belt for the miniature folded crossbow she had strapped on before leaving the Haven tonight. They didn't normally have to travel with projectile weapons, but Hayes's thugs seemed to favor them, and it was hard to slice someone's head off if you couldn't get closer than firing range. Several of the other teams were armed with full-sized crossbows, but she didn't like having to lug one along so she'd chosen a portable version.

Unfortunately its range and power were limited—there was no way she could hit anything two stories up.

"Faith!" one of the others called. "My transmissions are blocked—can you call out?"

Faith tried calling for backup, but only silence met her words. "What the hell . . . Star-one—my team is under heavy fire and needs immediate backup—" She switched to broadcast mode, but the result was the same; her com couldn't send out.

Cursing, Faith tried calling the Prime on her phone, but there was no signal—they were in the middle of the city. There should be signals for miles.

Up until now Jeremy's bag of tricks hadn't included jamming their communications. There had been attacks on humans, vandalism, fires, all sorts of nuisances, but nothing this coordinated. If he'd been saving the technology, that could only mean one thing.

Her team had walked into a trap.

They'd arrived at the coordinates where the SOS had originated from to find no other Elite in sight, but Elite 20 had found two warriors on the ground in the alley, already dead from multiple wooden arrows to the chest. Before they could find the rest of the missing team, the volley had started, and there was no time for further investigation.

She waited for either the arrows to stop or Elite 20 to report from the rooftop, but after several minutes she began to worry. "Eighteen, do you see Twenty or Sixty-six up there?"

Before Elite 18 could answer, something large and heavy struck the pavement a few feet from her. Faith leapt backward with a yelp as a second object followed it, and she realized with a sick lurch that the first one was Elite 20, who landed in a twist of limbs and blood, his eyes gaping open in death.

"Fall back!" she commanded. "Split up and regroup at the nearest rendezvous point!"

One of the others made it, though she couldn't tell who it was—she just saw someone make a run for it and narrowly avoid getting shot. That left only Elite 18 and Faith.

Suddenly the sounds of arrows hitting bricks stopped. Faith pulled her sword and waited.

She heard shuffling, a struggle, a grunt of pain. A moment later, footsteps from at least four different directions, growing nearer . . . five, six, seven . . . ten . . . twelve pairs of boots, halting just beyond her hiding place.

I'm surrounded.

She could take six or seven at once but not twelve. Not without an escape route available or at least a higher-ground advantage.

Faith sheathed her sword and stood straight, waiting, until one of the vampires stepped out where she could see him.

She and Jeremy stared at each other for a moment.

Then, she tried one last transmission through her com, speaking calmly: "Star-one, this is Star-three; cancel backup.

Do not send any additional Elite to this location. I repeat: Cancel backup."

Whether it went out or not, she never knew. The blow to her head sent her sprawling to the ground, the night around her gone black in an instant.

Miranda fell out of the Mist with a lurch but stayed on her feet and held back the nausea that always hit her after landing. Three years and she still couldn't do it without wanting to throw up.

David appeared beside her and took her arm as she swayed slightly. "Are you all right?"

She nodded and grounded as hard and fast as she could. "I hate Misting," she muttered. "Couldn't we just turn into bats or something?"

David smiled distractedly, his phone already in his hand. "The network signal is coming back online," he said. "I'm still not getting any . . . wait . . . I'm getting a homing signal from Elite Twenty-two."

Miranda's heart sank. The homing beacon went off only if the person wearing the com was no longer transmitting life signs.

He crossed the street at a run, and she followed, pulling her hilted stake just in case. As they reached the alley where Faith and the others had vanished, Miranda drew up short.

"Oh, God," she said.

There were bodies all over the alley, all of them Elite.

David had already reached the first fallen warrior and was checking for a pulse, but she knew by the look on his face that they were all dead.

Miranda counted seven total, three back in the alley and four in the middle of the pavement. The way two of them lay, limbs bent at unnatural angles with blood pooled around them, suggested they'd fallen from a height, but each one was run through with at least one stake.

The two other bodies had been shot full of crossbow bolts.

She leaned over one of them and closed his eyes . . . she knew him. She knew all of them. They had all pledged their lives to her and to David, and now they lay slaughtered in the street and discarded like trash.

David's voice was hard as he spoke into his com: "I need a body retrieval team to these coordinates immediately." He shook his head and said to Miranda, "The signal's weak here for some reason. I hope that went through."

"On our way, Sire."

"Good."

Miranda stood in the midst of the bodies, turning in a circle, trying to understand; there must have been an ambush, but why? Jeremy's thugs had never done anything like this. They caused mayhem and then disappeared, almost always attacking humans to draw out as many Elite as possible and keep them all busy. What had they accomplished here?

"Where's Faith?" she asked, panic seizing her heart. "Do you have her signal?"

David stared hard at his phone as if willing the screen to change. "No . . . she's not here . . . I can't raise her anywhere."

Miranda put her hands over her eyes and then pushed her hair back from her face. "She's dead," she said, choking on the words. "If she's not showing up . . ."

"Wait!" David interrupted. "I'm getting something . . . there she is! She's alive. And she's half a mile from here, in a building on Ninth Street." He looked up at her. "There are at least twenty other vampires in that building."

"She's bait," Miranda said. "They want us to come for her. We've got to get at least that many Elite down here."

David was already summoning as many teams as they still had intact to the location, and they headed for the building themselves; Miranda was glad he hadn't suggested another Mist. She needed a few more minutes before doing it again, or she'd probably pass out.

"What's the plan?" Miranda asked. "Charge in, swords blazing, and get ourselves killed?"

"No . . . let me get a schematic of the building . . . stop here."

They ducked behind a moving truck that was parked across the street from the building, and Miranda took a moment to look over the situation: It was three stories tall, one of the older, more run-down structures in this part of town; the ground floor was a boarded-up restaurant or bar of some kind, and most likely the upper floors had once been apartments. It looked like it had been empty for some time.

She saw shadows moving outside—guards. She edged back behind the truck, farther into the darkness.

"All right," David said, speaking both to her and to the team leader who was gathering the troops out of sight nearby. "Faith is on the ground floor, in the back. There are vampires scattered throughout the building, but most are on the first and second floors. There are five on the roof, one at each corner and another in the middle—assume those are crossbows. I want one team approaching from the east and another from the west, and the rest concentrating on the front of the building to draw as many of them away from Faith as possible. The Queen and I will go in the back. As soon as we have her, I'll send the signal to fall back."

"Yes, Sire. We'll be ready to go in in two minutes."

"Attack when ready," David replied. "I'll be monitoring."

He took a quick glance at the building and then moved back to stand next to Miranda. "We've got four full teams and two partials with members who were injured tonight— it's the best we can do on such short notice, but it should be enough. I'm not picking up any signals going in or out of the building—no remote detonators, not even a cell phone call. How do you want to go in?" he asked.

She shook her head. "I thought you were the one with the plan."

"I think we should split up," he said. "I'll take the roof and deal with the archers. You slip in from the back and find Faith."

"She'll be guarded," Miranda replied. "Even with a battle going on they won't leave her alone."

"How many can you take?" he asked.

"As long as I don't have to fight them all at once? As many as they've got," she said with determination, her hand closing around Shadowflame's hilt.

"All right. As soon as it looks like most of them are occupied, we'll go in."

Miranda watched the phone's screen as the red dots that represented the Elite moved closer to the building from all sides. The green dots, the non-Haven vampires, began to move quickly, taking position—one of their sentries must have spotted the Elite coming.

"Be careful," she told David. "We don't know what else he might have up his sleeve."

The Prime leaned over and kissed her. "You, too."

"Faith is going to be pissed at us for coming after her . . . she'll say we shouldn't have risked it."

David raised an eyebrow. "Do you agree?"

"Not for a second. We can't leave her there—if she's a trap for us, they'll kill her if we don't show. We can take that many vampires, especially with six Elite teams with us."

"You do realize he's got something planned. He must."

"Whatever it is, we can handle it." She held his eyes. "It's Faith, David."

David smiled, nodded. "Good. I'm glad we agree."

Miranda heard the first faint sounds of a struggle beginning across the street. The sound of steel meeting steel, a click and whistle of something flying down from the roof . . .

"It's starting."

David squeezed her hand. "Let's go. Call when you have her."

Miranda took a deep breath. "Have I mentioned I hate Misting?"

"You can go on foot if you need to."

"This way is better—they won't see me coming." She gave him an anxious grin. "Meet you on the other side, baby."

Then, she closed her eyes and *pulled*.

Twenty

She could hear, as she regained consciousness, the sounds of other vampires, weapons . . . orders being issued in low voices . . . the sounds of an army preparing for battle.

She hurt . . . God, she hurt . . . her entire body felt like it was on fire, burning from the inside, and if there had been anything in her stomach, it probably wouldn't have stayed there . . . if only she could just go back to sleep . . .

Her throat was raw and burning, too, as if she'd been screaming. Vision swimming, she tried to make sense of her surroundings, of anything.

An empty room, with a bar at one end. Old restaurant? The smell of fried food had seeped into the woodwork, and its undertone, coupled with the nausea she already felt, made her feel like gagging.

A cup of water was pressed lightly to her lips. She drank all of it greedily, trying to assuage the agonizing itch in her throat, and the cool liquid helped her come back to her senses somewhat.

"Try not to cough," came an accented voice. "No sudden moves."

She whimpered weakly as she realized whom the voice belonged to.

Hazel eyes met hers. "I'm sorry, Faith. I wish it could have been anyone but you."

She had to drag energy into her body by inches to even speak. "What did you do to me?"

Jeremy stepped back away from her, and she could see him a little more clearly. He set down the empty cup on the bar, and a few things registered at once: She was bound upright, she couldn't move her arms or legs, and there was a chemical kind of smell coming from somewhere nearby her that took a minute to place.

Nail polish remover . . . acetone . . . or whatever he had used to kill Monroe.

Her eyes focused on a pair of objects on the bar. One was a glass bottle of clear liquid with a bright yellow hazardous-materials sticker on the side, the other a syringe.

Jeremy sensed she was figuring it out, and said, "There are several containers of gasoline behind you. When the charge goes off, it won't be enough to bring the building down, but the fire will spread quickly and anyone on the ground floor will be killed."

He held up a cell phone. "This will tell me if you move. All I have to do is touch the screen, and it sends a signal to the detonator."

Faith closed her eyes, fighting helpless tears, thinking about the interrogation room at the Haven, its walls covered in the remains of 8.3 Claret. "I'm the detonator."

"You swallowed the charge while you were unconscious, and then I injected you. There's enough explosive in your body right now that all it will take is a tiny burst of electricity."

Jeremy met her eyes, and she saw regret there, and sorrow. "It will be quick," he said. "You won't feel anything."

Faith couldn't help it; her body hurt so much from the explosive poisoning her veins, and she had failed so utterly, that the tears fell even against her will. "Why?" she whispered. "Please, just tell me why."

He came to her again, this time dabbing at her eyes with the sleeve of his shirt. "Her name is Amelia," he said softly.

"Your lover?"

"My daughter," he replied. "My lover is long dead . . .

and our child, all I have left in this world, is chained to Hart's bed. As long as he has her, I am chained to him as well."

"He ordered you to do all of this . . . to start a war."

"Not in the beginning. He wanted to get back at Miranda for helping Cora. Cora was . . . very important to him, and now she is someone else's Queen . . . but more importantly, Hart discovered that Miranda and David are the linchpin of a greater plan that threatens everything he stands for. Now there is far more than simple revenge at stake."

"You're using me to lure them here so you can kill them both."

Jeremy nodded. "But Hart . . . there's something he didn't count on: Lydia."

"You knew Lydia?"

"Lydia asked Hart to help the Order, but he refused. She needed a Signet, you see, and thought his animosity toward the South would make him want to join her side. But Hart is no fool. He figured out that if the Awakening happened, the entire balance of power in the Council would shift— his enemies would become more powerful than anyone could imagine and the Council as we know it would cease to exist. To stop it from ever coming to pass, he wanted to have the Pair eliminated. When Lydia realized what Hart was planning, she sought me out and offered help. If I performed the Awakening, she would ensure that Amelia was returned to me . . . and Hart wouldn't know until it was too late. He would believe he had won."

"Then why go through with this? Why not ally with the South and all take on Hart together?"

"Not part of the deal," he said. "Lydia would only offer her help if I went through with Hart's plan to kill the Pair . . . modified, of course, to suit her own agenda."

Faith lowered her eyes, head bowed. "The Stone."

Jeremy lifted his hand and touched her face. "I never wanted any of this . . . you don't deserve it. Neither does your Pair. But we've all made our choices, and here we are."

"When you walk into a Haven, offer yourself to a Prime,

you seal your own fate," Faith said, remembering his words
to her what seemed like a thousand years ago, in her room.

"Things might have been very different . . . I wish they
had been. But some fires, once lit, have to burn until they
consume everything . . . and nothing is left of the world but
ash." He leaned in and kissed her softly on the forehead. "I
promise you, Faith, when this is over . . . what rises from
the ashes will be worth the burning."

Then he closed his eyes and faded from sight.

David watched the fight unfold for a moment before he
made his move; he opted not to Mist until he'd reached the
building itself so he could keep an eye on his Elite as long
as possible.

He knew that if she could see her warriors right now,
Faith would be proud; even without her there to lead them,
they swarmed the building with perfect timing and coordi-
nation, all sides attacking at once, the enemy reacting
exactly as David had hoped they would. Most of them
headed toward the outside walls of the building, either to
take on the first wave of Elite or to fire from above. Arrows
rained down all around the Elite, but they didn't falter, and
within two minutes three of the enemy were already dead.

The white dot that signified Miranda appeared just
inside the first-floor back door, in a short hallway that led
to storage rooms and then to the main restaurant area
where Faith was being held. There were still four guards,
but four was hardly an overwhelming number for the
Queen, who was moving toward them slowly.

She would be fine. He had no doubt of that.

David spun the display on his phone to show him the
roof again. There were only four up there now, the archers,
one at each corner. If he Misted right behind any one of
them he could kill him in seconds, take his crossbow, and
take out the others before they knew what hit them.

He took a few deep breaths to prepare himself for
another Mist . . . and frowned. *What the hell . . . ?*

One of the green dots kept flickering, as if its life signs were faltering, but suddenly it vanished from the ground floor and reappeared on the roof . . . it had to be Hayes, Misting up to the top of the building . . . but . . .

No, it couldn't be. The dot flickered again . . . and turned white.

David stared, unbelieving, as he realized what he was seeing.

But . . . it couldn't be. He couldn't believe it. Even after everything that had happened, it just . . . it couldn't be.

A Signet.

All right, girl . . . get ready.

The first guard was at the end of the hallway, facing away from her. Miranda drew the stake from her belt and moved up behind him, reaching out with her senses to touch his mind.

You're sad . . . so sad. Remember that time . . . that one . . . how depressed you were? You feel that way now. You can't even move, you're so depressed . . . You can barely even stand . . . Maybe the world would be better off if . . .

The vampire sagged sideways against the door frame, his hands over his face, his awareness of the room and his job fading into the gray heaviness of pain. The sadness sapped his energy, took him off his guard.

She clamped her hand over his mouth and slammed the other into his back, the stake biting through skin and muscle and ripping into his heart.

He made a gurgling noise and fell back against her. Miranda moved back, dragging him with her, and let him slide to the ground in the hallway where he wouldn't be seen.

Carefully, she pulled her stake and moved back to the doorway to get the lay of the land. The back hall where she had materialized led to another corridor of storage rooms, ending in another doorway to the now-defunct kitchen and from there out into the main room of the first floor. She could smell the grease and smoke from years of cooking and the fermented reek of old beer.

There was another guard at the kitchen entrance, then at least one more between there and the main room. She could hear the rush and shouts of fighting going on distantly, but if her Elite did as they were supposed to, they would keep most of the battle outdoors, drawing the enemy to the front and keeping their attention there.

The corridor was still too narrow for swords, but she touched the guard's mind and searched for a chink in his emotional armor as she had the first's. If she just went up and staked him the other guard might hear, and the commotion could alert whoever was holding Faith; they were probably waiting to kill Faith until they were sure the Prime and Queen were caught in whatever trap Hayes had planned.

As she moved closer to him, she noticed that the door to her right was a walk-in freezer with an external lock. She pulled on the handle, and it opened—good.

Miranda reached out to him. *Come to me. Come to me . . . now.*

She ducked into the freezer, which was empty but running. Most likely no one had thought to disconnect it when they got the power turned back on to use the building as their headquarters. They probably weren't worried about the electric bill.

Footsteps. The guard leaned cautiously into the freezer, no doubt wondering how it had opened itself.

She seized him by the throat and hauled him in with her, flinging him hard against the back wall of the freezer. Before he could make a sound, she had drawn Shadowflame, and his neck opened with a spray of blood, his head falling to the left while his body landed in a heap on the floor.

Miranda closed the freezer quietly behind her. Two down, two to go. She needed to take them out carefully, without alerting anyone else—she had gotten much better at group combat, but the odds were far more in her favor one-on-one. It was too bad she hadn't quite gotten the hang of using weaponized empathy on more than one person. She could handle a crowd only through music, and then they all felt the same thing. Now wasn't really the time to burst into song.

The kitchen wasn't the ideal setting for a fight, but it was better than the hallway. Her boots weren't entirely silent on the terra-cotta tiles, but the noise outside was growing louder and louder. A few more minutes and the Elite would break through the lines entirely and pour into the building. She needed to have Faith's guards dealt with by then.

Before she could reach out toward the third guard, he must have heard or felt her—he turned toward the kitchen, expression turning from surprise to outrage as he started to shout—

Miranda threw her stake, aiming for his throat rather than his chest; it took a lot more force to get through the sternum and rib cage, and she couldn't risk a miss.

His hands flew up to try to catch or deflect the stake and failed. He gave a strangled cry as blood burst from the wound, but the shock gave her all the advantage she needed, and she crossed the kitchen to him, yanked the stake back, and drove it into his chest.

By some miracle, the noise from the third guard's death didn't bring in any others. Miranda flattened herself against the open door and edged toward the main room an inch at a time so she could see in hopefully without being seen.

What she saw made her blood turn to ice with fear.

Oh, God. Oh, no . . .

"Faith," she said softly. "Faith, I'm so sorry."

There was no one else guarding the Second. Miranda knew, as soon as she saw what had been done to Faith, that there was no need to guard her.

Faith heard her voice and lifted her head. Her skin was greenish and sweat poured down her face; whatever Jeremy had shot her full of had to be toxic, and her body was trying to burn it off, but without fresh blood she couldn't heal, not as weak as she was. And even if she did, if Jeremy had done to her what he had to Monroe and force-fed her a charge, even if he didn't set off the explosive, the damage to her body could be catastrophic.

Miranda was at her side in seconds. "It's all right," she said, putting a reassuring hand on Faith's face. "I'm going to get you out of here."

Faith could barely speak. "You . . . have to get out," she said in a broken whisper. "He's going to . . ."

"No, he's not," Miranda insisted. She started examining the chains that held Faith upright against the containers of gasoline, and the wires threaded through them. Did they connect the detonator to the fuel, or were they just there to send a signal? "Faith, I'm not going to let him kill you. We're here to save you—do you hear me? Nobody's dying tonight except Hayes and his buddies."

"You don't . . . understand . . ."

"Save your strength," Miranda told her. "You're going to need it once we get you out of here . . ."

"You can't," Faith said. "If you move me, he'll know, and he'll set off the charge. Please . . . just go, before it's too late."

"I'm not leaving you here, damn it!"

Faith shook her head weakly. "You have to go. Get the Stone away from here, before . . ."

"The Stone doesn't matter, Faith. They can't do the ritual—Deven killed them all. The Stone is useless. Now, hold still while I—"

"Listen to me."

Miranda stopped and met her eyes. "Faith . . ."

Faith's eyes were full of tears. "He has the ritual. Lydia gave it to him," she said. "He's on the roof. All he needs is the Stone and you brought it right to him."

Her gaze lifted for a second, and Miranda saw the horror in her face just before she heard the click.

A second later, the first crossbow bolt hit Miranda's back.

The Queen lurched forward, dazed by the sudden impact, and by the next . . . and the next . . .

She looked into Faith's eyes again and held them as she

sank to her knees. A fourth bolt and a fifth punched into her back, all of them missing her heart, but each one sending pain coursing through her, overwhelming her senses, draining her strength.

"This isn't your fault," Miranda whispered. "It's not your fault, Faith."

The room was fading from her eyes, but Miranda held on to Faith's gaze as long as she could, trying without words to give the Second what little comfort she could.

She heard someone behind her say, "Sire, we have her."

And that was all.

David didn't have time to assess the situation as he Misted onto the roof. The second his feet hit the ground, one of the enemy vampires was already on him; he threw himself into the fight and threw the other vampire to the ground, drawing his sword and spinning to meet the next attacker.

Within two minutes he had killed all four of them. He shoved the last one's body aside and turned, blade ready, to meet the only other vampire on the roof . . . the Signet who had been waiting for him.

He blinked.

At the center of the roof, an altar had been erected out of discarded bricks and a piece of flat stone. There were two candles, one black and one red; several sheets of yellowed paper with diagrams and text written on them . . .

. . . and a hammer.

"I don't think we've been properly introduced."

David turned his head slightly to look at the fair-haired vampire. "No, we haven't."

He stepped toward David and gave a slight bow. "Jeremy Hayes . . . Prime of Australia."

David nodded. "David Solomon, Prime of the Southern United States."

Jeremy smiled slightly and walked back behind the altar, where he took a silver lighter from his pocket and set about lighting the candles. "I had a devil of a time figuring out where to set this up that the wind wouldn't blow them out," he said idly. "The parchment made it clear, however: We had to be outdoors beneath the new moon."

David let out his breath slowly, eyes moving down to the texts in front of Jeremy. "The Awakening ritual?"

A nod. "It has to be performed by a Signet. I think originally the idea was that the chosen Prime would do the ritual and sacrifice himself willingly. It really is a shame . . . I imagine when your boyfriend finds out he slaughtered the Order for nothing, he's going to feel terrible. As I understand it, Eladra was very fond of him."

"Eladra?"

"The High Priestess. Ex–High Priestess, now. You know . . . I've been loved, in my life, but I don't think anyone's ever been devoted to me enough to kill twenty-eight people. That alone makes me wish that you and I could have been allies."

David raised an eyebrow. "I doubt that, given how much you seem to enjoy blowing up my allies."

Jeremy smiled. "I had to see for myself if Lydia's theory about the connection among all of you was true. I had no intention of harming Janousek or his Queen—I merely set up the circumstances and then monitored his phone calls to see how all of you reacted. Knowing Lydia was right made all of this a little easier."

David started to move toward him, but just then he felt something—*pain*, and not his own. Three stories below, he felt Miranda being shot, this time by wooden bolts. He gasped, the world swimming around him, and held on to consciousness by sheer force of will. She was hurt; she was hurt and needed him—

"Stay where you are," Jeremy instructed. "She's alive. And she'll stay that way if you obey me. Try anything and both of you die."

A moment later the door to the stairwell opened, and three of the enemy vampires dragged something heavy out onto the roof.

One of the men hauled Miranda up at stakepoint. She

was half-conscious, blood running down both of her legs from the wooden shafts still sticking out of her back. As they got her to her feet, she woke up enough to struggle and snarled at the men holding her, writhing as hard as she could to win free of them.

"I would hold still if I were you, my Lady," Jeremy said. He lifted his hand, which held a cell phone. "One touch from me and the charge goes off."

Miranda froze, wide-eyed. "No."

"What's going on?" David demanded.

Miranda was the one who answered. "Faith's been turned into a detonator, like Monroe," she said. "She's strapped to fifty gallons of gasoline on the first floor."

"Look, this doesn't have to end badly," Jeremy said calmly. "If the Queen holds still, I won't kill Faith. If you hold still, I won't kill the Queen. Let's be civilized here."

David cast his eyes around the roof, looking for a solution—if he Misted to Miranda, Jeremy would set off the charge; if he went after Jeremy, the vampires would stake Miranda. There had to be something else. To buy time, he asked, "If you're a Prime, where's your Signet?"

Jeremy sighed. "McMannis is wearing it, of course."

"Then why is it lit up? If you're the Prime, it would go dark on him."

"Technology," Jeremy replied, shaking his head. "Did you know there have been two recorded instances of someone attempting to fake a Signet? In both, the crime was discovered because the rightful Prime came to claim his place. But if you were to, say, take a Signet from a Prime, and somehow rig it to glow, and then got rid of the true Prime, and had allies ready to swear you were the Signet's bearer . . . how would anyone know? It's not as if the Council works together or is connected in any way. Someone could rule a territory for years before anyone noticed."

David nodded. "Hart and McMannis deposed you."

Now, Jeremy smiled regretfully, coming forward once again. "I had the Signet around my neck for all of ten minutes before they made their move. And now Hart has the one thing that matters more to me than any of this . . . and as long as he has her, I am in his service. Lydia and the Order were going to help me destroy Hart, and McMannis, well . . . he's just Hart's hand puppet. Without Hart to back him, he would be easy to deal with, and I could regain my rightful place."

"Lydia's dead," Miranda ground out.

"I know. But that doesn't change anything. The help she promised me is waiting for me in New York. As soon as I've fulfilled my part of the bargain, they'll fulfill theirs."

"We can help you," Miranda said. "You don't have to do any of this—we can help you take Hart down."

"I'm afraid I can't take that chance," Jeremy replied. "I've already risked enough for the two of you."

"What do you mean?" David asked.

"As far as Hart knows, I'm killing you both right now."

"But you aren't."

"No," Jeremy answered, coming to stand in front of David again. "You, my Lord, get to live."

He reached up and took hold of David's Signet, flipping it over.

Jeremy's eyebrows shot up. "Or perhaps not."

"Looking for this?" Miranda asked, lifting her chin so her Signet fell forward slightly. "Lydia gave it to me, not David."

Hayes actually chuckled. "Poetic," he said. "I like it."

"What does the Stone really do?" David asked.

Before Jeremy could answer, a voice erupted from David's com: *"Sire, we've breached the building—what are your orders?"*

David looked from Jeremy to Miranda, to the altar, back to Miranda. The Queen was too weak to Mist. She was still bleeding. If his Elite tried to free Faith or come to the Pair's aid, Jeremy would blow the building and anyone caught down there would burn. Whatever happened, David wasn't going to let anyone else die tonight.

He lifted his arm slowly, making it clear to Jeremy he wasn't going for a weapon, and said into his com, "Execute

General Order Omega-Five," he said, broadcasting to the entire Elite. "I repeat: General Order Omega-Five. Retreat and abandon the mission. Regroup and await further orders."

Abruptly, the sounds of fighting down below stopped. *"But, Sire—"* the lieutenant began.

"That's an order," David snapped. "Situation unrecoverable." Then, with equal care, he pressed his index finger against his com, holding it there until it accepted his fingerprint and beeped. He spoke into it one more time: "Contingency Seven."

Another beep: command recognized.

Miles and miles away, the servers and network at the Haven would begin to shut down, the server room itself sealing to deny access to any invaders. Every computer, com, and phone connected to the Haven went instantly into lockdown mode—limited communication only on the network, no access to the programming code, no access to the sensor grid. The entire thing would be shut down in five minutes.

David lowered his arm, still staring at Jeremy, who waited patiently until he was done. The building was silent, the battle over. The Elite had run.

"Now," David said, "let her go, and you and I will discuss this."

"There's really nothing to discuss," Jeremy said. "She wears the Stone; it's all been decided. Fate's a strange thing, isn't it? Even with everyone conspiring to either save or destroy you, things unfolded exactly as they were foretold. I suspect Lydia thought she was saving you by giving the Stone to the Queen—if she had read the ritual, she would have known that whoever wears the Stone is the one who survives."

David lowered his eyes, afraid to look at Miranda. As soon as he did, she would see what he knew, what he had known, somehow, the minute Jeremy had introduced himself. Queens might have the gift of precognition, but Primes had the gift of knowing when they had been outmaneuvered.

"Let her go," he said again.

Jeremy looked down at David's Signet, then held out his hand. "She'll live. I give you my word."

"What is he talking about?" Miranda asked. "David, tell me what's—"

He didn't answer her but reached up and removed his Signet and handed it to Jeremy.

Jeremy took the Signet to the altar. He caught the eye of one of his guards and nodded.

David made the mistake of looking at the Queen as they started to drag her away. The minute their eyes met, she began to scream.

"No! *No!* Not without me! *Not without me!*"

David shut his eyes tightly, wishing he could do the same with his ears. She was still screaming all the way down the stairs and probably would keep right on until she could fight her way free. He knew she would—she would fight like a lion, whether Faith died or not, to save him— but he also knew that by the time she got away from them, as weak as she was, it would be too late.

"You're quite a remarkable man," Jeremy was saying. He laid the Signet on the altar and picked up the parchment. "Most Primes would never risk death to rescue a subordinate—not even a Second. They would have let Faith die and considered her a casualty of war. Of course . . . if it came down to a choice, a Prime would let his own Queen die a thousand times if it meant he could save himself."

David smiled. "You and I are not most Primes, are we?"

"No." Jeremy inclined his head toward the door. "She'll be held nearby until we're done here."

"And Faith?"

He shook his head. "I'm sorry . . . it must appear to Hart that both you and your Queen perished in the explosion. That's a lot harder without a bomb."

"She'll come for you," David said. "You know she will."

Jeremy bowed his head over the altar and said quietly, "I hope she can."

As soon as his head was down, David reached out and

seized the parchment with his mind; he jerked it off the altar and forced the edges of the paper into the candle flames. The paper was so old that the entire sheaf went up at once.

Jeremy didn't react quite like David expected him to. He watched the paper burn until it had fallen to ash and fluttered down onto the altar, and sighed.

"Smart move," Jeremy said. "Without the text, the incantation can't be performed, and without the incantation performed, the Stone can't be activated." He smiled. "Unfortunately for you I did that part already. There's only one step left to complete the ritual."

Jeremy picked up the hammer.

Twenty-one

Faith knew there was no time. She knew there was no hope. But she also knew she couldn't die without trying.

Her body wanted so badly to give out. The pain and exhaustion were killing her—perhaps not literally, not yet, but close enough. It would be so easy just to let it all go, to close her eyes and surrender to her fate, and when the bomb went off, she would never know what had become of those she loved . . . she wouldn't know anything, ever again, and at that moment she wanted it so badly . . . just to let go . . .

Then she heard Miranda screaming.

The men dragged the Queen into the room from the stairwell, and she was fighting with all the strength she still had in her bleeding body, so hard that one of the crossbow bolts sticking out of her back worked itself free and clattered to the floor.

The wild panic in Miranda's cries, the fear in her face— Faith took a deep breath around the pain and set her jaw. It wasn't going to end like this. She wouldn't let it.

She had to pray that she would have a few seconds, just long enough before Jeremy got the signal to blow the charge, to act. One chance.

They wrestled the Queen toward the front door of the restaurant. If Faith could distract the guards, Miranda could get away. That had to be enough.

Faith drew up what strength she could and threw herself forward in her chains. She felt the canisters behind her shudder and tip slightly—the weight of them falling should be enough to jolt the explosives in her body and set off the whole bomb. She jerked again and again, pulling forward and down as hard as she could, rocking the gas cans back and forth, back and forth. Each time she felt them tip a little farther, fall back a little farther. Each time, she grew weaker and weaker, but she didn't stop.

The ruckus of the cans rattling caught the attention of the guards as they were halfway over the threshold. She heard one of them shouting, heard Miranda snarl like a wild animal, and saw a blur of movement as the Queen fought her way out of their grasp.

In the half second before she fell, before fire consumed her, before the world exploded into light and then darkness, Faith caught the Queen's eyes and smiled.

The building shuddered. A blast of heat and fire blew out the windows on all sides of the ground floor, and the entire structure heaved.

David lost his balance briefly, and for one mad moment thought that, just maybe, Jeremy would fall over and he could reach the Signet before—

—the hammer came down.

He heard the stone shatter, saw shards of it flying through the air, catching the candlelight.

He and Jeremy both stared as the light in the Signet flared, sputtered, and went out.

David staggered backward, hands coming to his throat—it felt as if a giant hand had wrapped around him and was crushing his entire body, but from the inside out. He couldn't breathe—couldn't see—

But he could feel.

He might have screamed, but he would never know. Agony like nothing he had ever experienced tore every cell in his body apart, and he felt every last iota of energy, every ounce of power he had ever had, pulled from him, ripped from him, drained away, and flowing out—

—and down—

He could hear her screaming. He could feel her terror, her grief, as she felt him dying, felt the connection between them being torn in half, the Stone at her neck burning white-hot as his power funneled through it, through her.

"Please don't leave me—please don't go without me—"

He felt his knees hit the ground, then his hands. The floor was shaking. The building was shaking—but not from the fire that raged below. The earth was quaking.

I love you. I love you, Miranda. I will always l—

And as the world burned away, the Prime fell.

Cora screamed, falling to her knees, her whole body seized with a pain so intense she couldn't even name what part of her it originated from. She reached out toward Jacob, and their hands caught, but he had been hit, too—they both tumbled to the ground, their Elite clustering around them and calling out for help, as wave after wave of . . . something . . . struck the Pair, their Signets burning so brightly anyone looking into them was blinded.

"Hurry," Deven said. "There's still time. I'll head for the roof, you—"

The explosion drowned out whatever he was going to say, but he and Jonathan looked at each other, knowing what had just happened, and both started to Mist to the building, to do something, anything, before—

It hit Deven first. He sucked in a tormented breath and fell against the side of the car, face going ghostly white.

Jonathan felt it a split second later. Pain. He'd never been tortured, but in half a breath he understood why it made so many people confess to crimes they'd never committed. As if he'd been blown back by a blast wave, he crumpled against the car door, falling down beside his Prime, who had already lost consciousness.

Hold on to me, David. Hold on to me. Don't let go, don't—
    I can't—no—
    No . . . no . . . please, God, no . . .
    Please don't leave me . . . not now . . . no . . .
    We have to go together . . . we were supposed to go together . . .

The world was burning.

In that space between life and death, between darkness and annihilation, the Queen felt her beloved lose his hold on his body, on life. She felt him slip from her grasp, the warmth of their bond shattered like a brittle stone beneath a hammer stroke, leaving only shards that cut and bled.

What flooded through her was more than her own power, more than his—she felt it flowing into her, through the amulet that hung from her neck, her heart widening, her soul expanding until it tore, until she was beyond pain, beyond grief, beyond anything.

Far away she could sense her body. It was broken. Badly burned, bones cracked from being thrown into something by the explosion . . . wrung out from pain, so weakened by blood loss that it seemed a pitiful little thing, best left behind. If she went back to it, she knew how much it would hurt. She would have to feel again, have to remember . . .

"Miranda!"

No.

Someone was calling her name.

"Miranda! We have to get out of here! Miranda!"

A young voice, filled with fear, so fragile yet touched with such power, a voice she recognized.

Pain blossomed all over her body, and she struggled weakly against the hands that had taken her arms and turned her onto her back. Suddenly there was chaos, noise everywhere: fire burning, sirens, screaming. The stench of burning flesh, burning wood, burning . . . burning . . .

Nothing . . . nothing . . . let the fire take it. Let it burn.

She tried to turn away from the voice, tried to go back into the dark, but something stopped her. Something at once blazing hot and sweetly cooling . . . a kiss of moonlight on her forehead, softness enveloping her, lifting her up, filling her with light . . . with peace.

The Queen stared up into the light, but it wasn't light, not really: it was shadow. She felt a hand take hers . . . guiding her back to her body, promising her everything would be all right, but she still had work to do and had to be strong. She remembered that feeling, that presence, from a night when she had fought her way free of dark water, of death. Whether it was her own strength, or Someone Else's, she had believed in it then . . . she had to believe in it now.

As Miranda came to, Stella Maguire's pretty young face came into focus, and the Witch dragged the fallen Queen away from the fire, into the night.

The fire had reached the second floor before emergency crews arrived, but it was easily contained; the fuel that had fed it had already burned away, and aside from the remains of the restaurant on the first floor, there was little left inside to burn. The structure itself was mostly built of concrete and steel, and though it would have to be torn down and demolished, at least it was still standing as the Austin Fire Department finished putting out the blaze.

If there had been any bodies on the first floor, they were completely pulverized by the blast. There was nothing left. Ladder crews had done a quick check of the second floor but had to vacate the structure quickly when the whole thing lurched hazardously to the side. The building was abandoned, and unless there were vagrants living in it at the time of the fire, there were no bodies to find . . .

. . . except one.

As the night waned, sunrise only two hours away, the Prime of the Southern United States lay where he had hit the ground, his body waiting for daylight to set one last fire and leave only a scattering of ashes where once had been the most powerful vampire in the South. A casual onlooker unaware of the state of the building might think he was simply asleep, lying on one side, face turned into his shoulder, one hand stretched out on the sooty roof.

A shadow fell.

Hands shaking, Deven turned David onto his back and checked for a pulse, even though he knew . . . he had felt it. So had Jonathan.

David's eyes were closed, their deep blue lost to the world forever. He didn't look as if he'd died in agony, though they knew better.

They knelt on either side of the Prime. It was a while before either could speak.

"Did you know this was going to happen?" Deven finally asked, lifting his eyes to his Consort.

Jonathan was in tears. "No . . . not this. I was sure that we'd fixed it. I was so sure everything was going to be all right . . ."

Deven touched David's face, willing him silently to wake, as he once had with the body of someone else he had loved and lost just as suddenly. That time it had worked . . . he reached, desperate to find even the faintest trace of life remaining, and if found, draw it back into David's body . . . he reached until exhaustion overcame him, until Deven could feel himself trembling violently, and he had to let go.

"This wasn't supposed to happen," Jonathan went on hoarsely. "I swear I didn't know."

Dev lifted his hand from David and wiped the tears from Jonathan's eyes. "I believe you, love. This wasn't your fault."

"Wasn't it? Didn't we both do this, in the end?"

The Prime looked over to what was apparently the wreck of an altar; there were puddles of spent wax, and on the ground, discarded like trash, a shattered Signet.

"We did what we thought was right," Deven said softly. "I did what I thought was right. I just wanted to keep them safe. But you were right all along . . . none of it made any difference."

"What do we do now?" Jonathan asked, trying not to break down completely and sob.

Deven touched David's face one last time: eyes that had looked on him with both love and rage, lips that had touched his a thousand times, and those hands . . . how much of the world had they changed? What would become of the South now?

He forced himself to stand, to step away from the body. "Now we find Miranda," he said.

Jonathan swallowed hard. "She's dead. She must be. That's how it works."

Deven bent and picked up the broken Signet, holding it up where Jonathan could see the stone. "Maybe not."

The Consort frowned. "He broke it? But isn't that how you—"

"—break a Signet bond," Deven finished with a nod. "Break one stone, kill one half of a Pair. The other half goes mad from the shock and power imbalance and rarely lives more than a week. If that's what Hayes did, she could still be alive."

"Alive and in pain," Jonathan said. "Wandering around the city alone . . . We can't leave her out there, Deven. We have to find her. If she's going to die, it should be among friends, not alone."

"We will," Deven said, looking out from the roof into the city. "But for now we have to get indoors and hope to God Miranda is somewhere safe."

"We can't just leave him here like this . . ."

Deven took a shaky breath. "It's just a body, Jonathan. David is . . . he's . . ."

He couldn't say it. The tremor in his bones seemed to spread outward until he could barely even stand. He felt Jonathan's arms around him, and with the broken Signet in one hand, Deven clutched his Consort's shirt with the other, fighting desperately not to weep.

All around them, he could feel the Shadow World mourning.

"Come on," Jonathan said. "Let's go."

"Wait . . ." Deven bent over the body one last time and picked up David's hand, sliding the wedding ring off his finger. "Miranda will want this. And we shouldn't leave his phone here for some random human to find." He fished in David's pocket until he found the phone and stuck it inside his own coat.

Then he returned to his Consort's side.

The Pair disappeared from the roof, leaving the body behind to meet the dawn for the first time in 350 years. The night began to fade, the sounds of the city shifting subtly from late night to early morning, with the fire department personnel still working to make sure the building was roped off and there were no hot spots to put out. It was too risky to send anyone up to the third floor or the roof just yet—they were waiting for a structural engineer with blueprints of the building to tell them how best to proceed.

And just half an hour before sunrise, with no one to bear witness except the slowly lightening sky . . .

. . . David breathed.

From #1 *New York Times* bestselling author
CHARLAINE HARRIS

DEAD RECKONING
A Sookie Stackhouse Novel

With her knack for being in trouble's way, Sookie witnesses the firebombing of Merlotte's, the bar where she works. Since Sam Merlotte is now known to be two-natured, suspicion falls immediately on the anti-shifters in the area. But Sookie suspects otherwise, and she and Sam work together to uncover the culprit—and the twisted motive for the attack.

But her attention is divided. Though she can't "read" vampires, Sookie knows her lover, Eric Northman, and his "child" Pam well—and she realizes that they are plotting to kill the vampire who is now their master. Gradually, she is drawn into the plot—which is much more complicated than she knows.

Caught up once again in the politics of the vampire world, Sookie will learn that she is as much of a pawn as any ordinary human—and that there is a new queen on the board. . . .

M822T0111